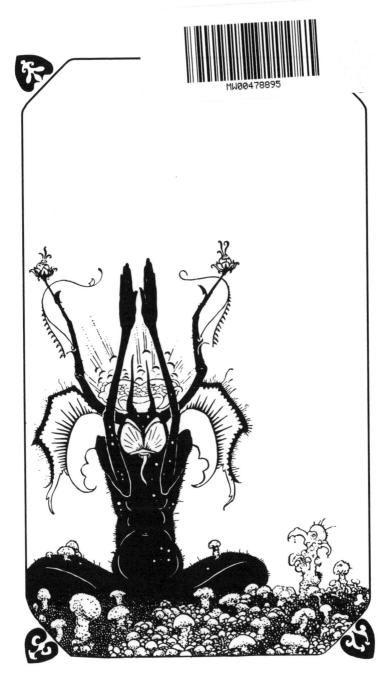

First published by Strange Attractor Press 2019
ISBN: 978-1907222-757

Design by Richard Wilkins
Illustrations by Sidney Sime

Strange Attractor Press
BM SAP, London, WC1N 3XX, UK
www.strangeattractor.co.uk

Distributed by The MIT Press
Cambridge, Massachusetts And London, England.
Printed and bound in the UK by TJ International.

Faunus

The Decorative Imagination
of Arthur Machen

Edited by James Machin

contents

Faunus
Foreword

Mark Valentine & R.B. *Russell*

The Friends of Arthur Machen arose in 1998, phoenix-like, from the ashes of a previous Arthur Machen society. The first incarnation was, for many years, much loved, and the new committee of The Friends was determined to replicate the social aspects of that original society, in part by continuing the tradition of memorable annual gatherings where members and guests ate and drank in good company while discussing the writings of Arthur Machen (and any other subjects that took their fancy). Possibly we succeeded only too well, as evidenced by our inability to remember some of those occasions over the years with any real clarity.

The committee also aimed to achieve a reliable programme of publications for members. The journal, *Faunus*, would be a mix of Machen's own writing, and an analysis of his life and work in reprinted and newly-commissioned essays. There would also be a newsletter, *Machenalia*, for social and other news. The majority of members, we were well aware, could not always travel to London or Wales to meet up with others, and they deserved two journals each year in return for their subscription, and a newsletter when appropriate. We had already published a couple of hardback journals under the auspices of the earlier society and we knew that it was possible to continue this programme, and perhaps, even, to augment it with occasional publications.

We were especially happy to include several items of previously unrecognised fiction by Machen. In our first issue we reprinted "The

Light That Never Can Be Put Out" (from the London *Evening News*, 14th February, 1916), a previously uncollected story in the tradition of "Munitions of War" and "The Happy Children" in which a commercial traveller has a strange encounter in Stratford-upon-Avon. We followed this in the second issue with "The Young Man in the Blue Suit: My Strange Experience in Kew Gardens" (from the London *Evening News*, 29th December, 1913), an anecdote in which Machen told how, when twenty years old, he met an eccentric new friend who convinced him of the futility of atheism and materialism—by arguing for them.

Gwilym Games, who looked after *Faunus* for us for several issues, unearthed from the vaults of a newspaper library several previously unknown legends of World War One, in the tradition of Machen's "The Bowmen", the story that gave rise to the myth of the Angels of Mons. Godfrey Brangham, another guest editor, offered readers choice chapters from Machen's medieval romance *The Chronicles of Clemendy*. And there was also the very rare Machen work, in an issue edited by Nicholas Granger-Taylor, which consisted of a single word.

The contents of *Faunus* certainly demonstrated the rich and eccentric range of Machen's curiosity and imagination. What other publication of a similar size could have covered Satanism, Angels, Shakespeare, Dickens, the Holy Grail, baseball, the Whitby jet industry, a cake factory, country lanes, Zeppelin raids, Scott of the Antarctic, the Celts, and the Occult?

But it was equally important, we believed, to include essays by and about Machen. We included older reminiscences by people who knew Machen or were inspired by him, but we did not want *Faunus* to be entirely backward-looking, and we always encouraged new analysis of Machen's writings by contemporary writers and researchers. From the start we determined that these should be erudite and scholarly, but also accessible to the general reader. There were aspects of some academic writing which we preferred to avoid. These included excessive footnotes and endnotes, the use of specialist jargon, and ponderous introductory and concluding sections. On the whole, we believe that we managed to temper the most excessive examples of this, while retaining the enthusiasm of contributors for their subject. And we were encouraged by how clearly and concisely argued the majority of the scholarly essays were.

One aspect of editing a journal which can only be properly appreciated by anyone who has attempted the job, is filling the ninety-six pages without blanks at the back when there is too little content (especially if a promised contribution has not materialised). Not meeting our self-imposed deadline for publication was not an option (this was a major failing of the previous society), and at this point the editors had to scour their own collections for photographs, illustrations, and literary items of a suitable length. We would like to record here the particular contribution of Rosalie Parker, who, uncredited, proof-read most issues for us.

And it may be mundane, but maintaining the membership database and posting journals and newsletters to a membership that has always been between two and three hundred members, takes time and effort. We were fortunate to have lots of help, including that of Rosalie, and the staff of the local post office who were very patient with us, especially in the days when stamps had to be licked, rather than coming ready-glued.

The Friends of Arthur Machen was set up with a determination to run the society accountably, and those left of the original committee were always apprehensive about handing on responsibility to others. However, when James Machin expressed an interest in the editorship, now with Tim Jarvis as co-editor, we knew that *Faunus* was passing into the hands of people we could trust to serve the membership well. And we were right!

A Friend of Arthur Machen writes
Introduction

Stewart Lee

Arthur Machen is best known, if he is really known at all, as a master of mystery and the macabre. But he was also an epicure, as well versed in the rites of the dinner table and the drinking den as he was in those of the sylvan grove and the temple of Nodens. The publicity sheet Machen wrote for the Sharwood's foods company in 1928, amongst the magnificent Machen ephemera included here, drives home his hatred of dull fare. "If a man says that he likes cold mutton, either he is demented or his wife beats him", writes the furious gastronome. And it is therefore only right that Machen's memory is annually consecrated with juicy meats, intoxicating drink, sulphurous tobacco, rich cheeses, sugary puddings and the thickest of custard.

The yearly dinner of The Friends of Arthur Machen, the society whose in-house journal *Faunus* birthed the book you have in your hand, sees an indefinable mixture of guests assemble by candlelight in the dining room of whichever of the writer's favourite old haunts has been selected for the year's event. They're all here, the usual crowd; artists, academics and antiquarians; writers, bikers, hikers and filmmakers; publishers, poets, old punks, and Goths; hippies, occultists and rare-book dealers; archivists, anarchists, rationalists, relic hunters and sundry admirers and chroniclers of the arcane in all its many and varied manifestations.

All of them are united by their admiration for the often-overlooked Welsh writer and mystic Arthur Machen, the threadbare son of a poor

Caerleon clergyman, who left the land he loved for the unknowable wastes of London in the 1880s, to seek his literary fortune. But he left instead an initially obscure and often derided oeuvre whose influence grows with each passing year, in no small part due to the efforts of the literary society dedicated to him. But people arrive at the temple of Arthur Machen by many different routes, having seen his white-haired presence shimmering at the edge of their field of vision, and found themselves wanting to know more.

I have rock and roll to blame for both my tinnitus and my love of Arthur Machen. I was a fan of the resilient Manchester punk band The Fall since my early teens, when a bruising encounter with the 7" single *I'm Into CB* on a 1982 John Peel show sealed my fate, and condemned me to decades of dedicated gig-going, by turns frustrating and exhilarating. Traversing the highways and byways suggested by the group's lyrical and musical allusions led me to Albert Camus and William Blake, and to Can and Captain Beefheart. And not least of all, to Arthur Machen.

I came to Arthur Machen, then, first and foremost as a Fall fan. I had read that Mark E. Smith explicitly referenced Machen's decadent 1894 novella *The Great God Pan* in the corrosive 1981 album track *Leave The Capitol*. "Pan resides in Welsh green masquerades", snarls the narrator, over the downward plughole spiral of the spindly guitar riff, as he derides that London, with its "vaudeville pub back room dusty pictures of white frocked girls and music teachers", and longs to leave the city's "Roman shell".

The lyric also quotes the title of a four-page Jack Kirby filler from a November 1959 issue of the horror comic *Tales To Astonish*, entitled "I Laughed At The Great God, Pan!" But the narrative thrust of the song, such as it is, seems more indebted to Machen's semi-autobiographical 1890s novel *The Hill of Dreams* than it does to *The Great God Pan*'s "incoherent nightmare of sex" (*The Westminster Gazette*, 1894). In the second Dark Age of the pre-Google era I knew none of this. The out-of-print canon of Arthur Machen had been placed, it appeared, like some sort of dangerous drug or an unsafe firearm, beyond reach.

In the early days of my stand-up comedy career, the long-since closed Tower Records in Piccadilly Circus, that didn't shut until midnight, was a terrible temptation. Its brightly-lit retail opportunities threatened to swallow each evening's meagre half-spot earnings whole as I headed drunk for the tube or the bus back to rented rooms in the same West London streets once walked by the would-be writer Arthur Machen.

And Tower's impossibly well stocked ground floor book section, full of obscure American fanzines and out-there small press publications, was especially problematic, its nightly siren calls threatening to pull me off course every time.

This was, of course, exactly the sort of metropolitan temptation the penniless provincial Lucian Taylor himself grappled with in *The Hill of Dreams*, exactly a century earlier, in a similarly inhospitable London, brilliantly decoded and accurately mapped in this volume by Roger Dobson. And like poor Lucian I too was dragged under one night in 1993 when I found a newly-published, and unusually affordable, Creation Classics paperback edition of *The Great God Pan*, my first Arthur Machen.

The book, illustrated with etchings by the occult artist Austin Osman Spare, boasted a preface by the counter-cultural historian, the late Simon Dwyer of *Rapid Eye* repute, and a foreword by an Iain S. Smith, from something called The Arthur Machen Society, which I seemed to remember Mark E. Smith had claimed to have joined at the age of sixteen. The puzzling narrative structure intrigued, the switching of storyteller perspectives was compelling, and slowly, and a little uncertainly if the truth be told, the book swells in its scope to encompass the apprehension of a vast and overwhelming hidden reality.

At first, I might have lazily filed this Machen character alongside Edgar Allan Poe or Robert Louis Stevenson, but it became clear he had something extra; a suggestion of things best left unsaid, of knowledge we should leave unknown, of happenings horrible and profound and best unseen, taking place in spaces in the narrative that Machen pointedly refused to illuminate. And now, for me, there was no way back.

But Arthur Machen was mainly out of print and Amazon was still only a glimmer in Jeff Bezos' tax-avoiding eye. I gave in to the primeval call of Hay-on-Wye and Charing Cross Road, the latter then still full of the same secondhand bookshops Machen's biographer John Gawsworth once rifled through daily to fund his drinking habit. A frustratingly incomplete 1922 edition of *The Secret Glory* was my next find, though I didn't read the excised final two chapters until I came across the 1991 limited Tartarus Press standalone edition of them years later.

Machen was exactly what I needed at that point in my life, and he continues to provide answers to questions I hadn't realised I was asking. We seek out books, someone wiser than me once said, to make us feel less alone, and I found Machen inspirational and comforting. As a stand-up comedian, I suppose you could say I work in the straitjacket of genre, but Machen shows us, that even when he was writing within the apparent confines of the Weird Tale, or the strict format of the light-hearted newspaper or magazine article, there was no reason not to grope towards the sublime.

Machen's horror stories might chill you, or seem laughably absurd even, but behind most of them lies an attempt to comprehend the totality of creation, in all its often morally-ambiguous glory. 1933's *The Green Round* anatomizes an existential disgust familiar to readers of his near contemporaries Kafka or Sartre, but in the form of an all but invisible dwarf, that scurries through the North London lanes and the sand dunes of the South Wales coast.

Machen's newspaper pieces, and the comical tracts he delivered to order, might seem whimsical, but 1924's *The London Adventure,* for example, details a writer at war with the very act of writing on demand itself, in a deconstructive feedback loop that already seems post-modern in the scarcely modernist world. The book that cannot be begun becomes the book itself, in a self-conscious strategy that subversively foregrounds the artist's act of creation over and above the work-for-hire demands of the commercial market. Machen, the scamp, cashes the check with a clear conscience and ridicules the terms of the contract simultaneously.

In the early years of my Arthur Machen odyssey, when his works still seemed elusive, the books themselves felt like holy relics, and the inscriptions in them suggested other untold stories. My copy of the essay collection *Dog and Duck* appears to have belonged to the Christian moral philosopher Austin Duncan-Jones (1908–1967), whilst the autobiographical volume *Far Off Things* hails "from the library of Caroline Duncan-Jones", a writer on Anglican church history, and presumably a relative. My 1905 edition of Machen's translation of Marguerite of Navarre's *Heptameron* was inscribed on its front page in 1910 by the Dante scholar Geoffrey L. Bickersteth, then resident in Marlborough. Indeed, the R.B. Russell essay included in this volume takes a dedication on a copy of Machen's *The Anatomy of Tobacco,* to the war correspondent Frank Vizetelly, as the starting point in a piece of literary detective work.

But it was a purchase made from Murder and Mayhem Books in Hay-on-Wye in 1994, of a 1915 copy of the cheap chapbook mega-seller

The Bowmen And Other Legends of The War, that made me realise that Arthur Machen had always been with me, all along. I instantly understood that I had always known this story, somehow. I had a vague memory of it, recast in brutal pixilated colour, but had forgotten the exact source, even though I had spent a lifetime replaying it in my head, and retooling its central conceit into English lesson creative writing exercises.

Gwilym Games, editor of the Arthur Machen newsletter *Machenalia*, told me that, to the best of his knowledge, "The Bowmen" never appeared in the exact form I recalled, and all the evidence suggested he was right. Machen's best fictions feel like stories that have always been there, born from earth and vapour, waiting to take shape, and so maybe my familiarity with the story was a false memory. In the end, after fruitless hours of search engine surfing and sci-fi bookshop crate digging, I found my long lost Machen memory in an unlikely setting and under a different name, and waited for a package from an Australian online comic book dealer to time-trip me back to my childhood self in a veil-rending flash.

We're in South Devon, in the Summer of 1975, and I am barely seven years old. From the time I was four or five, my father would give my mother, his ex-wife, a few days' respite from my precocious questioning every now and again, and we'd drive South along the M5 to stay with his parents in the seaside retirement gulag of Budleigh Salterton. My father did his best, but he never learned how to play, and his daily routine was inconveniently bisected by the opening hours of a hotel bar a little way along the South West Coast Path, and of country pubs in picturesque thatched villages further afield, where I would be left at lunchtime locked in the car outside with only crisps and coke for company.

But a seafront stall, replete with a revolving rack of the kind of disreputable American horror comic books that only found their way across the Atlantic as worthless ballast for ships, was an imaginative lifeline. I never normally mislaid the comics I'd collected, and I'm still carrying the first one I ever bought (*Captain Marvel* 38, from May 1975), but somehow this particular key component of my childhood went astray, probably binned by a parent who didn't recognise it as a sacred text, regarding it instead as rubbish.

DC comics' *Weird War Tales* issue 29 had been sitting on the seaside spinner for nine months or so, since September 1974, and the cover, a lurid Luis Dominguez drawing of a spectral nomadic horseman rising out of the sand to confront horrified German Afrika Korps riflemen, must have captured my seven-year-old imagination. I would have settled down to read it hungrily, I expect, on the Jurassic shingle, while my father surreptitiously spied on sunbathing women through a pair of binoculars that he euphemistically called his "birdwatchers", looking away innocently should the birds themselves turn to regard him.

The third of *Weird War Tales* 29's three sickly stories was entitled "The Phantom Bowmen Of Crecy", and when my belated replacement copy arrived from Australia in December 2015, some forty years after it was lost, I still remembered every frame off by heart, despite no longer knowing my own wife's mobile phone number. In Weird War world it's 1346 and a skeletal American GI introduces the story over scenes from the Battle of Crécy, an English victory in the Hundred Years' War, where the longbow first made its name; "Their bones had been dust for centuries and yet they returned to fight again," he says, ominously.

At Crécy the English bowmen swear an oath "never to rest so long as a single enemy threatens England" and at the moment of their victory over the French they are suddenly transported, in the form of hundred-foot-high ghosts, to the 1914 Battle of Mons. Here they dispel the terrified "Jerries", the enemy threatening England that their oath compels them to defy. "Who really won that victory?", asks the GI skeleton in conclusion, only to be answered by the tattered corpse of an English bowman, "Was it a thin line of men who had been dead for five hundred years?"

The story is of course an unattributed retelling of Machen's "The Bowmen", a morale-boosting ghost story published in the *Evening News* at the end of September 1914. But here it was stripped of nuance and poetry, and credited instead to one Jack Oleck, a jobbing horror comic writer, and brother-in-law of the Captain America creator Joe Simon. Oleck also briefly served as editor of *Interior Decorator News* in the 1950s, when the establishment of the Comics Code Authority made horror work untenable, the kind of practical decision Machen himself might have found familiar from his Sharwood's sauces days.

Did Oleck, my Machen gateway drug, know of Machen's original "Bowmen" yarn? Perhaps not. Machen's tale of the British forces' ghostly helpers quickly escaped its author's clutches and became common property, genuinely believed to be true by vast swathes of the British public, many of whom claimed to know men at the front who had witnessed the events described. When Machen himself pointed out that he was the originator of the groundless legend he was denounced by a clergyman as a traitor.

It's entirely fair to say that the myth of the "Angels of Mons" still remains more famous than its creator. Its most recent manifestation, in 2001, involved the Machiavellian media publicist Mark Borkowski, an opportunistic Stroud architect called Danny Sullivan, the advert director Tony Kaye, and a figure of £350,000 in regard to fake photographic evidence verifying the phenomenon.

The transmogrification of "The Bowmen" into an unattributed '70s horror comic seems trivial in comparison, and I wonder how many readers may have made their way to the Machen source because of Oleck's unlicensed appropriation, or Mark E. Smith's garbled incorporations, or even Mark Borkowski's monetised cynicism. Machen continues to haunt our culture, from shadows glimpsed in the films of Guillermo del Toro, in the psychogeographic shadings assimilated by the docu-novelist Iain Sinclair, and in the folk horror echoes of the electronic artists recording for the Ghost Box label, all of whom acknowledge his influence.

The material selected from *Faunus* in this volume maintains the unknowable aura that surrounds Machen, its academic investigations interrupted by plausible literary forgeries like Rosalie Parker's supplemental "White People" fragment, Timothy Jarvis' deliberately unreliable meditation on Machen's Stoke Newington fantasia "N", and the faerie sculptress Tessa Farmer's attempt to reverse-engineer the influence of Machen, the similarly-susceptible great-grandfather whose work she had never been aware of. Machen's a slippery ghost. He eludes us. The best of *Faunus* blows smoke towards the space he occupies invisibly and attempts to extrapolate his exact shape from hollows in a moving cloud.

At the turn of the century I was inducted, without my knowledge, into the recently re-booted Friends of Arthur Machen by the comic book creator and snake-worshipper Alan Moore. We found we had a shared interest in Machen, though Moore's ran much deeper than mine, after we met on a radio programme. Moore clearly logged that fact and stored it away, like a witch snatching a lock of hair to better curse its owner, and soon my own copies of *Faunus* started arriving, providing new pathways to Machen in each edition. Moore read me like an open grimoire chained to the sealed off section of a Cathedral library. He worked out what I needed, and set me on my way. And what I needed was Arthur Machen.

One of the stated aims of The Friends of Arthur Machen was to get his work back into print with a mainstream publisher. And in 2012 Penguin issued *The White People and Other Weird Stories* as part of its Penguin Modern Classics collection. Cautious email correspondences wondered if, under the terms of its own charter, it was now time for The Friends of Arthur Machen to disband. Sense prevailed, and arrangements for next year's dinner began to take shape. And as the ongoing publication of *Faunus* shows, Machen's world is a world without end.

Stewart Lee

writer/clown, Oxford, Bristol, Portsmouth, Salford, Birmingham, Cambridge, Brighton, Stoke Newington, September 2018.

sub ʀosa

ʀ.ʙ. ʀ*ussell*
originally ᴘublished in ꜰaunus issue ɪ

Reproduced above is the inscription found in a copy of *The Anatomy of Tobacco* (1884), one of Arthur Machen's most curious books. This copy belonged to Frank Vizetelly, a pioneering war-correspondent, friend of Garibaldi, and reporter of the American Civil War. Of more interest to us, however, is the fact that his brother was Henry Vizetelly, and the book was presented to Frank by the publisher of the *Anatomy*, George Redway.

Both Redway and Frank Vizetelly's brother, Henry, were publishers who mixed the risqué with the reputable, and were just two of a number of fascinating and often less than respectable characters with whom its author associated in his early years in London.

When writing *In the Eighties* Arthur Machen recalled how he "...got to know George Redway, of York Street, Covent Garden" and that "...he came to be the publisher of *The Anatomy of Tobacco*." Machen was setting out on the craft of letters by offering a less than promising manuscript. Redway (called "Davenport" in the last chapter of *Far Off Things*) was enthusiastic, but would not take the risk of publication. Machen's taste for the bizarre and arcane in literature was shared by Redway, who agreed to the publication of the *Anatomy* only after the author had obtained funds from old family friends.

Back home in Gwent Machen translated *The Heptameron* for Redway, but was soon in need of further employment. He returned to London to work for the publisher, and recalls that "...in 1885 I was cataloguing second hand books for him in a garret in Catherine Street, over Vizetelly's shop." How well Machen knew Vizetelly it is impossible to speculate. Vizetelly is principally remembered for his publication of Zola's *La Terre*, for which he received the longest of his various prison sentences. Machen says of *La Terre* that it is "...an obscene book that every judicious Bishop of Central France should put in the hands of newly ordained priests—if it is to be accepted that the physician ought to have some knowledge of the constitutions of his patients and of the diseases from which they are suffering." Machen also mentions Vizetelly directly in the Danielson *Bibliography*.

Machen described his place of work as "...a sumptuous and rich garret ...filled with that mysterious odour that used to prevail in oldish London houses that were not too carefully swept and washed and polished, and there day after day I worked, reading and annotating, and all alone." He gives some idea of the books that surrounded him in *Things Near and Far*: "It was as odd a library as any man could desire to see. Occultism in one sense or another was the subject of most of the books. There were the principal and the more obscure treatises on Alchemy, on Astrology, on Magic; old Latin volumes most of them. Here were books about Witchcraft, Diabolical Possession, 'Fascination', or the Evil Eye; here comments on the Kabbala. Ghosts and Apparitions were a large family, Secret Societies of all sorts hung on the skirts of the Rosicrucians and Freemasons and so found a place in the collection." A more detailed description of some of the books appears in the advertisement he wrote for Redway entitled *The Ingenious Gentleman Don Quijote de la Mancha*.

However, Machen says that he laboured amongst these, "...and much more than this". There were obviously further books on the premises, for Redway also ran an indecent lending library. The publisher issued a checklist of prohibited erotica, *Bibliotheca Arcana*, written by William Laird Clowes (author of *Confessions of an English Hashish Eater*). Among the titles advertised at the end of the *Anatomy* is *Phallicism, Celestial and Terrestrial*.

In the pursuit of better wages Machen was to move on from Redway, offering his services as a cataloguer to second hand booksellers Frank and William Kerslake and Bartholomew Robson. This time he was set to work in an ill-lit basement, and was soon asked to translate *The Memoirs of Casanova*. Machen refers to his employers as "The Brothers" in *Things Near and Far*, and suggests that they were perhaps as disreputable as Redway: "It may be mentioned that the firm dealt occasionally in works which would not be suitable for the 'centre table' of a New England parlour." They may well have been responsible for publishing *Gyneaocracy, a Narrative of The Adventures and Psychological Experiences of Julian Robinson*, just one year before Machen's *Casanova*. They had certainly produced, a few years earlier, a clandestine edition of the Earl of Haddington's *Select Poems on Several Occasions*.

If Kerslake and Robson were disreputable, their printer, Harry Nichols, was notorious. Grant Richards, in *Memoirs of a Misspent Youth*, says that Nichols was identified with the circulation of semi-erotic literature. With Leonard Smithers he was to become infamous for publishing the work of Oscar Wilde and Aubrey Beardsley and the celebrated *The Savoy*. The edition of Machen's *Casanova* was meant to have been strictly limited to 1000 copies, but according to Richards another 1000 sets were surreptitiously printed by Nichols. No action was taken against him by "The Brothers" (or Machen, who had invested at least £1000 in the publication). Grant Richards says that "…counsel's opinion was taken but apparently the case would have been looked upon as similar to the quarrel between highwaymen on Newmarket Heath. Justice would have refused to interfere."

At this time Arthur Machen was himself interested in the business of publishing. Both *The Chronicle of Clemendy* and *Thesaurus Incantatus* were published from his home address, 98 Great Russell Street. The pseudonym "Thomas Marvell" was employed for the publishing projects of the author and his friend Harry Spurr. They published *Clemendy* under the Carbonnek imprint, and were to use it again, as we shall learn.

Machen, of course, went on to make his name, if not his fortune, as a writer. But what of the above-mentioned "men about Machen"?

Henry Vizetelly was an old man when Machen knew him, and his last prison sentence finished him off. He died a broken man in 1894. George Redway's firm passed into the hands of receivers at the very end of the century and he went off to fight in the Boer War. He resurfaced, however, in *The Bookman* in 1932, offering 'Some Reminiscences of Publishing Fifty Years Ago'. The Kerslake, Robson, Nichols and Smithers partnership continued for a while (they published *The Secret Memoirs of the Duc De Roquelaure* uniform with the *Casanova*.) However, they were all to go their separate ways and only the name of Leonard Smithers survives to be associated with the 1890s, during which time he published some of the most important and beautiful books of the period. His decline into pirated works, pornography and vanity publishing was aided by a close association with the bottle, and he died in 1907. The activities of Nichols are recorded, although they are less than glorious. He prospered for a while, but the authorities took exception to his *Kavgnemia, or The Laws of Female Beauty* by Bell and *Mademoiselle de Maupin* by Gautier, and he made a tactical withdrawal to the United States. He continued to publish and deal in books, and appears as the instigator of the "The Great Beardsley Hoax". His attempts to publish and exhibit fifty Beardsley forgeries still has repercussions today (these poor imitations are, occasionally, still published under Beardsley's name). He thrived and prospered until his death in 1939, his poor reputation not greatly affecting his sales.

It would be wrong to over-state Machen's associations with these colourful characters who were part-time pornographers. Machen had been forced to take a number of dead-end jobs to make ends meet and he entered the seedy world of sub rosa literature through an interest in the arcane and a need to find a publisher. His translations of *The Heptameron* and *Casanova* were not pornographic, although desperate publishers and booksellers will always try to pass them off as such. However, Machen also indulged in one other translation, and it was published privately under his own Carbonnek imprint.

After he had finished *Casanova* (and before the memoirs were eventually published) Machen worked on the translation of *Le Moyen de Parvenir* by Béroalde de Verville. The book claims to be the table-talk recorded at a monstrous banquet attended by, among others, Julius Caesar and Martin Luther. He describes it as that "extraordinary and enigmatic book", and his translation was apparently too much for the printers. They found certain passages so obscene that they downed tools and refused go further than page eighty. It can be assumed that Machen funded the publication of the book himself, and despite changing printers from the Dryden Press to James Wade, he felt compelled to re-write the offending passages.

The question has to be, what would have happened if Arthur Machen had used another printer from the outset? It is unlikely that Harry Nichols would have had any qualms about printing Machen's one true pornographic work. If *Le Moyen de Parvenir* had been a success one can only speculate as to the future direction of Machen's career in literature as writer, publisher and translator. He was a relatively inexperienced young man, but he was enthusiastic and had some useful contacts. It happened, however, that *Le Moyen de Parvenir* afforded an introduction to Oscar Wilde, and Wilde inspired the translator to become the author of such society tales as "St John's Chef" and "A Double Return". *The Great God Pan* followed shortly afterwards.

sources
Craig, *The Banned Books of England*.
Danielson, *A Bibliography of Arthur Machen*.
Delectus Books, *various catalogues*.
Gilbert, *A.E. Waite, A Magician of Many Parts*.
Goldstone and Sweetser, *A Bibliography*.
Harris, *The Collected Drawings of Aubrey Beardsley*.
Curtis, 'Vizetelly & Co.', *PN Review 32*.

Arthur Machen—satanist?

Gerald Suster

originally published in Faunus issue 2

In their sterling biography of Arthur Machen, Aidan Reynolds and William Charlton state that in the wake of the death of his beloved first wife, Amelia Hogg, a death that came slowly and painfully via cancer, Machen was in danger of becoming a Satanist. The purpose of this essay is to examine this contention and by arousing controversy, to stimulate further debate, discussion, speculation and research on this contentious matter.

One of the many difficulties is that by the time Machen wrote his second volume of autobiography, *Things Near and Far*, he had adopted and embraced an unorthodox form of the Christian faith which may well have led him to evade the question. Those of us familiar with *Things Near and Far* must remain intrigued by the "process" he describes which led to so many mystifying results. But let us tackle that complex question in its due order.

Machen was the son of a clergyman, who appears to have been a gentle and kindly man, if somewhat absent-minded and impecunious. There is no evidence that in his early years, Machen was visited by any form of specifically Christian cruelty which might cause him to reject the faith of his forefathers. In *The Hill of Dreams*, though, a loathing is expressed for Low Church puritanism, a theme reiterated in *Dr Stiggins* and *The Secret Glory*.

In the Preface to one of his greatest works, "The White People", Machen has his hermit Ambrose declare that Sorcery and Sanctity are the only two ecstasies. It is surely obvious that the influence of London in the 1890s and Machen's period of cataloguing esoteric works for George Redway in the 1880s brought about a fascination with Sorcery, and Mark Valentine in his *Arthur Machen*, a fine work indeed, consistently makes astute remarks.

By the time that Machen came to write *The Great God Pan* and "The Inmost Light", he was familiar with and expert upon occult literature and was fascinated by these texts. In common with most young men of his time and of any time, he was obsessed by sex. His problem lay in the fact that Christianity condemned sex outside of marriage to be sinful: that Paganism discerned in sex a way of experiencing divine ecstasy; and that Christianity equated Paganism with Satanism. These paradoxes would later lead Machen into confessing that he had translated awe into awfulness. The fact remains that the brilliant works he wrote in the 1890s are suffused by sex.

In *The Great God Pan,* Helen, possessed by Pan, becomes a rampant and rapacious bitch-demon who devours and ruins all her lovers. In "The Inmost Light", Dyson discerns a similar unquenchable lust in the woman of Harlesden, whose body has been possessed by a daemonic entity as a consequence of the sinister Dr Black's experiment. The fiendish *femme fatale* of *The Three Impostors*, Miss Lally, is also called "Helen": yet Machen wrote to answer Paul England's enquiry some time after 1910: "'Helen' is not very interesting."

No? *The Three Impostors*, such a wondrous work, has "Helen" as Miss Lally and Miss Leicester, narrating "The Novel of the Black Seal" and "The Novel of the White Powder", the two finest tales in that extraordinary novel. In his interesting and worthy *The Supernatural in Fiction*, Dr Peter Penzoldt subjected these two tales to Freudian analysis. He came to the conclusion that "The Novel of the Black Seal" displayed Machen's terror of natural sexual forces as shown by "the Little People", portrayed as troglodyte disgusting degenerates: and that "The Novel of the White Powder" is simply a dramatisation of the late Victorian terror of the evils attendant upon masturbation.

For my own part, I am inclined to agree with Dr Penzoldt that "The Novel of the White Powder", along with "The Novel of the Red Hand" does display, among many other things, a classic, late Victorian complex of sin and guilt regarding masturbation—let us not forget the

Union with Self that is the principal spiritual horror of "The Novel of the White Powder"—but these tales are assuredly more than merely that. Freud once horrified an international conference of learned psychoanalysts by lighting a huge cigar and smoking it with evident enjoyment. "This may be a phallus, gentlemen," Freud declared, "but let us not forget that it is also a cigar."

Dr Penzoldt then proceeds—alas!—to become unintentionally hilarious by declaring that Machen's subject-matter is so disgusting, it cannot be fit for edifying literature. Let us take what good we can from this narrow perspective and pass on.

Of course, we note rape and sexual torture in "The Novel of the Dark Valley", sadism in "The Novel of the Iron Maid" and the burning of genitalia in "The Adventure of the Deserted Residence". The whole matter of *The Three Impostors* is accompanied by the narrator's cynical attitude towards the Satanic activities of Dr Lipsius and his three evil associates.

Machen's sexual obsessions can also be seen in his early short stories and in *Ornaments in Jade*, for the most part a work of quite exquisite poems in prose. Adultery is the theme of "A Double Return", which Oscar Wilde rightly admired. Pre-marital sex is the theme of "A Wonderful Woman". "An Underground Adventure" shows us the inability of some men to have sex even when it is offered to them enticingly. "Jocelyn's Escape" further explores the theme of adultery. "The Idealist" (again) has its focus upon male masturbation enacted as a holy sacrament. "Witchcraft" banishes sexual intercourse in favour of female masturbation that brings about the incubus. "Torture" is an uncomfortable tale of male sadism, attempted rape and impotence. "The Rose Garden", "The Ceremony" and "The Turanians" are all marvellously delicate tales of female sexuality, either masturbatory or full-blooded heterosexual, all delicately told, which would lead to "The White People".

In *The Hill of Dreams*, the hero undertakes a masochistic magical ritual, torturing himself in the love of the maid he lusts for from afar: and in the excruciatingly beautiful final chapters, Lucian Taylor lusts after a she-demon of the streets, transmuting her in his fevered imagination.

Machen was obviously fascinated by the erotic and was somewhat shy about the fact. Little is known about his first wife, Amy Hogg, other than she appears to have been an actress of the type then described as being "lively"; and one can only assume that Machen wrote so little about her because of the tragedy of her death and because he did not want to upset his second wife, Purefoy, who had rescued him from nervous depression.

It was after the death of Amy that Machen, "beside myself with despair and torment", essayed his mysterious "Process". The resulting three stages, which astounded him, he classified as "Syon"—a mystical ecstasy; "Baghdad"—an hallucinatory stage of mysterious happenings in London of which he could not make sense; and "Silly Fool" in which everything returned to the mundane and confounded his earlier high expectations. In later life, he declined to state what this "Process" was and such little knowledge as he gave out comes from a letter to Munson Havens. Here he described it as being akin to Hypnotism yet, he asserted that it would be of no use to him today since he was a married man.

I sincerely hope that I can start a fierce debate by venturing my own hypothesis, which is that his "Process" was some form of magical masturbation as outlined in "The Novel of the White Powder". In other words, for a time, and stricken in grief, Arthur Machen, translator of *The Memoirs of Casanova,* embraced the ecstasy of Sorcery. Around 1900, the German Ordo Templi Orientis was setting forth magical masturbation as its VIII degree, as I know, being a IX degree OTO. Furthermore, you can find this ancient technique, the way in which Ptah made the World according to Ancient Egyptian Mythology, in *The Book of Pleasure: Self-Love* (1910) by that extraordinary artist and writer, Austin Osman Spare, who claimed to have learned it from an hereditary witch, the latter being the subject of so many Machen tales. The spell, which probably came out of the many works of Medieval and Renaissance and Alchemical Magick that he had studied, probably had its effect on account of his Victorian horror of masturbation, his nurturing of the Sin Complex and his long abstention as his wife lay dying.

This extraordinary three-fold period which followed, of Syon, Baghdad and Silly Fool, bears a certain resemblance to the late Dr Timothy Leary's structuring of an LSD trip in terms of the Tibetan *Book of the Dead.* However, Machen did not have the mental tools to transmute the third stage he called "Silly Fool" into the loving acceptance of earthly life around us which is required.

Certainly, his experience of "Syon" had its parallels, as he noted, with the mystical ecstasies of the monks of St Columba. Having experienced the "Syon" and "Baghdad" stages myself, I can concur with his frequent bewilderment. It was during this period and not before his "Process" that he joined The Hermetic Order of the Golden Dawn, of which I have the honour to be an Adept, and he attained the Initiate's grade of Theoricus. Unfortunately, he found the majority of occultists then to be as insufferable as I do now and stated that the Golden Dawn shed no ray of light upon his Path.

The House of the Hidden Light, a series of letters written in collaboration with his life-long friend, the occultist A.E. Waite, does shed *some* light upon Machen's state of mind at the time. Ostensibly, these letters, written in a burlesque of the Alchemical authors, describe visits to pubs and endeavours to bed two girls. There are continuous sexual jests, as when Machen refers to sodomy—a practice he never essayed—and to the rites of Lilith—i.e. magical masturbation. Machen keeps hoping for another "annus mirabilis" such as occurred 1899-1900. Waite finally tells him to "put by these rites", since Waite was terrified of any Magick that might actually work.

In the "Silly Fool" stage, Machen reveals that the woman after whom he had lusted so much and to whom he had given a magical name, suddenly became very ordinary and he cursed himself "because I desired Desire".

I shall probably annoy my readers by stating, as my late, dear friend, the historian Francis King did, that Waite was a wretchedly bad influence upon Machen. So be it: and let us debate the matter. I regard it as being a grave misfortune that Waite persuaded Machen to embrace Christianity, thereby killing his creativity.

This matter can hardly be blamed upon Machen's excellent second wife, Purefoy, by every account a lady of strength and compassion, a woman who pulled Machen out of his introverted depression and who encouraged him to be a delightfully garrulous extrovert. According to Purefoy, Waite was just "a silly old fool" whom she tolerated for the sake of her husband. Quite.

Machen's problem was that he could see nothing other than a choice between Sorcery and Sanctity. Sorcery implied sex, often perverse, and Satanism. It was a rebellion against the Natural Order of God. This matter came to frighten him and he took the Path of Sanctity by publicly espousing Christianity and thus tended to minimise his earlier experience of the alternative paths to which he had been tempted, sublimating his sexual drive into a healthy relationship with Purefoy.

Of course, I find Satanism to be puerile. It is simply a rebellion against Christianity, a religion which many intelligent human beings must find to be equally puerile. As Voltaire pointed out, how can anyone believe that a boy born of a Virgin became from birth a God-Man and died for all our sins? Well: the excellent Arthur Machen came to do so.

This belief did little for his magical, literary skills. One can see this as early as "The White People" when Ambrose asks how one might feel were one's roses to sing or one's dog to speak in human accents. Personally, I would be astonished yet utterly delighted. Unfortunately, Ambrose has this harmless yet utterly fascinating matter displayed as the very essence of Sin. In just one respect, the hapless Dr Penzoldt is right: Machen could not break away from the Sin Complex aroused in him by the sexuality of Nature. We can see this again in his unsatisfactory work, *The Terror* of 1917.

Machen's middle-aged advocacy of Christianity was sincere; and would that there were more Christians like him! Yet he never again experienced the ecstasy that Sorcery had brought him in 1899-1900, referring in *Things Near and Far* to having returned to the darkness in which most of us dwell. In an Introduction to an abbreviated edition of *The Three Impostors,* published as *Black Crusade* in the 1960s, Julian Symons refers dismissively to Machen's post 1890s work "in which passion and frustration had been replaced by recollection." This remark, though astute, is not entirely fair.

Hieroglyphics is superb but manages to consider ecstasy without the Sorcery v. Sanctity dilemma. The *Autobiography* is magnificent but skates over the matter. Although I really like *The London Adventure*, I have to concur with Joshi: "the whole *London Adventure* is about Machen's not having written a book called *The London Adventure*." I have to admit that few other exponents of the English essay can delight me more than Machen. But what about his fiction?

The Secret Glory is a fine book indeed, but what a hodge-podge of conflicts within the author it reveals! I would argue that some of Machen's finest work of fiction was done in the last phase of his life, in the 1930s, when he brought his experience of a lifetime and considerable intelligence to creating from what appears to be an agnostic perspective, Christian though he undeniably was at the time.

"The Children of the Pool" is one of his worst stories, marred by Christian influence: after all, it is hardly very sinful to have gone to bed with the landlady's daughter. But "N" and "The Exalted Omega" and "The Cosy Room" are dazzling masterpieces. They are assisted in being such since he avoids the false dichotomy of Christianity v. Satanism or Sanctity v. Sorcery, in favour of sheer artistry that breaks through the crust of Christian dogma that had earlier imprisoned his genius. Perhaps this can be compared to what happened to his Rev Secretan Jones in "Opening the Door".

I must be among the few admirers of *The Green Round*, which is best read in conjunction with "N" and again features the Reverend Thomas Hampole, a character similar to Secretan Jones, who has glimpses of ecstasy despite himself. Machen was seeing less and less of that humourless pedant, A.E. Waite during this period of late creativity, which remains under-rated, even among admirers.

Satanism is merely an ignoble inversion of Christianity and it is unfortunate that Machen could not discern a nobler alternative to this dismal coin. It is even more unfortunate that Machen associated Sex with Sin and condemned another man of genius, Aleister Crowley, who admired Machen's works so much that he recommended them to his students in his "official" magical documents. Machen's scathing strictures regarding the "Oriental Occult Ass" and the Western "Occult Ass" are as true today as they always were: but it remains sad that he could only perceive holiness within the narrow, sin-obfuscated dogma of Christianity.

Although Christians who admire Machen are right in discerning a period in which Arthur Machen was a stout Defender of the Faith, this impulse prompted little writing that is memorable. Let us not forget the Agnostic Machen, the Man-of-the-World Machen, the Pagan Machen and the Satanic Machen. What a Man for all Seasons! This is just one among the many reasons why I hold him to be a major, not a minor writer: and I have insufficient space to consider the beauty of his prose and the wicked wit of his characterisation.

Some readers may be wondering why I have not mentioned Machen's beautiful novella: *A Fragment of Life*. Why not save the best for the last? Even though Machen was hampered by the Sin Complex in his quest for the Sangraal, this did provoke a tension within, whereby the true artist within him erupted, knowing the True way beyond Sorcery and Sanctity and enabling him to end his tale:

"And my love and I were united by the well."

A Reply to
"Arthur Machen—satanist?"

Mark Samuels
originally published in Faunus issue 3

It is strange that Mr Suster castigates Machen for his Christianity by promoting the idea that it was this faith which "killed" his creativity, for he allows that the finest of Machen's works is *A Fragment of Life* (I believe it is) but this was only completed once Machen was fully reconciled to Anglo-Catholicism. A careful reading of the work shows that the phrase "my love and I were united by the well" isn't necessarily sexual. It should be taken in the context of the description of the Holy Well as a "stream of cleansing to them that would be pure, and a medicine of such healing virtue that by it, through the might of God and the intercession of the saints, the most grievous wounds are made whole." It was not to "satisfy any bodily thirst". The union was surely one of spiritual ecstasy.

Mr Suster is quite right to point out that there are many examples of sexual activity in Machen's work and he often treats the subject with some fear and loathing. But this is hardly unusual for the period in question, and having translated Casanova, no doubt he was aware that the life of a sexual adventurer is one likely to end in disappointment—or worse.

Of course, to denigrate Machen's faith and claim that it was destructive to his writing ignores many of the fruits arising therefrom; not least such examples as "The Mystic Speech", the Preface to *Afterglow* and many other essays. Would we also have lost a very fine minor work, *The Great Return*, had Machen not returned to orthodox Christianity?

Wishing that he had remained a pagan ignores the part sacramental Catholicism played in thwarting the serious nervous collapse he feared after the death of his first wife. The re-emergence of this faith was one of three important changes that enabled him to re-fashion his life thereafter (the others being, of course, his marriage to Purefoy and his entry into the world of the stage).

As for Machen's prior dealings with occult matters, these are surely to be taken only as staging posts on his journey towards orthodox Christianity. He was simply fascinated, at first, by their mysterious appearance, though later he found them dreary and tiresome.

It is also important to emphasise, in view of Mr Suster's comments, that Machen was strongly opposed to the idea that the Christian Faith is primarily a series of moral injunctions. Machen regarded the faith as the key to all mysteries, as fulfilment for the soul that cried out for its source. The "sin complex" to which Mr Suster refers is something of a red-herring. As seems to be made clear in the discussion in "The White People" it is the notion of "true evil... (as) a lonely passion of the soul" which most concerns Machen and not "the merely carnal, sensual man (who) can no more be a great sinner than he can be a great saint." It is the person who hates life, who despises joy, the person who deliberately and with relish, seeks to become a monster and obtain unlawful power over others, who is the epitome of evil. The character of Helen Vaughan in *The Great God Pan*, for example, is monstrous not for her sexual appetite in itself, but for the destructive power which she exercises in using it to drive her victims to destruction. Of course, her background *is* rather unfortunate. In any case, it is in this definition of wickedness that we learn the meaning of Machen's dictum that "it is probable that there have been far fewer sinners than saints."

The "secret" behind Machen's view of morality is simply this: a lack of morality is ultimately unsatisfying. Eventually "the red roses and the ivory flesh of the girls had alike grown grey: meat and drink were bitter in the mouth." What followed the ennui in the wake of uncensured and exhausted pleasures was simply the desire for salvation. And good conduct to salvation is, Machen noted, as the rules of grammar to literature.

Finally, referring to the "rites of Lilith" mentioned in *The House of the Hidden Light*: Mr Suster states that these rites were a reference to "magical masturbation" and mentions that Waite advises Machen to "put by those rites." In fact, "Lilith" was Machen and Waite's secret name for Vivienne Pierpont (aka "The Shepherdess") an actress with whom Machen thought he might have fallen in love (see Machen's *Selected Letters*, p. 31). Machen says of these "rites":

> *"I have an appointment with her, which I shall keep alone, that I may thoroughly discover whether she have any Rite to administer."*

Waite obviously disapproved of Machen's involvement with her and the infatuation eventually passed.

A Palimpsest of the Three Impostors

Roger Dobson
originally published in Faunus issue 7

Throwing out a Mynydd Maen of ancient notebooks at the dawn of the Millennium, I undertook the laborious task of ploughing through them to determine if anything was worthy of preservation. Depressingly, very little was. From hundreds of doubled-sided leaves, only some twenty sheets and a pocket notebook devoted to Machen material seemed worth keeping. Among the heterogeneous collection are such things as the birth and death dates of Helen Vaughan (5th August 1865 and 25th July 1888), from the endnote often deleted from editions of *The Great God Pan*, but restored in the Tartarus Press edition of *Tales of Horror and the Supernatural* (1997) and the Creation Books version of *Pan* (1993).

Scribblings from Victorian street directories show that the Bun Shop, or Bun House, where R. Thurston Hopkins claimed he talked with Machen and (rather dubiously) with Ernest Dowson,[1] was at 417 Strand: it remains a wine bar and restaurant, Da Marco's. The news office of *The Globe* "where one sent one's early Turnovers",[2] as Machen states autobiographically in "N", was at 367 Strand, near the Lyceum Theatre. Alfred Denny's bookshop, famously mentioned in *Far Off Things*,[3] was at 304 Strand. The Spanish Restaurant where Machen dined was at 17 Beak Street, W1. There are notes on Winifred Graham's overcooked portrait of that "connoisseur of the occult" the Rev Montague Summers: "I wanted to sense the vibrations in the room where he worked, since his pen has brought to life every form of creepy horror. Ghosts and ghouls, vampires and other diabolical beings troop through his blood-curdling pages which are not mere fiction."[4]

A pasted-in advertisement from the Panacea Society warns that crime, banditry and the distress of nations will continue until the Bishops open Joanna Southcott's Box of Sealed Writings (see Revelation 11:19 and 4:4, which prophesies the Box and the Bishops—perhaps). The tragic prophetess Joanna is buried in St John's Wood, a few minutes' walk from 12 Melina Place. It was pleasing—and useful for a future edition of *The Lost Club Journal*—to rediscover the name of Daphne du Maurier's uncle Comyns Beaumont, the revisionist geographer who in *The Riddle of Prehistoric Britain* (1946) and *Britain—The Key to World History* (1949) argued that biblical events occurred not in the Holy Land but in and around (ahem) Edinburgh. As every schoolboy knows, "the islands of the sea" (Isaiah 11:11) refer to Britain. It makes one proud, doesn't it?

Some of the Machen notes relate to biographical and creative matters which do not appear to have appeared in print; so they seem worthy of an essay, albeit a rambling and disjointed one, in *Faunus*. Let's begin with the enigma of the "lost" Machen tale. On 1st February 1894, the 30-year-old Machen wrote to his prospective publisher John Lane, from 36 Great Russell Street, Bloomsbury:

> *My dear Sir,*
>
> *I have been thinking over our conversation last night, and I have come to the conclusion that it would not be advisable to bind up the story I told you with 'The Great God Pan', for though the two stories are different in many respects, they are conducted with much the same mechanism; Mr Clarke appears again with his 'memoirs'; the chief personage is not a descendant of the fauns but of the 'Little People'. Of course the working out is different, but still I think that the one story would spoil the other. But I find I have a number of short tales and sketches which have appeared in the St James's Gazette and other papers which would just double the book. I have them in a book and should be glad to show them to you when you please. I think you would like them.*
>
> *I remain, Yours faithfully,*
>
> *Arthur Machen*

This tantalising missive did not, for reasons too dim and distant to recall, appear in the *Selected Letters* (1988)—it can be found in one of the bound volumes of transcript letters at Newport Library—but it will immediately arouse the Macheniac's curiosity. *"Mr Clarke appears again with his 'memoirs'."* Surely Clarke and the "Memoirs to Prove the Existence of the Devil" appear only in *The Great God Pan*. And who is the descendant of the Little People? The likeliest candidate is Jervase Cradock, the unhappy half-human hybrid from the "Novel of the Black Seal", yet he is hardly the "chief personage": Professor Gregg and Miss Lally are the principal characters in the "Novel of the Black Seal".

Machen began writing *The Three Impostors* at 36 Great Russell Street in the spring of 1894, after he and Amy had returned from their two-year sojourn near Turville in the Chilterns. So at the time of the letter to Lane the concept for the Little People story may have differed considerably from the work the Bodley Head published in 1895. Transmutations may indeed have taken place. Could it be that the frame story of the romance originally involved Clarke rather than Mr Dyson? A few of Machen's rather interchangeable young gents about town appear in more than one story. Austin and Phillipps, bewildered by the Stevensonian mystery of "The Lost Club" (1890), resurface respectively in *The Great God Pan* and *The Three Impostors*. Villiers figures in *Pan* and "A Wonderful Woman" (1890). But Clarke does not appear to have been resurrected—at least not in print. Perhaps Machen realised that in Dyson, already established in "The Inmost Light" as a sleuth, literary man and student of the science of London, he had a more memorable character than the colourless Clarke (who seems to be some sort of businessman), and so a supernatural detective series was born. Clarke's Japanese bureau had been transferred to Dyson in "The Inmost Light". Machen himself possessed such a desk, and another fictional counterpart of this bureau may have been owned by Lucian Taylor some years before the events of *The Three Impostors*. (A few clues in *The Hill of Dreams* imply that Lucian's adventures take place in the 1880s. "Some Suggestive Dates in the Life of Lucian Taylor" is an essay yet to be written. The action of *The Three Impostors* seems contemporaneous with its composition: the fastidious Dyson is rather offended by the success of *Robert Elsmere*, which appeared in 1888, and the book appears to have been available for some time.)

There was perhaps another consideration for dropping Clarke. The "Novel of the Black Seal" is located around Wentwood and the Caermaen district: the *mise-en-scène* of *The Great God Pan*. A tale involving the Little People would presumably be set in Gwent, and perhaps Machen realised that to involve Clarke in another fantastical romance in the same territory as *Pan* would not only be artistically awkward but stretch credulity to breaking point. The letter shows he was concerned about the similarity between *Pan* and the Clarke sequel. Admittedly Dyson in "The Shining Pyramid" (1895) visits the region previously charted in *The Three Impostors*; though as the "Novel of the Black Seal" is ultimately revealed to be a hoax by Miss Lally, perhaps this coincidence doesn't really count. (It could be argued that not *all* her narrative is fictitious: Professor Gregg did disappear. One possibility is that Helen murdered him in order to get her hands on his collection of prehistoric artefacts for Dr Lipsius.)

One can only regret that Machen does not seem to have left a draft of the original tale. This would probably confirm whether the story was the palimpsest for *The Three Impostors* or whether it was an abortive separate tale. The letter to Lane may be too early for Machen to be writing the *Impostors*; though as he states in *Things Near and Far* he had rescued the "Novel of the Dark Valley" from the destruction wrought upon two books at Turville.[5]

To conclude the matter, Machen's next letter to Lane (3rd February 1894) was published in the *Selected Letters*:

> *I am sending you the pieces I mentioned in my last letter.*
> *They are all pasted in a scrap-book, and I have ticked with*
> *red pencil the stories and articles which seem to me most*
> *appropriate for the purpose.*
> *As a possible alternative to some of them, I also send a MS tale*
> *(10,000 words) called "The Inmost Light".*[6]

It was, of course, "The Inmost Light" which was bound up with *Pan* when Lane published the book in December 1894. The world had to wait many years before the tales such as "The Autophone", "The Lost Club" and "A Double Return" (all 1890) were collected in book form.

Other notebook jottings on Machen concern reminiscences by Edgar Jepson as related to Machen's young friend Colin Summerford, who, according to his diary for 1931, interviewed Jepson on Wednesday, 22nd July. Jepson's address is given in Colin's diary as 120 Adelaide Road—perhaps Adelaide Road, Hampstead. Jepson described Machen as "a bearded mage in those days [the 1890s] and only shaved when he went on the stage". Jepson's *Memories of an Edwardian and Neo-Georgian* (1937) mirrors the description used here.[7] The book contains that astonishing photograph of a heavily bearded, long-haired Machen, reproduced as the frontispiece to *Faunus 1* (Spring 1995), the "Rasputin" photograph perhaps it might be termed; though it would have been unwise to use this description in Arthur's presence.

Talking to Colin, Jepson referred to the great respect of the Benson company for Machen—"Ainley grovelling at his feet". This was the actor Henry Ainley, whose paths also crossed Algernon Blackwood's: Mike Ashley's biography of Blackwood will have a good deal to say on their relationship. Jepson's comment foreshadows, less politely, his statement in *Memories of an Edwardian* that "so deeply respected a member of that famous company was [Machen] that I have seen Mr Henry Ainley... when he was the most attractive *jeune premier* on the London stage, awed in his presence".

Jepson told Colin that all Machen's inheritance was spent in the last year of Amy's life in buying drugs to relieve her pain from cancer. One ostensibly puzzling line in the diary refers to Machen developing biceps like those of two navvies. There is a tragic explanation. In the 1980s Colin said that this was through Machen carrying the dying Amy around their flat in Gray's Inn. Some cryptic references occur in the diary: to what could "hill-dog" refer? Machen taking his bulldog Juggernaut out for long walks while composing *The Hill of Dreams* perhaps? "Monkey play" probably relates to *The Silent Vengeance*, Harry Grattan's melodrama, in which Machen acted at the Gaiety Theatre in 1901.[8] Readers may wish to ponder on one mysterious reference: "Olive's old journalist = Theo." Could this be Olive Custance, the poet who married Lord Alfred Douglas?

Finally, from the cull of those old notebooks, are two fragmentary letters from Machen to the artist and writer Frederick Carter: more fugitives from the *Selected Letters*. Machen attended an exhibition of Carter's work at the Leger Gallery, 13 Old Bond Street, W1 and wrote the following to Carter on 15th June 1932:

My favourite is The Old Actor! I like him very much. He is just the Illustration to the Anecdote Philosophical Inquirer into the Shakespeare Mystery[9]: "Pray, Sir, is it your opinion that . . . er . . . anything . . . has occurred between Hamlet and Ophelia before the curtain rises? The Old Actor "In my time, sir, invariably."

The "Old Actor" portrait of Machen appears in *Frederick Carter A.R.E. 1883-1967, A Study of His Etchings,* by Richard Grenville Clark.[10] At the end of the letter Machen told Carter that "when a new and exquisite edition of my books was called for" Carter alone would be the illustrator: "...and in the hour of that 'when', I will call for your art". In another letter Machen told Carter, then living in Liverpool: "Do not murmur against Liverpool: you might be forced to live in Manchester!" We know from *The Secret Glory* what Machen thought about that grimy industrial behemoth: Panurge is threatened with exile there for his misdemeanours.

In conclusion, the clear moral of all this rambling Machenalia is that the literary researcher should never dispose of any notebooks, no matter how dog-eared or space-consuming, without examining them. Who knows what revelations may be found within?

sources

1 R. Thurston Hopkins, "A London Phantom", Appendix D, *The Letters of Ernest Dowson,* ed. Desmond Flower and Henry Maas (Cassell & Co., 1967), pp. 440-43.

2 Arthur Machen, *Tales of Horror and the Supernatural* (Tartarus Press, 1997), p. 259.

3 *The Autobiography of Arthur Machen* (The Richards Press, 1951), p. 91.

4 Winifred Graham (Mrs Theodore Cory), "One of the Most Extraordinary Men of His Age", in *Observations Casual and Intimate, Being the Second Volume of That Reminds Me* (Skeffington and Son, 1947), pp. 74-83.

5 *The Autobiography of Arthur Machen,* p. 242.

6 *Arthur Machen: Selected Letters,* ed. Roger Dobson, Godfrey Brangham and R.A. Gilbert (The Aquarian Press, 1988), p. 217.

7 The passage relating to Machen from Jepson's *Memories of an Edwardian* was reprinted in *Machenstruck: Tributes to the Apostle of Wonder,* Selected by the Society of Young Men in Spectacles (Caermaen Books, 1988), p. 5.

8 For the plot of the melodrama, see Aidan Reynolds and William Charlton, *Arthur Machen: A Short Account of His Life and Work* (John Baker [Publishers] Ltd for The Richards Press, 1963; Caermaen Books, 1988), p. 86.

9 Perhaps a pun on *A Suggestive Inquiry into the Hermetic Mystery* (1850) by Mary Ann Atwood (née South). See *The Green Round* (Ernest Benn, 1933), p. 122, where it is suggested that the Rev Thomas Hampole corresponded with the author.

10 Reviewed by Mark Valentine in *Machenalia* (Autumn 1998), pp. 8-9.

The Immortal Story of Capt. Scott's Expedition
How Five Brave Englishmen Died

Arthur Machen, 1915

Published in Faunus Issue 7

Children: You are going to hear the true story of five of the bravest and best men who have ever lived on the earth since the world began.

You are English boys and girls, and you must often have heard England spoken of as the greatest country in the world, or perhaps you have been told that the British Empire (which means India, Canada, Australia, New Zealand, South Africa and many other smaller countries, as well as England, Scotland and Ireland) is the greatest Empire that the world has ever seen. Perhaps you have thought that great just means large or big and nothing else. It may mean that, but it means a great deal more than that. The Jews were a great people and so were the Greeks in the old days, and both Jews and Greeks lived in countries which were quite small.

So when we say that England is great we are not thinking of the size of the country or of the number of people who live in it. We are thinking of much more important things, and if you listen to the story that is to be read to you, you will find out what greatness really does mean.

You are to hear about five great men. Their names are: Captain Scott, who was their leader, Captain Oates, Lieutenant Bowers, Dr Wilson, and Petty-Officer Evans. These men are all dead, and they died after dreadful pain, in a dreadful place, called the Antarctic Region. You can find it on the maps and on the globes; it is the very bottom of the world. There, where the South Pole is, it is always cold, it is colder than anything that you have ever felt. There is no proper land there and no

27

water. The sea itself is frozen into waves of ice; the mountains are ice mountains; it is dark night there for many months in the year, and terrible snowstorms and bitter winds make it very difficult for anyone to keep alive for any length of time. At the South Pole, as at the North Pole, there are no living creatures, no grass, no trees, no flowers. There is nothing but ice and snow, and that dreadful cold that freezes off men's hands and feet, as if they had been burnt off in a flaming fire.

Nearly three years ago Captain Scott went on a voyage to this dreadful country. He and the officers under him and the sailors went in a ship called the Terra Nova, which means "the new land." The captain knew quite well what sort of a place he was going to, as he had been there before. So he quite understood the danger of the journey; he knew all about the awful cold; he knew how difficult it was to take enough food over the ice mountains and the snow deserts; he knew how often men got ill and died in these places because of what they have to eat there; and how the frost eats into their faces and their hands and feet. Captain Scott knew of all these dangers and hardships that would have to be borne, and his officers and men knew of them, too. But they went aboard the Terra Nova and sailed away to the South Pole. They sailed from the docks in London, going down the river on a June morning; down the river Thames, out into the English Channel, by Margate and Ramsgate and Dover. Then the Terra Nova sailed through the English Channel between France and England till it came out into the great Atlantic Ocean which divides Europe from America. Then the ship began to sail to the south.

It went by France and Spain and Madeira right out in the Atlantic, and went southwards by West Africa and the Cape of Good Hope. Still southwards the ship sailed by the West of Australia, by South Australia, till they got to New Zealand. All those places are marked on the map, so you can see what a long, long way Captain Scott and his men sailed on their journey to the terrible Antarctic Region. And still, though they had come all this way—fifteen thousand miles or even more—their real journey had not begun.

For they wanted to find the South Pole; that is, the very bottom of the world, the most southern place on it; and that South Pole is far south of New Zealand in the land of eternal ice and snow and cold.

And they took the ship down to that terrible country as far as they could, till the cold began to freeze the water into hard ice, and then they made the ship fast.

Some people wonder why Captain Scott and his men wanted to find the South Pole at all. There is nothing wonderful or beautiful to see there; only the ice and snow, which is all over the land. There is no gold to be found there, you cannot get money by going there; all that a man can hope to get in that place is hunger and cold and sickness, and very likely death itself. Why, then, did Captain Scott want to go there at all?

He went, first of all, because every man who is any good is curious about the world; he wants to know all that there is to be known about it. And it has been thought that by going to the North and South Poles we should find out all sorts of things about the heat and the cold and why the winds blow, and whether the ice is ever likely to move and come over the rest of the world as it once did, hundreds and thousands of years ago. To find out these things and other things of the same kind was one of the reasons why Captain Scott went to find the Pole, but there is another reason which is called the love of adventure, which is often a love of danger. It is this love of adventure and of doing dangerous things which has sent Englishmen all over the world, into the very hot places as well as the very cold places, wherever there was something new to be seen, or something strange to be seen, or something difficult and dangerous to be done. And people who have not got something of this spirit in them are very little good either to themselves or to anybody else.

So Captain Scott sailed down till he came to the frozen sea, and then when the right time came he and four of his companions left the ship and started in sledges for the South Pole. They found it, and they marked the place, and they found out all that there was to be found out, and then they turned back, hoping to go on the ship again and so sail safely to England.

Then their troubles began. It was much colder than they thought it would have been; they had terrible storms, and the ice was the roughest that had ever been seen. Then one of them, Petty-Officer Evans, fell ill, and tumbled on the rough ice on the back of his head and died soon afterwards. He was the strongest of them all, and his death was a great loss to them.

Then Captain Oates, who was an officer in the Army, became ill. He hands and feet were frost-bitten, and he was in dreadful pain. He could hardly walk at all, and yet he dragged his feet along over the snow and ice. He never grumbled; he was always quite cheerful and hopeful, even when his friends saw that he was so ill that he could never see England any more.

But at last Captain Oates knew that he must die, and he lay down to sleep one night in the tent, hoping that he might never wake again in this world. But the next morning he was still alive, and he went to the door of the tent and looked out. An awful storm of wind and snow was raging; and then, turning to his three friends, he said he was going out for a while, and might be away some time. He knew that he was going to die, and they knew it, too; but he went out to die in the storm because he did not wish Captain Scott and the two others to have the pain of seeing his death.

And now listen particularly to what is read next, because it was all written by Captain Scott himself as he lay dying in the tent of cold and starvation. He could not go any further, because of the storm, and there was no more food and no more fuel, so he knew that he and his two friends had to die. He passed the time by writing the story of their trying to get back from the South Pole; and here it is:—

> *The advance party would have returned to the glacier in fine form and with a surplus of food but for the astonishing failure of the man whom we had least expected to fail.*
>
> *Seaman Edgar Evans was thought the strong man of the party, and the Beardmore Glacier is not difficult in fine weather.*
>
> *But on our return we did not get a single completely fine day. This, with a sick companion, enormously increased our anxieties.*
>
> *I have said elsewhere, we got into frightfully rough ice, and Edgar Evans received a concussion of the brain. He died a natural death, but left us a shaken party with the season unduly advanced.*
>
> *But all the facts above enumerated were as nothing to the surprise which awaited us on the Barrier.*
>
> *I maintain that our arrangements for returning were quite adequate, and that no one in the world would have expected the temperature and surface which we encountered at this time of the year.*

On the summit in lat. 85 degs. to lat. 86 degs. we had minus 20 to minus 30.

On the barrier in lat. 82 degs., ten thousand feet lower, we had minus 30 in the day and minus 47 at night pretty regularly, with a continuous head wind during our day marches.

It is clear that these circumstances come on very suddenly, and our wreck is certainly due to this sudden advent of severe weather, which does not seem to have any satisfactory cause.

I do not think human beings ever came through such a month as we have come through, and we should have got through in spite of the weather but for the sickening of a second companion, Captain Oates, and a shortage of fuel in our depots for which I cannot account, and finally but for the storm, which has fallen on us within eleven miles of this depot, at which we hoped to secure the final supplies.

Captain L.E.G. Oates, 6th Inniskilling Dragoons, was the next to be lost. His feet and hands were badly frost-bitten, and, although he struggled on heroically, his comrades knew on March 16th that his end was approaching. He had borne intense suffering for weeks without complaint, and he did not give up hope to the very end.

He was a brave soul. He slept through the night hoping not to wake, but he awoke in the morning.

It was blowing a blizzard. Oates said; "I am just going outside and I may be some time." He went out into the blizzard and we have not seen him since.

We knew that Oates was walking to his death, but, though we tried to dissuade him, we knew it was the act of a brave man and an English gentleman.

After his gallant death, Captain Scott, Dr Wilson, and Lieutenant Bowers pushed northwards as fast as the weather, which was abnormally bad, would let them, but they were forced to camp on March 21 in lat. 79 degs. 40 mins. South; long 169 degs. 23 mins. East.

They were eleven miles south of the big depot at One Ton Camp, but this they never reached owing to a blizzard which is known from the records to have lasted nine days. When the blizzard overtook them their food and their fuel gave out.

Continuing his diary, Captain Scott writes of this blizzard:—

Surely misfortune could scarcely have exceeded this last blow. We arrived within eleven miles of our old One Ton Camp with fuel for one hot meal and food for two days.

For four days we have been unable to leave the tent, a gale blowing about us.

We are weak, writing is difficult, but for my own sake I do not regret this journey, which has shown us that Englishmen can endure hardship, help one another, and meet death with as great a fortitude as ever in the past.

We took risks——we know we took them.

Things have come out against us, and therefore we have no cause for complaint, but bow to the will of Providence, determined still to do our best to the last.

But if we have been willing to give our lives to this enterprise, which is for the honour of our country, I appeal to our countrymen to see that those who depend on us are properly cared for.

Had we lived I should have had a tale to tell of the hardihood, endurance, and courage of my companions which would have stirred the heart of every Englishman.

These rough notes and our dead bodies must tell the tale; but surely, surely, a great, rich country like ours will see that those who are dependent upon us are properly provided for.
(Signed) R. SCOTT, 25ᵗʰ March, 1912.

So these brave men died; and now you know what we mean when we say that they were great. They feared no danger, they never complained, they did their very best, each one was willing to give up his life for the others, and when they knew that there was no hope for them they laid down their lives bravely and calmly like true Christian gentlemen.

From a privately-published manuscript, whose origin and purpose is unkown. The date, 1915, is written upon its back, in pencil.

The Magician, The Bibliophile, and The Librarian

Adrian *Goldstone*

originally published in Faunus issue 10

It will make a little more sense if I start this story at beginning, my collecting of the books of Arthur Machen, my collaboration with Sweetser and others leading to the *Bibliography of Arthur Machen*. In 1959, when I was last in London, it had been known that for a short time Machen had been a member of a Rosicrucian order called The Hermetic Order of the Golden Dawn. Machen even mentions the order in one of his works but under a different name. Others in the order were WB Yeats, AE Waite, and Aleister Crowley. Later in life, Machen, whose father and grandfather were ministers and who descended from a long line of priests, felt badly about his association with the order and would not talk about it.

With me in London was Edwin Steffe, then playing in *The Most Happy Fella*. Steffe showed me a typescript of a book called *The House of the Hidden Light*. He said that it had been printed, that a copy was in the library of the late AE Waite held in trust for a mentally impaired daughter. It was alternate letters by Machen and Waite and was dated 1904. I based my conclusions on the fact that no copy had been seen for fifty-five years, that no mention of it had ever been made by people much interested in Machen and people very close to him. Also, the typescript had been prepared with great care. Usually no one pays much attention to a typed copy when a printed work was in existence. In all of this I was wrong.

I had been of a little help to Timothy d'Arch Smith in preparing his Montague Summers bibliography and one day he wrote to me and said that a collector of occult literature had indeed a copy of *The House of the Hidden Light*. A lot of correspondence followed, I suggested many times that I be allowed to make a microfilm of the book but no attention was made to my request. Finally, Mr Gerald Yorke, the owner of the book, brought it up to London and d'Arch Smith collated it for me for the bibliography. Mr Yorke's fee for allowing the book to be described was a copy of the Machen bibliography.

In due time the Machen bibliography saw print and I sent a copy to Mr Yorke. His son replied that Mr Yorke was on a world tour and I promptly wrote with an invitation to see if he was in San Francisco. However, San Francisco was not on his itinerary but he wrote thanking me for the book and inviting me to call him when I was next in London. I wrote him from Brussels and on my return to London found a letter from him asking me out on Wednesday the 12th, with the precise times of my arrival and departure. I had tried to get John Collett on the phone Sunday and Monday without success. I had the correct telephone number but the operator said there was no such number. I then wired Collett care of his library on Monday and he telephoned me. By that time our schedule was pretty full up, but when I told him of our plans to visit Gloucester, that suited him fine and I gave him Gerald Yorke's number so that he might call him. This brings us up to the start of our visit except that I have not explained the Hermetic Order of the Golden Dawn because I cannot.

We left Paddington at 9:15 am and arrived at Evesham at 11:14. Forthampton Court is on the Welsh side of the Severn River opposite Tewkesbury and twelve miles from Gloucester. At the depot in Evesham were Mr Yorke in a small car and John and Ella Collett in a small car also. They had not phoned of their arrival and I explained that I had not invited them but had thought that they would phone and ask permission to come. Mr Yorke said that if there was not enough to eat the Colletts would have to do without but there was no shortage.

We drove a little way through rolling green fields, some cultivation, some cattle, some sheep, finally we came to a small village. Yorke said, "We try to keep this village without change. I can do this because it belongs to me." Staggered by this statement, we were driven up to the house. The approach is through a long narrow lane of poplars to a cluster of houses; the group of houses containing the agent or overseer's house, servants houses etc. are at the back of the building. From the front and from each side, as far as the eye can see, is perfectly kept lawn. The trees—elm, yew and oak—are arranged that there are three separate vistas. All around are flower beds, raised in their own green houses. We saw several: chrysanthemums, Michaelmas daisies, cyclamen and roses etc.

The "Hall" is a tremendous room, about thirty feet with Norman arched ceilings about fifty feet wide and one hundred long, sparsely furnished. A square revolving bookcase is by a famous builder of the fourteenth century who also constructed a staircase in another part of the rambling building, no nails, all wood pegs. A large alcove with windows, installed by the present owners, gives the only light in the room. A magnificent fireplace is not in use, it would not start to heat the space, and the "Hall" is unused and left cold all the winter.

On the lower floor are many rooms connected by wide halls, tapestries and paintings, on the floors, except the "Hall" which is bare, are Oriental rugs. There are about four libraries on the main floor. Yorke pooh-poohs the books in these rooms which he calls the "House Library" but I saw a three-volume *Don Quixote*, in Spanish, bound in vellum. It had to be a very early edition as d'Arch Smith says there are many treasures there.

Other things of interest include a tomb of a crusader, feet crossed in the sign of the cross and a dog at his feet, this the stone on the top of the tomb. Originally in the church for about three hundred years, it has braved the elements for another three hundred years. Also, a medieval painting on wood, one of about five remaining in Great Britain, the National Gallery watches over it without cost to Yorke.

We lunched in the main dining room, just the kind of a room you would expect in this place; Mrs Yorke waited on us, but there was a girl in the kitchen. The dinner started with the main course, passed around family style; there were lamb chops, but it worked out fine, only John Collett and I had extra chops. The dessert was a kind of melted strawberry ice cream, served in a soup plate.

With our coffee in hand the ladies adjourned into the living room and the three men to an upstairs den where the principal collection was shelved. Yorke's only collecting interest is Aleister Crowley; he has everything! PLUS! Books, manuscripts, letters, typescripts, pressproofs, regalia, buttons, seals, costumes, everything connected with Crowley and the Order of the Golden Dawn and the splinter orders that Crowley was connected with or founded. No one could do a serious study of Crowley without access to this collection.

He then showed me *The House of the Hidden Light*, a very well printed book, on heavy hand-made paper. I was wrong in suggesting that the book was Crowley's. Yorke bought it, then showed it to Crowley who made notations in it. This was the book I had come so far to see. Later in looking over large scrap books of Crowley material I noticed a prospectus put out by John M. Watkins, 29 Charing Cross, London SW, of a book to be printed by the Cranford Press, Chiswick Road, with a page of the book they were offering. I immediately recognised one of the initials in a decorated square as the same one in *The House of the Hidden Light* and a careful inspection showed that they were identical and probably the Cranford Press printed *The House of the Hidden Light*, although there is always the possibility that two or more printers bought the type from the same type foundry.

Then to my astonishment Yorke told me that I could take the book back to London and have it microfilmed. He also gave me a copy of a typed monograph that he had written on the Golden Dawn and a list of the members, their names and temples. Machen was *Filius Aquarum I-U* (Isis Urania Temple No. 3); Yorke says that Machen was never more than a novice in the order under AE Waite.

Yorke's name does not appear on the list of names, but he knew Crowley personally and he has tried out the abacraballa and he says it works. He did his magic, picked up a tart in London and told her that she was going to get a diamond, and sure enough someone gave her a diamond soon after, not a good one, but a diamond just the same. Once in Wales while on a lone hiking trip it was pouring rain and he did magic to find a cave. Then went to a farmhouse to get dry and something to eat. He asked the farmer if there was a cave nearby and the farmer said, "right here". Yorke is looking for a bookplate that Beardsley did for Crowley, probably without Crowley's name on it. As a coincidence in *The House of the Hidden Light* are two letters from Sims the bookseller to Yorke telling of Sims selling to Lord Esher copies of *Thesaurus Incantatus* and *The Way to Attain* to the USA and the purchaser was me.

Dorothy was told of the help, or staff as it is called in England, that a married couple work for them, she as a cook, he the gardener; three women came in every day for cleaning, a stone mason and a carpenter work out their rent in upkeep of the place, but they really need a larger staff and could not get them. We took farewell to the magician and his wife and with the book clutched under my arm, the Colletts drove us to Newport, past Caerleon-on-Usk, Machen's birthplace, and the pub of the Three Salmons that he wrote about. Ella Collett whipped up a supper for us in no time at all and we left for London at 7.19 ending the story of the Magician, the Bibliophile and the Librarian.

An Exploration Beyond The veil
Guided By Arthur Machen

Tessa Farmer
published in Faunus issue 11

> *As the chemist in his experiments is sometimes astonished to find unknown, unexpected elements in the crucible or the receiver, as the world of material things is considered by some a thin veil of the immaterial universe, so he who reads wonderful prose or verse is conscious of suggestions that cannot be put into words, which do not rise from the logical sense, which are rather parallel to than connected with the sensuous delight. The world so disclosed is rather the world of dreams, rather the world in which children sometimes live, instantly appearing, and instantly vanishing away, a world beyond all expression or analysis, neither of the intellect nor of the senses.*
> [*The Hill of Dreams*]

Imagination. The realm where anything is possible. Dominated by children, we have all lived there, but inevitably as we grow older we must leave. As reason gradually overshadows our fantasies, the world and our senses become muted. Rationality quashes our willingness to suspend disbelief in order to enjoy the pleasures of wonder, as objects begin to lose their capacity for transformation.

I consider myself fortunate to still have access to this realm, a perquisite of being an artist. In my work I explore the realm of illusion and reality in the hope of finding an appropriate visual answer. I consider myself as a tool to realise possibilities of the imagination that would otherwise linger unseen, in spite of looking. A dandelion clock turns inside out, becoming a new species; a bumblebee buzzes by, ridden by a skeleton fairy. My aim is to reactivate the imagination by making suggestions of what could be, thus creating a gateway to this other domain. Something similar to the rabbit hole in *Alice in Wonderland*.

I only recently became familiar with the work of Arthur Machen. The timing was a little odd because he was my great-grandfather, and he wrote about fairies. When I began to create fairies, of macabre character, several years ago, neither my mother nor my grandmother commented. It took a stranger, an Arthur Machen enthusiast who came across my work, to point out the parallels between his writing and my own work. After all, it is often very difficult to see what is right under your nose. Machen creates with words what I anticipate through sculpture. He believed that imagination rather than intellect was the vital portion of the soul of man; his aim was to restore the sense of wonder and mystery into our perception of the world, by revealing the beauty hidden beneath the crust of commonplace things. He had a firm belief in another world beyond the shadows of this one, and strove to rend the veil, thus communicating the sense of this secret reality. I felt that I had found not only an ally, but also a guide into another reality.

I decided to visit the places that inspired Machen in his attempt to penetrate the veil, and where his most powerful stories are set. I hoped that through an immersion in these tales and in his native countryside I might gain access to the secret reality beyond the outward appearance of the world. And I felt that, in some strange yet comforting way, I had my great-grandfather as my guide.

* * *

Our journey takes us to South Wales, more specifically Gwent, where Machen was born in Caerleon-on-Usk in 1863.

> *I shall always esteem it as the greatest piece of fortune that has fallen to me, that I was born in that noble, fallen Caerleon-on-Usk, in the heart of Gwent. My greatest fortune, I mean, from the point of view which I now more especially have in*

mind, the career of letters. For the older I grow the more firmly
I am convinced that anything which I may have accomplished
in literature is due to the fact that when my eyes were first
opened in earliest childhood they had before them the vision of
an enchanted land.

[*Far Off Things*]

Just escaping the urban sprawl of nearby Newport, Caerleon is as I imagined it to be, a sleepy village with a close-knit community. The River Usk winds alongside the village; the ancient forest of Wentwood and undulating hills of Mynydd Maen loom in the background. Twyn Barlwm is the southern climax of this ridge, with "that mystic tumulus" at the summit, believed to be the tomb of some valiant chieftain. Surrounded by this lush countryside, the built-up village seems dull and grey in comparison until one comes across the remains of *Isca Silurum*, a roman settlement, amongst the houses and municipal buildings. Sections of the Roman wall that once surrounded the fortress still survive. The remains of the barracks which are surrounded by fences feel somewhat neglected and taken for granted. There is rubbish on the ground and I suppose it to be a gathering place for the local youth. It is difficult to visualise the scene in Machen's time, surrounded still by countryside rather than concrete. The urban development dilutes the spell of the British-Roman life that once engulfed his native land and the strange magic that Machen found in these cryptic Roman ruins. However, further afield just outside the walled area, is something more inspiring: the amphitheatre. This undulating earthwork, before excavation, was believed to be King Arthur's Round Table. Here we observe a gaunt young man deep in meditation. This is Lucian Taylor, protagonist of *The Hill of Dreams*, a story which Machen describes as "a 'Robinson Crusoe' of the soul".

> *I would take the theme of solitude, loneliness, separation from*
> *mankind, but, in the place of a desert island and a bodily*
> *separation, my hero should be isolated in London and find his*
> *chief loneliness in the midst of myriads of myriads of men. His*
> *should be a solitude of the spirit, and the ocean surrounding him*
> *and disassociating him from his kind should be a spiritual deep.*
>
> [*Introduction, The Hill of Dreams, Knopf, 1923*]

Lucian has indeed led an isolated existence. Due to poverty his father took him out of school at seventeen. Disgusted by the petty provincialism of the inhabitants of Caermaen (Machen's fictional name for Caerleon), whom he considered barbarous, he turned to the world of books for companionship and found solace in literature, feeding upon Dickens, Cervantes and Rabelais among others. He would roam the surrounding countryside, enraptured in the magic of the Roman ruins, desolate hills and archaic woods.

> *As the red gained in the sky, the earth and all upon it glowed, even the grey winter fields and the bare hillsides crimsoned, the waterpools were cisterns of molten brass, and the very road glittered. He was wonderstruck, almost aghast, before the scarlet magic of the afterglow. The old Roman fort was invested with fire; flames from heaven were smitten about its walls and above there was a dark floating cloud, like a fume of smoke, and every haggard writhing tree showed as black as midnight against the blast of the furnace.*
> [*The Hill of Dreams*]

The Roman fort—the "hill" of the title—is fictional, but is likely to have been based upon Lodge Hill, an Iron Age fort situated not far from Caerleon. On the hillside that shelters the Roman fort, Lucian encountered and fell in love with a farmer's daughter, Annie Morgan, who became his muse. When he found out that she had married he was more relieved than saddened as his idealised image of her could continue; indeed he was thankful to her as "the key that opened the shut palace, and now he was secure on the throne of ivory and gold". His love was not lost, but instead fuelled his dreams. Through the ancient memories of the dead civilisations which surround Caermaen and the magic incantations of literature, his imagination has developed to a point where he is able to cut himself off from humanity and pass into another sphere, dwelling as an observer in the exotic dream city where he sees the Romans among their vineyards and in the shade of ilex trees, and delights in the sensual experience of their rich pleasures. His imagination triumphant over harsh reality, he has elevated himself above the common level of life and come to understand the symbolism behind the alchemist's transmutation of lesser metals to gold.

To Lucian, entranced in the garden of Avallaunius, it seemed
very strange that he had once been so ignorant of all the
exquisite meanings of life. Now, beneath the violet sky, looking
through the brilliant trellis of the vines, he saw the picture;
before, he had gazed in sad astonishment at the squalid rag
which was wrapped about it.

Beyond the veil for Lucian then is enlightenment; perfection of
the self. The ageless wonders of nature have conjured another dimension
for him, and we sense the numinous beyond the common life. He is
becoming possessed by a pagan faun-creature; the lure of his Celtic
ancestors has drawn him into "outland and occult territory", into fairyland
where the "Little People" emerge from their caves; "He was beleaguered by
desires that had slept in his race for ages." That there is this other, unseen
reality reflects the Neo-Platonic view of the world that this reality of ours
at once conceals and symbolises a higher and greater one. The ultimate
reality of the universe is held to be an infinite, unknowable, perfect One.
For man Spirituality means the ascent from the lower sense-reality to the
higher spiritual reality, through the contemplation of nature; not of the
wonder of physical reality, but the wonder of the invisible spiritual reality,
believed to be the cause and ultimate meaning behind the physical reality.

We shall go on seeking it to the end, so long as there are men on
earth. We shall seek it in all manner of strange ways; some of
them wise, and some of them unutterably foolish. But the search
will never end… It is the secret of things; the real truth that is
everywhere hidden under outward appearances… There are
many ways of the great quest of the secret.
   [*"With the Gods in Spring"*]

I hear Machen's voice, urging us to depart and leave Lucian
Taylor in his meditation. He stresses that probing further into his
experience will not benefit us at this early stage of our journey. For
the meantime Lucian Taylor has provided a valuable insight into our
pursuit. I suspect we will encounter him again.

As we leave the village, the "hanging woods" and "domed hills" of
this strangely beautiful country begin to engulf us; to carry us away from

the familiar, closer to the unseen worlds that are pressing into ours. This land is certainly awe-inspiring. Machen calls it "occult territory"; this combination of beautiful scenery with a certain something that makes it seem unearthly. Being well acquainted with Welsh history—the Celtic myths, the land's mediaeval history, the Roman villages and forts—he superimposes this rich history on the landscape, evoking the haunted memories of the past and creating a fourth dimension, time, which is again accentuated by a fifth, his imagination. It is an enchanted land where ancient myths and mystical realms re-emerge through Machen's intense imagination. But we must be wary, as his is not a benign, sentimentalised vision of nature—there is darkness as well as delightfulness.

Heading deeper into the forest, there is a sense of some other semi-human species materialising through the different order of shapes, and lurking in the sinuous limbs, crevices and hollows of the ancient trees as if we are about to enter some elemental realm. I sense the danger of being tripped by wicked tree spirits, followed by muttering willow trees or led astray by fairies. The image of the amphitheatre lingers in my mind. It has an otherworldly presence, and not simply a historical one. It is organic, more an earthwork than a construction built by the hand of man. Suddenly I recall a description in "The Shining Pyramid", in which a young girl, Annie Trevor, vanishes without trace. Local people are fearful of a nearby hill which they believe to be a fairy castle and are convinced that she has been "taken by the fairies". Could the amphitheatre at Caerleon be a gateway beyond the veil, into another realm: fairyland?

> *Almost without warning the ground shelved suddenly away on all sides, and Dyson looked down into a circular depression, which might well have been a Roman amphitheatre, and the ugly crags of limestone rimmed it round as if with a broken wall… It did, in truth, stir and seethe like an infernal cauldron. The whole of the sides and bottom tossed and writhed with vague and restless forms… It was as if the sweet turf and the cleanly earth had suddenly become quickened with some foul writhing growth.*
> [*"The Shining Pyramid"*]

"I think not, my dear," Machen's voice comes to me again. "The amphitheatre is certainly far too close to civilisation. The Little People prefer their entrances far more remote and desolate. Perhaps we should venture to Grey Hill. That is where Annie Trevor was taken."

"The Little People" is the old name for the fairy folk, or the Tylwyth Teg in Wales, where they dwell in Annwn. This is an underground nether world region, commonly believed to be located deep inside the earth or in hills particularly near places linked with the dead, such as prehistoric burial mounds, or ancient ruins. Heaven for the ancient Celts, unlike that of the Christians, was not situated in some unknown realm of planetary space, but here on Earth. Sometimes it was a subterranean world entered through caves, hills or mountains and inhabited by many kinds of invisible beings, such as fairies and demons. Annwn, unlike most otherworlds in mythology, can be entered by the living.

Contained within the *Book of Taleisin* (Taleisin was allegedly a Welsh bard) is "The Spoils of Annwn", an obscure Welsh poem dating from perhaps the tenth century. It is the tale of a raid on the part of Arthur and his knights through Annwn, questing for a magical cauldron in the custody of nine maidens. Few men survived this dangerous expedition. Machen's own perilous quest was to achieve "ecstasy" in his writing. He defined this as rapture, wonder, awe, mystery; anything which signifies a withdrawal from the common life and common consciousness.

> *"You saw the appearance of those things that gathered thick and writhed in the Bowl; you may be sure that what lay bound in the midst of them was no longer fit for earth."*
> *"So?" said Vaughan.*
> *"So she passed in the Pyramid of Fire," said Dyson, "and they passed again to the under-world, to the places beneath the hills."*
> [*"The Shining Pyramid"*]

There are many theories on the origins of "those things"; they may be pagan nature spirits, fallen angels trapped in limbo, or the souls of the dead awaiting reincarnation; hovering somewhere between the physical and the spiritual, between life and death. We can be sure however that these are not the pretty minuscule creatures that dominated the Victorian era.

As we approach Grey Hill, above the forest of Wentwood, we consider Machen's essay "The Little People" (based on the myth of the Asiki, or Little Beings, in the French Congo), and he recounts an explanation of fairies as tribes of aboriginal troglodyte pygmies overcome and sent into the dark by invaders. They lurk in subterranean dwellings under the hills in the wildest and remotest countryside; beyond the boundaries of the known, in the darkness of our past. However they are supernatural rather than a lost tribe. Much of the folk lore of the world is but an exaggerated account of events that really happened and can be explained with reference to these goblin men who, unlike humans, have retained their primal link with the other world. Their closeness to physical nature links them with the bestial and the wild. Their need and desire for human energy forces them to abduct humans, sometimes babies, replacing them with changelings. In "Out of the Earth" such creatures, who wreak havoc in a quiet seaside village, are only visible to children and the child-like.

> *He peered over the green wall of the fort, and there in the ditch he saw a swarm of noisome children, horrible little stunted creatures with old men's faces, with bloated faces, with little sunken eyes, with leering eyes. It was worse than uncovering a brood of snakes or a nest of worms.*
> [*"Out of the Earth"*]

The creatures that we encounter in this strange borderland world, between dreams and death, are horrible and loathsome, responsible for abductions, murders and rape. So this was the fate of poor Annie Trevor. The young woman's miscegenation with the Little People, no matter how unwilling, rendered her unfit for life.

A retarded boy, the hybrid produced by intercourse between a mortal woman and a dwarf goblin man, played a role in the fate of Professor Gregg who also disappeared on this forsaken hilltop, in the "Novel of the Black Seal". Unlike Annie, who was abducted, his lifetime ambition was to penetrate the veil, seeking the ecstasy beyond. On the discovery of the "black seal", a stone carved with symbols that could not be deciphered by "ordinary" people, he became caught up in the lust of the chase after the unknown realm of the Little People that the stone half revealed:

"believe me, we stand amidst sacraments and mysteries full of awe, and it doth not yet appear what we shall be. Life, believe me, is no simple thing, no mass of grey matter and congeries of veins and muscles to be laid naked by the surgeon's knife; man is the secret which I am about to explore, and before I can discover him I must cross over weltering seas indeed, and oceans and the mists of many thousand years. You know the myth of the lost Atlantis; what if it be true, and I am destined to be called the discoverer of that wonderful land?"

[*"Novel of the Black Seal"*, *The Three Impostors*]

Unfortunately for Professor Gregg, an awareness of his potential fate was not enough to defy his uncontrollable desire to puncture the veil; a case of "curiosity killed the cat" indeed. At least his curiosity had been satisfied. Having unearthed the knowledge of the Little People, he was able to read the key of the "awful transmutation of the hills"; not in a literal sense, but rather the transformation of the conception of what lies within the hills. With this revelation came the secret held by the black seal, of human degeneration into primeval slime and animal form.

On reaching the summit of Grey Hill, we come across strange bowl-like pits, similar to that in which the hideous forms writhe in "The Shining Pyramid". There is something of awe mixed with the horror Dyson and Vaughan experienced whilst witnessing the Pyramid of Fire summoned in the earthy bowl by the Little People. This is a captivating combination of curiosity mixed with fear, their horror being created in part by their wonder. It is echoed at the beginning of "The White People", in the meandering discussion on the nature of sin and evil that takes place between two armchair philosophers, one an alter ego of Machen: "Sorcery and Sanctity... these are the only realities. Each is an ecstasy, a withdrawal from the common life."

Sin, apparently, is "an effort to gain the ecstasy and the knowledge that pertain alone to angels, and in making this effort man becomes a demon... The saint endeavours to recover a gift which he has lost; the sinner tries to obtain something which was never his." Only when moved by ecstasy can man peer beyond the veil and comprehend something of the glory and terror about him, but this is a violation of the natural order of things. If sorcery then is the tendency of sinners, this begs the question, is Machen a sinner? (I rather like to think he is parodying the abundant criticism he received as an outrageous and scandalous writer). What follows, to illustrate the theme of this conversation, is the diary of a naive young girl and a spellbinding stream-of-consciousness immersion in her experience. From an early age she was privy to secrets and sees "little white faces" around her cradle. Most likely these are fairies. Her nurse, a witch, introduced her to strange old rhymes and rituals, and she had a series of mystical visions involving supernatural presences in the woods. Here, on Grey Hill, the desolate landscape, the standing stone circle and the bowls in the earth resonate the dreamlike landscapes where she had adventures of her own in the wilds of the countryside, at once beautiful and bestial. Here mounds form patterns with hidden meaning, rocks anthropomorphise and nymphs and fairies emerge.

> *I went on into the dreadful rocks. There were hundreds and hundreds of them. Some were like horrid grinning men; I could see their faces as if they would jump at me out of the stone, catch hold of me, and drag me with them back into the rock, so that I should always be there.*
> [*"The White People"*]

The girl felt accepted and honoured by this mysterious world of dormant stones and it became her substitute for the society of ordinary people (as did Lucian's world in *The Hill of Dreams*), with whom she never wanted to share her secrets. Eventually, she committed suicide there. Perhaps this was her way of blinding herself to the mundane world; to become fully part of her imaginative dream world.

In the context of the conversation, her suicide is not a sin, nor a real evil, for although she crossed the veil, it was her indoctrination by her nurse that led to this, rather than her own ambition. Nevertheless, as we have seen, the perils of crossing the veil are extreme.

Earlier, as were approaching Wentwood forest, Machen pointed out the ruins of an old manor house, Bertholly. Now it is time to return to it, he tells us, so we can see where a terrifying act of sin occurred. The lonely house is enigmatic and beautiful even in its dilapidated state. Machen recounts his memories of the house:

It became one of the many symbols of the world of wonder that
were offered to me, it became, as it were, a great word in the
secret language by which the mysteries were communicated.
[Introduction, *The Great God Pan*, 1916 edition]

And so this house on the hill became the residence of Professor
Gregg during his pursuit of the Little People, and also the setting for
the horrors that take place in *The Great God Pan*. It is where characters
in both tales pondered the darker mysteries of the universe whilst gazing
upon the "occult territory" of the Usk Valley.

[*Dr Raymond*] *"I tell you that all these things—yes, from the*
star that has just shone out in the sky to the solid ground beneath
our feet—I say that all these are but dreams and shadows: the
shadows that hide the real world from our eyes. There is a real
world, but it is beyond this glamour and this vision... beyond
them all as beyond a veil. I do not know whether any human
being has ever lifted that veil; but I do know, Clarke, that you
and I shall see it lifted this very night from before another's eyes.
You may think all this strange nonsense; it may be strange, but
it is true, and the ancients knew what lifting the veil means.
They call it seeing the god Pan."

Pan is the goat-foot pagan God of death and rebirth, the horned
God of the wild places and father of all living things upon the earth
who causes fear in the hearts of man and beast. Machen understood
how paganism, driven underground by Christianity, could have become
a force for evil. Pan's retinue of fauns, nymphs and satyrs lurk in forest
grottoes, enticing the girl in "The White People" and possessing Lucian
in *The Hill of Dreams*.

In the quiet of Bertholly, Dr Raymond, witnessed by his friend
Clarke, performs a minor incision in certain nerve cells of the brain of a
young woman in order to break down the barrier between this world and
that beyond the veil. We see her awake with a look of great wonder upon
her face which is instantly replaced by hideous terror and convulsions,
after which she never recovers.

"Yes," said the doctor, still quite cool, "it is a great pity; she is a hopeless idiot. However, it could not be helped; and, after all, she has seen the Great God Pan."

Years later we come across a beautiful young woman of sordid depravity, who is responsible for the ruin and subsequent deaths of several men. Eventually Clarke, haunted by his past involvement with Dr Raymond, and two other men find this woman and force her suicide.

What I said Mary would see, she saw, but I forgot that no human eyes can look on such a vision with impunity. And I forgot, as I have just said, that when the house of life is thus thrown open, there may enter in that for which we have no name, and human flesh may become the veil of a horror one dare not express... Helen Vaughan did well to bind the cord about her neck and die, though the death was horrible. The blackened face, the hideous form upon the bed, changing and melting before your eyes from woman to man, from man to beast, and from beast to worse than beast, all the strange horror that you witnessed, surprises me but little... And now Helen is with her companions...

At the end of the tale we discover that Helen was Mary's daughter, and the god Pan her father. The "strange horror" of her descent into primeval slime is the hideous revenge measured out to the offspring of a god and a mortal. This gruesome demise is echoed in Welsh tales of men who crumble into dust on their return from fairyland.

As the veil of darkness begins to fall on us I become wary of this house and the horrors it has witnessed. We decide to return to Caerleon; the Little People lurk in the undergrowth on our route. Having learned that these beings are far more sinister than I once thought, our journey is swift. As we approach Caerleon, I recall Lucian Taylor, and I wonder what became of him? When we left him he was rapt in ecstatic mediation.

"Ah, dear Lucian. He sought what I did. To recreate his vision on paper..."

...to invent a story which would recreate those vague impressions of wonder and awe and mystery that I myself had received from the form and shape of the land of my boyhood and youth.

[*Far Off Things*]

In this land, and then in London, Lucian attempted to capture these emotions on paper, agonisingly analysing and recreating his visions. Tortured by his vain attempts to translate his spiritual visions onto paper, he became more and more immersed in his work; losing any desire to communicate with other people, "he realised that he had lost the art of humanity forever". He became paranoid, morbidly wondering if he was human at all; "he wondered if there were some drop of fairy blood in his body that made him foreign and a stranger in this world."

Eventually, with comforting thoughts of his beloved native Gwent, he returned to his dream, but this time, overcome by his imagination, he had no control over it. The once luxuriant Roman city became suffused with disturbing images of black magic and witchcraft, of the darkness and disillusion he had come to experience. He had descended from an ideal spiritual beauty to a fevered nightmare of depravity. Identifying himself with his art, and his inability to work out the alchemy of the word, he saw no other way out. He was found dead from a drug overdose; a neat pile of paper on his desk—his manuscript. "It was all covered with illegible hopeless scribblings; only here and there it was possible to recognise a word."

Although Machen denies it, the story of Lucian Taylor is highly autobiographical. He also suffered tremendously as a writer and endured the difficulties of being an artist. Days passed when he was unable to write a single word. At times, tortured by his quest for ecstasy he would experience euphoria followed by near suicidal despair. He set out his theory of literature, or rather his own literary goals in *Hieroglyphics*, stating that to be called literature, a work must contain ecstasy.

Literature, as I see it, is the art of describing the indescribable; the art of exhibiting symbols which may hint at the ineffable mysteries behind them; the art of the veil, which reveals what it conceals.

For him art was of the supernatural, the hieroglyphic was a metaphor signifying the high and hidden nature of everyday things, and ecstasy was the path to experience this. Was he himself successful in his quest?

Again and again Machen has striven to rend the veil, and at precious moments he has lifted a corner and let us peep through to the other side. He is skilled at unsettling rather than shocking; hinting at rather than demonstrating; suggesting rather than showing, until finally the picture you saw emerging all along becomes visible. Given the fates of his characters, it is almost a relief that we are not permitted a close view of the mysteries that were so clear to him. Perhaps we are seeking what should not be sought.

Machen felt he had never fulfilled his ambition, writing of himself, in *Far Off Things*: "He dreamed in fire; he has worked in clay." I would disagree. When immersed in *The Hill of Dreams*, I did indeed withdraw from this world, from the common life, into the mystical worlds of the Welsh countryside. Perhaps there was no need to journey to Wales in a hope of heightening this adventure. The experience was a glimpse, rather than a journey beyond the veil. But a glimpse is all we require, as the power of imagination paints the rest of the picture. Machen loved and revered his native Wales all his life, yet he never lived there again after moving to London. He saw this city as a challenge for a writer from the countryside and found the same magic in the seemingly barren city streets as in the narrow country lanes overgrown with fragrant wild flowers.

Although he felt that he had never succeeded in his quest for ecstasy, I believe that it is the actual journey that matters and the importance of things that are discovered and achieved along the way. I hope that Arthur Machen eventually realised this too.

We were skirting a wild little hill. It was a place of rough grass, winter withered; of bracken clumps turned brown; of brambles that had forgotten autumn berries, black and rich; of the twisted, ancient thorn tree, dark and dreaming of fairyland. And as we passed on our way, while the keen wind shook the bare, brown boughs as it went roaring down the valley to the brook, while the huge clouds rolled on to the sea; there I saw on the hillside, under a low black thorn bush rising from withered bracken, the green leaves and pale yellow blossoms of a daffodil, shaking in that high, cold wind.

[*"With the Gods in Spring"*]

The Great Return, The Great War and The Great Revival

Gwilym Games
originally published in Faunus issue 11

Prologue

> *But he gulped with astonishment as he spoke, for, indeed, the grey men were falling by the thousands. The English could hear the guttural scream of the German officers, the crackle of their revolvers as they shot the reluctant; and still line after line crashed to earth.*
>
> *And all the while the Latin-bred soldier heard the cry:*
>
> *"Harow! Harow! Monseigneur, dear saint, quick to our aid! St George help us!"*[1]

✳   ✳   ✳

> *And as the last breath was passing her lips, she heard a very faint, sweet sound, like the tinkling of a silver bell... And as the bell rang and trembled in her ears, a faint light touched the wall of her room and reddened, till the whole room was full of rosy fire. And then she saw standing before her bed three men in blood-coloured robes with shining faces. And one man held a golden bell in his hand. And the second man held up something shaped like the top of a table. It was like a great jewel, and it was of a blue colour, and there were rivers of silver and of gold running through it and flowing as quick streams flow, and*

there were pools in it as if violets had been poured out into water, and then it was green as the sea near the shore, and then it was the sky at night with all the stars shining, and then the sun and the moon came down and washed in it. And the third man held up high above this a cup that was like a rose on fire; "there was a great burning in it, and a dropping of blood in it, and a red cloud above it, and I saw a great secret. And I heard a voice that sang nine times, 'Glory and praise to the Conqueror of Death, to the Fountain of Life immortal.'"[2]

Two quotations from Arthur Machen, the first obviously from "The Bowmen", the second from *The Great Return*, works separated only by about a year. In both, the hallowed saints of mediaeval times return to work miracles: in the first to bring death by the thousand on the battlefields of France, in the second to bring life to one consumptive girl in the rural quiet of Wales. Machen regarded the first story as "an indifferent piece of work" and the second actually became one of his favourites. Yet Machen warned his publisher in advance that *The Great Return* would not sell. The reasons he offered for this later, that The Faith Press was obscure and might not advertise properly, seem reasonable enough. Yet the publisher must have thought Machen was being unduly modest, for his name was resounding from the hilltops in 1915; *The Angels of Mons: The Bowmen and Other Legends of the War* had just sold one hundred thousand copies, and *The Great Return* would be well advertised just through being serialised in *The Evening News*, which had a high circulation.[3] Why did not Machen simply advance a troop in the same style as "The Bowmen", to be included in *The Great Return* to ensure its success? After all, Machen did deploy a similar formation in "The Men from Troy", which appeared in *The Evening News* in September 1915 and subsequently in the second edition of *The Angels of Mons*, using Achaean heroes to reinforce the British in Gallipoli.[4] I hope to discover the answer to this question by exploring the roots of some of the ideas behind *The Great Return*, which is perhaps the best, if not the most well known, of Machen's stories from the Great War.

I   "we talked of the war, of course,
     since that is not to be avoided"

The First World War still casts a heavy shadow in its ninetieth anniversary
year and the Angels controversy is only one of the issues that still summons
attention, most notably in David Clarke's excellent new book, *The Angel
of Mons: Phantom Soldiers and Ghostly Guardians*. Yet, the controversy
about whether the Angels existed or not has distracted attention from
the effect of the dispute on Machen's other writings of the time. Machen's
war against the Angels and those supporting their authenticity led to
accusations against him of arrogance, avarice, disbelief and the worst sin
of all in wartime, being unpatriotic. All of these are strange accusations
against Machen, but it is particularly odd to think that the writer of such
an obviously morale-boosting tale as "The Bowmen" could be accused of
being unpatriotic.

Machen's early fictional works in wartime were fervent examples
of the enthusiastic, jingoistic and martial emotions that infected all of
Britain at the outbreak of war. Germany was an unproblematic target for
Machen, who unsurprisingly had little affection for "a country ruled by
scientific principles", while he loved France. Like many British people,
Machen's feelings were heavily influenced by reports of German atrocities
during their invasion of neutral Belgium where German troops killed
more than six thousand civilians, including women and Roman Catholic
priests, attempting to root out hypothetical resistance, which rumour
amongst the Germans claimed was orchestrated by Jesuits. Notorious
measures were ordered like the razing of the town of Louvain, resulting
in the burning of the priceless mediaeval university library and the church
of Saint Peter, and the shelling of Rheims Cathedral. These barbaric acts
were bound to rouse Machen's hatred and seemingly justified demonising
the "Hun", a process that had deep roots in Britain. Machen had even read
a copy of the earliest German invasion scare story *The Battle of Dorking*
in his youth in Caerleon. Unsurprisingly then besides true atrocities
newspapers readily added lurid second-hand reports of bayoneted babies,
outraged nuns and crucified children which were as unreliable as the
tales surrounding the Angels, though many, including Machen, did not
question them, especially after they were seemingly endorsed by the
official Bryce report in May 1915.[5]

Machen's contribution to winning what seemed to him a war against "savages" was to put his literary skills to work, though not on their highest level. Machen's fictional work asserted the justice of the allied cause in a number of ways. Firstly, he portrayed the Germans as monstrous, even shooting their own men as seen in the quote above (it should be noted that while British military discipline executed 346 soldiers in the war, the Germans killed seven times less); he recycled atrocity tales in the stories "The Soldier's Rest", featuring a bayoneted child, and later in "The Monstrance", where a German soldier, "who killed the old priest and helped crucify the little child against the church door", is slowly driven mad by "hallucinations". (Machen also casually mentions a slaughtered baby story, yet notably makes little moral capital of it, in "War and The Christian Faith".)[6] Secondly, his stories mobilised *en masse* all of Britain's literary and historical heritage into battle on the Allied side, conscripting not only Agincourt archers, but King Arthur, Wellington, St George, Nelson's sailors, Shakespeare, Greek heroes, and even the Spirit of Whit Monday. Obviously, the propagandist implication of Machen's stories is that God is clearly on the side of the *Entente* because their cause is just, and what is more, British Culture, symbolised through history, literature and legend, is more than a match for scientific German *Kultur*. So it might seem at first glance that Machen was simply following the remit (albeit in his own distinctive style) of his unloved employer, Lord Northcliffe, whose newspapers were centrepieces of Allied propaganda, helping to swell stories of German mayhem, and boosting Allied victories. Northcliffe later won the accolade of being blamed by General Ludendorff for Germany's defeat, which seems only fair, as Northcliffe had also been blamed for starting the war because of his longstanding promotion of German invasion scare stories.[7]

However, Machen's patriotism and attitude to the war was far from being simple; this war was for him part of a deeper, ongoing conflict, a confrontation between the forces of "sensible", scientific materialism and that of old-fashioned, romantic, literary mysticism. He summed it up nicely in a 1916 article in which he denounced anyone who supported the destruction of a beautiful, meandering, Pembrokeshire country lane for swifter transport as: "speaking on the Prussian side of the great quarrel that is now dividing the earth. The world is now fighting out the cause of the broad road and the winding lane, and I am glad that we are on the right side".[8]

Machen's position was full of intrinsic tensions; to see how profound they were we must go back to another story on the Sangraal, *The Secret Glory*, written almost ten years earlier. Here Machen furiously assaulted the Imperial British establishment embodied in the Great Public Schools. The most telling quote in retrospect is Machen's account of the life of the Old Luptonian, Captain Pelly who: "led the milder and more serious subalterns the devil's own life. In India he 'lay doggo' with great success against some hill tribe armed with seventeenth century muskets and some rather barbarous knives; he seems to have been present at the 'Conference of the Powers' described so brightly by Mr Kipling. Promoted to a captaincy, he fought with conspicuous bravery in South Africa, winning the Victoria Cross for his rescue of a wounded private at the instant risk of his own life, and he finally led his troop into a snare set by an old farmer; a rabbit of average intelligence would have smelt and evaded it."[9]

The entire Public School ethos was satirised by Machen in *The Secret Glory*: the cult of team sports; the sense of ingrained superiority; the unquestioning conformity; the "loyal co-operation" and "absurd observances" which supported their "main purpose to breed Brave Average Boobies", perfect for Army life as junior officers, and ready to die cheerfully. The existence of men like Pelly, churned out as a product, ready to join up in droves, was essential in creating the leadership nucleus of the new mass volunteer army Britain was to need in the Great War. At the time, the Public Schools were perceived both by themselves and others as saviours of the nation, and though some of their creations broke their conditioning, like Siegfried Sassoon and Wilfred Owen, most never questioned the war at the time.[10]

A particularly notable satirical passage in *The Secret Glory* celebrates the exceptional bravery of Old Luptonians, for which they won awards for gallantry out of all proportion to the size of the school. Indeed, it became a truism that whenever there was a dangerous, even suicidal mission to be undertaken, then a Luptonian was the man to ask. The Rev Rawson in his vitriolic review of *The Secret Glory* in the *Church Times* (July 13th, 1922) claimed the book was an insult to the valiant dead, and that Machen should be horsewhipped.

However, *The Secret Glory* was written before the Great War; in 1914 Machen was on the same side as the establishment he had previously questioned—indeed, it was one of Kipling's stories that helped inspire

"The Bowmen". As the war went on it became clear it was not to be won quickly, nor by any kind of chivalric ethos, whether that of Machen or of the Public Schools. Machen's mass mobilisation of British Culture was part of a war of mass destruction, a war in which science, conscription, and production were used on a mammoth scale to fight for victory. Britain became as martial and regulated as her Prussian opponent and inevitably adopted the principles of the "broad road" to speed victory, and old British ideals like volunteerism were abandoned. Machen realised the necessity of this reluctantly, as seen in his 1916 eulogy on Whit Monday, a typical piece of Machenean nostalgia for traditional revels that were dying out long before the war. There he accepts the temporary sacrifice of old-time holiday ritual to keep munitions factories running. Despite his willingness to make sacrifices, such developments were bound to irk Machen. One particular predicament for him was that Machen believed that the British Tommy would find that Heaven would be much like a good Tavern, as seen in "The Soldier's Rest". In that tale the Soldier asks in surprise, after drinking the "New Wine of the Kingdom" from a great silver cup, whether this is "the place they used to tell us about in Sunday School? With such drink and such joy—". Meanwhile the introduction of wartime licensing laws meant that Heaven on Earth was ever more difficult to find, for claims that drinking was impeding output of war materials gave the Temperance campaign new strength. As Lloyd George said in 1915, "We are fighting Germany, Austria and Drink and, as far as I can see, the greatest of these three deadly foes is Drink". Lloyd George was a prime mover in creating the Central Liquor Control Board in May 1915, which diluted drink, creating the infamous "Lloyd George Beer", and cut opening hours; the latter measure is still in force almost ninety years later.[11]

Writing *The Secret Glory* in 1907, Machen had connected the miseries of modern civilisation to the whole world being "overwhelmed with sobriety… the country itself at point to perish of the want of good liquor and good drinkers." The Graal here was symbolic of both mysticism and the companionship of good drink, while neglect of the "Everlasting Tavern" created "a curse—an evil enchantment—on the land of Logres because the mystery of the Holy Vessel is disregarded." Machen's views had not changed in 1917 when he said: "It is very well that men should live decently; but Galahad sought for something more than respectability.

He journeyed on a stranger adventure; he sought for a nobler chalice than the cup in which non-alcoholic beverages are contained." With King George himself taking the pledge, wartime Britain was truly becoming evermore like a Wasteland.[12]

As a newspaperman, Machen also realised more than most the true effect of the war on the Home Front through his exposure to news reports and travels through the country. He observed the sudden mania over German spies, the coming of the mysterious snow-booted Russians off to the front via Britain, and the increasing insistence on patriotic zeal. While the British public was seemingly growing ever more gullible and prone to panic, Machen knew personally that strict censorship was keeping the actual truth from them. It became clear in 1915 that the war would not be short, and that it was worsening. There were rumours of ever-increasing casualties; from January there were Zeppelin bombings on England that Machen observed first hand; there was the use of gas in April, and intensified U-boat warfare, including the sinking of the *Lusitania*, in May; and there were the false hopes raised and dashed by the Dardanelles campaign.[13]

All this meant Machen inevitably became more cynical and weary of the war and the effect it was having, though, it must be emphasised, remaining grimly committed to Allied victory over German savagery. The Angels of Mons controversy, fully developing from April 1915 onwards, intensified his feelings of disquiet, and they are most clearly encapsulated in his introduction to *The Angels of Mons: The Bowmen and other Legends of the War*, published in August. While much of the introduction is concerned with attempting to dispel the rumours of Angels by hogwashing the "evidence" supporting them, it is Machen's conclusion that goes to the heart of the matter for him, showing that anyone regarding him as a materialist sceptic was sadly mistaken:

> But, taking the affair as it stands at present, how is it that a nation plunged in materialism of the grossest kind has accepted idle rumours and gossip of the supernatural as certain truth? The answer is contained in the question: it is precisely because our whole atmosphere is materialist that we are ready to credit anything—save the truth... And the main responsibility for this dismal state of affairs undoubtedly lies

> *on the shoulders of the majority of the clergy of the Church of*
> *England. Christianity… is a great Mystery Religion; it is*
> *THE Mystery Religion. Its priests are called to an awful and*
> *tremendous hierurgy; its pontiffs are to be the pathfinders, the*
> *bridge-makers between the world of sense and the world of*
> *spirit. And, in fact, they pass their time in preaching, not the*
> *eternal mysteries, but a twopenny morality, in changing the*
> *Wine of Angels and the Bread of Heaven into gingerbeer and*
> *mixed biscuits: a sorry transubstantiation, a sad alchemy, as*
> *it seems to me.[14]*

Machen's reaction to the Angels of Mons phenomenon then was fuelled by his conviction that most wartime religion was proving just as materialistic as in peacetime; it was far too concerned with conveying the concept "jollity is wicked", and promoting causes like Temperance, than providing the true religious feeling he saw as essential.[15] The war in fact was the ideal topic for the sort of Puritan vehemence Machen had always disdained. Machen's fictional Bowmen appealing to Saint George were turned into real Angels to support the patriotic and religious pronouncements of not only Nonconformist ministers, like Dr Horton, an old enemy who had faced Machen in court at the libel trial of *The Academy*, but also Spiritualists, Theosophists, and probably worst of all in Machen's eyes, Low-Church Anglicans. With these allies, Machen's patriotism was being severely tested, and he was forced to retaliate.

For Machen the rite of High Mass verified above all else his longstanding belief in the concept of Christianity as a "Mystery Religion". Thus, it was natural for Machen's rejoinders to wartime materialism and false religion to focus on this. In "The Soldier's Rest", he had already showed a soldier achieving the Graal in a Heavenly Tavern through bravery. He developed this theme in two stories: "The Monstrance", published in June, and *The Great Return*, written between August and October. They are both constructed in very a similar manner; like "The Bowmen", the stories involve the return of the mediaeval past to the present, and they also both use false documents and a reportage style to heighten their effect. In "The Monstrance", the German trench smells of incense where none has been burnt, as does Llantrisant church in *The Great Return*; there is joint mention of a strange, red, rosy light; in both, an invisible bell is heard, St Lambert's and St Teilo's bell respectively (there was a St Lambert's in Louvain); in both, a mysterious visionary procession ends in a High Mass. However, in "The Monstrance", the culmination of the mass ends in horror for Karl Heinz, the German war criminal, and his cries lead to his unit's being "shot to pieces"; whereas *The Great Return* ends in joy for the Welsh congregation. For "The Monstrance" Machen was probably drawing on mediaeval tales of the supernatural punishment of those who desecrated churches. While it represents Machen's strongest condemnation of the German army, probably inspired by the recent publication of the Bryce report in May, it also clearly signals Machen's belief that the true Christian religion was a sacramental one. One can see Machen grinning at the thought of a Low-Churchman trying to use "The Monstrance" as the subject for a patriotic sermon.[16]

Yet, the use of similar supernatural events in *The Great Return* may show that Machen was not satisfied with his earlier tale. Perhaps he regretted a little using this sacred rite for hate-filled propaganda. Just as Machen had turned away from writing gothic horror after the 1890s despite his success, in late 1915 he clearly felt inspired to write a work very different to "The Bowmen" in tone, something that he suspected would be far less popular with a wartime audience. Perhaps at the back of Machen's mind was the dim hope that if through "The Bowmen" he could inspire thousands to believe in warring Angels, then maybe in another story he could inspire a return to the "eternal mysteries", the beauties of ritualism and simple joyful humanity which were essential to Machen's Christianity. Thus he retained a great affection for the idyllic *The Great Return*, while growing ever more dismissive of "The Bowmen", because the former represented his innermost dreams; after all, this was the vision of Britain that Machen thought was worth fighting for.

II   "Remarkable occurrences are supposed
      to have taken place during the recent revival"

One of the most engaging features of *The Great Return* is the description of the beautiful Arfonshire countryside, in reality Pembrokeshire, the location of Machen's beloved family holidays. In the early summer of 1915, in the midst of facing the sudden explosion of debate surrounding "The Bowmen", Machen contemplated an escape from London to Pembrokeshire: "I am groaning for the summer sea, and the smell of thyme on high cliffs, and the colour of rose heather mixed with Indian gold-gorse, for the Welsh accent, for many things that I like."[17] It is exactly these exquisite feelings evoked by a real landscape that are mentioned repeatedly in *The Great Return*. As so often in Machen's stories, the description of the beauties of a landscape he knew well are equated with mystical discovery; it is the concept of *perichoresis*, the interpenetration of the spiritual and material, which was so important to him. For example, in one of the most evocative passages in *The Great Return* Machen's feelings on escaping wartime London are shown wonderfully:

> *I went down to Arfon in the very heat and bloom and fragrance of the wonderful summer that they were enjoying there. In London there was no such weather; it rather seemed as if the horror and fury of the war had mounted to the very skies and were there reigning. In the mornings the sun burnt down upon the city with a heat that scorched and consumed; but then clouds heavy and horrible would roll together from all quarters of the heavens, and early in the afternoon the air would darken, and a storm of thunder and lightning, and furious, hissing rain would fall upon the streets. Indeed, the torment of the world was in the London weather. The city wore a terrible vesture; within our hearts was dread; without we were clothed in black clouds and angry fire. It is certain that I cannot show in any words the utter peace of that Welsh coast to which I came; one sees, I think, in such a change a figure of the passage from the disquiets and the fears of earth to the peace of paradise.*[18]

The story avoids the topic of the war, it is seen as a distant thing, best not mentioned: "At first they talked of the war, and I made myself deaf, for of that talk one gets enough, and more than enough, in London." Where the war is mentioned it merely provides a possible basis for explaining what seem to be supernatural events, "that scares and rumours and terrors about traitorous signals and flashing lights were current everywhere by land and sea."[19]

When I first read the story, it was these lights, chronicled by plain Welsh fishermen, which reminded me of similar tales from the Great

Welsh Revival of 1904-1905. I was later interested to learn that Machen had actually been inspired by these tales, as seen in this discussion of the origins of the story:

> *Another little matter is that of The Great Return. There is, so far as I am aware, no basis for a belief in the existence of the Grail: a subject which I "researched" with great ardour for six months at the Museum. I am glad you like the story. I like it; but my opinion is not generally shared. To my interest in the Grail you may add my liking for Tenby and the Pembrokeshire country; and to that Mrs Oliphant's Beleaguered City; with recollections of a violent Methodist revival in South Wales about thirty years ago: so violent, that people began to see lights shining where there were no lights.*[20]

Examining in more detail the revival so widely reported at the time exposes the extent to which Machen may have been influenced by these recollections. This year, 2004, actually marks the centenary of the Great Revival. It began in early 1904 in Cardiganshire and gradually spread further till the autumn, when it suddenly and spectacularly expanded right across South Wales and to a lesser extent into the North, until it faded away from mid-1905 onwards. It was the last in the series of revivals that had accompanied the ever-increasing strength of Nonconformity in Wales from the eighteenth century. Today its effects are still felt, as it gave birth to popular new evangelical denominations—the Apostolic Church and the Elim Movement—and triggered a series of other revivals worldwide, resulting most notably in the sudden spread of Pentecostalism in America. At its height, the revival in Wales led to massive prayer meetings, with every chapel in towns and villages full to bursting, occupied with people at prayer and song until the early hours, night after night. It made an estimated hundred thousand converts, in a population already full of ardent churchgoers. The effects on normal social life were dramatic: there was a marked decrease in reports of crime in the official figures, feuds were made up, debts were forgiven, "sinful" theatre groups and even rugby teams were disbanded. The temperance movement thrived; a Welsh publican of the time commentated: "Me and my missus were only saying last night as how our takings have fallen by the half this last fortnight. What's to become of the people if this goes on? The men must have a drop of drink if they are to do their work proper."[21]

The observations of one visitor, the famous editor WT Stead, give a further sense of the power of the revival:

Well you have read ghost stories, and can imagine what you would feel if you were alone at midnight in the haunted chamber of some old castle, and you heard the slow and stealthy step stealing along the corridor where the visitant from the other world was said to walk. If you go to South Wales and watch the revival you will feel pretty much like that. There is something there from the other world. You cannot say from where it came, or where it is going, but it moves and lives and reaches for you all the time. You see men and women go down in sobbing agony before your eyes as the invisible Hand clutches at their heart. And you shudder. It's pretty grim, I tell you. If you are afraid of strong emotions, you'd better give the revival a wide berth.[22]

The revival's chief public figure was the charismatic and mysterious visionary, Evan Roberts, a young former collier turned Calvinistic Methodist preacher, though he never actually finished his training. He was normally accompanied by a group of enthusiastic young female revivalists. Roberts' success shows how the revival broke down the usual Nonconformist divisions of denomination, gender and position. Even Anglicans, though less involved than Nonconformists, saw an increase in confirmations; the Bishop of Dorking spent three days incognito attending revival meetings, the revival was praised highly and publicly by the Archbishop of Canterbury, and it was seemingly prophesied by Dean Howells, Dean of St David's, in his final message from his deathbed in 1902. This ecumenical feeling should not be exaggerated though; the Anglicans most interested in the revival were Low-Churchmen, while Roberts' divine revelations led him on a number of occasions to refuse to address meetings in parish churches.[23]

The revival was accompanied by a number of unexplained and supernatural events, with Roberts and other revivalists being associated with acts of healing, telepathy, and clairvoyance. For example, here is

Roberts' description of one of his earliest visions which started off his part in the revival in November 1904:

> *And I heard a voice in my inward ear as plain as anything, saying, 'Go and speak to these people…' Then instantly the vision vanished, and the whole chapel became filled with light so dazzling that I could faintly see the minister in the pulpit, and between him and me the glory as the light of the sun in heaven.*[24]

Another vision of the time is perhaps of particular interest to students of Machen. In December 1904 a man claimed that, when walking home one night, he "beheld a faint light playing over my head and approaching earth… in the bright and glorious light I beheld there the face of a man, and by looking for the body in the light a shining white robe was covering it to its feet and it was not touching the earth, and behind its arms there were wings appearing, and I was seeing every feather in the wings, but they were not natural or material feathers, but the whole was heavenly beyond description." There was at least one other sighting of an Angelic figure in the revival, showing the use of this motif for visions in times before Mons.[25]

The Society of Psychical Research was so interested in all this it conducted a report on the revival. Possibly Machen had read it as it includes many of the phenomena used in *The Great Return*, though since they also are mentioned in mediaeval sources there is no certainty of this. Phenomena mentioned in the report include changes in countenance: one girl is described as developing "a Madonna-like face" and Evan Roberts' face is often mentioned as "shining"; in *The Great Return*, one who has seen the mystery has "an illuminated face, glowing with an ineffable joy." Travellers during the revival heard singing voices in the midst of the countryside, and in Machen's story, "there was a song upon the water that was like heaven." Also in the story, people "listened in the early morning with thrilling hearts to the thrilling music of a bell"; in the revival, "The Vicar of Llangadfan reports that three of his parishioners… heard bells chiming during service on Sunday morning, January 29th, 1905. The sound was over their heads, but no one else in the congregation heard it."[26] Another characteristic of the revival that aroused comment was the use of "pure idiomatic classical Welsh" by unlettered labourers and servants. A Welsh Professor claimed that they used "diction... more chaste and beautiful than anything I can hope to attain to". A young girl spontaneously prayed aloud using Scripture and old Welsh hymns, and her own words were spoken in Welsh that "would have done credit to the most scholarly theologian of the Welsh pulpit". In the story, the Welshmen have "fragments of the cloud of glory in their common speech", and they draw from old tales of saints for insights.[27]

The most famous set of unexplained events associated with the revival, and which Machen obviously knew of, occurred in North Wales with the sightings of mysterious lights connected to Mary Jones of Egryn, the Merionethshire seeress. Lights were repeatedly seen at night above chapels where the seeress preached; they might follow her progress, or mark the houses of souls that needed saving. In different sightings the lights varied in shape, appearing as stars, balls of fire or pillars; and in colour, such as yellow, white, and blood red. One description states seeing "three brilliant rays of dazzling white light stride across the road from mountain to sea, throwing the stone wall into bold relief, every stone and interstice, every little fern and bit of moss, as clearly visible as at noonday." Here is another typical account from a newspaper reporter: "Suddenly at 8.20pm I saw what appeared to be a ball of fire above the roof of the chapel. It came from nowhere, and sprang into existence simultaneously. It had a steady, intense yellow brilliance, and did not move... We watched the light together. It seemed to me to be at twice the height of the chapel, say fifty feet, and it stood out with electric vividness against the encircling hills behind. Suddenly it disappeared, having lasted about a minute and a half."

The Egryn lights were witnessed directly by a large number of people of good reputation; in more recent times they have often been reinterpreted as UFO activity. One explanation for the lights offered by Paul Devereux is that they are Earthlights created by geological electromagnetic forces along the Mochras Fault which runs through the area. One detailed study by Kevin McClure, who has also examined the Angels of Mons episode, came to the conclusion that considering the lack of electric lights and aircraft at the time the reports as a whole represented "the most remarkable anomalous phenomena in British history".[28]

Machen's description of similar lights in *The Great Return* comes to us in the manner of a newspaper report:

> *Two of those sailormen are precise as to the time of the apparition; they fix it by elaborate calculations of their own as occurring at 12.20 a.m. ...At first a red spark in the farthest distance; then a rushing lamp; and then, as if in an incredible point of time, it swelled into a vast rose of fire that filled all the sea and all the sky and hid the stars and possessed the land.*[29]

The light ends at the "old grey chapel of St Teilo" on Chapel Head. Machen clearly seems to be paralleling the old reports of lights.

The success of the revival gave a boost to the Welsh Language and represented the high water mark of Welsh Nonconformity's social and political influence, with chapel membership peaking at 549,000 in 1906. The vigour of Nonconformity went hand in hand with the triumph of the Liberal party, who in their victorious 1906 election won every seat, save one, in Wales, and added strength to the ascent of the voice of Welsh Liberal Nonconformity, Lloyd George, who was already in the cabinet. Machen's fuming reaction to this Liberal ascendancy in Britain in 1906 was the publication of his satirical *Dr Stiggins*. There was worse to come: Welsh Nonconformity was at long last in a position to finish off its most hated enemy; the final death knell of the Church of England in Wales was fast approaching. The Liberal reform of the House of Lords in 1911 meant the Tories could no longer prevent this, and in 1912 a Liberal government introduced a Disestablishment Bill; only the outbreak of war in 1914 delayed its final passage till 1920, when it made Wales the only part of mainland Britain to have no state religion.[30]

How did all this influence Machen's story, *The Great Return*? March 1915 saw more debates in Parliament on the delays to Welsh Disestablishment. It might seem the story was a riposte from a Welsh vicar's son, both to the Nonconformist revival and to Disestablishment, for here the return of the Graal creates a Great Revival of *ritualism* and the dissenters all return to the Church, the "old hive". Yet as always with Machen it is not so simple; there is evidence which indicates that the menace of Disestablishment meant little to him. Take his scathing reaction to a Bishop's worries in 1907 about the threat of Welsh

Disendowment, where he noted that there was no established Church in the time of the apostles—just the sort of response a Nonconformist might make. As the conclusion to *The Angels of Mons* introduction quoted earlier shows, Machen's continuing suspicion of the Anglican establishment was even greater than his dislike of dissenters. After all they did not know any better, while the Anglican hierarchy controlling Machen's own church had become corrupted by the Reformation and its own political ambitions, leading to its failure to promote true Christianity as he saw it. As the story makes clear, for Machen ancient Welsh Christianity was really represented by antique traditions and rituals, aged churches and old landscapes, and from this perspective its legislative status is irrelevant.[31]

Machen's use of the revival went beyond mere denominational rivalry. His longstanding interest in unexplained phenomena, and in what people choose to believe or disbelieve, had been intensified by his time as a newspaper reporter and most importantly by the Angels controversy. As he stated in *The Great Return*, "I have an appetite for these matters, though I also have this misfortune, that I require evidence before I am ready to credit them, and I have a sort of lingering hope that some day I shall be able to elaborate some scheme or theory of such things." Recollections of the supernatural events of the Welsh revival, perhaps inspired by articles he saw during the tenth anniversary year of 1915, may have led him to compare them to the similar miraculous events described in the Welsh mediaeval romances and Welsh saints' lives which Machen knew so well. Thus the idea occurred to him of combining them together in a story describing a hidden tradition of mediaeval spirituality in Wales. As Machen mentions in the story, his knowledge of the reverence still paid to relics in Wales, like the Nanteos Cup and the Skull of St Teilo, added to his scheme. He was not the only one to think in this way: the frequent appearance of crosses in visions during the revival was taken by one optimistic Catholic commentator in 1905 as a sign of a return to pre-Reformation spirituality in Wales.[32] There were other incidents in Wales which also perhaps inspired Machen's ideas, such as the visitations of the Virgin Mary to Gwent seen by the Anglo-Catholic mystic, Father Ignatius at Capel-y-Ffyn, Llanthony, in 1880.

This theme ties in with Machen's mixed feelings about Welsh Nonconformity and evangelism shown in the story, "their queer

Calvinistic Methodism, half Puritan, half pagan", as he puts it. Tellingly the narrator, seemingly Machen himself, is defeated in his confrontation with the Low-Church vicar of Llantrisant, being "justly rebuked" as a "railer" when mention of his Methodist "great-granduncle Hezekiah, *ffeiriad coch yr Castletown*—the Red Priest of Castletown", is brought up against him. The description of Hezekiah bringing a massive audience to the Eucharist clearly echoes the celebration of the Mass of the Sangraal to come. In that very rite a verse from a hymn composed by Charles Wesley is recited in Welsh; the combination of an ancient Celtic liturgy with a hymn from one of the founders of Methodism might seem strange. However, Machen here is referring to the fact that Methodism actually changed from the original beliefs of the Wesley brothers who endorsed both populism and the importance of sacramentalism. Tellingly, the most recent edition in Machen's time of the book in which that hymn appeared was by an Anglo-Catholic press in 1875. Machen here is also possibly referring to the use of old hymns which, as we saw, were such a feature of the revival. It should be noted that as Welsh Calvinistic Methodists did not necessarily hold the Wesleys in high regard due to doctrinal differences, the use of this hymn is perhaps an uncanny occurrence as noteworthy as the Methodist deacon's sudden knowledge of the Rites of the Graal.[33]

In all it seems that in this story Machen's affection for his fellow Welshmen, even dissenters, was such that he was willing to give them the benefit of the doubt, believing the threads of ancient ways lay hidden among them somewhere waiting. This is also seen in a later story, "The Gift of Tongues", where a Nonconformist valleys preacher unknowingly recites ancient rituals in his sermon. Machen's feelings can be compared with his close friend Caradoc Evans, who provided the Welsh phrases for *The Great Return*. Evans' notably vitriolic feelings for the parochial world of the Welsh chapel and rural life can be seen in *My People—Stories of the Peasantry of West Wales* and his other works. Since this book, which aroused a furious reaction in Wales, was also published in 1915 it may have played a role in Machen's development of his story. Certainly Evans, too, looked forward to the day when there would be not "a single chapel of the Dissenters open in the town", notably stating Wales would never be happy till every chapel was replaced by a pub, though his reasoning was more secular than Machen's. Nevertheless he and Machen certainly agreed on the value of good drink as well as the dangers of Nonconformist hypocrisy and puritanism.[34]

III   "ʙendigeid yr offeren yn oes oesoedd—,
       ʙlessed be the offering unto the age of ages"

Machen's use of a Welsh setting is ultimately tied to his theory about the Graal that it ultimately derives from a lost liturgy of Celtic Christianity. While both *The Secret Glory* and *The Great Return* use the same Grail materials Machen had gathered from the British Museum library in 1906, there are some differences in handling. In the former, the Sangraal represented an escape for a Machenesque solitary dreamer from a corrupt institution, but in *The Great Return,* an entire community is saved while Machen, the narrator, watches on. While in *The Secret Glory* Ambrose's discovery of the Graal inevitably leads to his Bloody Red Martyrdom, in *The Great Return* the Graal saves lives. In both stories, Machen uses details from Welsh myth and Welsh saints' lives mixed with evocative descriptions of the real Welsh landscape.

The importance of this mixture of reality, legend and Machen's vision can be seen by examining how many seemingly minor details tie together in the story. Take for example the different Fishermen mentioned in the tale, each evoking the Matter of Britain, ranging from saints to sailors and the pub "The Fisherman's Rest". The town of Llantrisant itself may have been based mainly on Penally, but it incorporates other elements. Machen on his holidays did not attend Penally church, because he hated the Low-Church services, preferring to walk with his family to the Roman Catholic church in Tenby. So it may be that Machen's disagreement with the Low-Church vicar in the story is based on a real meeting. Certainly Penally church does have three early Celtic crosses, though none of them feature ogham inscriptions. The interior of the Llantrisant church however is clearly based on nearby St Lawrence, Gumfreston church, a place that Machen believed may have been eighth or tenth century, which has no crosses in the churchyard but does have three ancient holy wells. This is Machen's description of the church in the story:

The Llantrisant church has that primitive division between nave and chancel which only very foolish people decline to recognise as equivalent to the Oriental icono-stasis and as the origin of the Western rood-screen. A solid wall divided the church into two portions; in the centre was a narrow opening with a rounded arch, through which those who sat towards the middle of the church could see the small, red-carpeted altar and the three roughly shaped lancet windows above it.

This description matches exactly the architectural design of Gumfreston. Machen's other writings reveal he believed that originally the wall was intended to help screen off the chancel during High Mass, as in Orthodox celebrations of Eucharist, signifying it was a "Holy Mystery"; in the story it seems as if "a veil of gold adorned with jewels" divides the chancel from the nave, like the curtain used in orthodox rites. Sadly for Machen's theory, the Iconostasis as an architectural feature of Orthodox churches only developed slowly into its form as a wall covered with icons separating the chancel from the nave in the twelfth century; prior to that it was more of a chancel rail. An authoritative modern architectural guide dates the Gumfreston chancel arch to the thirteenth century and believes the church's curious design is a result of piecemeal building.[35]

The name Llantrisant means "church of three saints" and Machen carefully replicates the fascination with threes found in the Welsh triads. Who are the three saints who appear in the passage quoted at the start of this article? One is obviously is St Teilo, mentioned directly in the story as the saint of the chapel on the old headland. St Teilo in his life was associated with a magic bell, which is such a feature of the story. Penally was also meant to be the birthplace of St Teilo, and the location of one of his three graves. In a posthumous miracle the kindly St Teilo replicated his body into three, so three Welsh churches could have the honour of burying him. The second saint is probably St David – *Vir Aquaticus*, "the waterman", as he was known. According to their lives, he and St Teilo were close colleagues, even related according to some lineages. The mysterious altar stone he carried would be the altar *Sapphirus* that Dewi Sant supposedly left at Glastonbury. The final saint, the holder of the Grail, is the most mysterious of all. In *The Secret Glory* it was St Teilo himself who was the Keeper of "a cup of wonders and mysteries, the bestower of visions and heavenly graces", but it cannot be him here. In his article, "The Secret of the Sangraal", Machen mentions that Cadwaladr the Blest, Saint and King, may have provided the basis for later grail knights such as Galahad. So it may be him, but equally it could be another Welsh saint such as Cybi, or Cadoc, or Gwnllyw. The mystery remains, as it should, a mystery.[36]

The same is true of the Liturgy of the Mass of the Sangraal, only partially recited in the story. The featured details of the mass and the liturgy are very similar to those used in *The Secret Glory*. Whether Machen was correct in connecting a lost Celtic liturgy to the Graal legends is a mystery, but he is certainly correct in saying the Celtic Churches differed in their liturgy from Rome, and this caused some disagreement between them. I believe one of the advantages of Machen's approach to the Graal materials is his willingness to incorporate them within a mediaeval mindset. Whatever their origins, the Grail legends as we have them in mediaeval romances are probably closer in feeling than anything else is to the type of hyper-sacramentalism which Machen believed in. He could not condense his long library researches on the Celtic liturgy into the story, nor did he wish to; instead he wished to convey their emotional impact for him.[37]

This personal vision is an essential element in the story. In *Things Near and Far*, Machen commentated that *The Great Return* contained an attempt to portray the feelings of "bliss", which he associated with the Graal and with the mystical experience he felt in Gray's Inn Road, an experience that had made life worthwhile again after his wife's death: "Thus in the story, and thus it was with me in fact, in that autumn and winter of 1899-1900." His experience cured his persistent headaches, so in his story it cured the fishermen of every "pain and ache and malady in their bodies". Because of this Machen particularly appreciated the irony of T.W. Rolleston, the Celtic mythologist, making a caustic review of the story in the *Times Literary Supplement* which criticised Machen for having the Grail revealed to ordinary people when Machen knew: "It may be low, but perhaps things happen in this way sometimes; and so with me".[38]

Crucially Machen extended this private dream in *The Great Return* into a wider sphere, inspired both by the Great Revival and by Margaret

Oliphant's *A Beleaguered City*, in which the bourgeois materialism of a provincial French town is faced by a religious mystery that embroils the entire community, which still at the end remains divided despite their experience. Machen is more optimistic; the people of Llantrisant are brought together by the "glow" that brings the forgiving of debts and reconciliation of old enemies, as in the revival. Yet for Machen there was a crucial difference, believing as he did, "We are not Christians in order that we be good; we try to be good in order that we may be Christians." These improvements in morality come about because individuals witnessed the celebration of the joy and beauty of the ritual of the Mass of the Sangraal. There is another characteristic difference; the final coming together of the community in Machen's story is signalled by the celebration of a marriage. Like the wedding at Cana, the marriage festivities are almost spoilt by lack of drink; in Llantrisant it is the unexpectedly generous donations of "a dozen of port" and a couple of cases of champagne that mean it all can go ahead splendidly, in contrast to the importance of Temperance in the revival and in wartime.[39]

To return once more to the war, it is interesting to note that Anglo-Catholicism in general also grew stronger during the war, even in Wales. Anglo-Catholics noted an increasing tolerance of ritualism in Britain, especially in the growing popularity of prayers for the dead, and hoped that the willingness to defend Catholic churches in Belgium signalled a significant shift in sympathies. This development helped lead to the first "Anglo-Catholic Congress", held in 1920, and the general growth of the High Church movement in the twenties. Thus Machen in one sense was part of a wider movement.

The war also marked a return of supernatural events to Wales. One famous Pentecostal minister who was inspired to begin his career by the Great Revival was Stephen Jeffreys. Supposedly during a service he held on 24th July 1914 in Llanelli, a mysterious vision of a lamb's head appeared on the wall of the church, and then transformed into a vision of Jesus as a "man of sorrows"; this was observed by many members of the congregation. When war broke out a month later, this vision was taken as a warning of what was to come. During the war, nowhere was the role of mass religion in giving the war-effort support more significant than in Wales, where the chapels turned it into a crusade. Given the traditional antimilitaristic feelings of Nonconformists and their admiration for

German Protestantism, this about-turn was somewhat surprising. Indeed, in 1906 Machen had the Nonconformist Dr Stiggins denounce those who "annoy our good friends at Berlin by the persistent building of vast ships armed with guns of great power".[40]

However, considering the political and religious ascendancy of chapel culture, the about-turn is perhaps not so unexpected. Like the other great Edwardian institutions such as the Public Schools, the chapels were complacent and felt compelled to defend a society which had served them well. Lloyd George, who debated long and hard before supporting the war, was crucial in bringing them along. His eloquence typified the war as a cause the chapels could endorse, to defend "gallant little Belgium" and to protect all "the little five foot-five nations" like Wales in the future. Lloyd George was happy to use religious imagery in his speeches too, even though privately he had long abandoned the beliefs behind it.

The Welsh were enthusiastic recruits for the army; more than 280,000 were to serve, 13.82 percent of the male population, higher than the rest of Britain. The war also resulted in a sudden upsurge in chapel attendance that had been declining since 1906. The 1915 National Eisteddfod at Bangor on St David's Day saw a noteworthy Lloyd George speech that eulogised Welsh military heroes, from the Hundred Years War bowmen to the present day, and celebrated the fact that eighty thousand Welshman had already heard the call to arms. When Lloyd George became Prime Minister in 1916, most of Wales became more firmly than ever behind the war. However, by the twenties, in a climate of industrial depression and social change and with the legacy of the "War to Save Civilisation" being increasingly questioned, the wartime belligerence of Welsh Liberal Nonconformity and its betrayal of its principles helped lead to its long-term decline against the rise of Labour. Just like the Public School, in retrospect the Welsh chapel had seen its Edwardian high noon blown away in the fury of the war.[41]

The crusading attitude of the chapels was exactly what Machen became increasingly reluctant to employ himself. His position shifted from the spiritual patriotism of "The Bowmen" and his later stories were no longer set on the front lines, nor were they necessarily so optimistic. Take the horrific "Out of the Earth", also set in Pembrokeshire, where Machen's Little People rejoice to see humanity—well, the Germans anyway—become as barbaric and violent as them. The fact the victims here and in *The Terror* were British rather than German is perhaps significant. In 1917, the essays in "God and the War" (later collected as *War and the Christian Faith*) notably neglect to discuss the supposed just or moral basis of the war. Instead, they explore Machen's understanding of human suffering, based on his Christian faith and belief that the world "isn't a very pleasant place, never has been a pleasant place, and never will be a pleasant place", and that "good things are born of torments". This meant that, along with the rest of the British public, Machen could endure the ever-increasing casualties, but it is markedly lacking in martial spirit. In fact, most of the essays do not even mention the war; instead, they return to Machen's long-term campaign against materialism and the failures of the Church. So while Machen never openly wavered in his support for Allied victory, like many others he was perhaps questioning the ethos behind it.[42]

Thus *The Great Return* represents Machen's most idyllic hope for the future in late 1915, an escape from war, not through bloody martyrdom or victory on the battlefield, but through the beauty of the land and mystery of ritual. Perhaps Machen's spirit may take some consolation from the fact that in modern Wales, while the Church in Wales and Nonconformity are both increasingly irrelevant, quite a number of Welsh chapels, those bastions of Temperance, have been turned into public houses. The Church in Wales also now pays far more attention to the legacy of the Age of Welsh Saints and the concept of Celtic Christianity than it did in his day. So, while I have explored some of the story's complexities and mysteries here, there is always more left unsaid. The time when the Mass of the Sangraal will resound once more across the land and sea may be still yet to come, but then at the last what do we know?

sources

1 "The Bowmen", *The Angels of Mons: The Bowmen and other Legends of the War*, 1st ed. (Simpkin, Marshall, Hamilton, Kent, [10th August] 1915), pp. 36-37; first published in *The Evening News [EN]*, 29/9/14.

2 *The Great Return* (The Faith Press, [December] 1915), pp. 66-7; first serialised *EN*, 21/10/15 to 16/11/15.

3 "The Bowmen", *The Angels of Mons*, 1st ed., 11. Aidan Reynolds and William Charlton, *Arthur Machen: A Short Account of His Life and Work* (Richards Press, 1963), pp. 115-116.

4 "The Men from Troy", *The Angels of Mons*, 2nd ed. (1915); first published *EN*, 10/9/15.

5 "The Bowmen", *The Angels of Mons*, 1st ed., p. 37. For an exploration of the myths surrounding German atrocities see James Hayward, *Myths and Legends of the First World War* (Sutton, 2002), ch. 4.

6 Niall Ferguson, *The Pity of War* (1998), p. 346. "The Soldier's Rest", *The Angels of Mons*, 1st ed., p. 44; first published *EN*, 20/10/14. "The Monstrance", *The Angels of Mons*, 1st ed., p. 62; first published as "Karl Heinz's Diary: The Story of a Battlefield Vision", *EN*, 9/6/15 (thanks to David Clarke for this detail). "War and The Christian Faith", *Avallaunius*, pp. 17, 23; first serialised *EN*, 7/11/17 to 7/12/17, with the title of "God and the War"; collected as *War and the Christian Faith* (Skeffington & Son, 1918).

7 "The Trail of the Zeppelin", *Faunus*, 4, p. 28; first published *EN*, 21/1/1915. "The Soldier's Rest", *The Angels of Mons*. "The Ceaseless Bugle Call", *EN*, 17/9/14. "Munitions of War", 1915; collected in *The Cosy Room*, 1936. "The Light That Can Never Be Put Out", *Faunus*, 1; first published *EN*, 14/2/16. "The Ghost of Whit-Monday", *Faunus*, 5; first published *EN*, 12/6/16.

8 "My Country Lane and My Critics", *Faunus*, 7, p. 6; first published *EN*, 31/8/16. Ferguson, *The Pity of War*, pp. 212-213, 217.

9 *The Secret Glory* (Tartarus Press, 1998), p. 41.

10 Peter Parker, *The Old Lie: The Great War and the Public-School Ethos* (Constable, 1987), pp. 34-40. *The Secret Glory*, pp. 12, 43-44.

11 "The Soldier's Rest", *The Angels of Mons*, 1st ed., pp. 49-50. John Grigg, *Lloyd George: from Peace to War, 1912-1916* (Penguin, 1985), pp. 229-237.

12 *The Secret Glory*, 137-142. "War and the Christian Faith", *Avallaunius*, 17, p. 40.

13 For panic and censorship on the Home Front, see Hayward, *Myths and Legends of the First World War*. David Clarke makes a similar point about this period in *The Angel of Mons: Phantom Soldiers and Ghostly Guardians* (Wiley, 2004), pp. 108-109. "The Trail of the Zeppelin", *Faunus*, 4, pp. 26-29.

14 Introduction, *The Angels of Mons*, 1st ed., pp. 26-27.

15 Ibid., p.9.

16 "The Monstrance", *The Angels of Mons,* 1st ed.,pp. 51, 56, 58-59, 55.

17 Arthur Machen, Letter to Paul England, forthcoming biography of Machen by John Gawsworth (thanks to Roger Dobson for letting me see this).

18 *The Great Return, p.* 19.

19 Ibid., pp. 26, 14.

20 Morchard Bishop, "A Chapter from the Table Talk of Arthur Machen", *Arthur Machen: Artist and Mystic,* eds. Mark Valentine and Roger Dobson (Caermaen, 1986), pp. 31-32.

21 *The Times,* 3/01/05. *The Times,* 6/2/05. John Davies, *A History of Wales* (Penguin 1994), pp. 505-507.

22 *London Methodist Times,* 15/12/04.

23 *The Times,* 6/2/05.

24 W. T. Stead, "The Revival in the West", in *The Revival of 1905* (London: "The Review of Reviews" Publishing Office, 1905), p. 45.

25 Quoted in Kevin McClure, *Stars, and Rumours of Stars: The Egryn Lights and other Mysterious Phenomena in the Welsh Religious Revival, 1904-1905,* Part 4 (www.magonia.demon. co.uk/abwatch/stars/stars1.html).

26 A.T. Fryer, "The Psychological Aspects of the Welsh Revival 1904-5", *Proceedings of the Society for Psychical Research* (December, 1905), p. 51. *The Great Return,* pp. 31, 44.

27 *The Times,* 31/1/05. *The Great Return,* p. 48.

28 "Signs in the Heavens or . . . ?" *The Daily News,* 9/2/05. Bernard Redwood, Report, *The Daily Mail,* February 1915. McClure, *Stars, and Rumours of Stars*, Part 2, p.5. Paul Devereux, *Earth Lights Revelation* (Blandford , 1990).

29 *The Great Return,* p.51.

30 Kenneth O. Morgan, *Rebirth of a Nation: Wales 1880-1980* (OUP), pp. 134-136, pp. 141-142. Roger Dobson, Godfrey Brangham and R.A. Gilbert, *Arthur Machen: Selected Letters* (Aquarian Press, 1988), pp. 221.

31 Grigg, *Lloyd George*, pp. 227-229.

32 *The Great Return,* 16. S.F.S., "The Welsh Revival", *The Month,* 105 (1905), pp. 453-465.

33 *The Great Return,* pp. 69, 24. "Sancho Panza at Geneva", *The Glorious Mystery* (Covici-McGee, 1924), 121-125. The verse is from Wesley's "Victim Divine, Thy grace we claim", *Hymns on the Lord's Supper* (1745).

34 "The Gift of Tongues" (1927), *Ritual and Other Stories* (Tartarus Press, 2nd ed., 1997). *The Great Return*, p. 72.

35 *The Great Return*, p. 58. Dobson et al, *Selected Letters*, p.106, p. 144. "The Charm of Old Churches", *Avallaunius*, **17,** pp. 11-12. "Iconostasis", *Blackwell Dictionary of Eastern Christianity* (1999). Thomas Lloyd, *Pembrokeshire: The Buildings of Wales* (Yale University Press, 2003), pp. 198-199.

36 *The Secret Glory*, 55. "The Secret of the Sangraal", *The Shining Pyramid* (Secker, 1925), pp. 112-114.

37 "The Secret of the Sangraal", pp. 116-122. *The Secret Glory*, pp. 53-54.

38 T.W. Rolleston, *TLS*, 27/01/16, p. 41. *The Great Return*, p. 55. *The Autobiography of Arthur Machen* (Richards Press, 1951), pp. 274-275.

39 Margaret Oliphant, *A Beleaguered City* (1880). *The Glorious Mystery*, p. 146. *The Great Return*, pp. 76-78.

40 *Dr Stiggins* (Francis Griffiths, 1906), p. 65.

41 Kenneth O. Morgan, *Rebirth of a Nation Wales 1880-1980* (OUP), pp. 159-161. John Davies, *A History of Wales* (Penguin, 1994), pp. 509-513.

42 "Out of the Earth", The Shining Pyramid (Covici-McGee, 1923); first published *T.P.'s Weekly*, 27/11/15. "War and the Christian Faith", *Avallaunius*, pp. 17,22, 24, 34-38.

Amelia Hogg —A Journey into Silence

Gill Culver & Godfrey Brangham
originally published in Faunus issue 12

Honour makes men faithful in keeping secrets.

The above words by Henry Cardinal Manning perhaps provide a clue to the extraordinary reticence that Arthur Machen exhibited with regard to his first wife, Amy Hogg. He was of course a man of the Victorian era, a man of high personal standards, where discussion of a previous marriage, which ultimately ended in tragedy, could be viewed as at best gossip, and at worst unseemly voyeurism. Naturally this is mere speculation, but his almost perverse avoidance of the subject does prompt the question—*why?*

Paradoxically, it is the very essence of secrets that they irresistibly attract attention, and so it is in this instance. Who was she, when and where was she born, how did they meet, what was she like? The questions tumble over each other, and yet each successive answer, no matter how hard won, precipitates another question. Again the reader might be justified in asking what her importance was in Machen's life—one can only conjecture. However, it was during their initial acquaintance, and subsequent married life, that Machen wrote most of the fiction for which he is now remembered.

After stating that, there remains the difficulty of knowing where to begin; so perhaps a chronological start might be appropriate, outlining the meagre facts known about her in Machen's own lifetime. Thereafter, the information that has been laboriously discovered in recent years can be added, perhaps to offer new insights into the tantalisingly vague history of Amy Hogg. A good starting place is Machen himself, where in *Things Near and Far* (1923), the second volume of his autobiographical trilogy, he inexplicably writes:

> *I was no longer the lonely man.*

This in fact refers to his marriage to Amy; yet later, the opposite occurs:

> *Then a great sorrow which had long threatened fell upon me:*
> *I was once more alone.*

He is, of course, speaking of the death of Amy on 31st July 1899; and that, apparently, is all we can learn from Machen himself—the entire twelve years of their married life summed up in two lines. It is only through other writers, friends of his, that we can glean more information about her. An early reference is made by Machen's closest friend in those years, Arthur Waite. In fact it was Amy who famously brought about the first meeting between them. Waite in his autobiography, *Shadows of Life and Thought* (1938), wrote the following, which we give in full, as it offers a rare glimpse of her background:

> *It may have been in 1886, when I was staying with my Mother at Worthing and working on the Levi book, or it may have been a year earlier, and in either case through attending the Roman Church, that my Mother became acquainted with some elderly Anglo-Indians, Mr and Mrs Hogg, who had a daughter named Mysie, a tall pallid girl, well-shapen but with little attraction in her looks. I had occasional talks with her and found that she had no horizon beyond that which was proffered and provided by Latin doctrine and practice. Seemingly also she had no interests beyond taking meticulous care of a brother who was some years older than herself and little better than childish. It is to be inferred that this indeed remained her vocation in life, after her parents left and so long as the brother remained. They are mentioned only because I*

heard a good deal about an elder sister, Amy Hogg, who was living in London and mixing much with authors, artists and actors. It was understood that she and I would prove to be kindred spirits, if chance brought us together as well it might, since she was always a possible visitor to Worthing and her parents for a few days, or so long as she could stand the place. Nothing happened, however, till the Summer of 1886, when she came down for perhaps a week and we took long walks together. She was taller and thinner than her sister, a free spirit, with a budget of living experience among people and things, in a circle utterly foreign to my own. She was emancipated, it seemed to me, in respect of religious belief and without further concern therein. As to Occultism, Spiritism, Psychical Research and the rest, no doubt we talked about them. I must have told her all I was doing and something possibly of my plans and hopes; but they meant nothing to her, except in so far as she was faintly and amiably wishful that success might smooth my path. Whether she herself had private means or some occupation in London to keep her craft afloat, I should not remember now, supposing that I heard then. She was quite of the type to have found her metier in light journalism and should have done well among women's papers. But personally I was much too detached to be at pains about such matters, and very likely I was never told.

Now, it was from Amy Hogg that I first heard of Arthur Machen, in special connection with her firm resolve that he and I should meet as soon as possible when I returned to London. May the Lord watch over her because of this good intent, and for the fact that she brought it about, I do not remember now. It was not until 1887, as witnessed by an inscription on a copy of his recent book, The Cosy Room, which reads thus on the first fly-leaf:

A.E.W. 1887

A.M. 1936

They subsequently met in London, under the dome of the British Museum on a dark January morning in 1887, to begin an enduring, lifelong friendship.

How Machen himself first came into contact with Amy is to an extent shrouded in mystery. John Gawsworth describes Machen's initial London residence, in 1881, as being Burlington Cottage, Turnham Green, the home of fellow Herefordian and author Lewis Sergeant. Certain literary soirees were held, and it was to these that Amy Hogg came. No doubt Machen was attracted to this unconventional and personable woman, but the degree to which they aspired to be friends is open to question. Yet it is an odd coincidence that the Census of that year lists her as living at 23 Clarendon Road, the very house to which Machen migrated in 1883. It doesn't require a great leap of the imagination to surmise that either she suggested he take up residence there, or he himself noted where she lived and simply followed her.

This 1881 Census is extremely important, as besides giving her occupation as a music teacher, it also reveals that she was born in Bengal, India, that she was unmarried and more importantly, that her age in 1881 was 36. The question of when Amy was actually born has caused great confusion amongst later biographers of Machen. It was he himself who created this, as on the marriage certificate and death certificates her age is at considerable variance. She was much older than Machen, and it may be assumed that they thought it more socially correct to minimise as far as possible the discrepancy in their ages.

During the middle years of the 1880s, Amy and Machen became closer, and eventually, in the parlance of the day, they could be described as "walking out together". In the spring of 1887, they were invited down to Caerleon, Machen's birthplace, by Maria, his elderly aunt. For Machen, it must have given great pleasure not only to show Amy to the family, but also to escort her around the countryside that meant so much to him and had proved the inspiration for much of his writing. In two letters to his friend Harry Spurr, he demonstrates the happiness he felt at the time:

[*15th July 1887*]

To our trusty and well beloved, Harry Spurr,
Greeting:
We arrived in these delicious solitudes on Saturday last, with
minds and bodies somewhat shattered by the horrors of the
excursion train; but the mountain air did soon refresh us.
On Monday we went for a good long walk to a place called

Wentwood Chase and ate our lunch under the greenwood tree. Tomorrow we go to a place called Uske; and propose to undertake several small excursions of the same kind till the time is up. I am devoting to a large extent to the consumption of tobacco and find that amusement more profitable than ever, since the scents of cavendish are mingled with those of meadowsweet and roses and honeysuckle...
Yours very faithfully
and infernally,
Arthur Machen

✻   ✻   ✻

[22ⁿᵈ July 1887]

Dear Spurr,
...I have certainly had splendid weather, and we have tramped about hill and dale, by mountains and river through this delicious land to our heart's content. We have tasted of the native beverage cwrw dda [i.e. "good beer"], as also of seidr: we have drunk from holy wells and the mountain torrents, we have laughed, sung and joked in a thoroughly Silurian manner. I have read out your letters to Miss Hogg, who approves of them altogether and sends you her kind regards. ...during my short holiday... things have been settled in the pleasantest way possible; the manner of which I will expound to you when we meet...
Well! Here's luck and to our merry meeting.
Yours very sincerely,
Arthur Machen
Silurist

Parry Michael in his MA dissertation on Machen (1941), comments that in the 1930s there were still people in Caerleon who remembered the couple making numerous visits there. In particular one local, a Mrs Pope, describes Amy as a gracious person, a little older than Machen, with a deep impressive voice.

The final sentence in the above letter to Spurr no doubt refers to the fact that Machen had proposed marriage to Amy and she had accepted. They were subsequently united on 31ˢᵗ August 1887 at Broadwater Parish

Church in Worthing. The ceremony was attended by Amy's family and also Arthur Waite. Their first home was at Great Russell Street, but where they spent their honeymoon is not known.

The couple stayed in France each year during the early years of their marriage and produced wine from a small vineyard in Touraine. The question of who owned a particular portion of this vineyard has previously been a source of conflicting opinion. Jerome K. Jerome, for instance, in his autobiography *My Life and Times* (1926), stated that the vines had belonged to his good friend Amy Hogg and that it was she who "sold the wine to the proprietor of the Florence Restaurant in Rupert Street". Arthur Waite, on the other hand, attributed ownership to Machen. Leasehold documentation now confirms that it was indeed Machen who held a lease in the vineyard at Les Perruches de Saint Martin.

In a letter to the publisher John Lane in September 1894, Machen reports:

> *I inspected the vineyard and I think the crop will be very fair. The wine will probably be drier than last year's.*

John Lane had a vested interest in the quality of the grapes that year, a portion of the crop being destined for his table, bottled as "Clos St Martin" by Azario, proprietor of the Florence Restaurant. This dining venue seems to have had a literary clientele and was almost certainly the same "little Italian restaurant in Rupert Street" mentioned in Chapter Six of Oscar Wilde's *The Picture of Dorian Gray* (1891). Machen's own fictional allusions to this local restaurant would no doubt also have been recognised as such by the initiated. One example of an implicit reference comes in the first paragraph of "The Inmost Light", when Salisbury is "slowly pacing down Rupert Street, drawing nearer to his favourite restaurant".

Machen himself dined at the Florence with Wilde more than once and, as Jerome recalled, Wilde also took his young male friends there prior to his downfall. Ed Cohen notes, in *Talk on the Wilde Side* (1993), that the restaurant consequently also featured in evidence against Wilde at his trial in 1895.

The Florence, however, has an additional significance here with respect to Amy and the creative circles in which she moved during the early 1880s. She frequented this restaurant, sometimes in the company of Jerome, who writes:

> *She had a favourite table by the window, and often she and I*
> *dined there and shared a bottle.*

Amy, as Waite asserted, was "mixing much with authors, artists and actors" in London. Indeed, prior to her marriage, the only three acquaintances we know of to date were writers; Jerome, Coulson Kernahan, and the poet, Augusta Webster. Regarding Webster, John Gawsworth, in *The Life of Arthur Machen* (2005), records an occasion when:

> *Machen had been to a dance at the Hammersmith House of*
> *a friend of Miss Hogg's, Augusta Webster, a poetess of repute.*

Webster was also a novelist and a feminist social campaigner. However, few of her letters or personal papers remain, and thus, as Christine Sutphin points out in her introduction to *Augusta Webster: Portraits and Other Poems* (1999), little is know of her "inner life". Similarly, Amy Hogg's personal history must be pieced together through scant and disparate sources.

Perhaps the most informative evidence we have comes from Jerome, who writes eloquently about her. In his memoir he recalls:

> *Arthur Machen married a dear friend of mine, a Miss Hogg.*
> *How so charming a lady came to be born with such a name is*
> *one of civilisation's little ironies… Amy Hogg was a pioneer.*
> *She lived by herself in diggings opposite the British Museum,*
> *frequented restaurants and Aerated Bread shops, and had*
> *many men friends: all of which was considered very shocking*
> *in those days.*

As an early female "settler" in male-centred urban territory, Amy is here aptly labelled a "pioneer". This alone is arguably good reason for researching the life of this unconventional woman and attempting a contextual understanding of her single life in London during the early 1880s, and even perhaps before then.

During the latter half of the nineteenth century, increasing numbers of middle class women were beginning to benefit from educational reforms and new career opportunities. In the wake of a growing gender imbalance in the population, more single women were also seeking careers in the city, acquiring a visible autonomy at work and leisure. The typewriter was soon to create a new female workforce, for which the innovative theatre matinee and numerous teashops constituted respectable recreational spaces. This unprecedented freedom for unmarried, middle class women in the growing metropolis was assisted by the popularity of the bicycle and improved public transport.

As Jerome implies, within the relatively liberal Bohemian circles of artists and writers in London, for Amy such freedoms may well have included a number of intimate relationships with men. During this period, the controversial issue of women's sexual freedom had become an area of conflict for feminists and "New Women" novelists. Whilst, for instance, "social purity" campaigner Sarah Grand did not condone sexual relations outside marriage, Machen's fellow Keynotes Series author "George Egerton" (Mary Chavelita Dunne), was to valorise a woman's right to take responsibility for her own sexual behaviour. This question was also occasionally implicitly addressed by Machen himself in his fiction. In *The Secret Glory*, the narrator declares:

> ...*Nelly began to tell me all about herself. She had never said a word before; I had never asked her—I never ask anybody about their past lives. What does it matter?... What is the hero that he should be dowered with the love of virgins of Paradise? I call it cant—all that—and I hate it; I hope Angel Clare was eventually entrapped by a young person from Piccadilly Circus—she would probably be much too good for him!*

Some of the author's *femmes fatales*, however, apparently symbolise ambivalence toward female sexuality. Dr Gail-Nina Anderson, in this connection, has recently highlighted Machen's characterisation of women in her illuminating article, "Arthur Machen and the *Femme Fatale*" (*Faunus*, Eleven, Winter 2004).

The multidimensional Fatal Woman was replicated in art and literature in a variety of forms toward the turn of the twentieth century.

Her emasculating potential resonated back and forth between literature and social discourse, in relation to the growing demands of modern women. Indeed, moral and political issues concerning women in the city and female suffrage were being hotly debated during the 1880s and 1890s, constituting a source of growing social ambivalence. Within popular culture, therefore, the literary trope of the *femme fatale* derived from myth acquired an ideological sisterly relationship with the iconic feminist New Woman of the city.

Associated contemporary tensions are reflected retrospectively in Jerome's memoir, wherein the author recalls an earlier time, prior to the invention of the typewriter, when "a woman in the city had been a rare and pleasing sight". This implied preference for exotic rarity with respect to the feminine was also later taken up from another perspective by Machen in *Far Off Things* (1922) and echoed in the context of 1920s London, which he considered to have been tainted by a "monstrous incursion of women". In the author's discomfort with an under-educated, feminised mass culture and its detrimental effects on hierarchies of taste in food and journalism, he cast a nostalgic eye back to the 1880s. There he contrasted a city of male-only clubs and restaurants, in which nurturing waiters served succulent meats and where the best newspapers were journalistically unsullied by female "matter", contained as it was in limited columns.

It may well have seemed contained to him in retrospect, but Machen's female "incursion" into city spaces, institutions and indeed journalism clearly had its roots in the early 1880s. This was already beginning to generate concern amongst those who anticipated an erosion of classed and gendered social spheres. By 1897, anxieties regarding the future of male employment and men's privileged position in the city prompted a contributor to *The Fortnightly Review* to warn in sensational terms of "a monstrous regiment of women which threatens before very long to spread throughout the length and breadth of … London".

Independent, single women like Amy in fact had less impact on male exclusivity in late nineteenth century urban life than the above would suggest. Moreover, low wages and the dictates of propriety often necessitated modest, shared accommodation and little privacy. It was not unusual, therefore, for spinsters like Amy to lodge with families or other single women. At 23 Clarendon Road, according to the 1881 census, she lodged together with a young Australian woman, Elizabeth Waller, in the apartment of Susan Edwards, a 49-year-old Irish widow of a naval officer.

As we know, Amy listed her occupation at the time as "a teacher of music", but it is doubtful that this source of income would have been sufficient to live on. As Paula Gillet's research has shown in *Musical Women in England* (2000), the music teaching profession at the time was heavily over-subscribed. It was also under-regulated and provided little security, even for women trained in the most prestigious establishments:

> *As early as 1875, the Year Book of Women's Work had done its best to dissuade its readers from following this path. "Musical Instruction", writes the Year Book, "…is given at so low a rate as practically to make the position of teacher in the profession of no avail in a remunerative view".*

The situation was exacerbated for women music teachers in general, by the preference for male tutors amongst the wealthy. The time and cost of travelling between private pupils, moreover, was not always compensated for. If Amy taught in a school or conservatory she might have had more security, but little chance to benefit financially. As Gillet points out, a later 1894 job manual considered £50 a year as "exceptional" and asserted that schools would pay as little as £25 for women music teachers.

Amy's family may well have been in a position to provide sufficient financial support. However, it is equally possible that this free-spirited, independent woman might have had to find means to supplement her income. In this regard, we repeat Waite's retrospective consideration that:

> *She was quite of the type to have found her metier in light journalism and should have done well among women's papers.*

This statement arguably justifies further speculation, particularly in view of Amy's literary circle, Machen's reservations about women's journalism notwithstanding. The thriving periodical market provided an area of opportunity for educated women, and women journalists often wrote anonymously or under pseudonyms, as did many of their male counterparts. Had Amy desired publication, she would have been well placed socially for potential opportunity. An obvious example would have been in her acquaintance with editor Lewis Sergeant, in whose house, according to Gawsworth, she was later to encounter Machen. Sergeant at one time edited *The Examiner*, to which, for instance, Amy's acquaintance Augusta Webster contributed a number of anonymous essays in the guise of the "domestic scholar". Webster also later became poetry editor for *The Athenaeum*, with which Sergeant was also associated.

There were a number of popular women's journals at the time and of these, the monthly *Ladies Pictorial* is mentioned in a puzzling postscript concerning Amy. This occurs in a letter from Machen to John Lane in 1894. It is worth quoting here, if only for the rare mention of our subject:

> *Mrs Machen has hunted in the back numbers of the Ladies Pictorial for "Penelope" but without success. She also consulted the pseudonyms in Hazell, but "Penelope" is not there!*

The letter's content elsewhere implies that Machen was writing in response to a meeting with Lane and not in answer to a letter. Therefore, whether or not of any consequence, the exact purpose of Amy's fruitless search may never be known. The "Penelope" in question, however, may well have been Phebe Lankester (née Pope, 1825-1900), whose son, Edwin, became Director of the British Museum. According to the Oxford DNB, she authored books on botany and health and contributed to journals under her own name. After her husband's death in 1874, she used the pseudonym "Penelope" for her popular journalism on women's issues.

In any event, Machen's letter was written prior to publication of *The Great God Pan* (1894), which another, similarly-titled paper, the weekly *Lady's Pictorial*, subsequently considered "gruesome and unmanly"—this was eventually recorded by Machen in *Precious Balms* (1924). More significant for us, however, is the fact that the same publication in 1885 had also expressed disapproval of the activities of the Playgoers' Club, to which Amy happened to belong at the time.

In this connection, Gawsworth duly inferred that Amy had been an "inveterate theatregoer" before marriage and we also learn from Jerome's memoir that:

> *She had been a first nighter, and one of the founders of the*
> *Playgoers' Club which was in advance of its time, and admitted*
> *women members.*

B.W. Findon confirms in *The History of the Playgoers' Club* (1905), that both Amy and Jerome became core members of the Club in 1884, at its founding by Heneage Mandell and Carl Hentschel. The club evolved initially through contact between men and women with strong literary and dramatic affiliations, who frequented the theatre pit and gallery at "first nights". Findon describes the first meeting which took place at:

> *Dane's Hill Coffee House, 266A Strand, at the corner of*
> *Holywell Street, with Dr Holden, a well-known entertainer*
> *and magician, in the chair... Nineteen young stalwarts,*
> *burning with zeal and fiery enthusiasm, assembled and*
> *breathed an atmosphere untainted with the fumes of alcohol,*
> *and pregnant only with the odour of Mocha and Orange Pekoe.*

A committee was formed that night and "Miss Hogg" was the only woman elected. As Findon records, "Hentschel always gallant was responsible for the election of the lady". Initially welcomed in theatrical circles, the club almost immediately attracted controversy. It claimed to have thwarted Henry Irving's plans for pre-booking in the pit and soon gained adverse attention in the press for insistence on loudly voicing criticism from the pit during performances, as Findon here relates:

> *The noisy demonstration, which attended the production of*
> *Twelfth Night at the Lyceum on July 8<u>th</u> 1884, was mainly*
> *placed to the credit of the Club, and its members were roundly*
> *abused in columns of the daily and weekly Press... "Yahoos,"*
> *"Rowdies", "Wreckers", "The Tailors of Tooley Street," and "The*
> *Pimply Crowd of Counter-jumpers" are a specimen of the*
> *epithets that found their way into print.*

The Playgoers held regular Sunday evening discussions and subsequently also lectures and "entertainments," attracting a number of well-known literary, theatrical and political figures. This incited derision from a contributor to the aforementioned *Lady's Pictorial* who, in two articles during March 1885, implied there to be a lack of independent thought amongst the "irresponsible... very stupid young men" associated with "the complacent body of amateur critics, calling itself the Playgoers' Club". The articles carried the valid criticism that the club's amateur integrity and critical impartiality was being compromised by these professional associations.

Nevertheless, for the tenth annual dinner in 1894, Aubrey Beardsley designed a menu and guest lecturers ranged widely to include such figures as Eleanor Marx and Oscar Wilde. In his biography, *Oscar Wilde* (1987), Richard Ellmann points out that Wilde was responsible for the membership of his friend John Gray, thought by some to be a model for Dorian. Moreover, through Gray, the Playgoers made the front page of the *Star* newspaper on the 6th February 1892:

> *Mr Gray who has cultivated his manner to the highest pitch of languor yet attained is a well-known figure of the Playgoers' Club where though he often speaks he is seldom heard.*

It may have been due to the club's associations with such decadent aesthetes that Max Beerbohm, in his series of "Club Types" in *The Strand* magazine the same year (Vol. 4), depicted the typical Playgoer as an effete individual in tight trousers and a cape. However, an American visitor, Mary H. Krout, in *A Looker-On in London* (1899), whilst noting the club's literary affiliations, also particularly recalled the presence of women and their debating skills:

> *...while the women were not quite so fluent and numerous as the men, those who did speak acquitted themselves with credit, coming to the point with great directness, and showing themselves liberally endowed with good sense and humor.*

The Playgoers' Club Minute Books, sourced at the University of Massachusetts, provide significant primary material, including scant but important evidence of Amy's early involvement in club debates. At the Third Meeting, April 22nd 1884, various club members, including Jerome

K. Jerome and Amy Hogg, had debated a motion concerning the play *Claudian* at the Princess's Theatre. Amongst criticisms of the production, one aspect in particular proved a source of scepticism for both Jerome and Amy. The following quotation contains the only known reported words of Amy Hogg, being justification enough for its inclusion here.

> *Mr J.K. Jerome... considered it too great a stretch of imagination to suppose Claudian to be under a curse... Miss Hogg said the curse was unchristianlike, & failed to see how Claudian became converted.*

Jerome, who was himself president of the club for five years from 1886, emphasised the female element amongst its members, but his assertion that the club was "advanced" in this respect is misleading. Although Amy's election to the committee implied a potential for gender equality at the club's inception, after only six months a decision was taken that would no doubt have necessitated her resignation.

According to Findon, the club had decided to move from the "non-spirituous" café environment to a more permanent venue and:

> *...as it was decided to conduct the club on the usual club basis, it was felt that the presence of ladies would militate against that end. Accordingly those of the fair sex, who wished to take some part in its doings were allowed to become "Associates" on payment of an annual subscription of five shillings, which gave them the right to be present at the weekly discussions.*

"The usual club basis" would probably have included alcohol and tobacco. Whether or not it was these pleasures that the presence of women were thought to militate against is not clear. Whatever the case, Amy, who is referred to by Gawsworth, perhaps significantly, as "charming and frank", no doubt expressed her own opinions on the matter. Indeed, the club Minute Books imply that she did not relinquish her status without question.

Of the three letters from Amy recorded in the Books, there is an indication of content on only one occasion. This occurs in the Minutes of the "Twenty-Ninth Meeting, 20th September 1885", a year after women were demoted to associate members. Here, the following instructions are given in response to a letter from Amy, which may suggest that the status of women was still a sensitive issue:

> *The Secretary was instructed to write to Miss Hogg, informing her that the Annual General Meeting was a purely business meeting, and that if any ladies associated with the club presented themselves, they would not be turned away, but would expected [sic] to take no part in the proceedings.*

Findon states, without explanation, that women were subsequently absent from the club entertainments for three years prior to 1889, when a "Lady's Concert" was held to encourage their return. By then, of course, Amy was married and living with Machen in Great Russell Street, and the nature of her relationship with the club after that is not known. Nevertheless, it is clear that after her marriage to Machen, her passion for the theatre was undiminished.

Sadly, by 1893, after less than six years of married life, the first clouds appeared on the horizon, in that Amy was diagnosed with breast cancer. The standard treatment in the late Victorian period for such a condition was surgical, a mastectomy, with laudanum the opiate of choice for controlling pain. Fortunately, as we have found, her illness did not yet exclude Amy from visits to France or excursions to the theatre and the Machens still entertained at home.

John Gawsworth asserts that a frequent house guest, "George Egerton", was particularly fond of Amy. He relates an "encounter on the pavement" between the two women when the Machens were living on the top floor of 36 Great Russell Street:

> *One day outside the house on the sweep of the curb, Mrs Machen ran into "George Egerton" ... They had met at Lane's Keynotes dinner and "George Egerton" was much attracted to Mrs Machen, who invited her to supper. The author of Keynotes remembers the occasion of her visits well—"Good gracious me," she said frankly to Machen standing puffing his pipe by the hearth, with Juggernaut the bulldog at his heels, "your ears are pointed like a faun's". Machen explained that this*

> *was a Monmouthshire characteristic, and they all drank the*
> *famous wine of Genille and talked Lane and Bodley Head over*
> *cold supper.*

The "wine of Genille" from Machen's vineyard no doubt also helped to lubricate discussions during literary gatherings at 4 Verulam Buildings, Gray's Inn. This was their home from October 1895, and neighbour M.P. Shiel, in "The Good Machen" (1933), recalled the convivial, literary community there as "an island in the sea of London":

> *Machen and Mrs often came to visit me—she taller than he, thin,*
> *amiable, fond of me. To me, beginning housekeeping, she gave*
> *council... The Inn then was quite a haunt of artists... and on*
> *Sunday afternoons quite a crowd of more or less literary people*
> *would fill Machen's large drawing room, filling it with smoke and*
> *sipping Benedictine which Machen presented with a certain unction*
> *and ceremony; "George Egerton" for one, was often among them,*
> *Mrs Shakespear (pretty! dark), who wrote novels and was in with*
> *me, and a family of reviewers, who still review—Sergeant—one*
> *of whom Mrs Machen meant me to marry, though I did not quite*
> *see eye-to-eye with her on that. Sometimes she'd take me about from*
> *guest to guest to exhibit the extraordinary length of my fingers—*
> *artistic, she said—I shrinking at the consciousness that the nails*
> *weren't clean.*

For Amy, such amusements must surely have become less frequent as her illness progressed toward the inevitable, tragic outcome that Machen so dreaded. Finally, on 31st July 1899, Amy's painful six and a half year struggle against death came to an end. Her death certificate confirms the cause to have been carcinoma of the breast with "numerous secondary deposits over the body" and further states that her husband was with her when she died. For a more personal sense of the end, however, we must again refer to Jerome, who writes movingly of a visit to the Machens' apartment just before Amy's death:

It was a Sunday afternoon. They were living in Verulam
Buildings, Gray's Inn, in rooms on the ground floor. The
windows looked out onto the great quiet garden, and the rooks
were cawing in the elms. She was dying, and Machen, with
two cats under his arm, was moving softly about, waiting on
her. We did not talk much. I stayed there till the sunset filled
the room with a strange purple light.

Aidan Reynolds and William Charlton, in *Arthur Machen: A*
Short Account of his Life and Work (1963), assert that Amy, born a Catholic,
was "received back into her church on her death bed", much to Machen's
satisfaction. His tragic loss, inevitable grief and appreciation of kind
friends are reflected in his response to letters of sympathy. The following
reply to Richard Le Gallienne was written only five days after Amy's death:

> [*5ᵗʰ August 1899*]
> *4 Verulam Buildings*
> *Gray's Inn, WC*
>
> *My dear Le Gallienne*
> *It is very kind of you to write to me.*
> *Everybody thinks, I know, that a letter of sympathy is a poor*
> *thing: I have felt that myself when trying to write one; but it*
> *is not so. Such a letter as yours does a great deal to lessen that*
> *awful sense of loneliness, which you know of—I am grateful*
> *to you. If you would come to see me I should be very glad: it*
> *would be an act of charity.*
> *Very truly yours*
> *Arthur Machen*

Edgar Jepson and his wife also proved to be patiently supportive.
In the following letter from Machen to Jepson, the mentioned visit to
Barnet probably refers to Amy's sister Mary Ann (Mysie), who was still
caring for her older brother.

> *Sunday* [*probably late summer 1899*]
> *Dear Mr Jepson,*
> *I want you to let me off the dinner at Roche's and to come*

and see me, either that night or any other night in the week—
Monday-Thursday inclusive. After that I shall be going to
Barnet for a fortnight, to my wife's relations.

I do not feel equal to going out to the restaurant. I am not by
any means well; the symptoms are indefinite, but the sensation
is disgusting! I hope you will pardon my defaulting and come
and see me—the sooner the better.

I enjoyed last evening very much, George Herbert writes that
it is a relief to a "poor body" to be listened to: and I am sure you
listened with great patience to some very wild stuff.
I hope to see you soon…

Whilst Machen's depression became a cause for concern amongst his friends, his bereavement also represented a release and new opportunity, as intimated by Gawsworth. The following extract from a letter, probably written during the winter of 1899 to Edgar Jepson, duly implies in Machen's usual cryptic fashion, that he was also enjoying new female company, no doubt with the help of Waite:

I do not know whether I shall see you on Sunday at Barron's.
Barron has very kindly asked me, but my coming depends on
a hypothetical syllogism, whereof the solution is in the hands
of the Shepherdess. "If A is B, C is D", and at present, so far
as I know the relation of A to B = ii, a Greek letter supposed
in Cambridge to be the symbol of the Indeterminate, though
the Cabalists say that ii should really be ii-He—the Hebrew
letter which, oddly enough (considering its name) expresses
the Feminine Nature, the "Great Deep" of Binah, the Waters
of Creation.

At this moment I receive a letter from the Fair Wanton,
informing me that she has been ruined by a Teapot, at 11.30pm
last night.

It seems strange…

The "Fair Wanton" referred to here was the young Hilda Wauton, an actress with the Benson Company. "The Shepherdess," being the actress Vivienne Pierpont, together with Waite's sister-in-law Dora

Stuart-Menteath, featured in the implied amorous adventures recorded in *The House of the Hidden Light* (1904).

Whether or not Amy ever acted herself, it is apparent that she had a suitable attribute in her "deep impressive voice". In any event, when Machen subsequently entered the theatrical sphere as an actor, he was also entering the world of his deceased wife's passion. On stage, furthermore, he would have been performing under the gaze of an audience that might once ideally have included Amy herself. Thus, whilst Amy's death effectively facilitated for Machen "another phase of life, almost a new world," as described by Arthur Waite, there is a sense in which this new beginning also comprised a certain continuity, in its tenuous link with the past.

At this distance in time it is naturally difficult to estimate the importance of Amy to Machen's literary career. Factually, most of his major works were written during their short life together, yet this period also corresponds with his early years, the years that normally mark the optimal span for creative activity. It is interesting to note that he himself penned the following in "With the Gods in Spring" (1923):

> *We are all white-haired now; we have been grilled and roasted*
> *and boiled and fried in the fire of life.*

Machen survived his fire, the most searing of all, the death of Amy after just twelve years of marriage. Aptly, one of his contemporaries, A.C. Benson, commented:

> *I wonder why we suffer so strangely—to bring out something*
> *in us I believe, which can't be brought out in any other way.*

His wounds were healed by the balm of meeting Purefoy Hudleston, their subsequent marriage, and the bearing of two children. This gave him the stability of a long and happy marriage, until their deaths in 1947.

Amy, on the other hand, has remained the "invisible woman" in Machen's life story, merely discernible in fragments and brief, secondary impressions. In his review article "Arthur Machen" (*The Nation and Athenaeum*, 11th November 1922), Forrest Reid considered that with

Machen's autobiographical "record of loneliness", *Things Near and Far*, the author had created a "sketch rather than a portrait" of a life. It follows that we may never appreciate the full picture until further textual silences can be filled with the hidden traces of Amy Hogg.

Within the nineteenth-century, Imperial and urban context, however, Amy's significance extends far beyond her marriage to Arthur Machen. Also, of potential interest is her historical position as a Victorian "Anglo-Indian", in the colonial cultural cross-currents of Empire. Important also is her role as an early New Woman on the Bohemian fringes, negotiating a way through male terrain in a climate of social change.

Thus it is hoped that before too long this ghost from the past will have greater substance and we will be able to present a fuller picture of this enigmatic woman. Amy was laid to rest in the western section of Highgate Cemetery. There beneath the trees, a granite Celtic cross still stands proud and unweathered against tangled undergrowth.

A Longing For The wood-world at Night

The sylvan Mysteries of Arthur Machen

Nick Freeman

originally published in Faunus issue 12

> *When they were alone together in the wood, Charlotte said:*
> *"Now you must show me the game. You promised."*
> *[Arthur Machen, "Torture", 1897]*

What connection might there be between Arthur Machen, Robert Holdstock and "The Teddy Bears' Picnic"? Readers of *Faunus* could and probably will propose numerous fascinating links, but for my purposes the answer is a prosaic one: woods. From "The White People" to *Mythago Wood* (1984) to Bratton and Kennedy's 1932 sing-along, the British woodland has often been construed as a magical, secretive place, a realm of dark gods and strange visions in which the reader is always "sure of a big surprise". However, Machen's contribution to the enchantment of British nature has rarely been acknowledged. Academic criticism has tended to focus on his importance as a gothic or horror writer, and even considerations of late Victorian paganism such as Patricia Merivale's *Pan: The Goat God* (1969) or Ronald Hutton's *The Triumph of the Moon* (1999) have concentrated largely upon the impact of his first novel.

At the same time, the tentatively "pagan" representation of nature has been attacked by those who have seen it as a betrayal of lived experience. Raymond Williams' influential *The Country and the City* (1973) is especially critical of those who filtered ideas about the rural and the pastoral through "a version of the classical tradition, which is so unlike any classical rural literature". The book singled out writers "who brought with them, from the cities, and from the schools and universities, a version of rural history that was now extraordinarily amalgamated with a distantly translated literary interpretation", and that connected "the honest past" with "the pagan spirit". Furthermore, Williams differentiated between wild "nature" and the British countryside created by thousands of years of agricultural usage. His argument, informed by both Marxism and his family history, is a compelling one, but because it fails to see "paganism" as anything other than a literary affectation, a matter of reference to "Fauns, Pan, centaurs, the Golden Age, ...immemorial history, presences, the timeless rhythm of the seasons", it cannot fully appreciate its significance.[1] I would like to suggest that although certain elements of Edwardian literature were prone to "intellectual projection" that ignored "authentic popular culture" in favour of a sentimentalised "Englishness", paganism was not simply a means by which middle class writers avoided pressing political and economic realities. It was instead a branch of mystical engagement with the world, the literature of which, despite what Williams would see as its political weaknesses, has become increasingly popular in recent years.

The "pagan" response to the countryside found in certain early twentieth century writers was never likely to win the approval of Marxist critics locked into the denial of transcendence. A more recent example is Robert Dingley, whose essay on Pan in Kath Filmer's *Twentieth Century Fantasists* (1992) argued that although writers employed the god to expose ideological contradictions in Edwardian culture, he actually removed these from their immediate context, rendering them natural and universal. In the same essay, however, Dingley showed the limitations of his approach in a reading of *The Great God Pan*. Quoting Machen's intention of passing on his "vague, indefinable sense of awe and mystery and terror" from *Far Off Things*, Dingley maintained that Machen "uses the image of the goat-god to encapsulate the threatening remoteness and isolation of the countryside".[2] This ignores Machen's own regret at translating "awe" into "evil" and fails to differentiate between Pan and a more generally pagan or magical conception of the natural world. Tellingly, it also ignores the "mystery" conjured by Machen's first sight of "the lonely house between the dark forest and the silver river". As Edgar Wind writes in *Pagan Mysteries of the Renaissance* (1967), "mystery" has a number of meanings "that tended to become blurred in antiquity, to the great enrichment and confusion of the subject". He eventually classified three distinct applications, the ritual, the figurative, and the magical, all of which are far more profound and elusive than modern understandings of mystery as an unexplained or inexplicable event.[3] The word was a crucial one for Machen, who, alluding to Henry James' tale "The Figure in the Carpet" (1896) in *The London Adventure*, wrote that "the pattern in my carpet" is "the sense of the eternal mysteries, the eternal beauty hidden beneath the crust of common and commonplace things". It is this sense of the numinous and the enduring that secular historicism is unable to appreciate or understand, and it goes some way to explaining why so much "pagan" writing on landscape is dismissed as escapist or fanciful. It is concerned not with immediate politics but with a mystical conception of the world that seeks deeper and enduring truths.

In *Genius Loci* (1899), Vernon Lee wrote, "I want to talk about something which makes the real, individual landscape—the landscape one actually sees with the eyes of the body and the eyes of the spirit—*the landscape you cannot describe.*" While a number of Edwardian and Georgian writers transformed the countryside into a fanciful Arcadia, Machen and his mystically inclined contemporaries viewed nature with what *The London Adventure* termed "purged eyes". They were not interested in what the distorting mirror of pastoral classicism might do to superficial observations, and neither were they especially attracted to naturalism's identification of native flora and fauna. Their landscape could not be described because it represented the ineffable. In some ways, these writers resembled the medieval theologians who believed that religious experience could not be reduced to linguistic terms. One could convey something of the surface, in this case, the setting for mystical experience, but the experience itself defied representation. Stories of Pan employ the notion of "panic" for an encounter with the divine which transcends language; tellingly, Mary in "The Great God Pan" is "a hopeless idiot", deprived of the power of speech, while the narrator of E.M. Forster's "The Story of a Panic" (1904) feels that his experience "blocked" "all the channels of sense and reason". In descriptions of landscape, however, words such as "mystery" and "silence" recur. This is not because, as is sometimes argued, writers suffered a failure of the imagination, but because their intuition defied explicit statement. It could be hinted at, alluded to, or implied, but only those prepared to offer a degree of sympathy, even indulgence, could properly appreciate it.

In descriptions of the natural world in writers such as Machen, Algernon Blackwood and W.B. Yeats, the perception of a deeper reality re-evaluated what Chas Clifton and Graham Harvey list as "nature, physicality, materialism, [and] embodiment". Vague intimations of this world came only to the imaginative, the "poets" who, in *The London Adventure*, "catch strange glimpses of reality... out of the corners of their eyes". Machen preferred poetry, myth and ritual to "religious dogma" or "scientific theory", just as Julian, in Machen's prose poem "Nature", prefers rhapsodic reaction to landscape to the analysis of his "wonderful and incredible passion". Machen responds to his surroundings in ways which, while powerfully suggestive to modern pagans, New Agers and environmentalists, are often anathema to traditional scholars.[4] This is not to "claim" Machen for modern paganism; merely to point out his affinities with certain aspects of contemporary belief.

The title of this essay comes from Machen's prose poem "Midsummer", written in 1897 but not published until *Ornaments in Jade* a quarter of a century later. In it, Leonard, a struggling writer, flees the "defilement and anguish" of the London streets and escapes to an old farm-house in order to find "the treasure he had long been vainly seeking". Inspired by the exquisite beauty of his surroundings, he at last completes his work, imbuing it with the "ecstasy" that Machen so prizes in creative art. The exultant Leonard finds himself "filled with a longing for the wood-world at night, with a desire for its darkness, for the mystery of it beneath the moon", and leaving his study, wanders outside. Here he feels "as though his soul were astray in a new dark sphere that dreams had foretold", and he lies in the moonlight in "the heart of the wood", witnessing at last a mysterious ritual performed by girls from the nearby village. Leonard's experience has all the hall-marks of the "withdrawal from the common ways of life" that Machen identified in *Hieroglyphics* as "the beginning of ecstasy". One could draw obvious parallels between Leonard, battered by the rumbling wheels of London and struggling with the expression of his thoughts, Lucian Taylor's *ars magna* and Machen at work on *The Hill of Dreams* in similar circumstances. One could also note the connections between this story and many other moments of analogous inspiration in the Machen canon; the exquisite description of "Rus in Urbe", for example, or the contrast between London's "black clouds and angry fire" and the idyllic Welsh coast of *The Great Return*. Unlike some of his contemporaries, Machen did not by any means reject urban life, but he never disguised the fact that his adult personality had been shaped by early exposure to what he termed in *Far Off Things*, "vague impressions of wonder and awe and mystery", and "the vision of an enchanted land" far removed from the Victorian city. The wild country of the Welsh borders left an indelible imprint on his character and imagination, informing virtually every aspect of his work from the weird tale to autobiography.

Apart from its obviously nostalgic appeal for Machen, what did "the wood-world" represent? As a number of writers and historians have argued, Romantic pantheism and tentative paganism were appealing alternatives to a Victorian materialist sensibility often identified with seemingly uncontrollable urban growth. Wordsworth had suggested in "Nutting" (1800), "there is a Spirit in the woods", and a hundred years later, writers and artists, as well as what would now be seen as campaigners for rural life, sought it from the Ancient Ireland of W.B. Yeats to the rural Sussex of Rudyard Kipling. "The cutting-off of man from Nature, whether wrought by Christianity, intellectual consciousness, industrialism and mechanisation, or by an insidious combination of all these forces, resulted in a civilisation based upon democracy and technology," observes Roger Ebbatson, categorising a "civilisation" for which, like many of his peers, Machen had at best guarded enthusiasm.[5]

The natural world, by contrast, represented the organic, the authentic, and the unadulterated, the rhythms of sun and season. Woodland, particularly ancient deciduous woodland that was neither "owned" nor "managed", predated the insistently "modern" world, and to stand in it was to re-connect oneself with enduring but increasingly overlooked realities, even the ancient gods themselves. Kipling's "A Tree Song" in *Puck of Pook's Hill* (1906) celebrated the everlasting England of "Oak, and Ash, and Thorn" in verses which Chas Clifton notes have become "incorporated into more recent ritual texts" and which have even been regarded as pre-Christian in origin.[6] In *Civilisation: its Cause and Cure* (1906), Edward Carpenter awaited man's rediscovery of "the old religions", when "once more in sacred groves will he reunite the passion and delight of human love with his deepest feelings of the sanctity and beauty of Nature". Although it lacks a woodland setting, Blackwood's "The Sea Fit" from his 1912 collection *Pan's Garden* was equally explicit on this point, maintaining that "the gods were not dead, but merely withdrawn", and "even a single true worshipper was enough to draw them into touch with the world, into the sphere of humanity, even into active and visible transformation". Classically educated men such as Carpenter inevitably drew upon Greek and Roman literature for their understanding and image of pre-Christian religion, but their works were not simply the "uncritical interest in myth" which so annoyed Raymond Williams. They were seeking instead a vocabulary that allowed the expression of spiritual intuitions and environmental sensitivity. As Edward Thomas noted wryly in *The Country* (1913), "Apollo, Woden, Jehovah, have been put away for the sake of unsectarian education. No wonder we are languid, fretful, and aimless."

Late nineteenth century Celtic writers were especially drawn to the connections between the wood and an immemorial or imagined past, intrigued by their potential role in the revival of Celtic culture. In his essay "Enchanted Woods" from *The Celtic Twilight* (1893), Yeats remarked that even as a boy "I could never walk in a wood without feeling that at any moment I might find before me somebody or something I had long looked for without knowing what I looked for", a sense that persisted into adult life and informed some of his finest work. "Fiona MacLeod" and "A.E." often struck a similar note in poetry and essays. MacLeod's *Where the Forest Murmurs* (1906) and *From the Hills of Dream* (1896), depict woodlands as places where the walker can feel "the breath of that other-world of which our songs and legends are so full", and become imbued with an "ecstasy" that causes one to "love the mystery one has but fugitively divined". A.E.'s "Dana", included in his *Collected Poems* (1913), tells of "the lonely wanderer by wood or shore", who has a moment of epiphany in realising how the goddess "can enchant the trees and rocks, and fill / The dumb brown lips of earth with mystery, / Make them reveal or hide the god". His parable, "A Priestess of the Woods" (1893), describes an encounter between a young woman who misunderstands the relationship between humanity and the natural world and a poet whose "proud assertion of kingship and joy in the radiance of a deeper life" transforms her forever. All three writers employ a common language of mystery and delight that, allowing for their differing spiritual paths, conveys notably similar visions or states of mind. Links between Machen and the "Celtic Twilight" are suggestive ones, even though in *Far Off Things* he was inclined to minimise the contribution of "the Welsh Celt" to "great literature", and Mark Valentine's biography of him rightly distinguishes between two very different approaches to the "Little People".

As John Clute points out, the journey into the wood marks "a passage from one life into another, one time to another, one place to another".[7] Kipling's "The Way Through the Woods", the poem which precedes "Marklake Witches" in *Rewards and Fairies* (1910), is a memorable example. A summer evening suggests a ghostly visitation or even a temporal slippage in which a woman canters through "The misty solitudes" as if knowing "The old lost road through the woods". The poetry and short stories of Walter de la Mare often depict similar moments, especially at twilight, when ghosts walk the woodland paths and nothing is quite as it seems.

Elsewhere, the passage from "one life to another" by way of ordeal or initiation is frequently imbued with sexual significance. Alison Prince, for example, entitled her 1994 biography of Kenneth Grahame *An Innocent in the Wild Wood*, a sylvan metaphor that suggests the writer's inability to meet the demands of adult life, specifically in his unsatisfactory marriage. Machen frequently associates woodland with the erotic. In "Midsummer", the woodland track leads Leonard "away from the world" and brings him into the presence of "things he had thought the world had long forgotten" as he watches, rather voyeuristically, the village girls in their mysterious ritual. *The Hill of Dreams* depicts Lucian's woodland experiences with an unforgettable imaginative intensity, even if his intimate relationship with bramble bushes alarmed Lord Dunsany. At the beginning of *The Great God Pan*, Clarke dreams he has wandered "from the fields into the wood", a journey into an "undiscovered country" where he encounters a hideous "presence" that is "the form of all things but devoid of any form", in an obvious anticipation of the sexualised horrors and deaths ahead. Woods do not belong to the "civilised" world and are not bound by its constraints. This explains, in some ways at least, the fear of the Wild Wood shown by members of the domesticated bourgeoisie such as Rat and Toad in *The Wind in the Willows* (1908), and the enthusiasm for it professed by modern pagans keen to reject such norms. The wood is the ideal setting for ancient and secret ceremonies, notably in the "black terrible woods" of "The White People", in which "the shape of the trees seemed quite different from any I had ever seen before".

Woods are places in which the rationalising intellect is likely to be overwhelmed by primeval urges, and Machen was far from the only writer of his era to imbue them with a lingering sexual charge. From the intense union of Paul and Miriam in D.H. Lawrence's *Sons and Lovers* (1913) to the eponymous protagonist's realisation that he is "at one with the forests and the night" in E.M. Forster's *Maurice* (1971, wr. 1913), woods are repeatedly sites of transgressive desire. E.F. Benson's "The Man Who Went Too Far" (1904), set in the ancient New Forest, sees a markedly homoerotic relationship between the artist, Frank Halton, and his friend Darcy. Forrest Reid's *The Garden God* (1905), depicts Harold Brocklehurst, deeply in love with his friend Graham, sitting on a fallen tree in "a little glen of trees and brambles" and pondering "a world where good and evil no longer stood so very far apart". This moral blurring or abandonment sometimes took disturbing forms. Rupert Brooke used the "holy three", "Night, and the woods, and you", in his poem "The Voice" (1909), although here the lover's arrival spoils the "magic" atmosphere and leads the speaker to wish her dead. A.E. Housman's posthumously published "Delight it is in youth and May", included in *More Poems* (1936), encourages a woman to follow the nightingale "Into the leafy woods alone" where "I will work you ill". "Torture", surely one of Machen's nastiest pieces, offers a similar scenario. The twisted schoolboy Harry, armed with a collection of home-made glass knives and a length of rope, lures a young girl to the Beeches, "a lonely wooded hill", in the hope of playing his "new game", although thankfully, he fails to fulfil his sadistic ambitions.

It would be simplistic and misleading to make a straightforward connection between a woodland setting and a pagan presence, but it is nonetheless important to recognise how often early twentieth-century fiction invoked a world in which the old gods lurk just beyond the reach of human experience. Those sympathetic to its atmosphere found woodland a site of extraordinary if elusive power, but those who are less reverential frequently pay the price. In Algernon Blackwood's novella "The Man Whom the Trees Loved" (1912), David Bittacy's love of the New Forest is opposed by his wife, who, significantly, is the daughter of an evangelical clergyman. Her fight with the trees sees her lose both her husband and her Christian faith. "The Fairy Wood" in Blackwood's "Ancient Lights" (1914) is "enchanting" in more ways than one and threatens those who would cut it down with the warning sign, "Trespassers will be Persecuted". Saki's stories are littered with the brutal and bizarre deaths of those seeking to own and even domesticate wild nature. "The Music on the Hill", his much-anthologised tale from 1911, depicts the garden of a country house where "a steeper slope of heather and bracken dropped down into cavernous combes overgrown with oak and yew". "In its wild open savagery," we are told, "there seemed a stealthy linking of the joy of life with the terror of unseen things." The oak and the yew connect the landscape with its pagan past: it is a place where "the worship of Pan has never died out" and where "the Wood Gods are rather horrible to those who molest them". "Watchful, living things of kindred mould" lurk in the "dusk-hidden wilderness of field and hedge and coppice" in Saki's novel, *When William Came* (1913), and numerous other instances could be cited from his work. In a memorable denunciation of "sanitised and politically correct" modern paganism, Kerri Sharp has noted the profusion of "workshops" at which "you may get to share some wine and look fondly at a few trees, but you'll probably have to listen to some embarrassingly bad prose and go home feeling faintly embarrassed with yourself".[8] Perhaps it is time for those who provide such mind-numbing experiences to acquaint themselves with Saki's work, or better still, ponder the nature of initiation and sacrifice after reading "The White People"!

Machen's wood-world was one in which, as Swinburne wrote in "The Palace of Pan" (1893):

> *The spirit made one with the spirit whose breath*
> *Makes noon in the woodland sublime*
> *Abides as entranced in a presence that saith*
> *Things loftier than life and serener than death,*
> *Triumphant and silent as time.*

It was a place of silence, withdrawn from what *The Hill of Dreams* calls the "roar" of the city, and governed by natural cycles rather than the ticking of the clock or the chiming of the church bell. It was also a place haunted by what Jocelyn Brooke identified in *The Scapegoat* (1948) as "the feeling of mystery, which haunts all woods", ancient gods and secret, mysterious rites. However, although similar material can be found in the work of his contemporaries, there are two especially important differences between them. Machen was well versed in the classics and the occult, but his mysticism was ultimately rooted in a highly personal version of the Celtic Church. Beautiful as his writing on nature often is, it pales beside the evocations of the Grail in *The Secret Glory*. Finally, Machen possessed a robust common sense that would have made him sceptical towards some aspects of today's nature mysticism, let alone its "workshops", tree hugging and "Iron John" "wilderness masculinity weekends" for stressed-out urban professionals. "Tennyson, you remember," he told Vincent Starrett, "says 'the cedars sigh for Lebanon,' and that is exquisite poetry; but Blackwood believes the cedars really *do* sigh for Lebanon and that... is damned nonsense!"[9]

sources

1 Raymond Williams, *The Country and the City* (Paladin, 1975), pp. 306-307.

2 Robert Dingley, "Meaning Everything: The Image of Pan at the Turn of the Century" in *Twentieth Century Fantasists*, ed. Kath Filmer (Macmillan, 1992), pp. 57, 54.

3 Edgar Wind, *Pagan Mysteries of the Renaissance* (Peregrine, 1967), pp. 1, 6.

4 *The Paganism Reader*, ed. Chas S. Clifton and Graham Harvey (Routledge, 2004), pp. 3-4.

5 Roger Ebbatson, *Lawrence and the Nature Tradition: A Theme in English Fiction 1859-1914* (Harvester Press, 1980), p. 30.

6 *The Paganism Reader*, p. 80.

7 John Clute, "Into the Woods", *The Encyclopedia of Fantasy*, ed. John Clute & John Grant (Orbit, 1997), p. 503.

8 Kerri Sharp, "Satan gets a manicure: Changing perceptions of pagan practice" in *Inappropriate Behaviour*, ed. Jessica Berens and Kerri Sharp (Serpent's Tail, 2002), p. 237.

9 Vincent Starrett, *Born in a Bookshop* (University of Oklahoma Press, 1965), pp. 248-249.

The ROSE Garden

Arthur Machen, with a preface by John Gawsworth
published in Faunus issue 13

Preface

From the "Prologue" to Strange Assembly,
Edited by John Gawsworth, London: Unicorn Press, 1932

To find such an exquisite tale as "The Rose Garden" uncollected in the works of Arthur Machen published in England, is good fortune for any Anthologist. No finer piece of descriptive writing ever came from his pen. Without strain or hint of forcing, it contains as much of the authentic Celtic twilight—peace on the wings of the morning— as ever a poem of Senator Yeats. On reading and re-reading new profundities of sense are revealed. Each word is significant, each phrase pregnant with a hundred unborn meanings. Written at the time of the conception and execution of the author's *chef-d'œuvre, The Hill of Dreams*, it might well serve as pendant to any of those delicate fantasias emanating from that Elysian "Garden of Avallaunius", where the only true and exquisite science is to be found. Machen since then has enriched our literature with stories such as "The Gift of Tongues", here published [in *Strange Assembly*], and books of autobiography, comparable only in our language to *The Opium Eater* and Sir Thomas Browne. Yet he has never adjudged to a more perfect nicety any series of paragraphs, as he has in this tale. "The Rose Garden" is as much a poem as "The Lotus Eaters", "The Dark Angel", or "Non Sum Qualis Eram Bonæ Sub Regno Cynaræ", and I am proud to be able, by placing it between covers, to give it a chance of permanence. So tattered has my own transcript become of recent years, from perpetual re-reading and the mishandlings of appreciative friends, that I must rejoice in this opportunity which, presenting itself at last, enables me to introduce it to a wider English public. Printed with other pieces in an expensive, and very limited, signed edition in America, this story has never found its way into any volume of Machen's published in this country.

John Gawsworth

The Rose Garden

Arthur Machen
Written 1897; first published in The Neolith Vol. I, August 1908;
collected in The Glorious Mystery, Chicago: Covici-McGee, 1924,
and in Ornaments in Jade, New York: Knopf, 1924

And afterwards she went very softly, and opened the window and looked out. Behind her, the room was in a mystical semi-darkness; chairs and tables were hovering, ill-defined shapes; there was but the faintest illusory glitter from the talc moons in the rich Indian curtain which she had drawn across the door. The yellow silk draperies of the bed were but suggestions of colour, and the pillow and the white sheets glimmered as a white cloud in a far sky at twilight.

She turned from the dusky room, and with dewy tender eyes gazed out across the garden towards the lake. She could not rest nor lay herself down to sleep; though it was late, and half the night had passed, she could not rest. A sickle moon was slowly drawing upwards through certain filmy clouds that stretched in a long band from east to west, and a pallid light began to flow from the dark water, as if there also some vague star were rising. She looked with eyes insatiable for wonder; and she found a strange eastern effect in the bordering of reeds, in their spearlike shapes, in the liquid ebony that they shadowed, in the fine inlay of pearl and silver as the moon shone free; a bright symbol in the steadfast calm of the sky.

There were faint stirring sounds heard from the fringe of reeds, and now and then the drowsy, broken cry of the waterfowl, for they knew that the dawn was not far off. In the centre of the lake was a carved white pedestal, and on it shone a white boy, holding the double flute to his lips.

Beyond the lake the park began, and sloped gently to the verge of the wood, now but a dark cloud beneath the sickle moon. And then beyond, and farther still, undiscovered hills, grey bands of cloud, and the steep pale height of the heaven. She gazed on with her tender eyes, bathing herself, as it were, in the deep rest of the night, veiling her soul with the half-light and the half-shadow, stretching out her delicate hands into the coolness of the misty silvered air, wondering at her hands.

And then she turned from the window, and made herself a divan of cushions on the Persian carpet, and half sat, half lay there, as motionless, as ecstatic as a poet dreaming under roses, far in Ispahan. She had gazed out, after all, to assure herself that sight and the eyes showed nothing but a glimmering veil, a gauze of curious lights and figures: that in it there was no reality nor substance. He had always told her that there was only one existence, one science, one religion, that the external world was but a variegated shadow which might either conceal or reveal the truth; and now she believed.

He had shown her that bodily rapture might be the ritual and expression of the ineffable mysteries, of the world beyond sense, that must be entered by the way of sense; and now she believed. She had never much doubted any of his words, from the moment of their meeting a month before. She had looked up as she sat in the arbour, and her father was walking down through the avenue of roses, bringing to her the stranger, thin and dark, with a pointed beard and melancholy eyes. He murmured something to himself as they shook hands; she heard the rich, unknown words that sounded as the echo of far music. Afterwards he had told her what those words signified:

> *"How say ye that I was lost? I wandered among roses.*
> *Can he go astray that enters the rose garden?*
> *The Lover in the house of the Beloved is not forlorn.*
> *I wandered among roses. How say ye that I was lost?"*

His voice, murmuring the strange words, had persuaded her, and now she had the rapture of the perfect knowledge. She had looked out into the silvery uncertain night in order that she might experience the sense that for her these things no longer existed. She was not any more a part of the garden, or of the lake, or of the wood, or of the life that she had led hitherto. Another line that he had quoted came to her:

*"The kingdom of I and We forsake and your home in
annihilation make."*

It had seemed at first almost nonsense—if it had been possible
for him to talk nonsense; but now she was filled and thrilled with the
meaning of it. Herself was annihilated; at his bidding she had destroyed
all her old feelings and emotions, her likes and dislikes, all the inherited
loves and hates that her father and mother had given her; the old life had
been thrown utterly away.

It grew light, and when the dawn burned she fell asleep, murmuring:

"How say ye that I was lost?"

Arthur Machen and the Legend of Drake's Drum

Bob Mann
originally published in Faunus issue 15

Eagerly unpacking my copy of the Tartarus Press edition of *Ritual and Other Stories*, I cast my eyes over the contents wondering where, faced with such riches, I could possibly start. I decided to leave the early prose poems until I had the leisure to savour them in the way they deserved, and turned, as a Westcountry loyalist, to the tale called "Drake's Drum".

This story, which appeared in *The Outlook* in April 1919, and was later published in *The Shining Pyramid* (Chicago 1923), is a coda to the series of Great War parables, all variations on "The Bowmen" of 1914, in which Machen sought, rather touchingly, to show that the heavens were on Britain's side. They are not, today, the stories his admirers most love, but their value to readers at the time cannot be denied (my favourite is "The Little Nations", in which armies of red and black ants are perceived to be enacting the fighting at Gallipoli in the corner of an old clergyman's garden).

"Drake's Drum" begins with a meditation on how, when waking from dreams, we sometimes have glimpses of the awesome reality behind ordinary life. Machen then relates a story to illustrate how this reality usually presents itself in symbols rather than in "logical and grammatical utterance." He tells a tale of an event that would have been fresh in the minds of his readers: the surrender of the German fleet off the Firth of Forth on 21st November 1918.

The action takes place on board *HMS Royal Oak*, a ship manned by sailors from Devonshire. Tension mounts as they approach the rendezvous.

Though the Germans have agreed to surrender, the British cannot believe that their enemies will give up without a last fight. Every man is therefore at his station "in a state of mind that is hard to describe."

The German ships appear, "looming through the mist." A group of officers on the bridge of the *Royal Oak* watches them, convinced that they are about to open fire. Then, says Machen, "the drum began to beat on the *Royal Oak*. The sound was unmistakeable; it was that of a small drum being beaten 'in rolls'."

At first, no one takes much notice, but as the sound persists, questions are asked and a search is made. Every man on board is in his place and the bandroom is locked: there is nowhere for the mysterious drummer to be. Even if he were hidden between decks, the sound could not reach the bridge. The Commander makes another inspection, but every man is at his battle station.

The British surround the German fleet, hemming it in. The drum continues to be heard, beating in rolls, at intervals throughout the process. "All who heard it are convinced that it was no sound of flapping stays or any such accident. The ear of the naval officer is attuned to all the noises of his ship in fair weather and in foul; it makes no mistakes. All who heard knew that they heard the rolling of a drum."

At two in the afternoon, the British drop anchor, totally surrounding the German ships. "The utter, irrevocable ruin and disgrace of the German Navy was consummated. And at that moment the drum stopped beating and was no more heard."

Machen ends in an exultant, if dark, major key:

> But those who had heard it—*Admiral, Captain, Commander, other officers and men of all ratings—held then and hold now one belief as to the rolling music. They believe that the sound they heard was that of "Drake's Drum": the audible manifestation of the spirit of the great sea captain, present at this hour of the tremendous triumph of Britain on the seas. That is the firm belief of them all.*
>
> *It may be so. It may be that Drake did quit the port of Heaven in a ship of fire, and driving the Germans across the sea with the flame of his spirit, drummed them down to their pitiful and shameful doom.*

Though not Machen at his greatest, it is an effective and memorable story. He writes as himself, in his role as a reporter who is merely relating and commenting upon a true event. This is a style he had now perfected, and it certainly helps to give the tale a sense of immediacy and credibility. It can also—as anyone who has written stories in this form for that very reason will know—make it difficult for readers, even those with a fairly sophisticated understanding of the differences between fact and fiction, to be sure whether or not it is "true". I had not read very far into "Drake's Drum" before I recognised it as a story with which I was familiar, though I had encountered it not in any edition of Machen's works, but in various studies and collections of folklore, as well as in the third volume of a highly respected history of the British Empire. Machen's story had, at some point, been taken as an account of a true event, and been passed down as such. I had even, I realised, played a small part in its dissemination, having referred to the phantom drumming in a local newspaper and in a visitors' guide to Devon and Cornwall. It was "The Bowmen" and the Angels of Mons again, but in this case Machen's commentators had not, apparently, noticed.

The legend of Drake's Drum was a natural, even inevitable, one for Machen to draw upon in his mystical-patriotic mode. Sir Francis Drake was a charismatic figure and a source of legends during his lifetime, as were his fellow Devon seadogs of the Elizabethan age. They were never entirely forgotten in later centuries, at least in the Westcountry and in naval traditions, but their transformation into heroes of the high Victorian Empire came about largely through the work of two Devon-born writers, the novelist Charles Kingsley, whose *Westward Ho!* appeared in 1855, and his brother-in-law the historian James Anthony Froude, whose books and essays provided unforgettable images of the Devon seamen as archetypes of English Protestant bravery, vision and enterprise: Drake climbing a tree in Panama, looking out over the Pacific and vowing to sail an English ship into that unexplored ocean, and finishing his game of bowls before beating the Armada; Sir Humphrey Gilbert, as his ship went down on his return from claiming Newfoundland, shouting encouragement to his men and reminding them that they were as near to Heaven by sea as by land. Tennyson's poem on the last fight of Sir Richard Grenville of the *Revenge* offered yet more uplifting imagery. The patriotic late Victorian and Edwardian, standing on Plymouth Hoe and thinking of the exploits of these immortals, could feel himself to be at the very heart and fountainhead of the Empire, and swell up with an almost religious sense of pride and destiny. Soon, the name of another local hero, perhaps the most heroic of them all, would be added to the pantheon: Scott of the Antarctic ("Children," wrote Machen, in a story read throughout the country on the day of Scott's memorial service at St Paul's in 1913, "you are about to hear the true story of five of the bravest and best men who have ever lived on the earth since the world began"). And if there was a single artefact that embodied this constellation of feelings and images, it was Drake's Drum.

The drum itself can be seen in the museum at Buckland Abbey, the converted Cistercian monastery a few miles north of Plymouth, which Drake purchased from Sir Richard Grenville in 1580. Made of walnut, standing twenty-one inches high, with Drake's arms painted on the side, it has been well authenticated as a 16th century side drum. It may have accompanied Drake on his epic voyage around the world in 1577-80, and was certainly with him on his last expedition in 1596 when he died and was buried at sea off Puerto Bello, Panama. It was brought back, with his Bible and sword, to his widow at Buckland, and has been there ever since, except for the years between 1938 and 1968, when, following a fire at Buckland Abbey, it spent a sojourn at Nutwell Court, near Exmouth, and another in a bank vault.

There are two main elements to the drum legend. The first, the belief that it can be heard beating to itself as a warning when England is in danger, is impossible to date; mid-nineteenth century collectors of folklore suggested that it went back as far as Trafalgar, but the written evidence is scarce. The link between the drum and Drake's actual ghost dates only from Robert Hunt's 1871 book *Popular Romances of the West of England*. He relates how an old lady at Buckland Abbey informed him that if Drake hears the sound of the drum, he rises up and has a "revel." This hardly fits the uplifting, patriotic legend as it developed later, but does sound like genuine folklore.

The other belief, that when England is in danger the drum can be used to summon Drake to her defence, is not a folk tradition at all, but derives from Henry Newbolt's poem *Drake's Drum*, published in 1895 in *St James's Gazette* and a year later in his collection *Admirals All*.

Despite the historical inaccuracies (Drake was buried not in a hammock, an item unknown in his day, but in a lead coffin), and the appalling attempt at a Devon accent, Newbolt's verses fitted the times perfectly; set to Charles Villiers Stanford's hearty tune, *Drake's Drum* became the classic Edwardian drawing room ballad. Every schoolboy knew that the great man was waiting, poised to return, the moment he heard his drum.

Another poet, Alfred Noyes, took up Newbolt's fancy that Drake had commanded the drum to be taken to Plymouth, and used for calling him when needed, in *The Admiral's Ghost*, and added another detail: that Drake was popularly supposed to have reincarnated as Nelson. In *The Times* of 28th August 1916, Noyes stated: "There is a tale in Devonshire that Sir Francis Drake has not merely listened for his drum during the last three hundred years, but has also heard and answered it on more than one naval occasion." He then claims that it was heard by the Brixham trawlermen as Nelson sailed past on his way to Trafalgar, "for all Devonshire knows that Nelson was a reincarnation of Sir Francis."

Machen was clearly familiar with Newbolt's poem, which he quotes in the peroration of his story, but he also draws on the earlier, more vague, tradition that the drum could sometimes be heard as a disembodied sound. This had been revived with the outbreak of war, so it became natural to associate any mysterious rumblings with the old seadog's relic. But linking the drum to the German navy's surrender in 1918 is an inspiration. Nothing could have reflected the spirit of the moment so perfectly, and Machen's use of a real ship, one that was indeed present, gives it even more the sense of a true occurrence.

HMS Royal Oak was one of five Royal Sovereign Class battleships built at Devonport between 1915 and 1917. At the surrender she was in the first Battle Squadron in the British line, to port of the German fleet. Machen's statement that she was manned entirely by Devonians is probably an exaggeration. Ships' crews were then recruited from the royal dockyards at Devonport, Portsmouth and Chatham; a man wishing to join the navy did so at the one nearest to home or within easiest reach. A Devonport ship would naturally have a high proportion of sailors from Devon and Cornwall, but not exclusively.

Jan Morris gives a characteristically vivid account of the surrender, which was widely reported around the world, in *Farewell the Trumpets* (1978), the last volume of her trilogy on the rise and fall of the Victorian empire. The day was clear and without fog; the seventy ships of the

German fleet were escorted into Scottish waters by a single cruiser, where they were met at the mouth of the Forth by the Royal Navy 'at its most complacent'—three hundred and twenty ships, twenty admirals and ninety thousand men. The British ships did not surround the Germans, but formed themselves into two parallel lines on either side of them. The sailors were, however, at battle stations, and all guns trained on the enemy. The defeated fleet was led to the entrance of the Firth of Forth, where it was ordered to drop anchor and the German flag hauled down. Seven months later, after Machen's story had been published, the German ships were taken to Scapa Flow and ceremonially scuttled. By coincidence, the *Royal Oak* also lies beneath Scapa Flow, as one of the first naval casualties of the following war.

In 1940, with that war in its early months, the well-known Westcountry Liberal politician Isaac Foot, father of the writer and some-time Labour Party leader Michael Foot, gave a talk for the BBC entitled *Drake's Drum—this land of ours*. Later, when Foot was Lord Mayor of Plymouth, this was printed as a pamphlet and distributed to the city's schoolchildren. It is an extraordinary production, as evocative of those times as a speech by Churchill. In what can only be described as a typical politician's blend of rhetoric, fact and blatant invention, Foot evokes the sound of the drum as a mystical presence forever audible to those attuned to it. "We in the West Country do not need to have the sound of the Drum *brought to us over the air*. We can hear it without that help."

"Some of you will recall," he continues, "that when, in November 1918, the German Navy surrendered and the British Fleet, after four years of constant action and ceaseless vigil, closed in around the enemy vessels, men aboard the Admiral's flagship [this was, in fact, not the *Royal Oak* but *HMS Queen Elizabeth*] heard the long roll of the drum. When, after careful search and enquiry, neither drum nor drummer could be found, they realised the truth and, by common consent, one man said to another 'Drake's Drum!'" Foot goes on to claim that the drum has been heard during every significant event in Plymouth history from the sailing of the *Mayflower* onwards. But it beats not only in the South West. "If you listen it is everywhere; in every land where Briton joins Briton to defeat the present menace of darkness and evil." The physical drum is no longer necessary; the sound is purely spiritual, unlimited by time or place.

In 1973 the Toucan Press, Guernsey, issued a booklet, *The Legend of Drake's Drum* by E.M.R. Ditmas, in a series called "West Country Folklore," under the general editorship of the respected Devon folklorist Theo Brown. It was intended as a scholarly series, as opposed to the uncritical, popular accounts of folk customs and beliefs flooding the market. Miss Ditmas gives a succinct account of the drum legend as it developed in the 19th and early 20th centuries. It was from her that I first read of the incident on the *Royal Oak*. Evoking the dark days of the First World War and the menace of German submarines, she comments:

> *Little wonder that men turned to the legend of Drake's vigilance. Rather startlingly, the legend seemed to be confirmed… when, at the time of the surrender of the German Fleet at Scapa Flow* [*notice the change of location*], *the beating of a drum was heard by the Captain, Commander and a number of other naval officers on board the Royal Oak, itself a West Country ship with a crew composed mostly of Devonshire and Cornish men. A thorough investigation was made at the time but the drum could not be traced and continued to roll at intervals until orders were given for the German flag to be hauled down.*

For Ditmas, this event is pivotal to the modern evolution of the legend, from being dependent on the physical proximity of the drum as a means of summoning Drake, to Foot's purely mystical, disembodied sound. As such it fits neatly into her argument. She is obviously unaware that it is a story by Arthur Machen.

I fondly imagined that seeking out Miss Ditmas' source would answer the question of when and how Machen's tale became a folk legend. She actually gives no source, merely advising us to "see the *Western Morning News*, 14th December 1964." When I did this, I found that it answered no questions at all. There are two items in the paper concerning the drum. One reports on the uncertainty of its future unless Plymouth City Council can afford to buy it (this is why it was in a bank vault at the time). On the opposite page a journalist writing under the name "Westcountryman" explains why it must be afforded. Calling it "the Westcountry's most legendary treasure," he goes on: "Probably the most famous story of Drake's Drum stemmed from the Firth of Forth in the early morning of the day the German fleet surrendered at the end of the Great War." He then tells a version of the now familiar tale. He cannot be Miss Ditmas's source, though, because he gets the location of the surrender right, without naming the ship.

I found I had three books on my shelves containing the story. Jan Morris uses it to great effect in her account of the surrender in *Farewell the Trumpets*, but says only that it was in the popular newspapers at the time, and when asked for more details she could not help. The well-known folklorist Christina Hole also includes it in two popular books published by Batsford in the 1940s: *English Folklore* and *English Folk Heroes*. In the latter, the drum is heard while the German ships are being sunk at Scapa Flow; in the former we are back at the surrender seven months earlier, but still in the wrong place. Miss Hole claims to tell the story "according to Douglas Bell," but he appears in neither acknowledgements nor bibliography, and I have been unable to find any trace of him.

I wondered if, perhaps, Douglas Bell was a member of the Folklore Society, in which Christina Hole was a prominent figure, who had either spoken or written about the incident for the society, thus providing her with the story. Unfortunately, no one at the Folklore Society has been able to answer my enquiry about this. Maybe he was just someone who had read Machen's tale without realising it was one, or heard Isaac Foot's broadcast. I am therefore unable to say when, and by whom, Arthur Machen's story was first confused with a real event, only that it happened some time in the twenty years between its appearance and the outbreak of the Second World War. It only needs one person, after all, to make such a mistake and put it into print, and it develops a life of its own, especially if it is, as Machen's tale most decidedly was, in tune with the elusive but very real spirit of the times.

What is surprising is not that the story was taken as a real incident —the way in which it is presented positively invites this—or that it exists in different versions, because that is the nature of storytelling, but that apparently scholarly and careful writers and researchers should have accepted it, at second or third hand, with seemingly no attempt to verify sources. And that committed folklorists, who might be supposed to take an interest in supernatural literature, should be unaware of a short story by a writer generally agreed to be a master of the genre. It is time, anyway, that Machen was given the credit for making an essential contribution to a legend which, unlike that of the Angels of Mons, still lives and resonates for many people, even in our jaded and cynical age.

some notes
on machen's sixtystone

christopher josiffe

originally published in faunus issue 18

In Arthur Machen's 'story within a story within a story', 'The Novel of the Black Seal' (contained, as it is, in the 'Adventure of the Missing Brother', itself a chapter in *The Three Imposters*), there is a mysterious reference to Ixaxar, the Sixtystone. The narrator, Miss Lally, who has been employed by the unfortunate Professor Gregg, to be governess to his two children, is browsing through Professor Gregg's library. A "fine old quarto…printed by the Stephani, containing the three books of Pomponius Mela, *De Situ Orbis*, and other of the ancient geographers",[1] catches her eye, and in examining the volume she recalls:

> *my attention was caught by the heading of a chapter in Solinus,[2] and I read the words: MIRA DE INTIMIS GENTIBUS LIBYAE. DE LAPIDE HEXECONTALITHO,—"The wonders of the people that inhabit the inner parts of Libya, and of the stone called Sixtystone." The odd title attracted me, and I read on:*
>
> *Gens ista avia er secreta habitat, in montibus horrendis foeda mysteria celebrat. De hominibus nihil aliud illi praeferunt quam figuram, ab humano ritu prorsus exulant, oderunt deum lucis. Stridunt potius quam loquuntur; vox absona nec sine horrore auditur. Lapide quodam gloriantur, quem Hexecontalithon vocant; dicunt enim hunc lapidem*

*sexaginta notas ostendere. Cujus lapidis nomen secretum
ineffabile colunt: quod Ixaxar.*

"*This folk,*" *I translated to myself,* "*dwells in remote and
secret places, and celebrates foul mysteries on savage hills.
Nothing have they in common with men save the face, and
the customs of humanity are wholly strange to them; and they
hate the sun. They hiss rather than speak; their voices are harsh,
and not to be heard without fear. They boast of a certain stone,
which they call Sixtystone; for they say that it displays sixty
characters. And this stone has a secret unspeakable name; which
is Ixaxar.*"[3]

The tale unfolds to reveal the survival in South Wales of an ancient
and malevolent race, elsewhere termed the "Little People". The connection
between this race, who still dwell in the Grey Hills near "Caermaen",
and those of many thousands of years earlier, is made apparent by the
strange, semi-wild (and semi-human?) boy, Jervase Cradock, who, in his
fits, utters "an inconceivable babble of sounds bursting and rattling and
hissing from his lips… an infamous jargon, with words, or what seemed
words, that might have belonged to a tongue dead since untold ages…"[4]

Machen has in fact composed a clever imitation of Solinus, who
genuinely does refer to a Sixtystone, but in the following way (Latin
version given here for the interest of those readers whose Latin is not as
rusty as my own):

*Quod ab Atlante usque Canopitanum ostium panditur, ubi
Libyae finis est et Aegyptium limen, dictum a Canopo Menelai
gubernatore sepulto in ea insula quae ostium Nili facit, gentes
tenent dissonae, quae in aviae solitudinis secretum recesserunt.
ex his Atlantes ab humano ritu prorsus exulant. nulli proprium
vocabulum, nulli speciale nomen. diris solis ortus excipiunt,
diris occasus prosequuntur ustique undique torrentis plagae
sidere oderunt deum lucis. adfirmant eos somnia non videre
et abstinere penitus ab animalibus universis. Trogodytae
specus excavant, illis teguntur. nullus ibi habendi amor: a
divitiis paupertate se abdicaverunt voluntaria. tantum
lapide uno gloriantur, quem hexecontalithon nominamus,*

tam diversis notis sparsum, ut sexaginta gemmarum colores
in parvo orbiculo eius deprehendantur. homines isti carnibus
vivunt serpentium ignarique sermonis stridunt potius
quam loquuntur.[5]

I have found English translations of Solinus rather hard to track down; I did manage to locate a 16th century version[6] by Arthur Golding[7] [given below with original spelling, which, I think, has its own charm]:

CAP. XLIII,[8]

Wonderfull things of the nations of Lybia, and of the ftone
called Hexacontalythos.

Whatfoeuer lieth between Mount Atlas and the mouth of
Nile called Canopitane, which beareth the name of Canopus
the Mafter of Menelaus fhip who was buried in that Lande,
which lyeth againft the faid mouth of Nyle, where Libie endeth,
and Egypte beginneth, is inhabitated by nations of sundry
languages, which are withdrawne into wayleffe wilderneffes.

The Athlantians

Of thefe the Athlantians are altogether void of manners meete
for men. None hath anie proper calling, none hath any speciall
name. They curfe the Sun at his rising, and curfe him likwife at
his going downe: and becaufe they are fcorched with the heate
of his burning beames, they hate the God of light. It is affirmed
that they dreame not, and that they utterlie abftaine from all
thinges bearing lyfe.

The Troglodites or Cauecreepers.

The Troglodits dig them cause under the grounde, and houfe
themfelves in them. There is no couetoufneffe of getting, for they
have bound themfelues from riches, by wilful pouertie.

The ftone called the threefcore stone, or the Sixtistone.

Onely they glory in one ftone which is called Hexacontalythos
fo powdred with diuers fparks, that the colours of threescore
fundrie ftones are perceived in his little compaffe. All thefe
liue by the flefh of Serpents, and beeing ignoraunt of fpeech, do
rather iabber and gnarre then fpeake.[9]

So Machen's pastiche draws upon ideas taken from two of Solinus' paragraphs: the hatred of the Sun espoused by the Atlanteans; and the Troglodytes' veneration of the Sixtystone, together with the primitive sounds they utter in place of speech.

That Machen both enjoyed writing such compositions, and had a talent for doing so, is attested by another piece, "Of the Isle of Shadows: and of the strange customs of the men that dwell there",[10] purportedly authored "by the shade of Sir John Maunderville", which again draws on accounts of early exploration and geography; in this case, the fabulist and traveller John Mandeville.

I first came across Machen's Solinus composition, not in his own *The Novel of the Black Seal*, but quoted in Kenneth Grant's *Hecate's Fountain*.[11] Kenneth Grant, secretary to Aleister Crowley in his latter years, and perhaps the most important post-Crowley occultist, often refers to Machen and H.P. Lovecraft in his "Typhonian Trilogies"[12] (of which *Hecate's Fountain* is the sixth volume; he also cites 'The Novel of the Black Seal' in *Outside the Circles of Time* and *Outer Gateways*). Grant's writings portray the fantastic *fiction* of both writers as having an underlying, occult *reality*, whether consciously or unconsciously. Thus, Lovecraft's Great Old Ones may be contacted and even summoned (should such an aim be desired!) by practising occultists, despite Lovecraft, in personal correspondences with friends, deriding magic as superstitious nonsense.

Grant notes that a Crowleyean magickal ritual, the Rite of the Ruby Star, refers to a stone in which is fixed "the Star of the Six". "This", he states, "may be an indirect reference to the *Hexecontelithos*, or Sixtystone, known to certain cthonian entities described by the histographer Solinus".[13] He then goes on to quote Machen's Solinus pastiche ("They dwell in remote and secret places..." see above and endnote 3). Grant attributes the quote to Solinus, noting that it was "translated by Arthur Machen and quoted in his 'The Novel of the Black Seal'". [14] So he has either been gulled by Machen (by virtue of the convincing qualities of the pastiche) and believed Machen's Latin to be a quotation from an ancient source; or he is aware that it is Machen's own, but is (mis)representing it thus for his own reasons. It should also, perhaps, be pointed out that Grant chooses to spell Machen's "Ixaxar" with a third "a", thus: "Ixaxaar". This is presumably because of the kabbalistic practice known as *gematria*, the substitution of letters by numbers (heavily employed in Grant's work as a means of establishing correspondences). The latter spelling yields the number 333, [15] a number of much significance in Grant's Typhonian OTO system.

Should it appear that I may be appearing to malign "Uncle Kenny" (as Grant is affectionately known), I should like to state that I have been a devotee of his writings for thirty years; his seemingly-autobiographical descriptions of magickal rituals make for very compelling reading. But some of his statements, as the foregoing may indicate, should be taken with a pinch of salt if considered as literal fact. [16]

Perhaps one could draw a comparison between Grant's writing and that of Arthur Machen, in that they both mix fact and fiction, and cite source material of dubious veracity. Finally, let us not be too harsh on Kenneth Grant; if—as I suspect—he genuinely believed Machen was quoting a 3rd century writer, then this is merely a testament to the skill with which Machen composed his "Solinus" passage in *The Three Imposters*; the passage is itself an Imposter...

sources

1 *The Three Imposters*. Arthur Machen. 1995. London: Dent. p. 58
2 Gaius Julius Solinus; 3rd century AD Roman grammarian
3 *The Three Imposters* ibid
4 *The Three Imposters* p. 64
5 Cap.XXXII. *Caii Julii Solini de Mirabilibus Mundi*.[online] http://www.thelatinlibrary.com/solinus.html
6 *The excellent and pleafant worke of Iulius Solinus Polyhiftor.* Translated out of Latin into English by Arthur Golding. Gent. Printed by I. Charlewoode for Thomas Hacket. London, 1587
7 1536-1605 (?). Thought to be a native of London. As well as Solinus' *Collectanea*, Golding translated Caesar's *Commentaries*, Ovid's *Metamorphoses*, and the works of the Roman geographer Pomponius Mela, who was a source for Solinus.
8 NB. These chapter numbers vary according to which Latin version is consulted; XLIII here is from the Golding edition; whilst Mommsen (1864) and Pancoucke (1847) have XXXI and XXXII respectively
9 *The Excellent and Pleasant Worke: Collectanea Rerum Memorabilium of Caius Julius Solinus.* Translated from the Latin (1587) by Arthur Golding. A facsimile reproduction with an introduction by George Kish, University of Michigan. 1955. Gainsville, Florida: Scholars' Facsimiles & Reprints. Cap. XLIII
10 From: *Ritual and Other Stories*. Arthur Machen. 1992. Lewes, Sussex: Tartarus.
11 *Hecate's Fountain*. Kenneth Grant. 1992. London: Skoob.
12 *The Magical Revival, Aleister Crowley and the Hidden God, Cults of the Shadow, Nightside of Eden, Outside the Circles of Time, Hecate's Fountain, Outer Gateways, Beyond the Mauve Zone, The Ninth Arch*
13 *Hecate's Fountain* p. 34
14 *Hecate's Fountain* footnotes p. 34 and p. 230
15 IXAXAAR = 10 + 60 + 1 + 60 + 1 + 1 + 200 = 333
16 *As Dave Evans said in a 2008 conference paper: "reading Grant is like taking a powerful hallucinogenic drug, there seems to be an urgent and elaborate message from 'beyond' to be found, but that it doesn't always come across in a linear or sometimes even in a linguistic fashion."] Crowleyan Echoes: Baraka and Fantasy. Dave Evans. [online] http://www.cesnur.org/2008/london_evans.doc*

Lucian in The Labyrinth

Roger Dobson

originally published in Faunus issue 25

One of Machen's accomplishments in *The Hill of Dreams* is the transformation of the waste places of London into regions as mysterious and mystical as his native land. Who else could set fiction in the environs of Shepherd's Bush and Acton without descending into banality and sordidness? The same technique is employed in *A Fragment of Life* and "The Holy Things", in *Ornaments in Jade*, where divine revelations occur in prosaic locales. *The Hill of Dreams*, in contrast, presents a darker vision. To paraphrase Wilde, anyone can be mystical in the country, but to do this in the heart of the stony metropolis stands as a remarkable feat. In the winter fog the city is transformed—transmuted to borrow a more appropriate Machenian term—into a mystic labyrinth: "All London was one grey temple of an awful rite, ring within ring of wizard stones circled about some central place, every circle was an initiation, every initiation eternal loss." Here the capital and the hill of dreams of Gwent become one. In Lucian's mind London mutates into the dead Roman city he has resurrected in his imagination, but this time to an arid wilderness of mist and grey stone. To Lucian it seems "the rocky avenues became the camp and fortalice of some half-human, malignant race who swarmed in hiding, ready to bear him away into the heart of their horrible hills". In Lucian's disordered psyche London degenerates into a nightmarish version of his homeland. Gwent was as Avalon for Machen, where he returned to heal his wounds after his terms of trial in London. Unlike Machen, Lucian is not permitted a return to his homeland: that would never do. Why? Because that would spoil the unrelenting atmosphere Machen is seeking to evoke. Lucian must be allowed no relief, no respite from his sufferings.

Readers can, if they wish, follow in Lucian's footsteps, and with a map trace his odyssey through western London. There is an argument for letting the locations in *The Hill* remain oblique, just as Machen leaves them unnamed in his novel: their mysterious nature perhaps makes them all the more beguiling; removing the veil may destroy the magic. Some readers therefore might wish to stop here and progress no farther.

Despite Lucian's wanderings, *The Hill* possesses a claustrophobic atmosphere, with the character's explorations limited to suburbia, perhaps because Machen wishes to mirror Lucian's mind and soul. The book focuses on the microcosm of a single consciousness, not the macrocosm that is London. It is a voyage into the mind of a solitary man. London is too immense a universe to be captured in *The Hill*. Even Mr Dyson, that profound student of London, can only hint at the city's immensity: "Yet I feel sometimes positively overwhelmed with the thought of the vastness and complexity of London... London is always a mystery." Machen writes in *The London Adventure* that the city has grown so vast that no man can know it or even begin to know it. Is this why we are never told of Lucian visiting Soho or Bloomsbury, Holborn or the Strand, the streets that knew Machen's tread when he lived in Clarendon Road, Notting Hill Gate? Lucian's London is narrowly circumscribed, consisting of the streets around Shepherd's Bush[1] and Acton Vale and the environs of Notting Hill. Machen names only a few localities in the three London chapters: Shepherd's Bush, Acton Vale, the Uxbridge Road, Notting Hill, while Islington, Stoke Newington and Hampton are alluded to in passing. His book is a romance not a travel guide, yet it is possible to identify several unidentified scenes.

To begin at the beginning of Chapter V: Lucian comes by "curious paths to his calm hermitage between Shepherd's Bush and Acton Vale". Why "curious paths"? Does this signify that he has lived elsewhere while trying to find a permanent refuge? The hotel in Surrey Street, off the Strand, where Machen and his father stayed in that famous June of 1880, for example? The hotel apparently appears, unnamed, in the "Novel of the Dark Valley" in *The Three Impostors*: Mr Wilkins, alias Richmond, says he stayed there on first coming to London from the West Country, though everything that gentleman says is suspect. Is he, like Lucian and his creator, really the son of a clergyman? It may be that the phrase in *The Hill* simply refers to Lucian's wanderings in the suburbs scouting for suitable digs. It is a tiny puzzle, never elucidated in the text. Lucian finds a "terrible 'bed-sitting-room'", in a western suburb: a "square, clean room, horribly furnished, in the by-street that branched from the main road, and advanced in an unlovely sweep to the mud pits and the desolation that was neither town nor country". Despite its silly wallpaper, Machen states that Lucian's room is a friendly place, and this subsequently proves significant. The Victorian terraced streets, running north off the Uxbridge Road, still stand today. "On every side monotonous grey streets, each house the replica of its neighbour, to the east an unexplored wilderness, north and west and south the brickfields and market-gardens, everywhere the ruins of the country..." These stony streets lie to the east and lie around Wormwood Scrubs and Old Oak Common to the north of Lucian's lodgings. The streets are patterned in identikit format, though in some the architect and builder have indulged themselves; some dwellings are larger, having elaborate porches with tall flights of steps. Whichever street Lucian inhabits, he lives near the southern end since he is able to see John Dolly, who proves so inept in providing details of Poe's old school at Stoke Newington, board the tram at the junction with the Uxbridge Road. Personally I think Lucian lives somewhere around Ormiston Grove or Thorpebank Road but Machen is never so specific.

Lucian ventures out for an hour each day between twelve and one while his landlady makes his bed and, Machen tells us, invariably walks east along the Uxbridge Road. His journey would take him past Shepherd's Bush Green, that "bald, arid, detestable" patch as Machen describes it in *Far Off Things*, Chapter V. Among the sights seen by Lucian along the way is "a church in cheap Gothic". Machen was notoriously fussy over ecclesiastical architecture. He dismissed the Brompton Oratory as a joss-house, and in his scathing remarks on Spiritualism in *The London Adventure* he scoffs at the humble "Mount Zion Chapel (Particular Baptist), Beulah Road, Tooting Bec". In *The Secret Glory* he heaps scorn on the 'Little Bethel' of the Nonconformists, while Lucian is affronted by the Independent chapel, "a horrible stucco parody of a Greek temple with a façade of hideous columns that was a nightmare". It is just as well that Machen did not live to see that modern monstrosity, the red-brick St Luke's Church, on the

Uxbridge Road near the junction with Wormholt Road; it looks more like a fire station. Is the "church in cheap gothic" in *The Hill* where the Darnells worship in *A Fragment of Life*? Machen attacks it in similar fashion as "a Gothic blasphemy which pretended to be a church". In *A Fragment of Life* St Paul's stands in a street near the imaginary Edna Road, Shepherd's Bush: "its Gothic design would have interested a curious inquirer into the history of a curious revival... it would have been quite difficult to explain why the whole building, from the mere mortar setting between the stones to the Gothic gas standards, was a mysterious and elaborate blasphemy." Darnell and his wife later find another church (Catholic or High Anglican?) to worship in. The sham Gothic church and its rituals are criticised because Machen is suggesting that the faith Darnell and his wife Mary initially follow is not the genuine mystery religion of Christianity but a fake substitute. To Machen, it bears the same relation to the faith that those works by Mrs Scudamore Runnymede, *A Bad Un to Beat* and *With the Mudshire Pack*, bear to fine literature. Does the church perhaps still stand today? It may be the Church of St Stephen and St Thomas located on the corner of Coverdale Road. Inside, its white plaster walls and calm are refreshingly peaceful after the roar of the Uxbridge Road.

Modern explorers of the Vale of Acton and Shepherd's Bush can still see the "corner publics", "the blatant public-houses", referred to in *The Hill* or ones very much like them: the Princess Victoria, the Queen Adelaide, the Coningham Arms, the British Queen and others. Walk east along the Uxbridge Road, from the junction with Old Oak Lane, midway between the Vale and Shepherd's Bush, and you will see the buildings that Machen and Lucian knew: Victorian stucco villas with elaborate porticos, "like smug Pharisees", turned into offices as their owners moved to more affluent districts. Nowadays the villas are interspersed with ugly modern flats, and the main artery is an array of food stores, kebab shops and takeaways.

As Lucian travels from the Uxbridge Road into Holland Park Avenue (unnamed) he would pass Royal Crescent where a young poet named Fytton Armstrong would one day dwell,[2] and skirt Clarendon Road, where Machen lived in his tiny cell in the 1880s. Progressing up the slope Lucian would reach Notting Hill Gate: "He had passed through the clamorous and blatant crowd of the 'high street', where, as one climbed the hill, the shops seemed all aflame, and the black night air glowed with the flaring gas-jets and the naphtha-lamps, hissing and wavering before the February wind."

At Notting Hill Gate, just after Ladbroke Terrace the incline—more of a gentle incline than a hill—levels out, a row of shops arises, now as in the era of *The Hill*. In Campden Hill Square, initially called Notting Hill Square, now like many of the surrounding streets a millionaires' row, you will see Evelyn Underhill's home at No. 50, where she lived from 1907-39 (plaque). Machen and Waite presumably visited her here. Violet Hunt, whom Machen also knew, lived at South Lodge at 80 Campden Hill Road (plaque). Holland Park Avenue leads into the "high street" of *The Hill*: Notting Hill Gate, where Lucian sees the clamorous public houses with their drunken orgies, symbolically contrasted with the sensuous memories of his Roman dream. Located along here, on the Gate's south side, was The Coronet Theatre, now a cinema, where Machen played the conjuror Bolingbroke, summoning the hosts of hell, in *Henry VI, Part II*. With his Stratford performance of the role this marked his farewell to the stage in 1909.

At the Gate Lucian has his fateful encounter with the bronze-haired prostitute who will lure him to his doom, as foreshadowed in the lines, "He knew that he had touched the brink of utter destruction; there was death in the woman's face, and she had indeed summoned him to the Sabbath." He flees from her down the hill, echoing the scene in the first chapter when he runs away after apparently seeing, or imagining he sees, the lovely face of the faun, the Queen of the Nymphs as she may be termed, gazing at him from between the boughs: a memory reprised in the last chapter.[3] The nymph has been replaced by a *femme fatale* even more perilous: the deadly Votary of Venus as we may think of her, or perhaps the Demon Lover would be a more fitting title. Machen quotes, a little imprecisely, a haunting line from "Kubla Khan", "By woman wailing for her demon-lover!", ironically foreshadowing Lucian's meeting with the prostitute. The woman herself ultimately becomes the Demon Lover, in an act of transmutation; just as Lucian himself, in a further instance of metamorphosis, fears he has become inhuman.

Machen never even tells us the nameless girl *is* a prostitute. "Kubla Khan" suggests a double allusion. Coleridge's masterpiece concerns an opium vision: "For he on honey-dew hath fed,/And drunk the milk of Paradise." Lucian is fated to meet the streetwalker again and she will become his mistress, though nowhere in the text does Machen state this explicitly: the reader must infer it from the events obliquely portrayed in the final chapter. In reality a lonely maiden might well invite a handsome young fellow to join her in a nocturnal walk. In Victorian fiction, and against such a saturnalian background, such an invitation can have only one meaning.

At the end of the novel, in a final transformation, the prostitute, her veils of glamour stripped away, reveals her cockney accent, with her "crool" and "ashaimed"; she becomes an infernal and reverse Eliza Doolittle. Whether she cares at all for Lucian is left veiled throughout; she cares for his legacy more. The "fiery street, the flaming shops and flaming glances, all its wonders and horrors lit by the naphtha flares and by the burning souls" are illuminated by a hellish radiance, echoing the "burning aureole" fashioned by Hawthorne in *The Scarlet Letter*, a sacred text for Lucian. His attempt to escape the Demon Lover through his work fails: lust and desire conquer him, and he pays a fatal price.

In a brilliantly conceived mimesis Machen echoes Lucian's amnesia, keeping obscure much of the action that occurs between the end of Chapter VI, when Lucian trembles before the bottle containing his drug on the mantelpiece, and the climactic events of Chapter VII. How he joins his fortunes to those of the streetwalker and their going to live in "the sad house in the fields" go unchronicled. Lucian cannot recall these events so the reader is not told. So often it is what Machen does not say that proves vital. As Thomas De Quincey writes in his *Confessions of an English Opium-Eater* (1822) "the opium-eater is too happy to observe the motion of time".[4] Or, in Lucian's case, too tortured. Readers must fill in these narrative gaps from clues embedded in the text. The shadow of De Quincey's *Confessions*, one of Machen's favourite works, lies behind *The Hill*. De Quincey's opium-fuelled rambles in London are referenced in the book. Machen never specifically names Lucian's drug, but could it be anything other than laudanum when much of *The Hill* consciously parallels De Quincey's classic? Machen may withhold the nature of the drug partly because this signals to the reader that here the darkness begins to gather.

Up to the end of Chapter VI Machen has provided a clear linear narration, chronicling the events of Lucian's life, but from the next chapter his hidden life begins and incidents are presented more obliquely. Where the art of the veil was concerned Machen was a master.

This involved the selection and omission of crucial plot details; readers themselves must determine what has happened. Not all readers appear to grasp this method.[5]

In the final chapter as Lucian sits "before his desk looking into the vague darkness he could almost see that chamber which he had so often imagined". He can almost see the chamber because he is *in* the chamber. The cottage fascinates Lucian when he discovers it, in flashback, in Chapter VII: he is already living there when the chapter opens. From minute clues in the text, and from *Far Off Things* and other writings, it is possible to speculate on the cottage's location. One bleak March day Lucian wanders north off "the high road", presumably the Uxbridge Road, and following a lane initially choked with "obscene refuse" eventually reaches open country and finds the house. His exploration can be seen as mirroring his wandering in Gwent in Chapter I. In *Far Off Things*, Chapter V, Machen writes of how the ravenous London suburbs trespass on the meadows and green pastures. He describes how "new, rabid streets are to rush up the sweet hillside and capture it; here the well under the thorn is choked with a cartload of cheap bricks lately deposited". Machen would be walking in the country only to be "confronted by red ranks of brand-new villas: this would be Harlesden or the outposts of Willesden". He had never experienced such things in Gwent. It was the "violent irruption of red brick in the midst of a green field" that startled him, just as Robinson Crusoe is shocked by finding that footstep on his desert island.

In *Far Off Things*, Chapter V, writing of his wanderings in the early 1880s, Machen states: "Then I became learned in Wormwood Scrubs and its possibilities. It was and is a very barren and bleak place itself, but in those days there was an attractive corner on the Acton side of the waste, that I was fond of contemplating." This corner is Old Oak Common. Machen refers to a "sort of huddle of old cottages and barns and outhouses with a fringe of elms about them". In *The Hill* an elm overshadows the cottage, and in his delirium in the final chapter Lucian hears its boughs moving in the wind. During his narcotic phantasmagoria Lucian's memories of his idyllic boyhood in Gwent and his harsh years in London fuse in his imagination; just as his memories of the rectory and the house in the fields merge, linked by the motif of the creaking elm—elms surround the Gwent rectory. "Truth and the dream were so mingled that now he could not divide one from the other." Caught in an amnesiac nightmare, Lucian believes he imagines the bough creaking since the street where he lodged previously, in his "calm hermitage", is treeless. "It was strange how in the brick and stucco desert where no trees were, he all the time imagined the noise of tossing boughs, the grinding of the boughs together." Lucian hears the branches moving because there is indeed a tree outside. Lucian cannot see the brass gas-jet by his bureau, not solely because it is dark but because the gas-jet was a fixture of his former cell. "He had only to get up and look out of the window and he would see the treeless empty street, and the rain starring the puddles under the gas-lamp, but he would wait a little while." All this is an illusion: though he knows it not, Lucian is trapped in the cottage's death chamber. These are subtle points in the text, and a careless reading may lead to error. The bungled synopsis of the book in *Masterpieces of World Literature in Digest Form* (Second Series: Harper & Row, 1952) is amusing: "His landlady, not hearing him stir for many hours, looked into his room and found him dead at his desk, his writings spread about him. Even she felt little sorrow for him, although he had made over his small fortune to her." For "landlady", read the Demon Lover, who certainly feels little sorrow since she has connived at his death. The *Masterpieces* précis also alters the plot somewhat: "Lucian called his land of make-believe Avallaunius..."

Like Lucian, the reader has no way of knowing how much time has elapsed between the end of Chapter VI and the beginning of Chapter VII, and the matter remains deliberately obscure. Lucian's death may occur six months after the publication of his tale *The Amber Statuette*, for that is the period in which he is working on his last manuscript, and it is difficult to imagine him not writing something. "Even about the little book that he had made there seemed some taint, some shuddering memory, that came to him across the gulf of forgetfulness." The *Statuette* conjures up the figures of the nocturnal orgies and reminds him of the life he is leading with the streetwalker, the naphtha flares illuminating the path to the cottage in the fields.

The events that occur after the publication of the *Statuette* are ambiguous, as Lucian suffers from amnesia caused by his addiction. One extravagant reading would be that the publication of the *Statuette*, and the "doubtful" incidents surrounding it, are illusory and part of Lucian's dream-fugue. "Dimly he remembered Dr Burrows coming to see him in London, but had he not imagined all the rest?" But this is the type of wild theory a critic would spin, merely to offer a fresh interpretation. "His mind was sluggish, and he could not quite remember how many years had passed since that dismal experience…" The dismal experience is Lucian's desolation suffered the winter after he arrives in London. Noting that Machen does not always say what he means, or mean what he says, it may be that, since this is Lucian's subjective view, the reference to years is ironic: months rather than years may have passed. Time for the addict appears distorted, De Quincey explains in his *Confessions*, that sometimes he seemed to have lived for seventy or a hundred years in a single night.[6]

Trapped in his semi-comatose state, Lucian's mind roams through the distant and near past. At the beginning of Chapter VII he awakes from "an utter forgetfulness" that has descended on him in the interval separating him from the scene introducing the laudanum bottle at the end of Chapter VI. There is irony in that passage in Chapter VI: "His only escape was in the desk; he might find salvation if he could again hide his heart in the heap and litter of papers, and again be rapt by the cadence of a phrase… He resolved that he would rise early in the morning, and seek once more for his true life in the work." These resolutions fail, and he becomes involved with the Demon Lover: her subsequent summons, though we are not privy to it, he does not refuse.

Does the cottage in the fields have a real-life counterpart? The house may be intended to stand on Old Oak Common, then as in Machen's day, an extensive patch around Wormwood Scrubs prison. The novelist and Machen admirer Peter Ackroyd lived nearby as a boy. Machen refers to the Wormwood Scrubs district as being a favourite haunt in his Introduction to *The Anatomy of Tobacco* (1926), reprinted in *Faunus* 11 (Winter 2004). Machen's memories of the 1880s were of a time when Acton seemed "more like a country town than a modern suburb". In *Mainly Victorian* (1924) Stewart M. Ellis writes of the cottage in *The Hill*:

> I always think this fateful house was suggested by Old Oak Farm and Friar's Place Farm—a sort of composite picture of two lonely houses beyond Wormwood Scrubs. But, as Mr Machen observed to me years ago, when we took a ramble together to revisit these two old farms, the house of The Hill

of Dreams was a thing of fantasy and does not need too close an identification.

The farm buildings may have inspired Machen with the idea for the cottage. For plot reasons it is essential that the house lies solitary in the fields; having a neighbouring farm would not do. Machen has perhaps played with geography in the way he does by placing the Roman fort at Common Cefn Llwyn near Llanddewi Rectory in Gwent. If the cottage in *The Hill* does lie on Old Oak Common then the fringes of the suburb Lucian sees may be Harlesden, the blatant new district that so disturbs Dyson in "The Inmost Light". Lucian notes the "'raw red villas'" of the suburbs, while Dyson is aghast at the red brick homes invading the green fields. Harlesden, beyond railway depots and industrial estates, is only a short distance from the northern end of Old Oak Common. One argument against the common being the site of the cottage is that Wormwood Scrubs Prison, still being built in the 1880s, lies nearby and of course nowhere does Machen allude to the prison in the text, though he does refer to the region's burning brickfields. "For a mile he had walked on quietly..." It is a minute but debatable point whether the cottage lies a mile from the high road, or if the mile referred to is the distance Lucian walks after the initially débris-strewn path becomes an attractive winding lane. The southern portion of Old Oak Common lies a mile north of the Uxbridge Road, but the latter reading would take Lucian deeper into the common and so nearer to the presumed suburb of Harlesden.

A further mystery concerns the decaying house that appears in the final pages, with its blotched stucco, skeletal laurels, blighted flowerbeds and fungus sprouting on the lawn: Lucian's glorious garden of Avallaunius has descended into corruption. In his delirium Lucian mistakes the house for the rectory, as the Demon Lover explains in her final dialogue: "He was carrying on dreadful, shaking at the gaite, and calling out it was 'is 'ome and they wouldn't let him in." The house is situated on the "same terrible street, whose pavements he had trodden so often". One infers that it stands somewhere in Notting Hill, since Lucian has gone to buy "paper and pens of a certain celestial stationer in Notting Hill".[7] Whether the house existed is probably now impossible to determine. As with the laburnum-shaded dwelling in "concealed Barnsbury", which does, or did, stand—it inspired the Hermit's house in *Hieroglyphics* (see Machen's letter to J.P. Hogan in the Reynolds and Charlton biography, pp. 179-80)—the address awaits unearthing. Can one hope that Machen letters existing in some archive provide details?

We rest on firmer territory with other allusions. Lucian "loved a great old common that stood on high ground, curtained about with ancient spacious houses of red brick, and their cedarn gardens". This seems to be Ealing Common, described in *Far Off Things*, Chapter V. Here Machen pondered on *The Anatomy of Tobacco*, mourning that his first book could not be better: "I stood by an old twisted oak, and thought of my book as I would have made it, and sighed, and so went home and made it as I could." On the road leading to the common was an oak tree and a pool where Lucian lingers. The "barbaric water tower rising from a hill" that he sees from a height, presumably Campden Hill, is the hill's Italianate water tower, demolished in 1970, which figures prominently in G.K. Chesterton's *The Napoleon of Notting Hill* (1904). In a poem in the book Chesterton writes:

> *This legend of an epic hour*
> *A child I dreamed, and dream it still,*
> *Under the great grey water tower*
> *That strikes the stars on Campden Hill.*

One closing puzzle: why did Machen have Lucian live off the Uxbridge Road, rather than in Notting Hill where he had dwelt himself? What follows is pure speculation without warrant from any of Machen's writings. Even as a very young man, Machen surely knew that he would one day write his autobiography. His notion for the memoir "A Quiet Life" had alarmed George Redway who counselled him to "defer the writing of *that* type of book until I was eighty or thereabouts"(*Far Off Things*, Chapter VI). He had a poignant tale to tell of his lonely struggles in London, and two wonderful scenic backdrops to work with: the metropolis and Gwent. If Machen had Lucian live in the Gate region the novel would perhaps have seemed inescapably autobiographical: Lucian must be Machen, critics would argue, whereas Lucian is very like his creator but is not *quite* Machen. As Machen informed Vincent Starrett in 1917, *The Hill* is not strict autobiography "since I am still alive": unlike Lucian he had survived into middle age. Also, he had already written of a struggling author in the district: Edgar Russell, the obscure realist in *The Three Impostors* lives in the fictitious Abingdon Grove. Russell, a realist rather than a romancer, could never be mistaken for a Machen self-portrait, even though, like Lucian and his creator, he experiences "the pains of literature" and lives on a starvation diet of bread and tea. Machen treats Russell's authorial battles semi-humorously. For narrative purposes it is important for Lucian to explore Notting Hill in all its strangeness, witnessing its Bacchic orgies in the way in which he roams through "outland and occult territory" in Wales. Had he lived on the doorstep of the Gate, in an unnamed Clarendon Road, say, the effect would not be nearly so dramatic. In Gwent Lucian walks in fairyland; in Notting Hill he wanders in nightmare. What a pity John Gawsworth did not quiz Machen about these matters of literary geography. If he did, he left no record in the biography, preferring to ask his hero such vital questions, thirty-six years after the event, as "In 1894 do you think *Casanova* appeared in Jan, Feb, March or April?" But at least, to borrow a phrase from "The Idealist" in *Ornaments in Jade*, such enduring puzzles provide "singular matter for speculation".

Endnotes

1 In 1908, a year after *The Hill* appeared in book form, the fairy-tale White City opened on land north of Shepherd's Bush. Machen writes of the City's decay in *Things Near and Far*, Chapter X, comparing its sham glamour to the gradual fading of the Baghdad and Syon illusion that London assumed for him during his *annus mirabilis* of 1899–1900. At the time of writing, Wetherspoon's pub in the West 12 Shopping Centre, overlooking Shepherd's Bush Green, has a photographic display of the White City.

2 Julian Maclaren-Ross, one of John Gawsworth's Redondan dukes, lived at various addresses in the district: 19 Holland Park Avenue in 1956; 37 Ladbroke Square and 39 Kensington Square Gardens in 1957; and 4 Dawson Place and 16 Chepstow Place in 1964. Maclaren-Ross was intrigued that 16 Chepstow Place features as the home of one of the victims in "The Suicide Club", one of Stevenson's *New Arabian Nights*, and wrote an unmade, updated film script based on the story. Albert Chevalier (1861–1923), the music hall star Machen admired, was born at 17 St Ann's Villas, off Holland Park Avenue (plaque).

3 The patterning of the novel can perhaps be stretched too far, but we can view the hill in Notting Hill in this scene as a mirror-image of the Welsh fort. The elements of the first half of the novel—the Roman city, the rectory, Lucian's illuminated manuscript, the tavern, Annie Morgan—reappear in grotesque forms in the second part. The Demon Lover can be viewed as Annie Morgan's evil twin. Most obviously, the novel's opening sentence is reprised in the final line. The symmetries even extend to Lucian moving to London halfway through the book. One can go overboard in noting parallels, but we can perceive the priests of Mithras and Isis, with their mystic theurgy, refracted in the "flatulent oratory" of the Independent Chapel. The exotic shops of the Roman Isca have their counterparts in the "row of common shops, full of common things" of Notting Hill. The lane in Gwent in Chapter VII, which Lucian retraces in memory "not knowing where it might bring him, hoping he had found the way to fairyland, to the woods beyond the world, to that vague territory that haunts all the dreams of a boy", may well mirror the lane off the Uxbridge Road leading to the fatal cottage.

4 The nymphs and fauns have a metaphorical status in the novel. A rationalistic reading would view them simply as figments of Lucian's imagination, but we know that in the wider context of Machen's fictional universe, where rationalism holds no sway, such supernatural creatures exist. This is akin to the case of the mansion Bartholly both being and not being the scene of Dr Raymond's experiment in *The Great God Pan*. Similarly, the episode in the fort when Lucian sheds his clothes in the summer heat and falls asleep is a masterly piece of ambiguity and evasion. While the scene has an undeniable sexual content, Machen draws a veil over precisely what happens and readers are free to interpret the incident as they wish. What other author has had it both ways in such fashion?

5 In his otherwise excellent study "The Shock of the Numinous: 'The White People'" (*Faunus* 6, Autumn 2000) J.S. Pennethorne is sceptical that the girl commits suicide, since "it doesn't tally with what we are told in her own words, and seems more to be Ambrose's (or Machen's) prim summation of an event that would not have passed the scrutiny of the age". What he has not taken into account is Machen's art of the veil. As it stands the girl's narrative provides only a partial

picture of her experiences and by the end of her narrative she is still in thrall to the unseen world; but "about a year" passes, by Ambrose's reckoning, before her suicide. During that time the delights of dabbling with the occult have turned to terror. What happens to the girl during that final year? That is the art of the veil.

6 In *Things Near and Far*, Chapter IX, writing about the mysterious process that healed the "horror of soul" which descended on him after Amy's death in 1899, Machen compared the urge to seek relief to that suffered by "a man with a raging toothache to get laudanum". In "The Opium of the Creators: Poe and Machen" (*Avallaunius* 15, Winter 1996: The Arthur Machen Society) Godfrey Brangham speculates on whether Machen experimented with the opium used to relieve Amy's sufferings. It seems unlikely that the visions of 1899 were opium-inspired since Machen himself, unless he was being uncharacteristically disingenuous, found them inexplicable.

7 The stationer had a real-life prototype; see *Things Near and Far*, Chapter II. In his Introduction to *The Chronicle of Clemendy* (Carbonnek: New York, 1923) Machen remembered it as Murley's. "Celestial" alludes to the Oxford Street druggist of the *Confessions* ("unconscious minister of celestial pleasures!"), who mysteriously "evanesced". De Quincey first obtained his tincture of opium, or laudanum, from the druggist while an Oxford undergraduate in 1804.

Interpenetrations
Ecstasy and Boundaries in The works of Arthur Machen

John *Howard*
originally published in Faunus issue 26

> *Holiness requires as great, or almost as great, an effort*
> *[as sin]; but holiness works on lines that were natural once;*
> *it is an effort to recover the ecstasy that was before the Fall.*
> *But sin is the effort to gain the ecstasy and the knowledge that*
> *pertain alone to angels, and in making this effort man becomes*
> *a demon... In brief, he repeats the Fall.'*
> *[Arthur Machen, "The White People" (1906)]*

The works of Arthur Machen published during a period of over forty years from, say, *The Great God Pan* (1894) to the best of the stories in *The Children of the Pool* (1936) contained and set forth a core set of beliefs and opinions which remained remarkably consistent during the course of a long life and literary career. And as such, these works—both fiction and what must be labelled nonfiction—can also be considered as expressing what may be termed a philosophy. Although I intend to concentrate here on Machen's fiction—which by no means comprised the main part of his literary work and certainly did not provide him with any form of secure livelihood—it is not always very distinguishable from his non-fiction.

Machen's three volumes of autobiography and many articles, written in the same style as much of the fiction, can seem to fuse reality with invention and a dreamlike speculation, making the boundaries between them as insubstantial and misty as a vista dimly discerned through one of the London fogs of the period. During the opening weeks of the First World War Machen deliberately crossed the border with "The Bowmen"; he also wrote his wartime novel *The Terror* in his best documentary and reportorial style, and it first saw serialisation in the newspaper he worked for. That Machen produced vast amounts of newspaper journalism for his employers makes the use of the term "story" for his output both as a reporter and as a writer of fiction doubly ambiguous—and therefore all the more appropriate.

Arthur Machen's beliefs and opinions, his philosophy, was reflected in his work through themes and imagery that also recurred over the decades. Themes flowed into and merged with each other like the London streets and districts, or twisting lanes winding over wild Welsh hills, both of which appear and reappear as images. Many stories concerned the consequences of the abuse of what should be the natural order: *The Great God Pan* and "The White People" are two examples. Machen distrusted the world he knew, considering it not to be natural but having fallen away from what it should be. Machen reserved a special distrust and scorn for the scientific progress of the nineteenth century and after, which he regarded as having led the world astray from the spiritual to the idolisation of the material.

Adherence to the Anglo-Catholic version of Christianity gave Machen added justification for his exaltation of the spiritual over the material, and so his revolt against the materialism of contemporary life. Machen saw humanity as a "sacrament": an inner soul manifested in an outer body. This was a natural unity not to be broken, but which was always under threat. The worst "sorcery" (which for Machen could often be equated with science) was that which destroyed the sacred link. In "The Inmost Light" Dr Steven Black's experiment on his consenting wife left her 'what was no longer a woman' and in consequence led to what amounted to his self-damnation and exclusion from the human race—crossing, with no possibility of return, the most important boundary of all. The long discussion between Ambrose and Cotgrave that forms the opening of "The White People" showed the way Machen meant to go on, as well as where he had already started from: "Sorcery and sanctity," said Ambrose, "these are the only realities. Each is an ecstasy, a withdrawal from the common life."

Machen had already written an entire book, *Hieroglyphics* (1902), in order to expound his theory of literature. He contended that it is the presence of ecstasy that distinguishes "fine literature" from something which, no matter how clever or interesting, will not be fine literature. Ecstasy (*ekstasis*, to be or stand outside the self, to be put out of place) is a movement or separation; for Machen efforts towards the recovery of ecstasy represented efforts towards holiness; a high calling for fine literature and those able and willing to create it. But when the "wrong" sort of ecstasy is sought, then the result is sin; the reader will not get fine literature but may nevertheless be enabled to dally with sin and all its alluring glamour at second-hand, and to come close to the demonic without actually quite going all the way. There is a boundary. If it is crossed, someone would be lead from sanctity to sorcery—trespassing from one reality into another reality—and the house of life would be riven asunder and the primal Fall repeated.

The crossing of boundaries to ecstasy—whichever boundaries to whichever sort of ecstasy—is possibly the most important preoccupation in Arthur Machen's work. The borderlands are where chaos and order meet, the ragged edge of reality and illusion (or perhaps true reality) where lives are touched and transmuted. By sheer indomitable will Machen attempted to impose order on life as he saw and lived it. He sought and showed hints of what he perceived as lying behind its commonplaces and confusions, sharing his views and insights with those who were able to discern his design. This is Arthur Machen's distinct, and lasting, contribution to fantastic literature.

Boundaries are where things happen—both mentally and physically. Significant events occur on or close to boundaries. Borders can symbolise tensions, and express them where they count: in coexistence, whether easy or not; exchanges hopefully leading to mutual enrichment; domination from one side or the other and possible destruction. Boundaries exist between states of life and environments. All of these are apparent in the life and work of Arthur Machen.

He was born and brought up in rural Wales and lived and worked for most of his life in London. His county of birth is itself a shifting borderland: a home at different times included in Wales as Gwent or in England as Monmouthshire. Machen spent his last years in the compromise of Old Amersham in Buckinghamshire, with its surrounding countryside and yet nearness to the suburban Metroland of Amersham-on-the-Hill and its station at the far end of the Tube. In his work these sort of differences in setting and background are received (or come to terms with) to some extent by Machen's technique of heightening the colours and deepening the shadows of the settings of his stories. There are places for ambiguities and seeing things, even if through a glass darkly: "And as I think the pure provincial can never understand the quiddity or essence of London, so I believe that for the born Londoner the country ever remains an incredible mystery."

Machen loved and revered his native rural Wales all of his life: yet as a place of residence he left it behind at the age of nineteen, never to return except for visits of longer or shorter duration. Machen's work is largely set in the countryside, yet he is as much an urban writer as a rural one. The city—London—is seen as a bright place of challenge to someone from the country. The country is seen as an idyllic place of retreat and escape. And yet neither is really the case. At times London was the "grey temple of an awful rite" and circled by boundaries to be crossed for which every crossing required an initiation that was "eternal loss". And, as has just been seen, the country, the "strangely beautiful" rural Wales, is also "full of mystery".

Machen seems constantly to have held his rural and urban sympathies in tension. No doubt this was a mixed attitude, held because of, as well as despite of himself. To say that, in terms of his literary career and output, it was a creative tension would be an understatement. Perhaps it was the product of alienation, or a seeking for something that never quite existed or was realised in Machen's life. He recalled his rural past with fondness, but it could be dull. The urban present was lively, and Machen celebrated that in his work. And to a mind such as his, always probing at the boundary between "sanctity and sorcery" there was still the ever-present possibility that either the rural scene or London could swallow someone and leave them remaining alive but no longer really a human being:

> *He had found himself curiously strengthened by the change from the hills to the streets. There could be no doubt, he thought, that living a lonely life, interested only in himself and his own thoughts, he had become in a measure inhuman.*

Machen's work spanned boundaries, the "twilight zones" between the more customary ways of seeing and experiencing places. Passages from a volume of autobiography such as *Far Off Things* and a work of fiction (which nevertheless contain strong autobiographical elements) such as *The Hill of Dreams,* resemble each other closely and are often in effect interchangeable. Machen described how, after moving to London, he "began the habit of rambling abroad in the hope of finding something that could be called country" and into regions that he recalled as a "sort of nightmare". And in the same way Lucian Taylor "tried to make for remote and desolate places, and yet when he had succeeded in touching on the open country, and knew that the icy shadow hovering through the mist was a field, he longed for some sound and murmur of life, and turned again to roads where pale lamps were glimmering..."

During Machen's lifetime, as the nation's population grew, its work patterns changed, and the transport infrastructure developed, the phenomenon of urbanisation became more noticeable than ever. As far as London was concerned, Machen was present during the time of its greatest expansion, from the growth of the later nineteenth century through to the tremendous explosion of urban sprawl after the First World War. This led to the swamping of Middlesex and large areas of other surrounding counties, with open spaces, fields, woodland, and much productive agricultural land in particular being covered with houses and roads. But it was the Victorian expansion of London, especially in the 1880s and 1890s that formed the background to so much of Machen's work, and especially the stories written during his great creative decade of 1889–99 (although in some cases they were not published until years later).

In a confused vision I stumbled on, through roads half town and half country, grey fields melting in to the cloudy world of mist on one side of me, and on the other comfortable villas with a glow of firelight flickering on the walls, but all unreal...

This example illustrates the sort of landscape Machen must have seen again and again on his constant wanderings around the western outskirts of a fast-growing London. It was the ragged place where town and country meet, the jagged line of a jumble of new streets and ravaged fields, and a place ideal for outrageous coincidences to occur with regularity, to form the setting for adventures stranger than can be imagined. The Prologue to *The Three Impostors* is a notable example. Two of Machen's cast of idler characters, Phillipps and Dyson, whose very idleness always allows them the time for things to happen to them and to pursue them, while exploring the "forgotten outskirts" of London see a deserted house from the road and wander up to it. It is in such a setting that a boundary into dark enchantments is crossed: "I yield to fantasy; I cannot withstand the influence of the grotesque... I cannot regain commonplace, I look at that deep glow on the panes, and the house lies all enchanted; that very room, I tell you, is within all blood and fire."

Here the house appears to stand as a stable remnant of the past—pleasant to look at, and in an apparently tranquil setting. But even this "picturesque but mouldy residence" is not what it might seem. It lies on a boundary and is itself a boundary. It is a place where past and present come together and where the future decays into the present on its way to becoming past. The stationary house can be seen as enclosing the boundary, and containing within it its own decay as it moves in transition backwards from its future. The house, seemingly serene, is a trap: in reality the setting for strange and terrible happenings.

Arthur Machen's boundary zones are places for seeking and finding: seeking that which should not be sought, and coming to terms with that which should not have been found. Where the edges meet or overlap sanctity and sorcery are closer to each other than can be healthy, and the commonplace is decisively lost: "...a veil seems drawn aside, and the very fume of the pit steams up through the flagstones, the ground glows, red hot... I see the plot thicken; our steps will henceforth be dogged with mystery, and the most ordinary incidents will teem with significance."

The subtitle of *The Three Impostors* is *The Transmutations*, which as S. T. Joshi points out, gives an indication of the different types and levels of transmutation that this complex novel reveals. Both human beings and landscapes are portrayed as undergoing transmutation; this usually involves entering the borderland, crossing boundaries and the sweeping away of previous conceptions.

Boundaries and ecstasy belong together; they intermingle with each other and transform those who seek and encounter them. Towards the end of his active literary career Machen wrote what was perhaps his most effective use of the theme of crossing borders and the transformation through ecstasy of those who do so. This is the idea of interpenetration or *perichoresis*, which literally means the area or space around about: in this case perhaps the boundary between the worlds, between reality and illusion, or two orders of both. Machen's work abounds in ideas of an unseen world pressing in on ours—and actually interpenetrating with it in usually the most unexpected and unlikely places, such as "ordinary" London suburbs, and with the most dire results.

As discussed above, buildings and roads in the shifting transition zone between town and country can be considered boundaries between the worlds. This also forms a connection with Machen's Christian faith and acceptance of a "Platonic" view of the universe. In this view the world as seen and experienced by human beings is in fact only the shadow of a perfect and unchanging reality, and usually veiled from sight; even so, there may be traffic between the two. According to the American critic Joseph Wood Krutch, Machen had "only one plot, the Rending of the Veil". Machen explored the concept of another dimension of reality—or, rather, reality itself—beyond the veil, the veil sometimes being rent asunder and the other side interpenetrating rarely with our world, and being perceived by a few people in the right place at the right time: "… we stand amidst sacraments and mysteries full of awe, and it doth not yet appear what we shall be. Life, believe me, is no simple thing…"

It is in the late story "N" where the idea of *perichoresis*, is most strikingly developed. "N" is a key story in Arthur Machen's large and varied output. But perhaps because it was a new story specially written in 1935 for *The Cosy Room and Other Stories*, a collection of otherwise reprint fiction published the following year, it can easily be overlooked and not accorded the importance it deserves. Three of Machen's company of habitual talkers, middle-aged and elderly men, meet from time to time in the rooms of one of them. They speculate as to why, over the years, there have been persistent hints and rumours of gardens and panoramas of "unearthly" or "astounding" beauty to be glimpsed behind the ordinary streets and through the windows of a place they think they know intimately, the thoroughly ordinary north London suburb of Stoke Newington.

One of the characters recalls a "shabby brown book" by the Reverend Thomas Hampole, *A London Walk: Meditations in the Streets of the Metropolis* (which had first been mentioned in *The Green Round*, published in 1933). In his book Mr Hampole refers to a conversation he had as a young clergyman with Mr Glanville, a member of his congregation who tells him about "a consequence, not generally acknowledged, of the Fall of Man". His doctrine was that the universe was "originally fluid and the servant of his spirit, became solid and crashed down upon him overwhelming him beneath its weight and its dead mass." During a last visit to Mr Glanville at his rooms, Hampole is invited to look at the view from his window. It is not what he expected to see in Stoke Newington; Hampole "uttered an inarticulate cry of joy and wonder." Hampole immediately feels a "swift revulsion of terror" and rushes from the house. Clearly a boundary had been removed, and Hampole's initial ecstasy was exposed as a manipulation from the demonic.

Through the skilful use of linked narratives, interconnected memories, pub anecdotes, second-hand reportage, Machen carefully constructed a documentary verisimilitude that is pervasive as well as being persuasive. When the men meet again and consider everything they have found out, the most likely explanation, it is hazarded, is "that there is a perichoresis, an interpenetration. It is possible, indeed, that we three are now sitting among desolate rocks, by bitter streams". The final words that follow are as redolent with horror, understated menace, and intriguing possibility as anything Machen ever wrote during the heyday of his literary career around the turn of the twentieth century.

At that time, in *Hieroglyphics*, Machen used the device of the narrator's visits to another of his talkative characters, a reclusive elderly man in his retreat, an old house in the "almost mythical region" of Barnsbury, then very much on a boundary at the northern edge of London. They discuss—or rather, the hermit tells the narrator—what it is that makes true literature. As has been seen, the deciding factor is the presence of ecstasy; in his book Machen put forward an entire literary theory, exploring the roots of ecstasy and defining another kind of boundary.

Machen sought the ecstasy which brings the boundary experience home at the deepest level, and makes the world and life within it into a place of darkness and glory, coexisting and interpenetrating with somewhere else through rendings of the veil:

*I recall the presence of that hollow, echoing room... and the tone
of voice speaking to me, and I believe that once or twice we
both saw visions, and some glimpses at least of certain eternal,
ineffable Shapes.*

In the final analysis Arthur Machen's best work, his fiction
of boundaries, seeks to test and cross those boundaries, explore the
consequences, and enhance, embrace, and communicate ecstasy.

Author's Note

This is a thorough revision of an article first published
more than twenty years ago. My thanks to Tom Miller for
(unwittingly) providing the impetus.

Sources

1 *The Terror* was first published in *The Evening News* (London),
October 16-31, 1916 and in book form by Duckworth in 1917.
2 "The Inmost Light" (1894) in *Tales of Horror and the
Supernatural*, Tartarus Press 2006, pp.175-6.
3 "The White People" in *Tales of Horror and the Supernatural*,
Tartarus Press 2006, p.111.
4 *Hieroglyphics* (1902) Martin Secker (New Adelphi Library)
1926, p.18.
5 "The Novel of the White Powder" (1895) in *Tales of Horror
and the Supernatural*, Tartarus Press 2006, p.56.
6 *Far Off Things* (1922) in *The Collected Arthur Machen* edited by
Christopher Palmer, Duckworth 1988, p.90.
7 *The Hill of Dreams* (1907), Tartarus Press 2006, p.167.
8 *The Three Impostors* (1895), J. M. Dent 1995, p.55.
9 *The Hill of Dreams* p.135.
10 *Far Off Things* in *The Collected Arthur Machen* p.146.
11 *The Hill of Dreams* p.157.
12 S.T. Joshi, *The Weird Tale*, University of Texas Press 1990,
pp.39-41. Joshi provides a list of the dates of writing, first
publication, and first collection in book form.
13 *The Three Impostors* p.47.
14 *The Three Impostors* p.6.

15 *The Three Impostors* p.13.

16 S.T. Joshi, *The Weird Tale* p.25.

17 Joseph Wood Krutch, "Tales of a Mystic" in *Nation* CVX (13ᵗʰ September, 1922), p.259. Cited in Wesley D. Sweetser, *Arthur Machen*, Twayne Publishers 1964, p.78.

18 *The Three Impostors* pp.50-51.

19 Thomas Kent Miller rightly draws attention to its importance in "Some thoughts on 'N'" in *Faunus* No. 26.

20 "N" (1936) in *Tales of Horror and the Supernatural*, Tartarus Press 2006, p.294.

21 "N" pp.295-6.

22 "N" pp.305-6.

23 "'The Secret and the Secrets' A Look at Machen's *Hieroglyphics*" in *Faunus* No. 5, Spring 2000, pp.3-12.

24 *Hieroglyphics* pps. 5, 8.

"This cackling old Gander"
The New Age and Arthur Machen

Mark Valentine
originally published in Faunus issue 26

The modernist magazine *The New Age*, edited by A.R. Orage, pursued a minor vendetta against Arthur Machen, sporadically over a five year period from 1911-16. The journal was the Edwardian organ of intellectual socialism and might be supposed to have had some sympathy with Machen's bitter views about the public schools and commercial values, and his bohemian sympathy with the underdog and the outcast. Even Machen's traditionalism ought to have appealed to them because *The New Age*'s brand of socialism was inspired in part by an anachronistic fondness for medieval guilds.

Ironically, the magazine's contempt for Machen seems to have been because he worked for the London newspaper *The Evening News*, owned by the powerful imperialist and reactionary Alfred Harmsworth, Lord Northcliffe, a *bête noir* of the left. For *The New Age*, "Harmsworthian" was a term of abuse. They could not know that Machen hated Northcliffe as much as they did, and took great pleasure in telling him (literally, and to his face) to go to hell, when royalties from his American revival released him from the need to carry on doing hack journalism.

In an anonymous column headed "Present-Day Criticism" in the issue of 2nd November, 1911, *The New Age* launched its first scathing attack on Machen's work for *The Evening News*. The particular stimulus seems to have been a crude piece of publicity they deplored:

An impudent circular has come our way, sent—why on earth to THE NEW AGE?—by the manager of the Associated Newspapers, Ltd. A page from The Evening News is enclosed as a specimen of the way they undertake "to sell books rather than to criticise them." We are invited to display the page in our office window and so encourage them "to continue educating the public to buy books rather than to borrow them." In effect we are to combine with the A.N. to trap the innocent into buying books uncriticised! What an idea!... We consider it downright disgraceful. The page of The Evening News begins with an exhortation to the "young fellow" not to be bullied out of reading what he likes, and, naturally, after so jolly a piece of advice, the huckster (Mr Arthur Machen) may safely mention a few well-known classics . . . without danger that that the young fellow will waste good money buying old rubbish like Don Quixote when he can choose "what he likes" from the flanking publishers' advertisements...

The columnist went on to list several of the titles advertised, including books by Nat Gould and Richard Marsh, summing them up as a "mind-offending mart".

Machen was next under attack six months later, in the issue of 23rd May, 1912, for venturing into labour politics. "A certain Mr Machen," the journal jibed, in its front page Notes of the Week, "who writes bad literary criticism for [*The Evening News*], has been turned on like a tap to supply views of the Industrial Unrest; and his most illuminating remark is the admission that he knows of no cure and does not see any hope. Pitt once withered an opponent by the words: "Whenever that honourable gentleman means nothing, I strongly recommend him to say nothing." We wish we could wither people like Mr Machen in the same way."

It must be said, however, that the paper was hard to please, for it was equally dismissive of many other commentators, including Ramsey MacDonald, Philip Snowden (a future Labour Chancellor), H.W. Massingham and Lord David Cecil.

Even when Machen had done a commendable thing, *The New Age* contrived to turn it into an occasion to lambast him. In its issue of 14th July, 1912, it reviewed Richard Middleton's *The Ghost Ship*, for which

Machen provided the introduction. The (unsigned) reviewer was quick to remind readers of their animus: "Our readers may recall our notice of an outrageous advertisement pamphlet sent us some time ago by a Harmsworthian company that requested us to put the paper in our office windows... Mr Arthur Machen's pen was put at the service of this disgraceful venture." His introduction, it scoffs, was only what was to be expected: "We need only remark that he affects to have discovered a man whose journalistic writings are quite well known, and that he froths in the regular Harmsworthian manner over a writer whose work was always gentlemanly, if not often of literary value."

But the magazine's most virulent attack came in its issue of 19th December, 1912. This was in the "Present-Day Criticism" column once again, and it commenced by reminding readers once more of the ill-advised publicity stunt "huckstered", as it put it, by Machen. Its target now was a column of descriptive writing Machen had done for *The Evening News* in which he strolls among the bookshops at Christmas. Machen evokes "the world of beautiful and delightful and ingenious objects... the spiritual and imaginative appeal of the bookshops". But to *The New Age's* columnist this was just another vulgar publicity stunt. "How can a man do it?" he demands, "How can a mortal man play such a silly part?... How—even for the money?" The true target soon comes out once again—"Mr Machen's aim is to give the impression of spontaneity in his peregrination of the very bookshops which are advertising in Harmsworth journals". More of Machen's (supposed) chatter with booksellers is quoted, before the columnist warms himself up for a final fusillade: "Here is a reviewer publicly making himself out a sillier ass than he would dare to be... What a business, what an unworthy business for an adult man, writing bunkum for a living!" And it offers a final insult for Machen, "this cackling old gander of Carmelite Street".

The same issue, incidentally, also included letters protesting at the paper's treatment of Richard Middleton, in a recent article: one of them was from Louis J. McQuilland, a fellow New Bohemian.

Some readers must have thought the Christmas attack on Machen went too far in personal vindictiveness. And the little feud is of particular interest because a young author leapt to Machen's defence. This was Eric Brett Young, the younger brother of Francis (who was later to be a popular novelist and poet). Their first book was a collaboration, *Undergrowth*

(1913), an excellent story about social turmoil and pagan survivals in a Welsh valley where a reservoir is being made. Francis Brett Young later acknowledged their joint debt to Machen, noting wryly, "the Machenery was obvious". Eric went on to become a local journalist and author of two novels, crime fiction with macabre and folkloric elements. He died young from polio, an illness he had borne since childhood. He had been a schoolfellow of Tolkien.

The riposte from Eric Brett Young appeared in *The New Age* issue of 9th January, 1913:

> *Sir—It is only fair to such of your readers as do not know Mr Machen's work, to point out that if he "writes bunkum for a living" (NEW AGE, DEC)—which concerns nobody but himself—he has also written (possibly for his own satisfaction) several works of extraordinarily exalted insight and imagination: and this concerns all lovers of the English language. If your reviewer had confided himself merely to attacking Mr Machen's puff (if, as I am inclined to doubt, it was actually written by Mr Machen) one would merely have regretted his discourtesy in omitting to mention the immeasurably superior work of the same hand. But in such phrases as "this cackling old gander of Fleet Street"; "like all writers who have gained a reputation by being, oh! so precious, he is really appallingly common and unimaginative"; your reviewer is on more general ground. He is taking advantage of an unfortunate lapse into bad journalism to attack the reputation of a supreme literary artist. It has been a common method of disparaging literary genius. But there is no reason why it should in every case be reserved for the disgust of the next generation.*
> *E. BRETT YOUNG*

The magazine's anonymous columnist was allowed to respond, and was unrepentant:

> *Our contributor replies: I do not understand the suggestion that Mr Machen does not write the articles signed with his name in The Evening News. He has never repudiated the signature*

to my knowledge. And on the reasonable supposition that he is the author of the bunkum what is the use of urging that the same writer is gifted with an "extraordinarily exalted insight and imagination," which he preserves for his books? A great man cannot make himself small at will. Exalted insight and imagination would out, even in a halfpenny paper. I have yet to read a work of Mr Machen's which shows either one or the other. His articles in The Evening News are simply his ideas with the disguise of pretty words, and they are, as I said, appallingly common and unimaginative. Supreme literary artist be damned!

Eric Brett Young did not continue the correspondence, but Machen found another champion in one J.H. Hobbs, in the issue for 6th February, 1913:

Sir—SUPREME LITERARY ARTIST. I am just recovering from the rude shock of an unexpected encounter with the above vigorous declaration, thundered forth by your reviewer in reply to Mr E. Brett Young. It settles a delicate question once and for all, and with the complacent assurance of a Jeffrey. At the same time, as a confirmed Machenian, I am curious to know which of the Machen books your reviewer has read, and if you could afford him a column or so in which to pour out his soul in undisguised contempt for such writings as Hieroglyphics, The House of Souls and The Hill of Dreams, I for one would gladly take the risk of reading every word of his "review".

Meanwhile, here are a couple of snippets for the defence. Of The House of Souls, Mr John Masefield wrote:

"Six remarkable stories, two of them the most remarkable stories that have been written in the present generation... Mr Machen is so beautifully sensitive to impressions of beauty—to impressions, that is, of living and eternal things—that his style is at all times exquisite and lovely."

And Mr T. Michael Pope, in Vol. 74 of The Academy said:

"He alone of modern novelists (it seems to me) possesses the

*needful qualifications of the true romanticist, for he alone
has a direct vision of great spiritual forces sustaining and
transforming the lives of men."*

*But, after all Messrs Masefield and Pope are persons of no
importance whatever; the one person of importance in this
particular corner of the critical vineyard being a certain
reviewer with a fine gift of "language" and more than a
tincture of self-conceit. J.H. HOBBS*

The magazine did not reply to this. But it had a regular column
called "Current Cant" which contained about a dozen recent quotations
that it deprecated. In the same issue as Hobbs' letter, it quoted in this
praise by Machen for Masefield: "It seems to me, that after all deductions
have been made Mr Masefield has brought a new spirit into English
poetry." This may have been meant slyly to imply that Machen and
Masefield were simply indulging in mutual admiration. In fact, this was
not the case: the two men did genuinely admire each other's work, but
did not get on in person.

The feud took a different turn in the issue of 27th February, 1913.
Machen had written a widely-admired *Evening News* article on the
memorial service for Captain Scott. The London County Council had
decided to make this available to teachers in its schools. *The New Age*
gave space to a correspondent to complain that teachers ought to be able
to tell the story of Scott themselves; that Machen did not know how to
write for children; and that his style was not good, with some examples.

In the following issue, Machen was included with about a
dozen others in a pastiche symposium, "Great Thoughts And Their
Thinkers", on the theme of "Are We Too Silly to Live?" This was a spoof
on the habit of other magazines of eliciting brief (unpaid) comments
from eminent writers to fill up space with symposia on general themes.
Those parodied here also included Galsworthy, Bennett, Snowden and
Cecil. The Machen parody is not very distinctive, consisting mostly of
defining terms and swiping at his liking for classic logic, but it concludes
by descending into mere insult, having him say, "I am myself quite
obviously feeble-minded!"

A few issues later (27th March, 1913), Machen was again quoted
in the "Current Cant" column for a description of a royal ceremony, and

quoted there once more on 17th July, 1913, for a column in *The Evening News* on "How to Write a Succesful Novel".

A different attack started in the issue of 22nd January, 1914, with a pungent notice of *The Great God Pan*. The contributor to a column headed "Readers and Writers" launched off with the following:

> *I cannot think what it is in Mr Arthur Machen's The Great*
> *God Pan that procured the sale of more than the copies to his*
> *friends; for assuredly it is one of the baldest black-magic stories*
> *ever written. Yet since the first publication in the rotten period*
> *of 1894, it has gone into several editions, and is now reprinted*
> *in shilling form (Grant Richards).*

The book was "morbid", concerned "the stinkpools of human psychology", and was the work of a "farthing journalist" either "unscrupulously profiteering" (this seems rather at odds with the "farthing" epithet) "or himself morbidly affected". The columnist is not sure if Machen was a practitioner of the "sordid ceremonies" of "obscene cranks" recently in London: he suspects him only of the "suburban séance". The story is not even plausible: it presents "the doings of a fool and a maniac", and he has already wasted enough time on it.

This is just the sort of criticism Machen relished at the first appearance of his book, and quoted with gusto in *Precious Balms*. As he remarked of a similar notice then, it says too much, rather alluring than deterring a certain sort of reader. And Machen is once again in good company: the reviewer finds Wells' *The Island of Dr Moreau*, "one of the filthiest books ever published", which probably did its sales no harm at all.

As if it had exhausted its spleen for a while, *The New Age* laid low for almost the whole year, but the attack was resumed in passing on 26th November, 1914, by the critic "R.H.C." in reviewing books by James Stephens (*The Demi-Gods*) and Algernon Blackwood, "another bugaboo writer" (*Incredible Adventures*). He condemned both, along with (for good measure) the work of W.H. Hudson, "the horrible Mr Crowley" and Wyndham Lewis. R.H.C. claimed that in each case faulty work in their early, acclaimed, books prefigured later, much worse work, just as "Mr Arthur Machen in *The Great God Pan* prepares his descent into the squalor of *The Evening News*."

An unusual note of approval came in passing from the paper's military columnist, "Romney" in the issue of 3rd December, 1914. "A work of imagination," he noted, must contain an element anciently called "inspiration", adding: "The best phrase of all has been suggested by the much-despised Mr Arthur Machen—"ecstasy" he calls it..." Alas, perhaps in retaliation, Machen was back in the cant column the following week, quoted praising Russian soldiers. He made five further appearances in that column in 1915-16.

A review of T.W.H. Crosland's parody *The Showmen* in the issue of 20th January, 1916 gave the opportunity to sneer at "the absurd acceptance" of the Angels of Mons as literal fact and to snidely agree it was "at least credible" that Machen had told the truth without knowing it. It was not, however, a very warm review of the book.

The journal rounded off its five year campaign against Machen with a contemptuous review of *The Great Return* in the issue of 24th February, 1916. This starts: "Marvellous! Halfpenny Marvellous!"— Machen's value seems to have doubled from the farthing of before—and continues, "The things that Mr Machen can discover in the papers would strike us dumb with amazement." Alluding to "The Bowmen," it says: "We have scarcely recovered from the effects of the "Cupid's Own"... against Von Kluck's cohorts' before being asked to "turn to Wales" for a "temporary return" of the Holy Grail, which (it is suggested) perhaps fled when it knew Machen was coming to investigate. The notice concludes with what looks like an ugly anti-Semitic jibe, asking if Machen could next find "the Wandering Jew in Lombard Street" (known for its banks and financiers). Perhaps that tells us as much as we need to know of the character of the anonymous columnist.

acknowledgement

This essay was only possible thanks to the work of The Modernist Journals Project, a joint project of Brown University & The University of Tulsa, which has made available content from *The New Age* online.

The Nurse's Letter—
The White People

Rosalie Parker
originally published in Faunus issue 27

15th October 18—

Dear Mr Ambrose,

Your friend has found me, after some months' searching I understand. He says that you would like me to write down in a letter everything I know about the girl who died, and the time I spent as her nursemaid.

I don't really see why I should. What purpose will it serve? It seems a long time ago, and it was a very different life to the one I live now. I've tried my best to forget about my employment in that house. When I heard that the girl was dead, I confess I was very unhappy, but I hadn't set eyes on her for several years.

Why would you want to rake over the past? What is there in our story to catch the interest of a London gentleman like you? I was a common country servant—and she is dead, and that's the end of it.

I left that house when her father accused me of something I'd rather not mention—something of which I was wholly innocent. He had taken against me, because of some things that had occurred, and some things I had said, and he found a way of getting rid of me, so that he did not look at fault. He is a lawyer, and good at arranging things. Since then I have moved around quite a bit, but I've set myself up now in a cottage with some livestock and a vegetable patch, and I make my living selling produce at the market. Sometimes I give advice and help to those that need it, and, if they are pleased to, they make it worth my while.

I didn't want to be a servant, but there was no helping it. I was fourteen when I went to work at the house. I was good at my lessons and stayed at school until then. But I had six brothers and sisters and my mother was struggling to make ends meet with one field, a cow and some casual work. I'd always had the run of the lanes and the mountain. My great-grandmother lived alone in a cottage on the high slopes and since I was a very young girl I visited her every day, helping with the chores, listening to her stories and watching the way she worked. She taught me many things. She showed me that it is possible to help people get better (or worse) by making them believe that you can. She taught me how to listen, and to speak only what needs to be said. She lived a long, hard life and she was generous with her knowledge.

The girl's mother was still alive when I became her nurse. She was a kind mistress, but sickly, and she died soon after giving birth to a dead child—a brother for the girl, and a much longed-for son for the father, if he'd lived. She and I heard the girl speaking her own strange language, and had seen her odd ways—the counting and the touching, the habit she had of not looking you in the eye—but her mother didn't scold her. She understood the way her daughter was, and loved her the more because of it.

In his grief the father shut himself away and closed his eyes to the child. It was left to us servants to bring her up. He didn't want to know anything about it, and he seemed at first to have nothing but disdain for me. Once, I knocked on his study door and talked to him about her. He covered his face with his hands and said he paid me to make sure she was clothed and looked after, and dismissed me as soon as he could. (Not before I had seen him looking at me through his fingers.) There was some talk in the servants' quarter after that, of his neglect of her, and of other things, but what could we do?

I took her with me wherever I went. She was quick to learn, but she didn't say much. She took pleasure in my stories of kings and huntsmen, and women who wanted to marry, or not marry, and take all the power for themselves. Her face would become rapt, her eyes round as an owl's. Most of the tales I told her I had heard myself from my great-grandmother. I showed the girl how to make the clay figures and set them to work, how to sing the secret words, and make the pots and pans in the kitchen jump around to our bidding—the old lore my great-grandmother had passed on to me. At least the master's disinterest meant that we could wander where we would. I taught her the names of the trees and the flowers, and showed her the places I knew as a girl, the rocks and hollows, pools and streams. I became fond of her, and I looked after her well. Once or twice, I own it, I would meet up with a young man I was seeing then. He was a blacksmith from the village, a tall gentle boy who was in love with me. I was a good-looking young woman in those days, with grave dark eyes, white skin and black hair like a raven's wing. But I'd always make sure that the girl was safe. She was well cared for, I tell you.

The only time I spoke to her roughly was when the little talk she had became too outlandish—when she spilled secrets to the other servants, or thought her dreams were real. Once she told her father one of my great-grandmother's stories—about a ghost—and he was beside himself. He summoned me and accused me of poisoning her mind with my ignorant wickedness and filth, treating me like something dirty he had found on the sole of his shoe. I managed to persuade him it was just a harmless story—I still had some influence over him then—and he soon lost interest, in her at least. At those times she was more moonstruck than was good for her—or me—and I tried to frighten her back into herself, warning her of the hollow pit and the dangers that awaited her there. I should have been more gentle, I can see that now. Now that it is too late.

There was a time I dreamed I could help her, that he would set me up or marry me and I could make sure he gave her a future. I thought I might be a lady and he would clothe me in fine dresses and shawls and I would learn to speak in an educated way like him, and read the books in his study. But I mistook his passing fancy for love, his promises for troth, and I should have known better—but my head was turned, like many a woman's before me, and since. He soon tired of me and found a way to dismiss me, and the girl was left to her own devices, and died.

The men from the village said that she was found lying in front of an old statue, a Roman image—one of their gods from the old times. I find that very hard to fathom. That was not a thing I knew about, or showed her in our wanderings in the woods. I would never have taught her to worship a man carved into a piece of cold stone. Or the Devil, either, despite what some people say.

I don't like to think of her being frightened and alone and drinking the poison. She was a fine person, and someone should have been taking care of her. Sometimes I wake in the night and think of that.

You can do what you like with this letter. It will make no difference now. I hope that she, too, has found a place where she might learn to be content.

Yours sincerely

Backward Glances
Machen in the Mid 1920s

Nick Wagstaff
originally published in Faunus issue 27

On 12th February 1924 Arthur Machen wrote to Munson Havens, one of his enthusiastic correspondents from the USA, saying:

> *I have been busy during the last few weeks in an odd employment which is getting customary and common with me—signing sheets of limited editions of my books. First there came 1000 sheets of The Chronicle of Clemendy, an odd, rare book of mine the Alexandrian Society of New York are reissuing. Then 1200 signatures for Ornaments in Jade, which Knopf of New York is publishing some time this spring... So, on the whole, I am getting rather sick of the sight of my own signature; and yet, at the same time, profoundly grateful that I dropped my full style many years ago. I don't believe that I have signed myself "Arthur Llewelyn Jones Machen" since 1880—save in joke, by way of giving people a slight surprise.[1]*

The words used in this extract strike a positive tone. The potential sale of his books is full of promise, and he ends this piece with a playful remark about the style of his signature. I find this an interesting passage, because it does not hint at the reality of his circumstances. In 1924 his professional life was in difficulties following the end of a decade or so of working as a journalist with *The Evening News*, and late in his career he is doing his best to earn a living as a freelance writer and aspiring to secure his reputation as a literary figure. His statement in the letter about the release of limited reissued editions of his early works gives us a feel for one of the most important matters affecting him in the mid-1920s. Put straightforwardly the important matter was that if there was going to be any transformational change in his fortune in ensuing years it would have to come about through careful selection and republication of his back catalogue of work. The mood of the writer during these middle years of the 1920s tends to be one of looking back.

Let us imagine tip-toeing into Machen's home at Melina Place, St John's Wood in the poor light of a wintry afternoon in February 1924. After a while the figure of the author might be made out, looking a little like Prime Minister Asquith, premier of the UK in the early part of the First World War, as he moves to and fro across the room. The criss-crossing figure also has a resemblance to the hermit described in the preface to Machen's book *Hieroglyphics*, who in near-dark paced up and down constantly in the void centre of his room. He is caught at a moment in his favourite house, set in his favourite garden in St John's Wood. His movement across the room might indicate an energetic, purposeful and optimistic tread. Equally he might be seen to be disconsolately patrolling his bedroom, taking stock of what he feels to be a disappointing level of achievement gained from his sixty years of life. The grey failing light does not allow us to come to a conclusion about his disposition and attitude. There he is looking out over his garden, taking a break from working at his desk, and exercising his aching wrist, before renewing the struggle to pick up his pen and carry on with the business in hand. The business in hand being one of signing inserts to go into USA reproductions of editions of his early books. He has steadfastly been signing off each tiny piece of paper as he slogs through the mound of autograph sheets in order to satisfy his American publishers. He has to do this because there are possibilities and some hope—he must have fervently believed in that hope—of making income from it. This effort is necessary as part of a survival plan to provide earnings for his family.

Three years earlier the author had resigned from the Evening News after writing a premature obituary of Lord Alfred Douglas, editor of *The Academy* (a journal for which Machen had written before the First World War). Unfortunately, Douglas was still alive, and he sued the Evening News for damages over unfavourable comments in the obituary. Having been displaced from his customary grind in Fleet Street Machen was forced to retreat to his London home on the look-out for work in the world of writing. At this moment in early 1924 he is working through a period when he might be spending too much effort on such distracting matters as signing autograph sheets for small print runs of his books. In the same letter quoted above Machen writes of the "signing business" that "I quite appreciate its good consequences from the business point of view". But as he concentrates on this immediate work, there might be a sense too that he is moving further away, step by step, from the inspirational spirit that delivered his famous, extraordinary and sensationalist fictional work of the 1890s. At the same time he is distracted from further developing his deep scholarship of the Holy Grail legend and his attempts to capture the essence of profundity and excellence in literature, as expounded in *Hieroglyphics*, 1902. He probably knows from his gruelling experience of a decade or more as a daily journalist in Fleet Street that his hard won reputation as a good hack has drained his energy, but hopes that his gift with words might allow him a few more creative opportunities and enough money to survive on. He may also hope that his record of achievement as a writer will be secured and that he will gain international standing.

As he pauses in his task of signing insert sheets he looks out over his favourite garden in St John's Wood, thinking about planning his next reception party for supporters of his literary endeavours. In those few years in the mid-1920s, after his relationship with the *Evening News* ended, he attracted an audience of American enthusiasts for his work. He hoped it might be possible for him to cash in on his literary record, and that his republished works from the 1890s and early 1900s would sell well in the USA. At this imagined pause in his work, he might be surveying the pear tree and the lilacs in his garden, looking forward to their spring flowering. He might also be examining the territory of Dog and Duck, the game he invented for his St John's Wood garden.

We see him now as an author who rarely provided satisfaction to his literary critics, and he rarely appealed to a wide readership. It is not often that an author publishes a book about the unfavourable critical reactions to his lifetime's work, but Machen did in 1923 with *Precious Balms*. Concern about external critical reaction was not the major inhibition to his work. Machen was always highly critical of his own efforts, and could rarely deliver a piece of work that met with his own exacting standards. As he wrote in another letter to Munson Havens, dated 1st April 1924, "Nearly all of my books have been written with extreme difficulty; I might almost say with anguish".

I am suggesting that 1924 might be seen to be a turning point for Machen. On the detrimental side he had no salary, he had no fictional material to develop, he was struggling to come up with fresh ideas for non-fictional writings. But on the plus side, there was much interest in his works in the USA and demand for his output was being met by USA publication of material written and published in the UK years before. Added to which he hoped that publication of his entire works in the UK Caerleon Edition 1923 would boost his name to the domestic market. USA visitors were making their way to his door in London to meet him in person, giving him a hope that he might become recognised internationally as an important author and that income would flow. As a fall-back he was spending his spare time concocting more strenuously demanding versions of his famous punches for his own enjoyment and that of his guests. It must have been difficult for Machen to assess how the mid-1920s would shift. With hindsight it is clear that the hints of achieving literary fame, just perceptible in 1924, would evaporate. He struggled on as best he could to make-do.

Let us return to my fanciful setting of his home at St John's Wood in February 1924, where we see that Machen's approach to gaining a livelihood in the mid-1920s was to attempt to do several things at the same time. His strategy, as might be expected of an experienced foot-soldier in the world of Fleet Street, was manifold. Machen, an accomplished master of journalism, wrote in one of his late period "autobiographical" stories that "a journalist has two offices—to proclaim the truth and to denounce the lie".[2] He had delved into the enormous scope provided by this journalistic "office" over many gruelling years, and a writer of his stature could be relied upon to explore several disparate strands at the same time with determination. He had several avenues in mind.

a) His best opportunities were to encourage his UK and American publishers to promote his complete backlog of works. He hoped credit would be given to his stock of works, and that royalties and more commissions would flow from that series of publications.

Unfortunately his willingness to sell his rights cheaply in the USA posed fatal problems to income production. He hoped that the American market in the early 1920s, which had been given a taste of his works promoted by Vincent Starrett, would build. For UK readership he bundled together articles written earlier into several volumes, such as *Dog and Duck* (1924), *Dreads and Drolls* (1926) and *Notes and Queries* (1926).

b) In the mid-1920s he set out to pick up opportunities to write new non-fiction pieces in newspapers and journals, and in this way add to his volume of thoughts, articles and essays on life and literature. He did this, for example, by writing for *The London Graphic* in 1925-26 and by offering his services to *The Observer*, which eventually employed him in 1926–27 to write a weekly column. He was also approached to write a book on "The Canning Wonder". He took this on and the book was published by Chatto & Windus in 1925. Some Machen enthusiasts might regard this as a nemesis product in the author's career, but he did the job required and earned money from the venture. Nowadays few people see *The Canning Wonder* as a distinguished piece of his work. It was written to order to earn much needed income, and he dealt with it by writing rapidly after years of training as a daily journalist on a major newspaper.

c) He alerted himself to opportunities to write new and commissioned fictional pieces, but as it turned out he wrote little new fictional material in the 1920s. In *The London Adventure* written in 1923 and published in 1924, he essentially confessed to his inability to deliver the grand imaginative romance of London he had fondly imagined for so long. That great project and related works would never materialise. His admission meant that there would be little creative fiction from his pen in future. A handful of short stories, such as "The Islington Mystery" (1927) and "Johnny Double" (1928) emerged in collections in the 1920s. Otherwise the 1920s was a fictional desert for him. When forced by commissions a decade or so on he would make determined efforts, as in *The Green Round* (1933), and *The Children of the Pool* (1936), to produce fresh material.

d) He encouraged American supporters and anyone else to provide him with literary support and personal donations. Munson

Havens, the recipient of the February 1924 letter quoted at the outset, was one such person. Montgomery Evans was another avid champion of the mature writer. The Hasslers" volume of selected letters between Machen and Montgomery Evans[3] shows how often Evans provided material support to the Machen family in the 1920s through to the end of the Second World War, by means of food packages, cash and other kinds of donations.

e)   He wrote new introductions to republished collections of his works to add new insights to his output. By such means he hoped to attract new readers. For example, Machen had written a new foreword to *The House of Souls* for its 1923 third printing by Alfred A. Knopf in the USA. The content of the US foreword to *The House of Souls* was entirely different from the UK volume of the same name. He was also in the business of writing prefaces to works by other authors, an example being *Mainly Players: Bensonian Memories* by Lady Benson (1926). (In the early 1900s Machen had been a member of the Benson Company.)

f)   He made himself available to review books. A few years on in the decade he managed to become a reader and reviewer for Ernest Benn Ltd, the British publishers. It was a role that lasted until 1933, and provided a line of income. Moreover this association led to Ernest Benn Ltd publishing *The Green Round* in 1933 as part of its Ninepenny Novelist series.

In general, Machen had to make the best job of surviving in the limited financial circumstances he had come to. His wife, Purefoy, in her memoirs[4] casually mentions selling off family goods to the pawnbroker in the 1910s, so it seems that Machen and his family were accustomed to scaling down their possessions at least a decade before the mid-1920s. In Purefoy's account she and her husband kept some distance from any transaction with the pawnbroker by asking their lodger to do the deed by discreetly flogging off the family spoons on their behalf. By the mid-1920s things had got worse in the Machen household: he had no regular income and he had a family to support. In this imaginary intervention in an afternoon of February 1924, Machen is seen to return to his desk, bend over to look at the books and scraps of work scattered around him, and then with reluctance become focussed again on dealing with the pieces of insert paper he is obliged to sign. The hope of fame, offered to him tantalisingly in the mid-1920s, flickered briefly but never came to anything much. He appeared in 1924 to have exhausted a limited palette of creative energy, exercised in a decade or so of colourful, determined and skilful writing between 1890 and the early 1900s. In his primary works of the 1890s and 1900s he managed to carve out a distinctive place in literary achievement, which is better recognised now than in his own day. As the 1920s progressed his reputation as a writer peaked in the American market and then dropped rapidly. He was buoyed by supportive efforts of enthusiastic American visitors to St John's Wood, but that happened briefly. His signature statement of the 1920s might be captured in another letter to Munson Havens, written by Machen on 4th July 1924:

I have worked very hard for very little all my life, and now I am sixty-one.

Years on there was a rescue attempt by literary celebrities to grant him a small income in recognition of his literary endeavours. A grant awarded in 1928 was reinforced by another award in 1933, which allowed Machen and his wife to live out their last years in something above the poverty line. The financial support granted to Machen in his late career was welcomed gladly. But overall there was a sense of the family on a path to financial failure from the early 1920s, distressingly in line with the example set by his clergyman father. Machen's experience in 1924 was one of coping without a salary. Owing to the amount of his published material that appeared in the UK and the USA in the early 1920s he might have felt a degree of optimism about a long delayed positive reception to his endeavours as a writer. A favourable uptake in his readership would have offered a reliable income stream. It is clear that the mid-1920s saw a remarkable number of Machen's books published in the UK and USA, but these were almost entirely works reissued from pieces written many years earlier. The imaginative content of his earlier works and the intellectual endeavour of his non fiction pieces stand to this day, but financial rewards eluded him. Over the years, in constant ebbs and flows of literary fame, Machen has at least managed to receive grudging acknowledgements of his contribution to late nineteenth- and early twentieth-century writing. Some literary historians, enthusiasts and a wide casual readership would say that Machen deserves greater recognition in literary history.

This essay has attempted to imagine Machen's predicament in 1924. The eternal themes Machen wrote about throughout his long career were produced and set against his own personal financial hardship over several decades, and his financial problems multiplied in the 1920s. During his most productive years of writing in the 1890s, Machen had a small family legacy to sustain him in his creative life, but by the 1920s, when he had responsibilities for raising a family, the private income had been stripped away and his salary had gone. After he left his work as a daily journalist he had to struggle with a future full of uncertainties and deprivation. Machen, having managed to cope with poverty through many years of hardship, would have had little trouble in recognising where he was placed. In the mid-1920s he turned repeatedly to the extensive output of his previously written material. He looked, with less ease, to his ability to write high quality literary outputs in the future, realising that his best creative years were behind him.

When I attempt to visualise Machen in 1924 and try to get a feel of his trajectory through the mid-1920s I am drawn to his 12th February letter to Munson Havens with its message of the writer engaged in a sound business practice of promoting his works to international buyers, but there are underlying reservations. I feel that Machen felt that stylistic trends were going against him, that his appeal to a new audience was limited and that his works were becoming unfashionable.

I am taken with the notion of Machen seated in some kind of waiting room in a state of anxiety, waiting for an assessment of his financial situation and reputation. Yet there would be no clear verdict in 1924, nor would there be in 1925 or 1926. Several possible outcomes were imaginable ranging from success to failure. As he glanced back in February 1924 he felt that he could reflect upon a massive amount of material he had written over his career. He would acknowledge the varying quality of his prodigious output. The key question was whether or not the best of it would meet the appetites of readers as the second quarter of the twentieth century was about to begin.

In the mid-years of the 1920s Machen might have been tempted to look up his "Strange Roads" essay of 1919, in which he wrote:

*I do not know how to put my impression into definite words,
but, somehow... the very thorn trees that grew in the fields had
about them an aspect of concealed mystery.*

As he knew, all too well, thorns grow everywhere and extensively.
Any upbeat views he had of his achievement and prosperity in the 1920s
would be checked by the mysterious thorns and stinging nettles that he
often used as symbols in his writings.

sources

1. *A Few Letters from Arthur Machen*, Letters to Munson
Havens, The Rowfant Club, Cleveland, USA, 1932. This letter
is dated 12th February 1924, p.20 in the 1993 edition, The
Aylesford Press.

2. "The Happy Children", *The Masterpiece Library of
Short Stories*, London Educational Book Company 1920.
Republished in *Tales of Horror and the Supernatural*, Richards
Press, 1949

3. *Arthur Machen and Montgomery Evans, letters of a literary
friendship*, 1923-47, edited by S.S. Hassier and D.M. Hassler,
Kent State University Press, 1994.

4. *Where Memory Slept*, Purefoy Machen, Green Press Round, 1991.

At a Man's Table
The Truth About curry

Arthur Machen

Publicity sheet for Messrs J.A. Sharwood & Co, 1928
Published in Faunus issue 28

"I should uncommonly like to be in the dining room at home," writes Charlotte Brontë, in Brussels, to her sister Emily, at Haworth, "or in the kitchen, or in the back kitchen. I should like even to be cutting up the hash… and you standing by, watching that I put enough flour, not too much pepper, and above all, that I save the best pieces of the leg of mutton for Tiger and Keeper… To complete the picture, Tabby blowing the fire, in order to boil the potatoes to a sort of vegetable glue."

No wonder they were melancholy at Haworth Parsonage; no wonder they died young; no wonder old Mr Brontë dined by himself on a special diet. The unhappiness of the Brontës had ample grounds for its existence. One cannot eat horrors and be happy.

It is, of course, true that cold mutton constitutes one of the graver difficulties of life. In itself it is uneatable; even the Brontës, with their terrible cookery, recognised that. If a man says that he likes cold mutton, either he is demented or his wife beats him.

cold Mutton

Cold mutton is a difficulty, then, but like other difficulties, it may be overcome. And the best way is a curry; the only medium I know which can quench and abolish that dank and clammy flavour which afflicts the palate and the soul more grievously than many of the drugs of the apothecary.

But there are curries and curries. It is odd enough that this dish, one of the simplest in all cookery, should be so often ruined in the making.

I have known excellent cooks, sound and admirable in soup and fish, roast and sweet, come to the saddest grief over their curries; serving up horrid greenish messes of hard meat swimming in a thin and acrid juice, surrounded by a rim of rice, boiled a la Tabby into a kind of vegetable glue. And yet, as I say, there is no difficulty. Anybody can make a curry. And the way is thus:—

In the first place, cut up that sorry gigot of cold mutton into pieces as large as a well-grown walnut. And as you cut, take away every fragment of skin and of fat and of sinew. Now scatter your curry powder (Ventcatchellum's) over the pieces of meat with a liberal hand. Roll the meat in the powder, see that each lump is covered with curry. And then fry it to a rich, dark brown, and put it into a pot or casserole.

Then take onions. Slice them and chop them finely, and in such quantity that the plateful of sliced onions is as large in bulk as was the plateful of meat. Fry the onions well, with a leaning to darkness in the colouring, and add them to the meat in the pot. Add furthermore a small teacupful of stock, or milk, or water. Stir all together, set on the hot plate, and bring to a boil.

So far, I think all has been plain, direct, British. There has been no pandering to Continental subtleties or refinements; no command to make the fire of olive wood or the prunings of the vine. And the business continues on straightforward lines, but its order must be strictly followed without varying or turning.

The curry is boiling freely. Slide the pot gently away from the utmost heat of the fire, and find by experiment the place where it will simmer with two unctuous and reluctant bubbles; two and no more.

And now keep an eye on that pot and on the fire, and take care that the work of the two bubbles continues for two hours. And then take the pot off the fire—and think of tomorrow. For the precept of Mme D'Anstrel, superior of the Convent of the Visitation at Belley with regard to chocolate, applies also to curry.

"Monsieur!" said the religious lady to Brillat-Savarin, "when you wish to drink good chocolate, let it be made the day before in a porcelain coffee pot, and left overnight. The night's rest concentrates it, and makes it velvet to the tongue. The good God cannot frown upon this small luxury, for life is Himself all excellence."

So with our curry; and if it has been cooked in an iron pot, it should repose for the night in porcelain. The next day, within about an hour of the meal—curry is, properly, a dish for lunch—skim off the fat, again bring to a boil, again soothe down to the two fat bubbles. Rice is boiled so that every grain retains its individuality, and serve, not round the curry, but in a dish apart.

And, in helping the happy guests, make first a bed of rice on each plate, and then add the curry; dark, velvety, delicious. "Green label" chutney is the best accompaniment, and with it you may take, if you will, poppadoms, Bombay ducks, and a little powdered mint.

It is, I think, almost a solemn thought that this exquisite dish is a transmutation of that dark, nauseous, and repulsive cold gigot of mutton.

Notes on Gawsworth's Account of Arthur Machen's Funeral

Gwilym Games & James Machin
originally published in Faunus issue 29

Arthur Machen's funeral was held on 17th December 1947, two days after his death. Janet Machen had stayed with her father all summer but it was clear his illness was serious. During that time he made his will and he was also visited by a Welsh vicar, Reverend Gordon Lewis Phillips of St Mary's Northolt. Phillips began his ministry as a curate at St Julian's in Newport, which endeared him to Machen, and Phillips heard his confession and gave him Holy Communion.

conversion?

It was Mrs Ione Massada, a friend of the family, who arranged for Machen to be established in the Roman Catholic private hospital St Joseph's in Candlemass Lane, Beaconsfield, run by the Sisters of the Bon Secours de Paris. It was founded in May 1936 from a pre-existing nursing home which had been located on grounds belonging to the famous local Catholic convert G.K. Chesterton. Chesterton and his wife were friends of the hospital, and his last public engagement before his death was opening the hospital. St Joseph's later became a nursing home once again before it closed in 1998.

While at St Joseph's Machen received a number of visits from a Roman Catholic priest, a former acquaintance of Chesterton. It seems these visits helped give rise to the idea Machen was received into the

Roman Catholic Church, and Gawsworth's account gives a clear indication that the notion was promoted by Machen's Roman Catholic friend Colin Summerford. It was apparently Summerford who provided some information for *The Times* obituary (16th December 1947—see *Faunus* 24), a glowing eulogy to Machen, which ran the day before the funeral and concluded:

> *From the days of his researches into the legend of the Holy Grail he was always deeply interested in problems of theology and ritual and became a Roman Catholic in later years. His place in English literature is as assured as that of almost any writer of his day and was duly recognized in 1932 by the award of a Civil List pension. He fished perhaps in a small pool, but his line went deep.*

Gawsworth's account suggests that after discussion at the funeral Machen's family and friends quickly endeavoured to set the record straight. John Lancelot Davenport (1908–1966), journalist, author, and screenwriter, was an old friend of the family, a friendship formed via his father Robin, a songwriter. The following letter appeared in *The Times* on 24th December:

> *Mr J. L. A. B. Davenport writes—*
> *In your sympathetic and perceptive obituary notice of Arthur Machen you state he became a Roman Catholic in his later years. He would have wished to be described as a Catholic: but would, I think, have been distressed by the suggestion that he ever deserted the Anglican Communion in which he was baptised and to which he remained faithful all his life.*

Nevertheless this mistake in *The Times* was copied in many other notices of Machen's death. A Catholic periodical, the *Universe*, repeated the story, though the most notable instance is the long obituary published in the *Catholic Herald* on 26th December, written by Machen admirer Father Brocard (Michael) Sewell (1912—2000) which treated the supposed conversion at some length:

After the dangerous spiritual explorations of his younger days Machen settled himself firmly in the Christian faith, the elements of which he had received from the Anglican Church of Wales through his father, a clergyman of that denomination. The philosophy and theology in his books is thoroughly Catholic, and his detestation of Protestantism was intense. But his Welsh origins made him look back lovingly to the old Celtic Church of Dewi Sant, and with corresponding aversion to the "Roman" Church of St Augustine of Canterbury. But he was quite out of place in the Church of England, which he satirises with tremendous gusto in his beautiful novel The Secret Glory. Eventually the Mists cleared away and he entered his true spiritual home.

Nothing would have pleased this humble man and great writer more than to know that after his death his works (so neglected in his lifetime) were appreciated by his brethren in that Faith of which he was a life-long defender, although he only embraced it formally a few years before he died.

Sewell's claim was refuted in a letter written to the *Catholic Herald* by Machen's son Hilary, published 2nd January 1948:

Sir,—There is one misstatement in Dom Sewell's discerning note on my late father which requires correction.
To the end of his life Arthur Machen remained in communion with the Church of England, and was at all times a stout defender of the Anglican position.
HILARY MACHEN.
Lynwood, High Street, Amersham, Bucks.

Father Brocard Sewell, a Machen enthusiast throughout his life, was at this stage of his career an Augustine Canon. He later settled as a Carmelite monk and achieved public recognition for his editing of the *Aylesford Review*. Sewell's ongoing interest in Machen's religious views can be seen in his later biographical writings on Machen and unsurprisingly he never wavered in his belief that Machen would have found a good home in his church, though he came to accept that Machen would not have agreed.

An Ecumenical Matter

Machen's self-identification as a "Catholic" (rather than a "Roman Catholic") should be seen against the backdrop of nineteenth-century church history. The Catholic Emancipation Act in 1829, which allowed Roman Catholics to become MPs for the first time since the Reformation, led to a controversial expansion of the involvement of the Roman Catholic Church in public life in Britain, inflaming the long-standing British tradition of violent prejudice against Roman Catholicism (or "Popery" to use the contemporary pejorative). It reached an almost hysterical pitch, resulting not only in the violent rhetoric of dissenters, low and broad churches, but in actual acts of violence and civil disturbance, with the lingering shadow of the Inquisition contributing to a widespread perception that the "foreign" Roman Catholic Church's nefarious agents were conspiring to relieve England of its liberty.

Roughly contemporaneous with this was the re-invigoration of the Church of England that became known as the Tractarian or Oxford Movement. Reacting in part to the threat to the established church from the growing popularity of dissenting movements, and the perception of the institution as simply another secular arm of the state, populated by a complacent, careerist clergy, Newman, Pusey, and others had sought to re-establish the Church's moral authority, emphasising its apostolic succession and seeking renewed engagement with the laity at parish level. Newman's emphasis on centuries of dogma and theological discussion as proof of a "living" church (a progressive church that had not come to a standstill at the time of the compilation of the gospels) led inevitably and often irresistibly to the suggestion that the true Church of England (the Apostolic Church), was the pre-Reformation Church, and therefore a "Catholic" one.

While Machen's particular religious focus was of course the Celtic Church, his enthusiasm for tradition and violent antipathy for the Reformation place him firmly in the tradition of those Victorian medievalists such as Augustus Pugin, John Ruskin, and Thomas Carlyle who valorised the age before the Reformation as a sort of prelapsarian idyll of "true" religion and pre-industrial social harmony. Like Machen after him, Carlyle saw the Reformation as precipitating a disastrous shift in the national psyche: "It is no longer the moral, religious, spiritual condition of the people that is our concern, but their physical, practical, economical condition, as regulated by public laws." In a 1907 article in the *Academy* Machen was even blunter, describing the Reformation as "that Masterpiece of Hell and Death":

> *I cursed the "Protestant Reformation" then with heart and soul; and still do I curse it, and hate it, and detest it, with all its works and in all its abominable operations, internal and external; I loathe it and abhor it as the most hideous blasphemy, the greatest woe, the most monstrous horror that has fallen upon the hapless race of mortals from the foundation of the world.*

Machen's self-identification as a "Catholic" was, rather than an indication of conversion to Rome, a sign of his sympathy with Anglican dogma, respect for Apostolic tradition, antipathy for the dissenting churches and what he perceived as the worldliness of Protestantism, as well as his pronounced dislike of Puritanism wherever he identified it.

However, the confused and confusing distinctions and nuances differentiating High Anglicanism and Roman Catholicism were muddied further by the series of high-profile and controversial conversions to Rome, from Pugin up to and including many of Machen's contemporaries, including Aubrey Beardsley, Oscar Wilde, and G.K. Chesterton. Machen's refusal to follow suit makes it clear that despite Machen's admiration for certain aspects of the Roman Catholic communion there were strict limits, and indeed he shared the traditional Anglican suspicion of many of its claims. While he could admire Cardinal Newman, one high-profile Anglican convert to Roman Catholicism, Machen regarded Cardinal Manning, another convert, who became the Head of the Roman Catholic Church in England and was responsible for the major expansion of the Church, with deep suspicion. Newman and Manning notoriously clashed over the new doctrine of Papal infallibility amongst other matters, Manning being strongly in favour. Speculating on the respective destinations of the two Cardinals after death Machen quipped, "I hope they are in very different places", reflecting his hostility to the wider claims of the Roman Catholic Church.

Like many other Anglicans since the Reformation Machen focused on the fact that Britain had a longstanding Christian tradition prior to the arrival of St Augustine. This gave the Anglican Church an independent validity and indeed perhaps even a special mystical purity through its ties to the land and the monarchy, which was a central aspect to Machen's faith. It is clear Machen regarded "the Church of Rome", as he called it, as but one aspect of a universal Catholic Church which included other churches with apostolic succession, like the various Orthodox Churches. Machen of course hated the Protestant "corruptions" he identified in the Church of England, but his hatred of these corruptions did not mean he would ever leave what he saw as his "true spiritual home". Indeed, the very suggestion of Brocard Sewell that his thinking was obscured by "mists' would have infuriated him. While Machen's son Hilary conceded that his father's "whole attitude to the Catholic Church was curious", he was also—and not surprisingly given his father's views—adamant that "contrary to popular rumour at the time of his death, he was never anything but a High Church Tory".

Funeral Attendees

The organist of course was Machen's good friend, the novelist Frank Baker. Other notable participants were other old friends Norah Hoult, the novelist, and Peter Llewelyn Davies, a publisher of Machen's work. Davies is perhaps best known for his childhood connection to J.M. Barrie, hence Gawsworth styling him "Pete Pan" after Davies' famous literary namesake. Lyn Harding, who sent a telegram, was a Welsh actor (real name David Llewellyn Harding) who came from Machen's homeland, from St Bride's on the Gwent levels. He was well known for his Shakespearean roles and film work, often playing villains. He was a friend of Conan Doyle and produced a stage production of "The Speckled Band" where he appeared as the villainous Dr Roylott, later reproducing that role on film as well as appearing in other films as Moriarty. Machen would have known him from his short time acting with Sir Herbert Beerbohm Tree's Company. It is also worth noting that Una Machen, the wife of Machen's son Hilary, was the daughter of Samuel Chad Hope Hodgson who was the eldest brother of the author William Hope Hodgson. A brief summary of Rev Gordon Lewis Phillips' career from

Crockford's clerical directory follows:

> *Monmouth. Curate St Julian Newport 1937–40, Rector of St Mary's, Northolt 1940–55. Chaplain University of London 1955–68. Rector of Bloomsbury 1956–68. Dean and Vicar of Llandaff 1968–71.*

The wreath

The five names on the wreath to Machen, probably organised by Gawsworth, are of interest. Henry Savage was one of Machen's old friends from the New Bohemians, E.H.W. Meyerstein (1889–1952), the literary scholar and poet, was another friend of Gawsworth and an admirer of Machen. He wrote a poem in Machen's memory. Frederick Carter, the artist and writer, was another old acquaintance of Machen.

The admiration of David Hay Petrie (1895–1948) for Machen is interesting. Hay Petrie was a Scottish character actor who will be familiar to anyone who has seen older film adaptations of Dickens. Petrie's many notable film roles include Quilp in *The Old Curiosity Shop* (1936) and Uncle Pumblechook in David Lean's *Great Expectations* (1946). Petrie also appeared in various films directed by Machen admirer Michael Powell. Gawsworth was a good friend of Petrie, but a direct connection to Machen perhaps dates to Alfred Hitchcock's *Jamaica Inn* (1939). This featured the villainous Sir Humphrey played by Charles Laughton: Petrie played Sir Humphrey's groom while Machen's Amersham neighbour, the director, writer, and novelist Edwin Greenwood—author of the thriller *Skin and Bone* (1939), referred to by Gawsworth—appeared as "Dandy", alongside Emlyn Williams (another admirer of Machen), as part of Sir Humphrey's savage crew of wreckers. Greenwood was to die of an illness not long after filming, possibly due to a chill he contracted on set.

Arthur Machen's Funeral

John Gawsworth
 originally published in Faunus issue 29

Arrived Amersham station 11.05 am. Called on Hilary 11.50, he was alone. Later Janet arrived with a bottle of brandy, then Colin Summerford, then Oliver Stonor, his sister, Mrs Masada [sic], the Blackmores (mother and daughter neighbours) and John Davenport. Wires from S.T. War [Sylvia Townsend Warner] and Lyn Harding. Thence in two cars to church, following the coffin. The Rev Phillips officiated. Summerford gave me bay leaves from garden of convent where Machen died. In the churchyard I was joined by Peter Davies, and Frank Baker who had played the organ. Chief mourners Hilary, his wife Una and daughter Ann and Janet (Davis). Summerford and the RCs poured water into grave. Walked over to Kings Arms with Martin Travers, architect, who had married Molly (Edwin Greenwood's widow).

Talked to Stonor and sat at lunch with him, got on famously: he has some 600 AM letters and is not a Summerfordian (or Davenportian). He writes novels now with Gollancz under the pseud. "Morchard Bishop". We had some drinks and then sat down 19 to lunch.—to wit—

Norah Hoult
Percy Hazleden
Frank Baker
Colin Summerford
Hilary Machen

Una Machen (his wife)
Janet Davies
Rev Phillips (of Northolt)
Miss Greta Blackmore (at school with Janet)
Myself
Mrs Martin Travers (former Molly Greenwood)
Martin Travers
Anne Machen (H's daughter)
Oliver Stonor
Mrs Barbara Pickup (Stonor's sister)
John Davenport
Pete Davies (Pete Pan)
Mrs Ione Masada

I had already, when alone with Hilary, discussed the matter of *The Times* stating AM had been converted to Rome. He denied it and promised to write to deny it that night, then when John Davenport arrived he said he had already taken it upon himself to do so, and had phoned *The Times* and that they had promised to print his protest. Summerford, naturally, was not pleased—but the truth will prevail.

Hilary said AM had only begun to fail about 6 weeks ago, when his mind began to wander and the local doctor suggested he was moved to a nursing home at Beaconsfield.—the place was no good and in a few days he was moved to the nuns of St Josephs where he died at 8am on Monday 15. Hilary and his wife had taken over from Janet in August when Janet had returned to Bristol. Stonor felt Machen had not been so happy with his daughter in law as with Janet and that the friendly neighbour Mrs Blackmore had borne this out with her opinion. Janet had acquired the Rev Phillips for the service as AM had liked him (Welsh) and enjoyed his tales of his ministry in Newport. A memorial service is to be given by Phillips at St Thomas off Regent St, on Dec 31. Stonor was delighted he had not been "won over"—after 84 years—to Rome. There is no literary executor, but Summerford will, presumably, "aid" Hilary and Janet—Stonor very much desires me to step in and warmly pleaded with Janet that I should: I merely promised all aid at all times that the Estate could demand of me. There is a rumour of a Penguin edition of *The Hill of Dreams* on the way: AM was very pleased with his 80,000 sale of *Holy*

Terrors. Copies arrived (too late for AM to see) of the Spanish (South American) edition of *The Three Imposters*.

Mrs Travers informed me her late husband Edwin Greenwood's *Skin and Bone* had appeared in Swedish with AM's Preface and Stonor mentioned AM—before the war—had contributed to his forward *The Free Critic* and that Robert Hillier had contributed (? June 1947) an article by AM to *Atlantic Monthly* (Alyse Gregory had shown him a copy). Janet recalled an article on Wordsworth in Wales. Other new material is *Casanova* Preface, Introduction to Hando's book on Monmouthshire, and a page in Oliver Sandys' *Caradoc Evans*. It appears that Mrs Blackmore (a great card-playing friend of Mrs Machen's) was of great service around the time of his death (Palm Sunday '47) taking charge practically completely. Stonor desires to edit The Letters.

Inscription on wreath—

*In fond and respectful remembrance from five admirers of his
immortal art
Henry Savage
Frederick Carter
E.H.W. Meyerstein
David Hay Petrie
'John Gawsworth'.*

Arthur Machen, Anglicanism and the Legend of The "celtic" church

Mark Samuels
originally published in Faunus issue 31

As to your entreaty for us to listen to you, we waive it; yet do return to you this our answer. Our realm and subjects have long been wanderers, walking astray, while they were under the tuition of Romish pastors who advised them to own a wolf for their head (in lieu of a careful shepherd), whose inventions, heresies and schisms be so numerous that the flock of Christ have fed on poisonous shrubs for want of wholesome pastures. And whereas you hit us and our subjects in the teeth, that the Romish Church first planted the Catholic Faith within our realms, the records and chronicles of our realm testify the contrary; and your own Romish idolatry maketh you liars; witness the ancient monument of Gildas;[1] unto which both foreign and domestic have gone in pilgrimage there to offer. This author testifieth Joseph of Arimathea to be the first preacher of the Word of God within our realms. Long after that when Austin [viz. St Augustine of Canterbury] came from Rome, this our realm had bishops and priests therein, as is well known to the wise and learned of our realm by woeful experience, how your church entered therein by blood; they being martyrs for Christ, and put to death, because they denied Rome's usurped authority.
[Reply of Queen Elizabeth I to the plea of five Papal Bishops seeking the reconciliation of Western Christendom]

> *…the same difficulty embarrasses High-Churchmen or so-called 'Anglo-Catholics' today. It is impossible for them to give a clear definition of their position, because they, while abhorring the word Protestant, are essentially Protestant in refusing unity and in preferring a national religion, which can include any degree of heresy, to an international religion which excludes all heresy… They remained (though they would not have admitted it) thoroughly anti-Catholic, because they rejected that one part of Catholic doctrine which is its essential—the combination of unity and authority.*
> [*Hilaire Belloc, Characters of the Reformation, 1936*]

> *It is the old blood calling to the old land.*
> [*A Fragment of Life, Arthur Machen*]

prologue: The Historical Background Prior to 597

Christianity probably first came to these Isles via Roman merchants or legionaries.[2] The first English Catholic saint is Alban, a Roman legionary, who was martyred sometime during the 200s. In the early 300s the Faith was adopted by the Emperor Constantine and legalised across the empire. By 314 there was already established an episcopacy in Britain, and representatives from Lincoln, York and London travelled to the Council of Arles in Gaul. After 410 the Roman Legions were withdrawn to defend Imperial Rome from the sackings of Visigoths.

The church in Britain called for assistance from the Papal See against the Pelagian heresy and requested that two bishops be sent. St Germanus of Auxerre and Lupus of Troyes were sent over in 429. Then, in 446, the church in Britain again requested assistance. On this occasion they also wanted aid in the struggle against Saxons and Picts, so apparently St Germanus returned (reputedly with Severus of Trier). The historicity of this second visit is contested by some scholars.

Thereafter, until the arrival of Pope Gregory the Great's envoy, St Augustine of Canterbury, in 597, historical records are almost a complete blank except for the account of St Gildas written sometime in the 540s. As an historical source it is virtually worthless, being a series of homilies and lurid descriptions of the raids of barbarian pagans, riddled with later interpolations. It does not mention the legend of Joseph of Arimathea founding Christianity in Britain however, instead speculating it was brought to the Isles late in the reign of Tiberius Caesar (d. 37). By whom, he does not say, and probably it is impossible to know. All attempts to do so derive from the realm of legend, not historical fact, and have proved to be speculations or propaganda of much later origin.

Of capital importance is the point that until the time of King Alfred the Great (848—899) there was scarcely any concept of an England as a nation in and of itself. The idea of Wales as a nation unto itself only consolidated when in 1057 Gruffudd ap Llywelyn united Powys, Dyfed, Gwynedd and Glamorgan into one kingdom.

Looking back into this period of history we must not read back from the perspective of being English or Welsh when considering tribal allegiances of the Dark Ages in Britain.

It seems the little kingdoms and tribes warred and interbred, Saxon pagans, the Cymri, the Picts, the Irish, and so on, all amongst fighting one another in a shifting series of territorial alliances and disputes, leading to the withdrawal of the monasteries to the more tranquil western fringes of the Isles. The Christians were, thus, cut off from the rest of western Christendom on the European mainland by the pagan Saxon pirates having established little kingdoms on the east coast.

Hereafter, we have more or less a period of 150 years of isolation of the church in Britain from mainland Europe, until St Augustine arrived in order to firmly consolidate Christianity across the southern and eastern pagan tribes of the Isles, a task beyond the powers of the few existing Bishoprics who were only partially in situ and the inclination of the more numerous monasteries.

It is clear that the church in Britain seems to have developed a few local customs peculiar to itself (in the matter of monastic tonsures, for instance) after separation from the body of Christendom for about a century and a half, but the events of 429 and 446 show, indeed, that the church in Britain was willing to put down even so lacklustre a heresy as the Pelagian one.

It is well to recall that Christendom stood defenceless after the might of Imperial Rome and its legions had lately fallen to the Asiatic hordes of Attila the Hun. It was the lone, isolated, holy Catholic church of the fifth century, assailed by the Asiatic and Germanic Vandal warrior forces of pagan barbarism. It was the beleaguered Petrine bishopric, threatened from all sides, yet still holding fast to a unity upon which the very survival of western Christendom and civilisation depended.

Such is the general position of the church in Britain up until the arrival of Augustine.

celtic saints and Anglo-welsh Kings: The paradoxical catholicity of Arthur Machen

Arthur Machen's true religious views have been known to cause consternation even amongst the most devoted admirers of his work. There are some, like the militant atheist, who desire to bang their head against the nearest wall when reading of them—there are some, like the professional occultist, who will try and lever diabolism into the equation—and then there are even some, the followers of liberal intellectual fashion, who cast over them a hazy pall of bohemian or pagan "spirituality" in order to obfuscate them altogether. Nevertheless, the most interesting of these "some"—to me at least—are those who take Machen's religious views for what they are; "Orthodox", Anglican, deeply sincere and yet deeply contradictory.

It seems to me unsurprising that a number of Machen's (Roman) Catholic friends thought it probable he would eventually go over to Rome. The list of artists who had done so throughout the 1890s is almost interminable.

The sequence seems to be as follows.

In 1896, the Papal Bull *Apostolicae Curae* had been issued by Pope Leo XIII in response to the question of the validity of Anglican Orders. It caused a minor sensation in England. The issue in part arose from the growth of the Oxford Movement in the Church of England, with its high profile conversions and reconsecrations of already high-ranking Anglican clergymen such as Newman and Manning. Pope Leo XIII set up a commission of scholars with varying views so that the question could be re-examined. After due deliberation he pronounced that Anglican orders were "absolutely null and utterly void".

In July 1899 Machen's first wife Amelia Hogg was reconciled upon her deathbed with the (Roman) Catholic Church of her childhood, to, as his friend A.E. Waite said, Machen's "great satisfaction".

Later the same year, in a torment of loneliness and despair after her death, he underwent a self-induced mystical experience (more of this later) and joined the Hermetic Order of the Golden Dawn. Machen did not linger long in the society (later dismissing it as shedding no light on his path), and derived more benefit from his entry onto the stage in 1901.

Significantly, a year later, again to Waite, Machen made his most definite close approach to conversion and declared "I believe I am committed sub conditione to go over to the Latin Church."[3]

Not that it was always thus. Machen's worldview as a young man, that is, up until the summer of 1883, was decidedly secular and "liberal". He described how he had once supported Gladstone, and wrote verse in the Swinburne manner ("in it there were certain violences... about kings and priests").[4] The verse does not survive. *The Anatomy of Tobacco*, written also in 1883 and finished in the autumn of that year, is in part an amusing satire on Medieval Scholasticism and *a priori* considerations but ends on a distinctly non-materialist note. He does not seem to have been much of a church-goer during the period, even after his marriage to the (then) very avowedly bohemian Amy in 1887.

And, of course, there is *The Chronicle of Clemendy* to consider, finished late in 1886. It is difficult to make a case for this picaresque and mildly risqué series of tales being, in any significant sense, concerned with deep religiosity or the beauty of the Gwent landscape. In fact, all the locations could easily be transposed to Medieval France or Italy. Its prime focus is on ribaldry, the amusing antics of Knights and Ladies, ale, wine, and the drollery of monks.

And here is a curious thing, for towards the end of the 1890s, Machen became something of an indifferent Welshman. It is well to recall he was only half-Welsh by blood and had freely adopted the maiden name of his lowland Scottish mother. Perhaps it might also be pertinent to recall the fact that his birthplace, Monmouthshire, was "border country", and was also considered by some authorities to form part of England.[5] Indeed, its exact status was not finalised until well into the second half of the twentieth century.

So it is clear he became much more cosmopolitan after his marriage to the free-spirited Amy, almost, even, a London man of letters, being familiar with the likes of Jerome K. Jerome, Oscar Wilde, M.P. Shiel, John Lane, and living in the comfortable surroundings of Gray's

Inn. When, at this time, he mostly referred to his homeland in his work it was in vague terms of "the West" even in such masterpieces as *The Great God Pan* and *The Three Impostors*.

There is one exception, however, and it is a mighty exception. His most definite literary statement of his Gwent identity: *The Hill of Dreams,* written during 1895 to 1897. Here it cannot be said that the setting is vague, that the landscape might easily be set anywhere in the Celtic fringes. There are too many clear, stark, autobiographical references and deep love and appreciation of Gwent to gainsay the question. And yet, *The Hill of Dreams* is almost nostalgic. Gwent becomes a symbol of a lost, magical land. The novel is elegiac, a farewell to his youthful self and to the past, in the form of Lucian Taylor. For though the young artist and mystic Lucian Taylor finally dies alone in abject poverty in London, Machen had himself lived on into early middle-age, was happily married and now had an independent income.

So too we must consider the matter of his remarks on the then-contemporary "Celtic literary renaissance" which were little short of scathing. He dismissed the movement in an article of 1898 thus;

> *the fanatical race-theorist… has seized upon their productions as so many triumphantly significant sprouts from his absurd genealogical tree. If every syllable written by men of undoubted and undiluted Celtic blood were to vanish tomorrow from our literature, the achievement of England would remain splendid and illustrious as ever… our English immortals hold their session on white thrones forever, unvanquished, eternally crowned.*

But perhaps an even more startling pronouncement, in view of his later views, from the same article, is this;

> *…the original Arthurian Legend was feeble enough certainly when it issued from Wales, for it lacked Guinevere and Lancelot, and the San Graal, and yet this rude story of a British chieftain and his Saxon wars became in the hands of Englishmen and Northmen the supreme and Royal book of the Morte d'Arthur.*[6]

I believe a sea-change came with the rewriting of the fourth chapter of *A Fragment of Life*.[7] In May 1904 this final chapter had been published in Waite's *Horlick's Magazine*. Machen recognised, quite rightly, that it was unsatisfactory and so, shortly after receiving it in print, he set about revising the text. The result, a completely reworked fourth chapter that first saw publication in his collection *The House of Souls*, was nothing less than a triumph. In it Machen reconnects spiritually with his Welsh roots, turning the story of Edward Darnell, an obscure London clerk, into a celebration of mystical heritage reaching across the centuries.

The dull materialism of Darnell's existence is routed utterly by a sense of ancestral connection and splendour. Here Machen begins to make the first tentative use of Celtic myths and legends of Welsh saints that led to a deep interest in the question of the Holy Grail.

> *It would be impossible to carry on the history of Edward Darnell and of Mary his wife to a greater length, since from this point their legend is full of impossible events, and seems to put on the semblance of the stories of the Graal.*[8]

Meanwhile, at the same time, his friend Waite was engaged upon his own research into the origins of the Grail legend. And it seems to have been this correspondence in 1905, along with *A Fragment of Life*, that formed the catalyst for Machen to begin his own Grail research.

> *I wish you could send me the collections you have made on the Graal. In the first place I should very much like to read them; and secondly, coming fresh to the subject, points might strike me which might prove useful in the investigation. But, I think we ought to know more about the survival of the Gnostic Sects; and I am inclined to doubt whether the Manichean sect is the only possible origin. There are other Gnostic heresies which might easily have lingered in the Syrian hills—which, perhaps, are there now.*[9]

He rapidly found himself deeply immersed in a six months study of the origins of the Grail legend in the British Museum and began to form and articulate his own theory about the "Celtic" Church.

Looking back at his mystical episode of 1899 from the vantage point of 1905, during his researches into the Grail and the "Celtic" Church, Machen uncovered a curious parallel in history. Twice he makes clear reference to it:

> *It was with a singular surprise that I read, in St Adamnan, many years afterwards, how St Columba's monks, toiling in the fields, experienced now and again the very sensation—if it be just to speak of it as a sensation—that I have described. They, too, weary with their work of reclaiming the barren land of their isle, would know that sudden glow of joy and strength and courage; and they believed it was the prayer of their Father in God, Columba, strengthening them and inspiring them, as he knelt before the altar of the Perpetual Choir.[10]*

> *I have never forgotten my almost incredulous amazement when I found out, seven years afterwards, that some of these experiences had also been experiences of the monks of St Columba's congregation at Iona.[11]*

The monks at Iona were, or so Machen thought them, Celtic and not Roman monks.

The seeds that had been sown in *A Fragment of Life* grew into a doctrine. Machen went on to swallow whole the then-popular historical theory about a separate native "Celtic" Church.

He soon made a dramatic volte-face: the possibility of his "going over to Rome" suddenly vanished forever, for in February 1906, his studies concluded, he flatly declared to Waite: "in the Popish Church as the sole custodian of the Faith or Sacraments I utterly disbelieve!"[12]

It is true that Brocard Sewell maintained that Machen was a *anima naturaliter catholica* who upheld orthodox Catholic doctrinal and moral teachings.[13] And it is also true that Machen still railed bitterly against the Anglican bishops and fashionable moral posturing of the C of E. The Anglican church had sunk into what he derided as the creed of "Mr Feeble Goodygoodyman with his passion for the obvious, the moralising moral, the everlasting commonplace."[14]

But in this question of the "Celtic" Church, Machen unwittingly ended up actually championing a Protestant historical fabrication. He adopted, as had the English Protestant establishment which had carefully cultivated the legend in official history, the "Celtic" church as the native religion of these Isles, and viewed the Papal mission headed by St Augustine as collaborators in a "Saxon" or English takeover of the Isles.

It is here necessary to familiarise the reader with Machen's own words on the subject. Amongst his more striking claims are the following.

He tells of "the war between the Roman and Celtic churches".[15]

He tells of "the decay and ruin of a great Church, which once posted its outposts to the very gates of Rome and spoke with the Pope on equal terms... the sacramental legend of the vanished, or almost vanished, Celtic Church".[16]

The Irish Abbot of this "Celtic" Church who spoke with such authority was St Columbanus.[17] He it was who, Machen tells us, had "addressed the Holy Father as an equal, not without a hint that any case of error or heresy on the part of the Chief Bishop of Christendom would meet with due correction from the Celtic monk."[18]

Now St Columbanus had founded other monasteries elsewhere on the continent. He had written to accuse Pope Boniface IV of Nestorian tendencies in 612, insisting that his order was not schismatical or heretical but Catholic. But it is clear from this he writes as an insider, not an outsider, and was concerned that it could cause a scandal for the See of Peter. Indeed, he was a frequent letter writer to Popes. Earlier, in 602, he had written to Pope Gregory I pleading with "the Holy Pope, his Father" to use his authority against the bishops in Gaul, where he had set up more monasteries and caused a rumpus. It is true that the rule (that is, the monastic customs) of St Columbanus was more severe than the more usual rule of St Benedict. So, too, did St Columbanus differ in the date of the celebration of Easter.

Yet what the example of St Columbanus demonstrates is not the existence of a separate "Celtic" Church independent of Papal primacy, but only the very common tribal disagreements that prevailed across Christendom.

Rome, at no point, sought to stamp a "Celtic" church out as heretical, as it did with the Arians, nor did it view it as a deadly rival as it did later with the very real Albigensian Church. There are no Papal edicts against the "Celtic" Church simply because, as a separate unity, it had no existence.

Some adherents of the idea of a "Celtic" Church cite the Synod of Whitby of 664 as the moment when it was finally "subjugated" by Rome. This, however, was only one of a series of similar councils held throughout Christendom to harmonise the most important date in the Christian calendar, Easter. Moreover, at the end of such councils, it was customary for all present to acknowledge that St Peter, and his successors as Pope of Rome, had final authority over Christendom (an acknowledgement, as usual, affirmed in Whitby).

One of the other common claims often made concerning the so-called "Celtic" Church is to draw an analogy between the position of this "Celtic" Church and the Eastern Orthodox Church in its relations with Papal Rome.

The schism threatening to split Christendom into two, between Papal Rome and the Eastern Orthodox Church, reached a climacteric in 1054, that is, some five hundred years after the supposed conflict between the "Celtic" Church and Papal Rome. The divide between Papal Rome and the Eastern Orthodox church was a consequence of a series of factors, but perhaps the most decisive of all was the final transfer of the Imperial Roman Empire to Constantinople in 476, after the last western Roman Emperor was deposed.

Thereafter, Christendom slowly began to separate into Western Latin and Eastern Greek bishoprics. The full process of separation took place over several hundreds of years, and it was during this period, at various junctures, that the Eastern Orthodox Church disputed the doctrine of Papal Supremacy. Without Papal Supremacy, unity itself was impossible, as history later clearly demonstrated. By the 1450s the rupture between the two was regarded as definitive.

Now for those of my readers whose instinctive reaction is to recoil at the very notion of "Papal Supremacy" there are two points to be made. Firstly, we are talking about spiritual and not temporal primacy. Secondly, it is not possible to "read history backwards" and view the struggle as one of centralisation (the Latin See) and democracy (the Greek Sees), and follow up by mumbling something about the sinister nature of Ultramontanism under one's breath. For it was in Constantinople that the concept of the Emperor-Pope ("Caesaropapism") first arose under the Byzantine Emperor Justinian I. The glamorisation of Eastern Orthodoxy, in the west, is frequently the last resort in which to exhibit an acceptable anti-Papal mania that has always been culturally endemic in the "official" English Whig-Protestant version of history (of which more later).

Machen himself elaborates upon the misleading Eastern Orthodox "parallel", claiming that the "Celtic" Church had its own liturgy of an Eastern Orthodox origin rather than of the western Latin Rite,

> ...the Celtic Church was really the work of the fifth century and was organised by [the] Gallican missionaries; and that being granted it follows necessarily that the churches of Britain and Ireland were of the type that is called Oriental.[19]

Here Machen is referring to the Syrian-Greek rites of Jerusalem and Antioch which today we would term Eastern Orthodox and the "Gallican missionaries" refers to the visits of St Germanus of Auxerre in 429 and 446. But in no sense can these two visits be regarded as "missionary" work. In the first case, it is clear St Germanus was invited over by the existing British church, was suggested by a synod of bishops in Gaul, and with the sanction of the then Pope Celestine.[20]

However, since there are no records of a specific Celtic liturgy, that is, a liturgy common to all the churches in the British Isles, the question of diverse rites across western Christendom has no real significance. Most of the fragments that remain are from Ireland (the "Stowe" Missal) and the rest are often contradictory to it, and to each other. Even within the Irish fragments alone the order of the Mass cannot be reconstructed.

Machen's own conclusions were not so circumspect:

> "...the Romances celebrate and glorify the curious and ancient quarrel between Roman and Celtic Christianity... the anti-Celtic fervour of the Roman Authorities was so thorough that there is no such thing as a Celtic Liturgy in existence...[21]

One needs here to be quite clear on the serious charge Machen makes; that Papal Rome had eradicated all trace of this "rival", unified, Celtic liturgy of Ireland, Scotland, Wales and Cornwall. There is simply no historical evidence for such a radical claim.

Certainly, there were alternate liturgies in existence around the same time as the Roman rite (for example the Ambrosian, Gallican and

Mozarabic rites) but the very fact of their existence did not signify any challenge to the idea of the primacy of Rome.

It is generally agreed that the religious communities in Britain had developed diverse rites as a consequence of their 150 year near-isolation from the rest of Christendom. But the aim of Rome was not the deliberate eradication of a pre-existing rival liturgy, but to unify what was a multitude of confusing local customs.

Machen outlines his organisational theory as follows:

> *The hagiology of the British Church begins, for all practical purposes with the post-Roman period, and tells how Pelagianism having overwhelmed the island, certain saints from Gaul came over, routed the heretics, and established orthodoxy. It has been suggested that for Pelagianism we should read Paganism, and that the two saints, Germanus and Lupus were, in reality, the evangelisers of Britain... Celtic scholars have wondered how an imaginative people could have been attracted by the heresy of Pelagius—which is more stupid and unenlightened than the common run of heresies—and the answer may be that the British never were attracted by this new theology of the fifth century.[22]*

This account is worth comparing with one in the most popular books of the Victorian era on the subject, *The Liturgy and Ritual of the Celtic Church* (1886) by Frederick Edward Warren[23] (pages 100-101):

> *There are no substantial grounds for impugning the orthodoxy of the Celtic Church. Certainly Britain like the rest of Christendom may have been partially tainted... with Pelagianism in the fifth century, which was the cause of a joint visit by joint bishops... the real difficulty here is to understand how the rationalism of Pelagius can have had even a passing attraction for the naturally superstitious and mystic Celt, not how Germanus succeeded in stamping it out.*

But whereas Warren employs a visionary national trait as part of his argument for orthodox continuity in an independent "Celtic" Church that did not require Papal influence, Machen employs the same visionary national trait as an argument for the "Celtic" Church's establishment outside of Papal influence!

What Machen did not see was that the spurious legend of an independent "Celtic" Church was a by-product of the rewriting of history at the time of the English Reformation and the establishment of an English empire within the British Isles. The process that began with a disagreement between Henry VIII and Pope Clement VI over the monarch's wish to annul his marriage to Catherine of Aragon finally ended with the establishment of an alternative, national-spiritual rival to the Papacy.

There were attempts at the English Reformation to get around this difficulty of there not being a native British church independent of Papal Rome. So it was that the Protestant exile William Tyndale's theological ideas, such as the word of the King being God's word, inspired Thomas Cromwell (effectively the minister for Erastian propaganda in Henry's court) to set to work one John Bale (1495—1563). As well as producing a number of distorted historical plays, it was he, in his later tract, who co-wrote, with the infamous John Foxe, the book *Acts and Monuments* (1563), which cast the Papal mission of 597 as the work of the Anti-Christ assailing the true church of Christ, the native Anglo-Welsh church.

The appeal to patriotism is one of the most persuasive forces to affect the mind of man. He can be made to swallow almost any lie if it lends glory to his own nation.

What did Machen mean when calling himself a "Catholic"? Principally, he meant he felt he belonged to the Catholic Church as much as any "Papist". He meant "Catholicism" without Papal Supremacy. And, in Anglicanism, that meant the national King or Queen was the Head of the Church. But one has to bear in mind that to the end (1547) Henry VIII regarded himself as Catholic. He was firm in his loyalty to the Mass. Machen may have castigated Henry VIII for the part he played in the English Reformation, and he did so heartily, but his own national Catholicism is indistinguishable from that monarch's. However, the break with Rome, which may have been repaired within a generation, was then fostered by those noblemen who eventually benefited most from it, particularly in the destruction and looting of the abbeys, and seizure of the lands. The period of 597 to 1534 was thereafter rewritten as being one of Papal occupation. By the time of Elizabeth I, the break was turning permanent, and the vision of England and Wales as being fully Protestant took firm hold and the final rupture was achieved when Bishops began to be consecrated to secure the perpetuation of the English Reformation and not with the historicity of Catholicism in mind.[24] Unbroken sacramental continuity was no idle concern for the likes of Machen. Knowing how vital this point was, it was necessary therefore he doggedly adhered to this idea that Anglican orders were still valid.[25]

Without them, there could not still subsist within the C of E communion any sacraments at all, save that of lay baptism. If the sacramental nature of Anglicanism was really broken during the English Reformation then what remains is nothing more than a masquerade imitating rituals that have lost their core sacramentalism, even in the "High Church" or "Anglo-Catholic" wing.

Indeed, he must have realised that all of his arguments against the dissenting churches, that whole school of endless subdivision after subdivision, which he regarded as noxious fungi, could equally be turned against his own Anglicanism.

The conclusion: in which no conclusion is reached

These are regarded as old, tedious quarrels. What were vital questions to Machen and his contemporaries, are more likely to raise a yawn in the new age of spiritual darkness wherein intellectual secularism has culturally triumphed over all its foes except Islam (with whom it may well be forced to make an eventual political accommodation). Perhaps the last serious literary flourish of such debates in England was Evelyn Waugh's heavy-handed attempt to shock John Betjeman out of his Anglicanism in 1946. Much of their mutual distress stemmed from the fact that each saw the other as belonging to a "sect".[26]

The conclusion of the Second Vatican Council in 1962 opened up a fresh dialogue between Rome, the world, and the rest of Christendom, but shared communion remains a distant prospect. Closed communions persist to this day not only in Roman Catholicism, and in some denominations of the Protestant churches, but also in the Eastern Orthodox church.

Machen's opinion of the changes in the Anglican church since his death in 1947 would doubtless have been even more condemnatory than in his lifetime. But I am not sure he would have found the post-Conciliar Roman Catholic Church a much more pleasant prospect to contemplate. As for the "Celtic" Church, that legend now persists hardly anywhere aside from the far fringes of Christianity with its autocephalous, *episcopi vagantes*. The key issue of licit apostolic succession in such instances has become so muddied as to be almost impossible to determine, at least by this poor scholar.

I almost wrote that perhaps Machen would have turned Eastern Orthodox had he been born a hundred years later, but, thinking it over, I am not sure either that he would have thrown in his spiritual lot with what is, since the end of Soviet communism, little more than a Pan-Nationalist Church. After all, seven-eighths of all Eastern Orthodox adherents today are Russian. And Machen's views about Russia do not bear reprinting in this august journal.

Endnotes

[1] Attributed to William of Malmesbury (1095-1143?) not Gildas (500-570?).

[2] The spurious notion of Joseph of Arimathea having founded Christianity in Glastonbury shortly after the crucifixion is now generally regarded as a later interpolation by that abbey's monks into William of Malmesbury's *De Antiquitate.*

[3] Selected Letters (1988), p.32.

[4] "The Young Man in the Blue Suit" see *Faunus* #2, Autumn 1998.

[5] See, for example, the entry for "Monmouthshire" in *The Encyclopedia Britannica,* Vol. XVIII, 1911, p.728.

[6] "The All-Pervading Celt", Arthur Machen, *Literature*, 8th January 1898.

[7] Machen states *A Fragment of Life* was partially based on an 1890 tale called "The Resurrection of the Dead" published in a society journal whose name he since forgot. The tale has not been discovered.

[8] *A Fragment of Life*, Tartarus Press, (2000), pg 105.

[9] *Selected Letters* (1988), p.36.

[10] *Things Near and Far* (1923, 2nd Knopf edition) p.197-199.

[11] *The London Adventure* (1924, Village Press ed 1974) p.13.

[12] *Selected Letters*, (1988), p.39.

[13] *The Aylesford Review*, Winter (1959-60).

[14] *The Glorious Mystery* (1924), p.144.

[15] *The Secret of the Sangraal* (1995), p.5.

[16] *The Secret of the Sangraal* (1995), p.232.

[17] Not to be confused with St Columba of Iona.

[18] *The Secret of the Sangraal* (1995), p.29.

[19] *The Glorious Mystery* (1924), p.26.

[20] See Prosper of Aquitaine's *Epitoma Chronicon* c.429 for a direct contemporary source. Bede's *Historia Ecclesiastica gentis Anglorum* c.731 partially derives from it.

[21] *The Glorious Mystery* (1924), p.25.

[22] *The Glorious Mystery* (1924), p.12.

[23] Machen mentions having exchanged some letters on the Celtic Church with Warren, see *Selected Letters* (1988), p.104.

[24] Ordinations according to the *Edwardine Prayer Book* rite.

[25] "If a clerk in holy orders of the English Communion is not a Catholic priest he is one of the most melancholy humbugs and imposters that the world has produced." Ecclesia Anglicana II, *The Glorious Mystery* (1924) p.171.

[26] Cf "The C of E is The Catholic Church... and English Romanism is sectarian." Quote by Betjeman in 1963, and "you are being allowed to see a glimpse of the truth broad enough to damn you if you reject it now... it is doubtful how many formal heretics really commit the sin of heresy—of seeing the truth and denying it." Letter from Waugh to Betjeman, 9th January 1947.

The Great Pan-Demon:
An Unspeakable Story

Arthur Sykes
The National Observer, 4th May 1895
Published in Faunus Issue 31

"Libet mihi efficere ut membra tua horreant" dixit Puer Pinguis.
DICKENSIUS

[*The following narrative was discovered among the manuscript papers of the late Dr Frankenstein, the well known symbolist and diabolist of Vigo Street. It has been deciphered and translated with some difficulty from the original chemist's Latin, with which the author sought to veil his incredible experiences. The date "Kal. Apr. 1895," appears on the right hand corner of the MS. Below this is a barely legible motto, written in pencil, which may be read as Cred. quant. Stuff.*]

I have grave doubts as to whether the scientific world is yet ready to accept my astonishing physiological discoveries. I prefer, therefore, to commit them to the obscurity of a dead language, an appropriate medium and repository for these secrets of the charnel-house. It is possible, however, that my friend and literary executor, D., may at some future time consider that the psychologic moment has arrived to strike therewith a fresh keynote. In that case, I beg to disclaim in advance all responsibility for any mental alienation undergone by the reader, or any violence done to his sense of literary art and of verisimilitude.

For some years past I had been engaged on my *magnum opus*—the Demonic Origin and Properties of the Pineal Gland or Median Eye. In the course of my laborious investigations I had made not a few perfectly appalling discoveries, which I hesitate to communicate, even in the language of symbols. But the functions of one particular brain-cell had always baffled my attempts at elucidation. This cell, which I found to be only present in persons of marked cataleptic tendencies, is of microscopic dimensions, rarely exceeding 1-1000th of a millimetre in diameter. None, even of the leading brain-surgeons, had hitherto noticed its existence. I was determined, therefore, not to be beaten, and, if necessary, to dedicate my whole life-work to research in this direction. I felt, from incidental scientific evidence (which I dare not specify or even hint at) that, under certain conditions, the reaction of this cell, situated in the exact centre of the pineal gland, to a cerebro-chemical stimulus would produce the effect I had so long striven to obtain. This result was simply the transformation of a corpse into a devil.

I was in my dissecting room late one night, busily engaged, after a somewhat imprudent evening meal, in completing an experiment on a fairly fresh cadaver, that of a full-grown male idiot. I had obtained the required pineal cell from a hydrocephalous female subject, who had died of peripheral-epileptic dyscraniorrhagtis, and whose autopsy I had just attended. This I treated in vain with a long series of acid and alkaline reagents, and was almost giving up in despair, when the thought flashed across my mind that I had not yet tried tetramyldiethylbenzoamidochloroxaltriphenylbromine. I rushed for the phial, and with a quivering hand poured a solution of this elixir mortis over the cell. On placing it immediately under my microscope, I began to notice an indescribable and mysterious organic change. Seizing a three-drain basanometer in one hand and a No. 2 Poupart's hodospore in the other, I rapidly transferred the already metabolising cell to the point of a compound Eustachian probe. I then inserted it behind the fifth antero-posterior convolution of the cadaver's cerebellum through an aperture previously trephined in the skull, and sank down in an operating chair, exhausted with excitement, to watch the effect.

I had not long to wait. As I gazed, I was hypnotized by the horror that slowly unfolded itself before my eyes. No hashish-vision, no ghoul-dream of Doré, could image the thing, or rather, the unnameable

No-thing that was incarnated in my presence, the offspring of my own brain, the creation of my own hands. I watched, with staring eye-balls and blanched lips, the gradual evolution of the inert mass into the embodiment of the Utter Diabolic. It shrank at first to a Devil-embryo, foul, repulsive, androgynous, abortional, a fœtus-product of the obscenest union of ægipans and hell-hags. Thence the Devil-babe, my bantling, grew and grew, instinct with the very Negation of life, endued with the death-energy which causes after-growth of a dead-woman's hair, or the gestation and coffin-birth of a corpse-mother's child. But I must not tell of all its hideous series of transfigurations, of its passage through the forms of satyr and sphinx and she-centaur, while in its cyclopean eye, directed towards myself, there gradually dawned a horrific light, a Satanic intelligence.

Meanwhile, though my gaze was directed on the object before me and its awful adolescence, I was conscious of a horrible alteration in my surroundings. I was in the centre of the lost Pleiad, the abode of damned souls. Possessed now of a sixth sense, that of molecular actinism, which superseded all the others, and of yet a seventh, the knowledge of all evil, I cast off the limits of time and space. I heard and smelt and tasted with my eyes, and smelt and tasted and saw with my ears, and thought unthinkable thoughts. I cannot record my impressions in this state as my concepts were not reducible to the terms of any known or possible language. The totality of evil flashed in the millionth of an instant in the universal Lost Soul, the multiplex occupant of chaos, of the annihilated limbo of the universe.

I may not describe the entities which were the malevolent denizens of the lost Pleiad. They were existent and non-existent simultaneously, but are only comprehensible to the owners of a seventh sense. But I was actinically aware of an addition to their number—the result of my experiment. This was announced by audible letters of fire, burnt into my brain with inconceivably cold and foul-smelling sounds, and written in the language of Hell. What the actual words were I must not relate, but I give their Latin equivalents in the form of an inscription:

> DIVO.M.PANJANDRO.
> SEU.DIABOLO.ABSURDISSIMO.
> HANC.CLAVIFORMEM.NOTAM.
> POSUTT.BODLEIANUM.CAPUT.

Whilst I considered over their point and application with what now appears to have been remarkable self-possession, the shape was executing an infinite medley of synchronous quick-turn changes, from Venus of the cross-roads with her beauté de diable to the most bestial Harpy or Tanith with the direst attractions of hellish repulsiveness. He-she-it transfixed me with a lurid leer, with a cobra glance of quenchless lubricity, and the octopus-tentacles of a noisome lust-fury wound themselves round my very soul. I felt myself drawn from out my vitals downwards, and ever downwards, under the influence of a malignant and monstrous Bodily-Head, and plunged for a million years into unfathomable malebolge. I fell from Hades to Hades, and underwent all the torments of Inferno in each. At last I reached the bottom of the Bottomless Pit. I opened my eyes, and found myself on the floor of my dissecting room, at the foot of my operating chair.

Well, I had learnt at any rate the secret of Death Life, and had seen the Great Pan-demon in his own pandemonium…

[*Here the MS. rather abruptly ends. It should perhaps be added that the writer finished his days in a private establishment for patients suffering from demonomania.—Translator's note.*]

"a wilder reality"
euhemerism and
arthur machen's "little people"

emily Fergus
originally published in Faunus issue 32

> And as the "worms" and dragons of the ancient songs, and
> the "roc" of the Arabian tales are doubtless memories of the
> iguanodons and plesiosauri and pterodactyls, so the wildest
> myth may prove to be founded on a, perhaps, wilder reality.
> [*Arthur Machen.*]

Little people are everywhere in Machen's tales. They scamper and crawl across the pages, playing major (and largely malevolent) roles in "The Shining Pyramid", "The Novel of the Black Seal" and "The Red Hand", all written in 1895. They are the subjects of "The Turanians", one of the elegiac prose-poems collected as *Ornaments in Jade*, written in 1897, and they appear in "The White People" of 1899. Even in *A Fragment of Life* one makes an oblique and fleeting appearance when a "horrible boy" with red hair appears suddenly with "a dreadful face, with something unnatural about it, as if it had been a dwarf". Machen continued to write about little people throughout his life in fiction: they materialise in "Out of the Earth", first published in *T.P.'s Weekly* in 1915, in "Opening the Door", written in 1931, and in his final novel *The Green Round* (1933). He also wrote articles about them during his career as a journalist, from 1887 to at least 1924. Scholars have tended to focus on Machen's "little people" mythos as representative of fin-de-siècle anxieties about decadence and degeneration. I want to suggest, rather, that the negative emotions of "fear" and "anxiety" inevitably ascribed to degeneration theory have occluded other, more hopeful and spiritual readings of Machen's texts.

The anthropological theory of euhemerism was widely-known and widely-accepted during the last two decades of the nineteenth century. Indeed, Carole Silver contends that even by 1883, it was "almost taken for granted that the dwarfs, trolls, and fairies were folk memories of prehistoric races of small people". However, euhemerism has been insufficiently taken into account when considering these little people narratives. There is a theory that belief in mythological dragons is rooted in the ancient presence of pterosaurs, and other dinosaurs, who left their fossils behind for early man to discover. Similarly, euhemerism suggests that the myth of fairies, elves, dwarfs, and so on is based on the prehistoric existence of a race of real little people. Hounded out by the taller, more powerful Celts, these "Turanians" hid under the hills, appearing only at night, dancing by moonlight for exercise, and occasionally stealing food, and sometimes even women or babies, from their oppressors. The euhemerist hypothesis that a race of smaller-than-average people had colonised Western Europe before the incursion of taller, Aryan or Celtic, tribes, appeared to embed fairy fantasy in a firm scientific base, and certain accounts, published during the 1890s, maintained that these people still lived, largely hidden in inaccessible areas of Morocco, the Pyrenees, and Switzerland. Euhemerist ideas have been an under-recognised aspect of the mixture of weird imagination and science that characterises the late-Victorian gothic. Machen, as well as other writers of weird fiction at the fin de siècle, such as Grant Allen and John Buchan, was particularly influenced by the work of the euhemerist anthropologist David MacRitchie who deemed euhemerism the "'realistic' interpretation of such traditions". The interpretation of Machen's "little people" stories takes on a very different quality when read through a euhemerist rather than a degenerative lens.

Machen made no secret of his belief in the euhemerist hypothesis. In 1898 he reviewed the euhemeristically-inclined *Folklore and Legends of the North* for *Literature*, and made the following comment:

> *Of recent years abundant proof has been given that a short, non-Aryan race once dwelt beneath the ground, in hillocks, throughout Europe, their raths have been explored, and the weird old tales of green hills all lighted up at night have received*

confirmation. Much in the old legends may be explained by a reference to this primitive race. The stories of changelings, and captive women, become clear on the supposition that the "fairies" occasionally raided the houses of the invaders... We might deduce the whole mythology from a confused recollection of the relations existing between the tall Aryans and the short Turanians.

Machen is so often presented as anti-materialist, it seems perhaps strange that he was so convinced of the truth of what was, after all, seeking to establish itself as a *scientific* theory. But really, it was an article of faith for Machen not that the material world is of less value than the immaterial, but that the material and immaterial worlds are indivisible.

When Machen writes, in "The Novel of the White Powder" that all the elements of our world "are each and every one as spiritual, as material, and subject to an inner working", he encapsulates his belief that the spiritual and the material are not divided, that each contain elements of the other. Dr Raymond, in *The Great God Pan*, quotes from Oswald Crollius, a somewhat obscure seventeenth-century alchemist, saying, "In every grain of wheat, there lies hidden the soul of a star". Machen returned to this quote in his autobiography, calling it "a wonderful saying; a declaration, I suppose, that all matter is one, manifested under many forms". This amalgamated worldview, where the real contains aspects of the unreal, the mundane aspects of the fantastic, was key to Machen's understanding and acceptance of euhemerism as a basis for interpreting belief in fairies, and that it was this belief that primarily animated his "little people" mythos, rather than anxiety about degeneration. Machen was convinced of the truth of a euhemeristic interpretation of the widespread belief in the "little people", in which they were a matter of historical fact, rather than a figment of supernatural imagination. Perhaps this conviction, and his evident delight in it, was due to euhemerism's innate revelatory quality. Unlike the unveiling of tawdry theatrical mechanisms that mimic stage magic, euhemerism, with its sourcing of fairy-fantasy in the literally earthly discoveries of archaeological digs, has at its heart the demonstration of the indivisibility of the material and the immaterial. Contained within the material exterior is the magical truth, like the soul of a star in a grain of wheat, or a green hill, beneath which hide an unexpected tribe of little people.

Machen's little people also function as exemplars of his theories about literary ecstasy and spiritual transformation, their existence deployed by the author to demonstrate the universe's essential mystery. S.T. Joshi has noted that there is awe mixed with the horror experienced by Machen's narrators when they come into contact with the little people, which Joshi ascribes to their embodiment of Machen's dichotomy of both "sorcery and sanctity", each "an ecstasy, a withdrawal from the common life".

By suggesting that prehistoric hominids have lived as "savage survivals", hidden and unknown, as modern, urban humanity evolved, the idea of atavism is reframed so that it becomes a quality of endurance rather than a random event, the renascence of a transgressive, ancient mythic force in contemporary society. Machen's "little people" are not degenerated, but re-generated, surfacing as material warnings against the lazy acceptance of superficial appearances ("The Red Hand"), or of mistaking ancient, pagan ritual for uneducated superstition ("The White People") and underestimating the power of ancient artefacts ("The Novel of the Black Seal"). Although frequently dangerous, they are not always so: in "The Turanians", for example, there is little hint of threat, except to bourgeois complaisance. And they are always symbols of powerful longevity, as ur-human as they are ab-human, and equally representative of Machen's concept of the indivisibility of the material and immaterial worlds, of the universe as a "tremendous sacrament", as they are of degeneration anxieties.

"The Novel of the Black Seal" will be so well-known to readers of *Faunus* that it needs little introduction here. The superstition surrounding the "little people" of the hills around Caermaen is set up by Professor Gregg's early reference to local fairytales: of "a servant-girl at a farmhouse, who disappeared from her place and has never been heard of", the unexplained death of a child, and of the killing of a man by "a blow from a strange weapon". There is the "Pomponius Mela" manuscript, which Miss Lally translates as speaking of a folk who dwell "in remote and secret places", who "hate the sun", and who hiss rather than speak. There is, of course, the Black Seal itself, and finally, there is Jervase Cradock, with his curious provenance, his access to the "secrets of the underworld", his transformative, tentacular abilities, and his hissing speech, which seems to link him that "race who had lagged far behind the rest". Jervase is clearly of that race himself, a race in which atavism is complicated by enhanced admission to the supernatural. The attention to local superstitions, Professor Gregg's profession as a celebrated ethnologist, the archaeological artefacts that point the way to the people of the Grey Hills—including the Black Seal—embed the story and Professor Gregg's quest firmly in anthropological euhemerism.

Machen adds two elements of fantasy to the basic euhemerist construct: the supernatural abilities of the "little people", and their continued existence. Neither element is presented as solely horrific. Jervase's tentacle is certainly grotesque, and Gregg is, indeed, left horrified, "white and shuddering, with sweat pouring from my flesh" at the sight. But before he actually witnesses the episode, he is convinced that it is not supernatural, that Jervase's body may be an example of that human flesh which is "the veil of powers which seem magical to us", powers that are "survivals from the depths of being". Afterwards, he has considerable trouble convincing himself that Jervase's tentacle is indeed as natural as the action of "a snail pushing out his horns and drawing them in" again, yet—or, perhaps, therefore—determines to go and meet "the 'Little People' face to face". And although he fully expects not to return, he willingly pursues his curiosity to its ultimate end, and his determination to proceed is equally fired by the anachronistic longevity of the little people. This Gregg denotes as both as horrifying and as fascinating as the idea that one of his "confrères of physical science, roaming in a quiet English wood, had been suddenly stricken aghast by the presence of the slimy and loathsome terror of the ichthyosaurus, the original of the stories of the awful worms killed by valorous knights, or had seen the sun darkened by the pterodactyl, the dragons of tradition". Gregg's mixed reactions are "a strange confusion of horror and elation" that resolves into a "passion of joy" that he has made this incredible and exciting discovery. Gregg is figured as a heroic hunter of essential, spiritual reality, as a daring quester after ultimate truth, which is the existence of the fantastic, the immaterial, behind the material veil. His disappearance is no failure: he has found what he sought, even if he has paid with his life.

The survival of an ancient race into the modern world can certainly be figured as atavistic, but it can also be read as a measure of endurance, of permanence and even of nobility. In his prose-poem "The Turanians" Machen makes his "little people" much more marvellous than monstrous.

"The Turanians" is the fragmentary tale of a young girl, Mary, who is transfigured by her brief association with a member of the wandering tribe. By conceiving his Turanians as wild rather than savage, Machen gives them immediate access to nature, and figures them as more spiritually evolved than their ignorant, "civilised" contemporaries. Machen's "little people", whether threatening or not, are always the keepers of a lost connection with the sublime, and he often used them to illustrate the essential permeability of the boundary between the natural and the super- or preternatural worlds. "The Turanians" begins: "The smoke of the tinkers' camp rose a thin pale blue from the heart of the wood." With this wording Machen hints that the tinkers' camp is the heart of the wood, which puts them at the heart of Machen's transcendent world of natural mystery. For him, the woods about his home in Gwent were "a kind of fairyland", and ancient woodland encapsulated the glamour and fascination of the unknown: "Paths full of promise allured me into green depths... And so I crossed Wentwood, and felt not that I knew it, but that it was hardly to be known". Into this mysterious woodland comes Mary, on a hot summer's day, the forest path offering a cooler alternative to the "brown August fields", the spreading oaks shading "a winding way of grass that cooled her feet". Mary is a fey, sensitive girl, whose dramatic imagination is of concern to her mother, but which also marks her out as a Machenian fellow-traveller, one whose super-sensitive mind is worthy of exposure to a higher consciousness.

In *Hieroglyphics*, his essay on ecstasy in literature, Machen wrote that in great literature "[W]e are withdrawn from the common ways of life; and in that withdrawal is the beginning of ecstasy". In "The Turanians", Mary's walk down the forest path, from her comfortable, safe home, and into the wild wood, denotes just such a withdrawal, and signals her openness to another, transcendental, experience. Away from her mother, Mary is free to indulge her emotional and sensual connection to the natural world: she walks "in a green cloud"; the strong sunlight makes "the tree-stems, the flowers, and her own hands seem new"; the familiar wood-path has become "full of mystery and hinting, and every turn brought a surprise". "[T]he mere sense of being alone under the trees was an acute secret joy", and when she loosens her hair, she sees that it "was not brown but bronze and golden, glowing on her pure white dress". She begins a process of transfiguration—trees to flowers, new hands, brown hair to bronze—which prefigures her transformation to the preternatural via the natural when she sees her reflection in a woodland pool as a "smiling nymph".

Mary hears "strange intonations" emanating from the camp, which suggest the Turanians are in tune with both nature and the divine. Their song is "almost chanting", pleasing Mary "with a rise and fall of notes and a wild wail, and the solemnity of unknown speech". This speech, unlike Jervase's hissing, is in harmony with the woodland sounds—the drip of the well, "the birds' sharp notes, and the rustle and hurry of the woodland creatures"—but also has a ritual, prayerful resonance as "the voices thrilled into an incantation". Mary lacks the courage to go and talk to "these strange wood-folk" and is "afraid to burst into the camp"—and the sense here is clearly that she is not afraid of them, but afraid to disturb their incantatory, curiously religious meeting. Instead, she waits under a tree "hoping that one of them might happen to come her way". Mary's lack of fear and the lexis of devotion—"intonations", "chanting", "solemnity", "harmony"—as she draws nearer the gypsies' camp marks the Turanians as unworldly, mystical, perhaps holy, and certainly not monstrous or threatening. The Turanians are soon described in more detail: they are "people of curious aspect, short and squat, high-cheekboned, with dingy yellow skin and long almond eyes", the typical anthropological description of the ancient, short-statured Turanians. The camp includes a "swarm of fantastic children, lolling and squatting about the fire, gabbling to one another in their singsong speech", but "in one or two of the younger men there was a suggestion of a wild, almost faunlike grace, as of creatures who always moved between the red fire and the green leaf". In this context, the faun reference seems much more benign than it does in *The Great God Pan*, and their place "between the red fire and the green leaf" positions them somewhere between man and nature, or nature and the divine, perhaps as interlocutors.

Most intriguing, however, is the notion that these people "were in reality Turanian metal-workers, degenerated into wandering tinkers". The use of that most loaded of fin de siècle terms, "degenerated", is both problematic and highly suggestive. What does Machen mean by it in this context? The word inevitably has an evolutionary (or devolutionary) quality, and may suggest a certain amount of physical degeneration: perhaps their smallness of stature is a sign of this, although the

Turanians, to whose race they belong and from whom they have "degenerated" were believed to be a dwarf race anyway. Perhaps their movements, specifically "lolling and squatting" and in a subsequent description, their appearance as "a procession of weird bowed figures… one stumbling after another" while "the children crawled last, goblinlike, fantastic", might be a sign of physical degeneration, although it is equally probable that their figures are "weird" and "bowed" because each carries a "huge shapeless pack". It might refer to a certain mental degeneration, although the fact that they are "gabbling to one another in their singsong speech" does not suggest, surely, that their language is meaningless, merely that Mary cannot understand it. It certainly does not refer to any kind of moral or spiritual degeneration, given that Mary is not frightened of them, and they are repeatedly framed as profoundly connected both to nature and to the spiritual. Rather, I think "degenerated" here is used primarily in a social, a hierarchical context. They are now called gypsies, but they were "Turanian metal-workers… their ancestors had fashioned the bronze battle-axes, and they mended pots and kettles". It is clearly a higher calling to be making battle-axes than mending kettles, and implies that the Turanians were very far from being a race of squat monsters and were highly evolved, skilled and war-like (historically a sign of status), however "goblinlike" their children. We are to take from this, I suggest, a notion that, despite their unconventional appearance, these Turanian tinkers, with a historical authority implied by their warrior caste and their strong connection to both the natural and the preternatural, are at least equal in evolutionary status to Mary.

Mary's eventual encounter with the young Turanian—which, as it involves Mary's heart leaping as a young man walks towards her in the middle of a misty wood as the sun goes down, we assume to be sexual—leaves her both happy and transformed. The process of transmutation which started in the wood, becomes material: while her hands before only "seemed" new, and her hair's brown colour was modified by the sun, now, in the privacy of her bedroom, she holds a green stone (perhaps a more benign version of the Black Seal) "close to the luminous ivory, and the gold poured upon it". Through this ecstatic encounter, Mary's skin has become the "luminous ivory", and her hair, previously bronze, has become gold. She has been transfigured, from being merely human, into natural materials (ivory, gold) mined and worked through her contact with the Turanians into something rich, valuable and numinous.

Much later in his career, Machen included a tale called "Opening the Door" in the collection *The Cosy Room and Other Stories*, published in 1936. Written in 1931, this tale revolves around the Reverend Secretan Jones, a retired gentleman "understood to be engaged in some kind of scholarly research... a well-known figure in the Reading Room of the British Museum" who lives in Canonbury. One day, he goes out for a walk and disappears for six weeks. When he returns, to a relieved welcome from his housekeeper, he has no memory of his absence, and no sense that he has been away at all. A "newspaperman" who has interviewed Jones and become friendly with him relates the story. During their conversation, Jones reveals that he has for some time been suffering from "absences": putting papers carefully away then discovering them somewhere completely different, losing his sense of direction, books disappearing then reappearing inexplicably.

> *One afternoon I was in a very miserable and distracted state. I could not attend to my work. I went out into the garden, and walked up and down trying to calm myself. I opened the garden door and looked into the narrow passage which runs at the end of all the gardens on this side of the square. There was nobody there—except three children playing some game or other. They were horrible, stunted little creatures, and I turned back into the garden and walked into my study. I had just sat down, and had turned to my work hoping to find relief in it, when Mrs Sedger, my servant, came into the room and cried out, in an excited sort of way, that she was glad to see me back again.*

He has no idea why this happened. The journalist suggests a nervous breakdown. However, Rev Jones shows him a pressed flower and explains that he had picked it that day in the garden, and when he returned "it was quite fresh". Rev Jones admits that some dim memory has been returning to him of his sojourn:

> *In a day or two there was a vague impression that I had been somewhere where everything was absolutely right. I can't say more than that. No fairyland joys, or bowers of*

bliss, or anything of that kind; no sense of anything strange
or unaccustomed. But there was no care there at all. Est enim
magnum chaos.

His interlocutor notes the meaning of the Latin is "For there is a great void", and nothing more is said. Two months later, the Reverend goes to a farm near Llanthony in the Black Mountains as his nerves have been troubling him. Three weeks after this the journalist receives an envelope, addressed in Secretan Jones' writing. "Inside was a slip of paper on which he had written the words: *Est enim magnum chaos.* The day on which the letter was posted he had gone out in wild autumn weather, late one afternoon, and had never come back. No trace of him has ever been found."

What is the point of the three "stunted" children in this tale? It would work perfectly well without them. They are clearly not children at all, but little people, "horrible, stunted little creatures", "creatures" signifying their not-quite-human ontology. They should be a sign of ill-omen, positioned as they are in the narrow passage between the urban gardens and… what? The "passage" is surely a metaphorical boundary between this world and some other, between "here" and "there". But Jones' returning memory seems to signify that "there" is a kind of peaceful paradise, specifically not an enchanted fairyland, but a state of being without care, almost transcendental. So we have two conflicting stories here: the horrible, demonic little creatures playing on the borderland between our world and, presumably, theirs, should signify that this other world is unpleasant, hellish. But it seems their world is a place free from human care. The "great void" is not to be feared after all. Thus, Machen's little people, framed as euhemeristic survivals rather than degenerated throwbacks, demonstrate a range of attributes: permanence in a changing world, an unbreakable connection with both nature and the supernatural in a landscape of increasing materialism, and physical proof of the fantastic nature of the universe. Jones' willing disappearance can be compared to that of Professor Gregg, and indeed to Mary's walk in the woods: these "victims" may be regarded rather as spiritual "seekers", who have been shown the way.

postscript: machen and the dwarfs of the val de ribas

It is likely that Machen first read of the theory that a "race" of dwarfs still inhabited parts of Europe in 1887, although he later protested that the idea was "wildly improbable". He was at this time a journalist, de facto editor of *Walford's Antiquarian Magazine*, and already interested in anthropology, reviewing *Palaeolithic Man in N. W. Middlesex* by John Allen Brown favourably for the August 1887 edition. In the following issue he contributed an article entitled "The Allegorical Signification of the Tinctures in Heraldry", and in the same edition, in the "News and Notes" section, is this short paragraph:

> *A strange anthropological discovery is reported to have been made in the Eastern Pyrenees. In the valley of Ribas a race of dwarfs, called by the people "Nanos," is said to exist. They never attain more than four feet in height, and have high cheek bones and almond eyes of the Mongolian type. They marry only amongst themselves, and are of a very low intellectual type.*

Machen may even have contributed the paragraph himself. According to Gawsworth in his biography of Machen, the "Heraldry" piece was the only article signed by him during the months he edited the magazine, although he "contributed in a general way to everything that was going on in the paper: 'The Collectanea', the obituary notices, the news and notes; even the book-reviewing came within his province". Whether or not he actually wrote the paragraph, as editor it is hardly possible that he did not read it.

A few years before this was published, in the early 1880s, a Canadian called Robert Grant Haliburton was travelling in Morocco when he heard stories of a "little people" living south of the Atlas Mountains. After a decade of investigation, on September 2nd 1891, he presented a paper in London to the Oriental Congress on the existence of what he believed to be a "race" of dwarfs living in the foothills of the Atlas range in Morocco. This sensational news was reported in the *Times* on September 3rd. Several fellow-folklorists and explorers immediately and vigorously contested Halliburton's theory, so in 1892 he produced a pamphlet on the subject, because his original paper had "attracted so much attention and so much discussion". In it, he detailed his evidence and refuted claims that sightings of these dwarfs had been the province of only a few "stray Englishmen". The *Journal of the Royal Asiatic Society of Great Britain and Ireland*, giving notice of its publication, suggested that "it is difficult to see what negative evidence… could be of much value against the carefully authenticated enquiries set out in this little book. Mr Haliburton deserves the thanks of historical students for the trouble he has taken in the matter".

Later that same year, Haliburton came across a back issue of a defunct periodical, in which there was a piece about the 1887 discovery in the "valley of Ribas" of a race of curious dwarfs. In 1894, when Haliburton and MacRitchie worked together, MacRitchie visited the Val de Ribas on Haliburton's behalf, uncovering the original paper by a Professor Morayta in which he claimed to have discovered them. It is tempting to think that the defunct periodical may have been *Walford's Antiquarian*, and the piece either written by, or edited by, Arthur Machen.

Gawsworth, John.

> 2013. *The Life of Arthur Machen* (Hayward, California: Tartarus Press)
> Haliburton, Robert Grant.

> 2009. *The Dwarfs of Mount Atlas*, ed. Chad Arment (Landisville, Pennsylvania: Coachwhip Publications).

Joshi, S.T.

> 2007. "Introduction", The Three Imposters and Other Stories, Vol. 1 of the *Best Weird Tales of Arthur Machen* (Hayward, California: Chaosium): xi–xix.

Machen, Arthur.

> 1887. *Walford's Antiquarian*, August: 111–2.

> 1895 [2007]. "The Novel of the White Powder", *The Three Imposters and Other Stories* (Hayward, California: Chaosium): 196–213.

> 1895 [2007]. "The Novel of the Black Seal", *The Three Imposters and Other Stories* (Hayward, California: Chaosium): 139–175.

> 1898 "Folklore and Legends of the North", *Literature*, 24th September: 271–4.

> 2003. "The Turanians". *The White People and Other Stories* (Hayward, California: Chaosium): 53–55.

1926 [2007]. "The Little People". *Dreads and Drolls*: 104–107 (first published in the *Graphic*, Vol. CXII, 11th July 1925: 64, titled "The Little Beings of the Forest").

"Opening the Door", *The Cosy Room and Other Stories*, (London: Rich & Cowan Ltd) 1936.

1951. *The Autobiography of Arthur Machen*, Parts I and II (London: The Richards Press).

1988. "A Fragment of Life", *The Collected Arthur Machen*, ed. Palmer: 23-88 (London: Gerald Duckworth & Co. Ltd).

MacRitchie, David.

1890. *The Testimony of Tradition* (London: Kegan, Paul, Trench Trubner & Co. Limited).

Silver, Carole G.

1999. *Strange and Secret Peoples: Fairies and Victorian Consciousness* (New York: Oxford University Publishing).

"A Perichoresis, An Interpenetration": Musings on 'N'

and the Representational Poetics of strange Fiction, found in a Notebook Discovered in Newington Green

Timothy J. Jarvis
originally Published in Faunus Issue 33

> *Towards the end of September last year, I was sitting on a*
> *bench in Newington Green, eating an ice cream, when I saw*
> *something fluttering in a clump of coarse grass near by. At first*
> *I thought it might be a wounded bird, as there was something*
> *frantic about the motion, but when I crossed over, examined*
> *it, I saw it was only a small notebook, pages riffled by the wind.*
> *As I stood there, the gusts died, the notebook fell open, and*
> *amid the close scrawl on one of the pages uppermost I spotted*
> *the enigmatic phrase, "I believe that there is a perichoresis, an*
> *interpenetration." I knew it as a line of dialogue from the very*
> *end of Arthur Machen's story, "N", and, intrigued, picked up*
> *the notebook, took it back to the bench, began to read. It was*
> *slow going making out the crabbed hand. The book is all but*
> *filled, though most of the jottings are reading notes and plans*
> *for essays that are of limited interest. But the final pages of*
> *scribble take a turn for the strange. I present a transcription of*
> *them here, with very little in the way of comment. I feel they*
> *speak for themselves.*

Earlier today, *the writer of the notebook records*, I sat down on a bench in
Newington Green to drink a cup of coffee, read a while. As I did so, I
noticed a sheet of lined paper, torn, I think, from a reporter's notepad,

wadded up and wedged between two slats of the bench. Curious, I tugged it out and unfolded it, read the text scrawled there. I copy it out here:

It has been a habit of some years to sit in Newington Green and look upon life. One bright day, a few weeks back, I was doing just this, looking about me, watching children playing, people exercising their dogs, a young couple sharing a bag of chips, a small group swigging at cans of cider and smoking. Leaning back, I looked up at the ancient London plane that shaded me. I then felt a sensation I can only describe as a shudder, like an earthquake, but deeper, a tremor at the core of things, and I was suddenly aware I wasn't looking up at gnarled and leafy branches any more, nor at patch of blue sky, but at stampeding grey clouds fleeing a crescent moon that hung in the east, skull down, horns up, in rut. I gawped about. I no longer sat on a bench in Newington Green, but on a rock in the midst of a waste strewn with bones. Among these bones, I saw the skulls of animals and birds, the skulls of cattle, sheep, and swine, birds' skulls, some of which I thought I could identify by their beaks, a raven's, a cockatiel's, a hoopoe's, a skull I think was a large dog's, or possibly a badger's, a stag's skull, with branching antlers, and a hippopotamus's, with vicious incurving tusks. But there were human skulls too. A great many human skulls. Other rocks jutted, here and there, from the plain, and near at hand there was a sluggish stream, waters roily, yellow. I could hear faint yowling and scent the salt tang of blood or brine and the cloying perfume of bindweed flowers.

Filled with dread, I staggered to my feet, stumbled a few paces, then, losing my footing, sprawled across the scattered bones.

I blacked out for a moment, and when I came to, I was back in Newington Green, and the young couple who were eating chips, stood over me, looking down, concerned. They helped me to my feet, I assured them I was fine, went on my way.

I was convinced I'd had a stroke, but after some tests, was pronounced perfectly sound, physically. And I feel I'm sane. But,

*since that day, I've seen that place several more times, always
in the vicinity of the Green. Each time I spend a bit longer
there. My terror shifting to awe and curiosity, I have explored.
From what I've been able to tell, that dread plain is stark and
grim and bone-strewn in all directions, but I've always been
thrown back to the everyday world before I'm able to get far.*

*But I think I've now learnt the secret to entering that place
at will, and staying there as long as I want. And leaving it
when I choose. In case I'm wrong about that last, I leave this
note here as something to anchor me to this world, call me back.*

This text has disturbed me, *the writer of the notebook goes on*, though
I'm not sure entirely why. Perhaps because it seems somehow to hint at
more than it tells, as if those strange words were not in fact revealing, but
mercifully cloaking. And I'm sure it seems familiar.

*There are a few pages of jottings about other matters here, before the
writer returns to the subject of the note.* I've lived a long, fairly dull life. Five
years ago I retired from my job as a lecturer in Literature and Critical
Theory at a provincial redbrick university and moved back to London,
where I was born and grew up. My retirement has been quiet, I've few
friends, and I spend my days working in the garden, pottering about the
streets of the neighbourhood, or researching and writing in my study or in
the reading rooms of the British Library. I'm working on a semi-fictional
treatise on instances of mystical visions in the literature of modernist
London, though it's more a hobby than a serious project.

But, though my life has been uneventful, I've known the rare and
odd through literature; my finding that strange scrap of text may not
have precedent in my experience, but it does in my reading. It's got me
thinking again about my work on Gothic fiction, and in particular of the
research I undertook, late in my career, on the strange or weird tale. This
scion of the Gothic emerged in the late-nineteenth century and is, in the
popular imagination, most closely associated with the group of writers
who wrote short stories for *Weird Tales* magazine, in the 1920s, '30s and
'40s, including H.P. Lovecraft and a number of his circle, and also with
the tradition of cosmic horror that is Lovecraft's legacy.

The strange or weird tale tends to be defined as a break with the
traditional Gothic and its strategies of revenance, its monstrous Others

who are ghosts or ravening feudal despots. The Gothic was a psychological abreaction, a return of the horrors of the medieval period in a fictional form that evoked a sublime terror. The original period of Gothic literature is generally thought to have ended in 1820, with the publication of Charles Maturin's *Melmoth the Wanderer*. But, though the oppressions of feudalism were, in the West, remote by the beginning of the Victorian age, the supernatural fiction of the era continued to deal largely in returns, revenants and bestial survivals of darker times, often put to flight by the light of progress.

But then, towards the close of the nineteenth-century, there was a shift in the epistemological conditions that underpinned Western ideology. While in most areas of culture fidelity to the rational tenets of the Enlightenment was maintained, a new paradigm arose in the more abstract areas of thought: mathematics, physics, and cosmology. These new paradigms eroded some of the certainties of scientific progress, of empiricism. Despite this, though, the prevailing models remained rational, and the irrationalities of the new sciences were banished; Riemannian geometry, entropy, quantum indeterminacy, and so on, were effectively occulted, deemed crypto-discourses, they were hidden from plain sight. It was those circumstances which gave rise to the new offshoot from the Gothic branch, the strange or weird stem, a form of fiction that was a complex set of responses to the shift taking place. It explored the possibilities suggested by the revolution in the sciences, and the vast gulfs of time and space they opened up. Its supernatural blurred the boundaries between science and hermeticism, for the new scientific discourses were so strange and incomprehensible to most they seemed a kind of occultism. The fictions both revelled in and cowered from the things the new abstruse sciences told of: the voids, the abysses, the gulfs of time, the other spaces and dimensions. They no longer offered sublime terrors that returned the reader to the world with a stronger sense of self and social duty as the early Gothic had; in fact, dissolution in despair or ecstasy awaited the protagonist of most strange or weird tales.

The rupturing event of the Great War followed, and the ideology of the Enlightenment was dealt another severe, perhaps, this time, mortal, blow on the bloody mire of the Somme; the dread side of rationality reified in the slaughter wrought by machine guns and poison gas. There was a general turn back to the religious: to a Christian God who'd guided the allies to victory, for some; for others, who sought to come to terms with the loss of so many, to spiritualism, which was bound up with the intellectual rupture in the sciences. This all intensified the strange or weird mode.

The strange or weird tale, then, can be defined against earlier supernatural fiction's depictions of revenance. As China Miéville has argued, "[t]he Weird is not the return of any repressed," rather it "impregnates the present with a bleak, unthinkable novum" (2009: 513).

But this bleak, unthinkable novum, does not, in truth, exist. The scrawled note I found, and the strange or weird fictions themselves, the places and creatures they tell of, are not real artefacts, locations, or entities, but texts, forms of representation. How then can the strange affect be explained? What is the representational praxis, or poetics, of the strange or weird tale?

I've returned several times now to Newington Green, hoping to see the person who left the note. I don't know, though, by what token I'd recognise them, perhaps some strange quirk of behaviour. But, in any case, no one has caught my eye.

So the strange or weird tale can be defined against earlier supernatural literature. But what does this mean for its poetics? One of the best known accounts of the poetics of the nineteenth-century supernatural is Tzetan Todorov's 1970 structural analysis of the genre, *The Fantastic*. In this work, Todorov famously defines the fantastic as inhering in a hesitation between a rational and a supernatural interpretation of an event. For Todorov, the fantastic hesitation operates as a challenge to a particular regime of representation, as a critique of the Enlightenment doctrine of empiricism. The fantastic hesitation posits observation not as a sure way to understand the world, as the empirical method would have it, but as fallible. As Todorov argues: "The nineteenth century transpired... in a metaphysics of the real and the imaginary, and the literature of the fantastic is nothing but the bad conscience of this positivist era" (168).

Todorov also claims the shift in scientific and philosophical discourses away from empiricism and towards uncertainty and phenomenological approaches at the end of the nineteenth century brought about the end of the genre of the fantastic. He argues that:

*Today, we can no longer believe in an immutable, external
reality, nor in a literature which is merely the transcription of
such a reality. Words have gained an autonomy which things
have lost… Fantastic literature itself—which on every page
subverts linguistic categorizations—has received a fatal blow
from these very categorizations. But this death, this suicide
generates a new literature. (168)*

As strange or weird fiction is a response to the same set of
conditions, it might be thought that the new literature Todorov describes
is the strange or weird tale. But that doesn't appear to be the case. Todorov
describes his new literature of the fantastic, as a *"generalized fantastic*
which swallows up the entire world of the book and the reader along
with it" (174). In the generalized fantastic, the world described in the
text is entirely bizarre, and, according to Todorov, "obeys an oneiric
logic… which no longer has anything to do with the real" (173). His
example is Franz Kafka's novella, *Metamorphosis* (1916). The feature of
Metamorphosis that, for Todorov, exemplifies the new literature, is what
he terms adaptation: the progressive naturalisation, over the course of the
story, of the central supernatural event, Gregor Samsa's transformation
into a vermin. Adaptation also shifts the fantastic from the external world
to the central character; Todorov quotes Sartre, who writes of Kafka's
fiction that "there is now only one fantastic object: man" (174).

For Todorov, what Kafka's corpus does is illustrate a paradox at the
heart of literature. It overturns the naive idea that language corresponds
directly to reality: "Words are not labels pasted to things that exist as
such independently of them" (175). But in doing so, it comes down on the
side of language and humanity. In Kafka's stories, and other similar works
of fantastic modernism, there is a focus on language and its poverty, its
inability to represent, and we end up with oneiric texts outside of which
there is nothing.

This approach to the fantastic can be linked to what Graham
Harman has called the "linguistic turn" of the twentieth century, the
idea that the world is structured like a language. Harman argues that
the linguistic turn is an attempt to replace "an obsolete 'philosophy of
consciousness,'" to effect a shift in our understanding of our place in
the world:

> *Instead of an aloof human subject that merely observes the*
> *world while managing to keep its fingers clean, the human*
> *being now appears as a less autonomous figure, unable to escape*
> *fully from a network of linguistic significations and historical*
> *projections. (Harman 2010: 93)*

However, Harman argues that this attempt to resolve the problem of anthropocentric ontology, an understanding of the nature of being that puts humankind at the centre of things, doesn't go far enough. As he puts it:

> *Even if we replace the lucid, transcendent cogito with a murkier,*
> *more cryptic human thrown into its historico-linguistic*
> *surroundings, there is still a fixation on a single unique rift or*
> *correspondence between human and world. (Ibid: 134)*

The philosophy of the linguistic turn is still in thrall to the Copernican revolution of Kant, which put humankind at the centre of the world, and placed the emphasis of philosophy on phenomena, on humankind's relation to things. And this is why the solution to Todorov's paradox of literature, which he calls the new fantastic, still has the human embedded at its heart, for all its strangeness.

But there is another possible solution to Todorov's paradox. That is to focus not on language's inability to represent the real, but instead on the way the real withdraws from representation. This is the way the strange or weird tale works. The strange or weird tale responds to the same shift in representation as the generalized fantastic of Todorov, but retains the formal structure of the fantastic. Its protagonists are not bizarre, but generally ordinary, and the strangeness is located out in the world and gradually revealed throughout the narrative, rather than being disclosed at the outset and progressively naturalised. But unlike the nineteenth-century fantastic, the strange or weird tale is not suspended between delusion or trickery and a true encounter with the unearthly, between a rational and a supernatural explanation; instead, its supernatural is usually unveiled by reason and brings about madness and dissolution when encountered. The question its plot poses is not, "What is the nature of experience?", but "What is the nature of the real?"

But how does the strange or weird tale pose this question given that it is, of course, nothing but text on a page? What are its descriptive strategies or representational poetics?

I've just realised what the scrap of text I found reminds me of. It recalls the end of Arthur Machen's late tale, "N" (1936), a story which concerns Stoke Newington, just up the road from Newington Green. I was back on the Green today, and I discovered, in the grass, the skull of a bird with a very long curved beak, almost certainly not a native bird, perhaps a hoopoe.

Of course, the strange or weird tale developed not just in opposition to the nineteenth-century fantastic, but also to the realist tradition, which, as Roland Barthes has claimed, is strongly defined by its representational poetics. In his 1968 essay, "The Reality Effect", Barthes argues that the main representational praxis of realism, "the reality effect", is a disingenuous convention. He uses a tripartite model of the linguistic sign to analyse how this works. His claim is that, in the poetics of realism, a proliferation of insignificant background details produce a text that appears to refer directly to reality, to concrete things, or referents, when what it actually refers to are mental conceptions, or signifieds, of concrete things. This gives the false impression that these texts simply reproduce objective reality, when, in truth, the real referent, the thing in the world, is elided, and all that is signified is realism itself.

The representational strategies of speculative fictions mark their difference from realist texts. Many speculative fictions are entirely fantastical, bearing no relation to reality. In these texts, the referent is elided—their signifiers are fantastical, only denote mental concepts, signifieds, that have no basis in reality.

But there is another kind of poetics of representation. Some texts use a strategy that is a hybrid of the mimetic and the fantastical approaches. Realism and fantasy exist side-by-side in these narratives.

This can produce texts in which the signified and the referent neutralize each other, leaving only the signifier, the word not tethered to any thing. Barthes briefly discusses such texts at the end of his essay. He writes, "the goal today is to empty the sign and infinitely to postpone its object so as to challenge, in a radical fashion, the age-old aesthetic of 'representation'" (1989:148). It is not clear precisely what is meant here, but it can be assumed Barthes is discussing modernist literature, texts such as

Kafka's *Metamorphosis*. The thing Gregor Samsa becomes is just language, a signifier with no object; it has no real life referent and we can't form any mental image of it, because it is so strange. Indeed, in the original German, the word Kafka uses for the thing Gregor becomes is *Ungeziefer*, which means literally, "unclean animal not suitable for sacrifice" or simply "vermin", and has none of the specificity of the terms "insect", "beetle", or "cockroach" which are often used in English translations. Because the unthinkable thing Gregor becomes exists in a world of ordinary objects, of violins, paintings, and apples, a bizarre vibration is set up—this is one version of the radical challenge to representation Barthes refers to.

The strange or weird tale also combines the realistic and fantastical poetics of representation. But its descriptive language is not plain, terse, and vague in the moments when the veil is rent and the fantastical is revealed. In fact there is, in these moments, most often a surfeit of very specific words, an ecstatic or dread tangle in which language is pushed to the very limits of sense. The fantastical elements are not naturalised, words are not left untethered to things. In strange fiction, language collapses when it encounters the weird thing, is not just unable to denote a "real", but cannot even function as a language.

Miéville has characterised the descriptive prose of weird fiction, its "frenzied succession of adjectives," as being, "in its hesitation, its obsessive... stalling of the noun, an aesthetic deferral according to which the world is always-already unrepresentable, and can only be approached by an asymptotic succession of subjective pronouncements" (2009: 511-512). Eugene Thacker, in his *Tentacles Longer Than Night* (2015), echoes this, arguing that characters in weird fiction, when faced with the weird, "resort to what is really an apophatic language, the language of negative theology," that is, they attempt to articulate the weird by approaching it obliquely, through stating the things it is not (112).

Generally we associate this poetics with what Miéville has termed "Weird Fiction's revolutionary teratology", its depictions of monstrous others (2009: 513). This is unsurprising; Lovecraft, in whose work the weird element is most often represented by dread entities from the outer reaches of space, is still the most visible of all strange or weird writers. But the text I found in Newington Green generates a strange affect simply through the depiction of a barren alterior place. This poetics is equally applicable to the description of settings. Indeed, even in the story that presents Lovecraft's most famous "monster", "The Call of Cthulhu", Cthulhu's dwelling place, the island of R'lyeh, is as significant as Cthulhu itself, as the Great Old One can only awaken when an earthquake causes R'lyeh to rise and must return to dead dreaming when the island sinks again. And perhaps the weirdest, most terrifying description of Cthulhu is not that of its teratological form, "[a] pulpy tentacled head surmount[ing] a grotesque and scaly body with rudimentary wings," but the image we get of Cthulhu when it is finally encountered: "A mountain walked or stumbled," (Lovecraft 1999: 141, 167). An image which tropes the monster as a landscape.

Machen's "N" is a text that generates its strange affect almost entirely through the description of place. Three old friends meet in rooms in Holborn to talk about the "old days and the old ways". In the course of their conversation, Perrott, the owner of the rooms, tells of a beautiful park in Stoke Newington that a cousin of his, a "stodgy" experimental farmer, once described to him. "'I know every inch of that neighbourhood, and I tell you there's no such place'," one of the others, Harliss, who grew up in Stoke Newington, a man of "business stock," asserts. But Perrott and the other man, Arnold, are of a more poetical bent. To them, Stoke Newington, perhaps only four miles distant from the cosy rooms where they meet, is, "unfriendly and remote," and to talk of it is, "as if one were to discourse of Arctic explorations, and lands of everlasting darkness" (Machen 2010: 1, 11, 9, 11).

Arnold is drawn to investigate the matter of the park. His interest is piqued by the discovery, in an otherwise mundane and moralising treatise on walking in London, by "a pious and amiable clergyman," the Reverend Hampole, of an account of a rapturous and terrible view seen from the window of the house of one of Hampole's parishioner's, Glanville, where there should only have been dull suburban streets. Hampole then relates Glanville's strange notion that "that which we now regard as stubborn matter was, primarily... the Heavenly Chaos, a soft and ductile substance, which could be moulded by the imagination of uncorrupted man into whatever forms he chose it to assume." This thesis the reader assumes to be linked to the visionary prospect his window affords. Hampole feels it "more in accordance with the doctrine I had undertaken to expound than much of the teaching of the philosophers of the day, who seemed to exalt rationalism at the expense of Reason"

(Ibid: 12, 17). Here, then, we see the strange or weird tale's suspicion of Enlightenment rationality, and also a new kind of relationship to the empirical data of the senses—the prospect of the beautiful park is neither delusion nor strictly real, there's no fantastic hesitation, but a new relationship to the ultramundane. Or perhaps an old relationship, in a modern context—a visionary mysticism.

In the course of his investigations, Arnold hears the story of a young man, an escapee from an asylum, who also apparently saw a transfiguring scene from a Stoke Newington window. When Arnold regales the others with his findings, Harliss dismisses them, and Perrott makes a claim for the actions of coincidence as a solution to the mystery. But Arnold is not to be put off. There is a further incident, something he himself witnessed and that is more persuasive, which he tells the others of. Then he offers his thesis: "I believe that there is a perichoresis, an interpenetration." Arnold takes the term perichoresis from Christian theology. It is a technical term used to describe the relationship between the human and divine aspects of Christ's nature. Arnold's use of it in "N" is to describe the relationship between the "real" and the "fantastic". It indicates the possibility of the fantastic coexisting with the real, not demarcated from it; it indicates an interwoven real and numinous. Here the real and the fantastic aren't bound together to naturalise the fantastic, as was the case in Todorov's generalized fantastic, but rather to enweird the real. And terror, as much as awe, is the result. "It is possible, indeed," Arnold goes on to say, "that we three are now sitting among desolate rocks, by bitter streams… And with what companions?" (Ibid: 33).

And it is this image, of course, that led me from that strange text I found to "N".

The term perichoresis is also used in Christian theology to describe the interpenetration of the three parts of the trinity. And triads abound in "N", from the three old raconteurs at the heart of the story, to the paintings of the three choir-boys and three charity girls reminisced about at the opening. And Arnold's case is initially made on the basis of three witnesses, three who've had a vision in Canon's Park, Stoke Newington: Perrott's "stodgy" cousin, who saw merely beauty, not ecstasy, the Reverend Hampole, and the madman. But then, after Perrott counters by evoking the "marvellous operation of the law of coincidences," Arnold relates his final incident. He tells of a fourth "witness", who he encountered when he returned to have one last look at the place, a young man, looking for her "who lived in the white house on the hill," who is, Arnold tells us, "lost also and for ever" (Ibid: 32-33).

This fourth term, which upsets the patterning of threes throughout the story, must be significant. And it must be significant that it is this fourth that is carried away, lost forever. The triads recall the tripartite sign of post-structuralist linguistics. What then is the additional term? Is this the strange or weird sign? With four parts instead of three? With a lost, receding, and inaccessible numinous, or, to use the Kant's term for that which is beyond our senses, *noumenal* referent alongside the 'real' one?

Thacker has identified two main strategies of the apophatic poetics of strange or weird fiction. In the first, which he terms minimalism, "language is stripped of all its attributes, leaving only skeletal phrases such as 'the nameless thing,' 'the shapeless thing,' or 'the unnameable.'" The second is the strategy of hyperbole, "in which the unknowability of the unhuman is expressed through a litany of baroque descriptors, all of which ultimately fail to inscribe the unhuman within human thought and language" (2015: 141). He argues that when these two approaches are used together, they generate a weird epiphany in which not just language, but thought falters, an epiphany that points to the limit of thought.

Hampole's account of the prospect he sees from Glanville's window, is an example of the ecstasy of this weird epiphany. It begins in excess, in "astounding beauty," which robs Hampole of speech: "In deep dells, bowered by overhanging trees, there bloomed flowers such as only dreams can show." And ends with the collapse of language: "A sense of beatitude pervaded my whole being; my bliss was such as cannot be expressed by words" (Machen 2010: 20).

But this ecstasy quickly induces dread, as it points to the limits of human thought, and so to something beyond thought:

> And then, under the influence of a swift revulsion of terror,
> which even now I cannot explain, I turned and rushed from
> the room and from the house... In great perturbation and
> confusion of mind, I made my way into the street. (Ibid: 20)

And this vision has its particular power because of the way it is overlaid on the mundane:

*The familiar street had resumed its usual aspect, the terrace
stood as I had always seen it, and the newer buildings beyond,
where I had seen oh! what dells of delight, what blossoms of
glory, stood as before in their neat, though unostentatious order.
(Ibid: 20)*

Again, this is the enweirding of the real; the real is shown to have
always already been interpenetrated by the fantastic.

It seems mystics and poets and madmen and lovers are those
compelled and transfigured by the strange, while "stodgy" men and men
of "business stock" are not. And, when representing the fantastic, strange or
weird tales employ language that is akin to ritual chant or poetic metaphor
or delirium or lover's talk; strange discourse operates in a heightened
register that causes the collapse of the linguistic sign. As words, signifiers,
are inadequate to express the strange thing, the noumenal referent, they are
piled on to meaningless excess, producing a bizarre ambiguous signified,
or text, a linguistic chimera. This is the sign of the strange or weird tale.
It is not the empty sign of Todorov's generalized fantastic and Barthes'
literature of the infinitely postponed object, in which language is used with
precision to express only itself, where the sign breaks down on the side of
the signifier. In the poetics of the weird or strange tale, the sign collapses
on the side of a noumenal referent, an inaccessible fourth term.

The strange or weird tale, then, is a challenge to the twentieth-
century critical theoretical orthodoxy of linguistic relativism and its
human protagonist. Its representational praxis gestures at a strange
unknowable, always receding, noumenal.

And the single letter of Machen's story's mysterious title points
to this. As Donald R. Burleson notes in his essay on the tale, "Arthur
Machen's 'N' as an Allegory of Reading" (1990), "it is significant, then,
that in 'N' we find the very grapheme that initiates words of negation
in all Romance, Germanic, and Slavic languages." For Burleson, though,
"[t]he text, by its remarkable title, promises to dwell upon textuality and
thus upon (as an instance of textuality) itself, *mise en abyme*, like the
heraldic picturing of a shield upon a shield" (1990: Unpaginated). I would
suggest that, following Thacker, the title might instead indicate the text
is apophatic, that is, it points, by negation, to that which lies beyond and
outside all text.

The strange or weird tale's gesture at the noumenal, at that which lies beyond thought, explains the sense of awe and terror it generates, and also its appeal for contemporary thinkers who wish to challenge the anthropism that has dominated Western philosophy since Kant. And despite a critical focus on the radical teratology of the weird, this representational praxis can perhaps be seen even more vividly in depictions of strange places, than it can in those of weird monsters, who can be more easily recuperated and visualised. Cthulhu can be made into a soft toy, but nothing so cosy can be done with the paradisiacal fragment of Machen's "N".

I've kept returning to Newington Green, compelled somehow. For all that my research has been into literary texts, it has begun to take on a very real element. I've started to see that other place, flickering at the edges of my vision…

And this is where the notebook ends, with a tantalising, or perhaps hackneyed, ellipsis.

Endnotes

Barthes, R. 1989 (1968). "The Reality Effect" ("L'effet de réel"), in *The Rustle of Language*, trans. R. Howard. Berkley and Los Angeles: University of California Press, pp.141-148.

Burleson, D. 1990. "Arthur Machen's 'N' as an Allegory of Reading. Lore " http://www.lore-online.com/index.php/component/content/article/43-vault/80-mm4-2

Harman, G. 2010. *Towards Speculative Realism: Essays and Lectures*. Alresford, Hants: Zero Books. Paginated eBook.

Kafka, F. 1992 (1916). "Metamorphosis", in *Metamorphosis and Other Stories*, trans. W. & E. Muir. London: Minerva, pp.7-64.

Lovecraft, H. 1999. "The Call of Cthulhu", in S. Joshi (ed.), *The Call of Cthulhu and Other Weird Stories*. London: Penguin, pp.139-169.

Machen, N. 2010 (1936). "N". Leyburn, North Yorkshire: Tartarus Press.

Miéville, C. 2009. "Weird Fiction", in M. Bould, et al (eds), *The Routledge Companion to Science Fiction*. Oxford: Routledge, pp.510-515.

Thacker, E. 2015. *Tentacles Longer Than Night: Horror of Philosophy, Vol. 3*. Alresford, Hants: Zero Books.

Todorov, T. 1975 (1970). *The Fantastic: A Structural Approach to a Literary Genre* (Introduction á la littérature fantastique), trans. R. Howard, with a foreword by R. Scholes. Ithaca: Cornell University Press

Biographies

Gill Culver was a Londoner who sadly passed away at quite a young age. She loved folk music and played the guitar. Her other great interest was in pre-suffragettes; those ladies of the late-Victorian age who rebelled against male domination. This attracted her to Arthur Machen's first wife, Amy Hogg. Gill was an intrepid researcher and uncovered many unknown facts about the life of Amy Hogg.

Roger Dobson (1954–2013) edited *The Life of Arthur Machen* by John Gawsworth (2005) and co-edited Machen's *Selected Letters* (with Godfrey Brangham and R.A. Gilbert, 1988). He also wrote the Machen entry for the *Oxford Dictionary of National Biography*. His essays on Machen, M.P. Shiel, Yeats and others have been collected in *The Library of the Lost* (Tartarus Press, 2015).

Tessa Farmer is an artist based in London. She was born in 1978 in Birmingham and is the Great Granddaughter of Arthur Machen. Working with organic materials, she creates complex installations in which evil skeleton fairies battle with insects and other animals. *In Fairyland*, a critical study of her work edited by Catriona McAra, was published by Strange Attracor Press in 2016.

Emily Fergus is studying for an MPhil at Birkbeck, University of London. Her thesis identifies the fairy-euhemerism that flourished in the late nineteenth century as the chief explanatory model behind the 'little people' who feature so prominently in Machen's weird fiction, thus challenging the dominance of the trope of 'degeneration' as his principal inspiration, and examines more broadly the roles little people play in both fact and fiction throughout the nineteenth century.

Nick Freeman teaches English at Loughborough University, where he does his best to initiate students into cults of decadence, weirdness, and the occult. He has published widely on late-Victorian literature; his first book, *Conceiving the City: London, Literature and Art 1870-1914* (2007), featured a significant discussion of *The Hill of Dreams* while his second, *1895:Drama, Disaster, and Disgrace in Late Victorian Britain* (2011, paperback 2014) looked at *The Three Impostors*. He has been a FOAM member for almost twenty years.

John Gawsworth was the pen name of poet, writer, and editor T.I.F. Armstrong (1912–1970), who befriended Machen in the 1930s, industriously recording details of Machen's life and work before writing a major biography, eventually published in 2005 by the Tartarus Press.

Gwilym Games is Local Studies Librarian for the City and County of Swansea, and is a former editor of both *Faunus* and *Machenalia*, the Friends of Arthur Machen newsletter.

Adrian Homer Goldstone (1897–1977), a Californian book collector, wrote (together with Wesley Sweetser) what is still regarded as the definitive bibliography of Arthur Machen, published by the University of Texas Press in 1965.

John Howard was born in London. He is the author of several books, including *Buried Shadows* (2017) and *Inner Europe* (2018, with Mark Valentine). He has published essays on various aspects of the science fiction and horror fields, and especially on the work of classic authors such as Fritz Leiber, Arthur Machen, August Derleth, M.R. James, and writers of the pulp era. Many of these have been collected in *Touchstones: Essays on the Fantastic*.

Timothy J. Jarvis is a writer, scholar, and teacher of creative writing with an interest in the antic, the weird, the strange. He also co-edits *Faunus*. His first novel, *The Wanderer*, was published by Perfect Edge Books in the summer of 2014. Short fiction has appeared in various venues. He currently lives in Bedford, a small town in the hallowed/cursed M1 corridor.

Christopher Josiffe is a librarian, researcher and writer whose articles on European witchcraft, Spiritualism, African diasporic magical traditions, folklore, magick and psychical research have been published in various journals over the past ten years. His first book, *Gef! The Strange Tale of* *an Extra-Special Talking Mongoose* was published by Strange Attractor Press in 2017. He is currently writing a biography of Dr Eric Dingwall, the paranormal researcher, sexologist and intelligence agent.

James Machin co-edits *Faunus* and teaches at the Royal College of Art, London. His book *Weird Fiction in Britain, 1880–1939* was published by Palgrave Macmillan in 2018.

Bob Mann was born in Totnes, Devon, where he still lives. He is a writer, editor and publisher with a deep interest in history, topography, folklore and the ways in which creative artists explore the sense of place.

Rosalie Parker co-runs independent UK publisher Tartarus Press with R.B. Russell, with whom she has won four World Fantasy Awards. *The Old Knowledge* (Swan River Press 2010), *Damage* (PS Publishing 2016) and *Sparks from the Fire* (Swan River Press 2018), collect together her short stories, which have also appeared in a variety of "best of "and other horror and weird fiction anthologies.

R.B. Russell is a publisher and author who has been collecting Arthur Machen for nearly forty years. He is a founder member of the Friends of Arthur Machen.

Mark Samuels lives in Kings Langley, England. He is the author of six short story collections: *The White Hands and Other Weird Tales* (Tartarus Press 2003), *Black Altars* (Rainfall Books 2003), *Glyphotech & Other Macabre Processes* (PS Publishing 2008), *The Man Who Collected Machen* (Ex Occidente 2010, rpt. Chomu Press 2011), *Written in Darkness* (Egaeus Press 2014, rpt. Chomu Press 2017) and *The Prozess Manifestations* (Zagava Books 2017), and two novels: *The Face of Twilight* (PS Publishing 2006) and *A Pilgrim Stranger* (Ulymas Press 2017). His latest book is a compilation of essays on authors of weird fiction under the title *Prophecies and Dooms* (Ulymas Press 2018). Hippocampus Press is scheduled to release a 'Best of Mark Samuels' collection, *The Age of Decayed Futurity*, edited by S.T. Joshi, in late 2019.

Gerald Suster (1951–2001) was born and raised in London and educated by himself and by Trinity Hall, Cambridge. He had twenty-nine books published, seven internationally, including non-fiction works on such varied subjects as the Tarot, boxing, military history, the occult roots of Nazism, the Hell-Fire Club and Aleister Crowley. His novels of supernatural terror include *The Devil's Maze*, a sequel to *The Three Impostors*; *The God Game*, in which Machen is one of the principal characters, and *The Labyrinth of Satan*, in which Machen has a vital, cameo role.

Arthur Alkin Sykes (1861–1939) wrote several parodies of contemporary writers, including Rudyard Kipling, Anthony Hope, and George Egerton, as well as Machen. These were collected in the 1896 book *Without Permission: a book of dedications*.

Mark Valentine is the author of studies of Arthur Machen (Seren, 1995) and the diplomat and fantasist 'Sarban' (Tartarus Press, 2010). With Roger Dobson, he co-edited booklets about Machen under the Caermaen Books imprint, and later co-edited *Faunus* with Ray Russell. He also writes supernatural stories, and essays on book collecting. Recent titles include *The Uncertainty of All Earthly Things* (Zagava) and *Inner Europe* (Tartarus), a shared volume with John Howard.

Nick Wagstaff has written several essays for *Faunus* since 2010. These are largely about Machen's journalism in the *Evening News* and *The Observer*, but he has also discussed *The London Adventure* and Machen's introduction to Richard Middleton's *The Ghost Ship* (1912). Nick has retired from a career in university administration spent mostly at The Open University and is involved in local heritage conservation matters.

Strange Attractor Press 2019